STARF

Dear Jade,

Welcome to the Court of the Fallen!

You're in for a wild ride ☺ Thanks so much for your support!

All the love xx

Fern Cole.

By Fern Cole

BOOK I | THE COURT OF THE FALLEN

Cover design by Fern Cole

Edited by Pinpoint Editing

ISBN (Paperback): 978-1-9192483-3-2

ISBN (eBook): 978-1-9192483-0-1

ISBN (Hardcover): 978-1-9192483-4-9

First Edition

www.ferncole.co.uk

info@ferncole.co.uk

Printed in Great Britain

Trigger warnings

Starfallen is an adult romantasy containing explicit sexual content, violence, murder, self-harm, sexual assault, and death.

All characters are eighteen years or older.
Reader discretion is advised.

Visit my Instagram linktree for:

♡ Starfallen playlist on Spotify

♡ Discord channel to discuss all things Starfallen, connect with other bookish friends, share book recommendations, etc.

♡ Fable book club, where you can discuss each chapter as you read. (Please be careful before you go into each chapter, as there might be spoilers!)

♡ Etsy shop for bookmarks, signed edition, and more.

♡ See *@ferncoleauthor* on Instagram for more.

To my street team, you can finally get on that table.
To the rest of you, normal-ish people,
You won't look at tables the same way again.

Prologue

I wear grief like a torn silk dress and shattered diamond crown.

It clings to my bones, haunting, hollowing, possessing me, a ghost flickering behind my grey eyes.

At first, I was numb, in an out-of-body haze.

Words reached me like echoes underwater. None of them made any sense.

And when they did, I refused to believe them. To hear them.

Once the denial faded, reality hit me all at once.

No more smile, no familiar warmth wrapping around me like a soft blanket, not a single breath left to brush my skin.

Everything had been ripped away from me in an instant.

Declan is gone—just like that.

It's been a month since my boyfriend died.

A promising young man with a bright future, all of it ruined by alcohol and a few careless words that landed at the wrong table.

He was beaten, stabbed outside a tavern, and left to die in a filthy alley.

And I've been stuck ever since, drowning in waves of sorrow, crushing pain, and guilt.

I wander in the dark, pacing and panting, unable to find my way home.

It's my fault.

I know it's all my fault.

And people go on with their lives, doing whatever it was they did when Declan was still alive, whilst I can barely scrape the broken pieces of myself off the floor.

I see him everywhere in my home—in the empty space beside me when I wake in the morning, and behind my closed eyes at night. A stupid attempt to steal sleep, to shut down long enough that this shell of a body still functions to breathe through the next day.

There were so many words I should have said.

So many words I'll never get to say.

Some days, I stand on the edge of a cliff, screaming into the raging wind, begging the Gods to give me a reason.

Why?

Why him?

All I'm left with are unanswered questions and sleepless nights.

I pray to the stars, wishing for things that will never come true.

I wish Declan and I could still fight. I'd yell at him for leaving me, for storming out for a drink after our argument.

But most of all ... I just wish he was still alive.

But stars don't grant wishes.

Not the ones that shine in the night sky, anyway.

There's only one place that does: the Court of the Fallen.

A realm built from fallen Fae, exiled starbeings, appearing only during celestial events—eclipses, blood moons, meteor showers.

And when it does, the Fae of that court host twisted little games, cruel competitions and trials, most likely watched with wine-stained, wicked smiles.

Seven desperate humans. One prize.

Win, and a wish is granted.

Any wish.

Chapter 1

Another pie from the neighbour.

So many fucking pies.

Because apparently, when you're grieving and haunted by your own depression, people show how sorry they feel—how much they pity you—by baking you pies.

I understand that they give me food to make sure that I still eat when I can't find the energy to do anything but pace restlessly and listen to the creaking of my own floorboards.

But fuck me.

I can't take another look from their pitying eyes or hear the gossip carried on the wind when they think I'm too in my own head to listen.

Cassandra's drunk in sadness. Her eyes are hollowed. Lost about half her weight.

Maybe she'll set herself on fire in the middle of the night.

Not that what they're saying isn't true.

But if I die, I might as well die trying to bring Declan back to life.

I have two weeks to train before the coming eclipse—the one a crooked, probably fake seer predicted—and that's about the only reason I shove some protein into my mouth and make an effort to drag my feet out of the house this morning.

The sun is blaring through the leaves turning shades of orange and red. The ground smells faintly of damp after the rain. White smoke rises from the vent of the house next door, replacing the damp smell with something garlicky and spiced, heavy enough to exorcise a vampire.

I'd say it's a beautiful autumn day, but my boyfriend is still dead.

I'm half tempted to knock on the neighbour's door to thank them for the pie, but then again, I can't be bothered to sit through tea when they ask how I am, to which I will lie: I'm okay.

Everyone lies when asked if they're okay.

They could be going through a heartbreak, jobless, mourning a dead goldfish, but they're all "okay."

Hardly anyone bothers others with their problems, because no one actually wants to listen.

So, I just settle down the washed-up pie plate with a simple thank-you note on their doorstep, and make my way to town.

A whole season has changed since Declan died.

It sounds so crazy to think that.

I remember how hot it was that night, how I tossed and turned in bed because I couldn't sleep, both from the heat and from the fight. Declan stayed over sometimes, but he had his own place. I'd thought he'd just gone home.

But he never did.

Before I knew it, autumn had crept in—grey clouds, cold wind, and rain, washing away some of the pain, but not the guilt.

Never the guilt.

Everyone still looks at me like a lost little puppy they don't know where to return. They tilt their heads, place a hand on their heart, and use their softest voice when they talk to me like if they breathe too hard, I might turn into dust.

I wish I lived in a big city, where no one knows anyone.

Where no one cares about the people around them.

But it's in this damn town that I met Declan.

A bell rings as I open the wooden door of the blacksmith's shop. The only experience I have with hunting is from playing hide and seek as a kid. I've never held a sword, or any other weapon really, apart from kitchen knives.

Declan was a peaceful man, destined to be a scribe. He didn't hunt or fight either.

Ironic, considering there was nothing peaceful about his death at all.

I have no idea what awaits me at the Court of the Fallen. No one does. Even the rare few who make it back seal their lips. I suspect the rules go something like: win, and a wish will be granted—but speak of the court, and all will be taken away.

I don't know if I'll have to fight, solve a puzzle, dance my way to death, or fuck a Fae to win—or all of the above.

If I'm even chosen to begin with, since there is an overwhelming number of dark souls just begging to be collected.

I can't blame them, really.

We're a miserable little breed, swallowed by poverty, depression, and lust.

But learning how to wield a dagger sounds like a good enough place to start.

The shop owner's gaze follows me like a hawk as I gather decent-sized daggers and dump them on the counter. He glances at them, then drags his gaze back to me.

"I don't think it's a good idea to sell you these, Cassie."

"Why?" I frown. "Promise they're not for slitting my throat. I could just use a kitchen knife if I wanted to do that—do you really think I'd drag myself out here to spend a fortune?"

Paul sighs. "You haven't left the house in weeks, and now you fancy a whole new set of knives?"

"Yes." I smile. "A new hobby." Hoarding knives.

"If you're thinking of going after those bastards who killed Declan ..."

"Please," I cut him off, my voice cold. "I don't even know who they are."

And hurting them wouldn't bring Declan back.

I'm not stupid enough to waste my energy with that.

"Still, I don't think this is a good idea ..."

I roll my eyes, not even trying to hide my frustration. "Fine, I just want to throw them at a tree trunk, okay? Let off a little steam. Now, will you please sell me the damn daggers?"

Paul blinks, assessing if what I said was true.

It is true—just not the "letting off a little steam" part.

"We're all worried about you, you know," he says at last. "Promise me you won't do anything stupid?"

Depends on how he defines "stupid."

Letting anyone know about my plans would definitely be a stupid thing to do. Especially when I don't even know what those plans are.

Plus, why go through the hassle, when chances are I won't be picked anyway?

But I smile like a nice girl I used to be. "Promise."

And Paul pretends to believe it.

The daggers feel like a dead weight in my bag.

Maybe the alternative is to walk off a bridge and let their weight drag me to the deep—so I could meet Declan on the other side.

But I kind of want a coffee.

I stop at a café a few streets down from Paul's shop and take a deep breath. I don't really want to come here, but it undoubtedly has the best coffee in town.

Mainly because I used to make it myself, exactly how I like it.

Problem is I work—*worked*—here.

Worse, Declan and I met here.

And Susan and the others always give me that sad look. The one that says: *poor thing, still broken.*

Or maybe it translates to: *bitch, snap out of it and get back to work*—but I'm just too despondent to tell the difference.

It's just a coffee. I can do this.

I push the door open. The familiar scent of tea leaves and coffee beans used to be the closest thing I had to home.

Now, it smells like a graveyard.

In and out is all you have to do.

I exhale as I walk up to the counter, where Susan looks up to meet my eyes. She straightens, her eyes lighting up, and the next thing I know, she steps out and throws her arms around me, welcoming me home.

I swallow the invisible lump in my throat.

"It's so nice to see you, Cassie," she says softly, pulling back to look at me like she's not sure I'm even real.

I give her the faintest smile. "It's nice to see you too, Susan."

I think.

I can't really tell what I'm feeling most of the time.

Like I'm just a shell, controlled by someone else.

I feel guilty even smiling.

My boyfriend was murdered in cold blood—I should never smile ever again.

"How are you, hm?" Susan caresses my cheek the way a mum comforts her child. Her touch is warm, but fails to reach my cold, cracked heart.

"I just need a coffee, and I'll feel better."

She doesn't know how low I feel, so that wasn't a lie.

A coffee might lift me two centimetres off the ocean floor—but that's still *better*.

"Of course, honey. Anything for you." Susan rubs my arm, nodding towards the counter. "Want to make it yourself? On the house."

Even better.

I nod and murmur, "Thank you."

It's muscle memory for me to make coffee at this point. I push myself through the counter door and stand where I usually did for the past year and a half. It's not necessary a dream job, just practice for the future—for when I save enough money to open a small café of my own, which will probably be about ten years down the line, if I'm lucky.

Now I've spent some of that carefully saved money on the daggers.

I take my time making the coffee. It's not like I have many plans these days. My main goals right now are to get to the Court of the Fallen, win whatever nightmare trials they throw at me, and wish for Declan to not be dead.

Or die trying.

But first, coffee.

I pour my very strong coffee in a takeaway cup—a silent sign to Susan, who's been secretly watching my every move, that I don't plan on staying.

I take a careful sip.

Gods, that is to die for.

"I've been thinking," Susan says before I can open my mouth to awkwardly tell her that I'm leaving, now that I've got what I came for. "Maybe you could come back part time? Just a few hours a week, until you're ready to go full time again?"

I press my lips into a thin line.

Well, this is awkward.

I was thinking about quitting. Don't want her waiting around for a dead soul when she could easily hire someone to take my place.

Susan told me to take all the time I needed. It's been a month, and this place usually gets slammed. They could barely manage with me here full time. Now, they're short-staffed, and Susan still hasn't hired someone new because she's kind enough to wait for me.

All I'm doing is disappointing her.

I let out a soft sigh, my gaze drifting to the table where I first saw Declan. The memories crash like waves—the first time our eyes met, the way he smiled at me, how he nervously told me about the book he was reading just because I said the cover looked interesting.

I was never interested in the book.

The rest is history.

"I don't know, Susan," I murmur. "I don't think I'm ready yet."

I don't know if I'll ever be.

"Please, just hire someone." I swallow, trying to not break down again. I've done enough of that in the past month. "Don't wait for me."

Susan seems disappointed. There's sadness in her eyes, the same kind that's probably carved into my face.

"I understand." She nods. "But I want you to know that you'll always have a place here."

And I'm grateful for that.

I'm just too exhausted to show it.

So, I whisper a thank you, and I walk away.

I spend most of my time in the next two weeks in the woods. Every morning, I drag myself out of bed at dawn and run, pushing a little further each day. Then, I chug enough protein to maybe build whatever muscle I can in the limited time ... or at least just gain back some of the weight I've lost.

In the afternoons, I train with the daggers. I build my own makeshift target out of hay and old wood, mark the ground, and start hurling blades like my life depends on it.

Not-so-spoiler: I miss. A lot.

The first two days are honestly embarrassing. I lose more energy picking daggers off the ground than actually throwing them. But by day five, something clicks. I finally get the hang of it, and the blades start landing.

So I decide to challenge myself by moving further back.

I consider archery, too, but then I figure maybe it's smarter to get really good at one thing, instead of being just okay at both.

Quality over quantity.

Fingers crossed it will save my life.

Because today is the day the seer predicted the eclipse.

I make sure to eat—who knows what the Fae eat, anyway—and I let myself have all my favourite snacks, just in case I never get to have them again. Everything is prepared, on the off chance I actually get selected for the trials.

I write letters to my parents and my brother, Noah. They have been so worried since Declan died. I can't bring myself to say goodbye to them in person, because I'd probably end up ugly crying, and they'd all know something is seriously wrong.

I'm not stupid. I know something is seriously wrong with me.

But they can't save someone who doesn't want to be saved.

The problem is, I don't know when this eclipse is meant to happen.

If it actually is.

So, I sit in the woods, waiting for the sky to do a trick.

Minutes tick by. Then hours.

The sun is setting.

I was told the sky would bleed, but so far all I can see are streaks of orange and pink.

Well, shit.

Should have known the seer was full of shit.

The woods are now completely dark, stars flickering above—just like what the seer will see when I pay her a visit tomorrow with a big, fat punch to the face.

There goes my only hope of existing.

I drag my feet home, slow and miserable, not even caring if a wolf jumps out and mauls me to death on the way. And to add insult to injury: rain starts to pour down a minute into the walk.

Great.

Just when I thought it couldn't get any worse.

By the time I reach home, I'm drenched and shaking. All I want is a very hot bath—but the lights are already on inside. I lost count of how many times I checked that everything was off this morning, so unless Declan is back to haunt me for failing the mission ...

It's Noah.

And he's holding the letter I left for him.

So, yeah. Today could actually get so much worse.

"What the fuck, Cassie?" my brother asks, his voice is low, furious.

I clamp my lips together, tight, dripping in the doorway and shaking even harder. Noah is twenty-six, three years older than me, and he usually treats me like a little princess—unless he's angry.

It's rare, but when he is, I usually hide.

That's not really an option right now.

"What is this?" he snaps, stepping closer and waving the letter. "A goodbye note? Joining the Fae trials? What the hell were you thinking!?"

I bite my bottom lip. It takes me a minute to finally open my mouth. "It doesn't matter. It's never going to happen anyway."

"Doesn't matter?" Noah's voice spikes, sharp enough to make me flinch. His eyes soften as he realises how loud he is, but he barrels on. "You're talking about going to the Court of the Fallen and bringing back your dead boyfriend. Cass, what is wrong with you?"

What is wrong with me?

I stare at him, rage flooding through me like fire under my skin. "My boyfriend is dead—that's what's wrong with me!"

Now Noah is the one flinching.

"Everyone carried on as if nothing happened—even his family, his sister, for gods' sakes!" I snap, finally letting out the emotions I've buried for the past month and a half. "I don't understand how. Why is it so easy for them? Why isn't anyone trying, like me?!"

Noah's expression shifts. Anger drains from his face, replaced by that look—the same quiet, sad one everyone's been giving me since it happened.

I can't bear it anymore.

I just can't.

"Cass ... it's not easy for anyone," Noah mutters, pulling me into his arms, not caring that I'm soaking wet. "I only knew Declan for half a year, and it still wasn't easy for me. It sure as hell wasn't for his family. But it's the only way we know to move forward." He pulls back enough to meet my eyes. "And I know you don't want to hear this ... but you're going to have to try to let go, too."

"But what if I don't want to ..." I sniffle, my voice threatening to break.

"I know you don't, and no one's asking you to forget about him." My brother sighs, brushing the raindrops from my cheek. "Just ... take it one day at a time."

That's easier said than done.

I don't know how to.

It's impossible for me to reply to that, so I just bury my face in Noah's chest, quietly letting the tears run free, breaking in his arms.

This is the first time I've cried in two weeks. I never let myself go there. My focus has only been on the training—but now that's all gone, too.

I've been desperately clinging to a thin, invisible thread of hope.

He's really gone.

And I can't bring him back.

It takes me a while to calm down again. Only when my lips start turning blue from the cold do I finally stop and drag myself into the bath to warm up. Noah's still there when I come out, as if he didn't trust I wouldn't drown myself in the tub.

"I'm going to burn these," he says, tossing both letters into the fireplace. The flames eat the papers in seconds. "Get some rest, Cass. I'll come back to check on you tomorrow."

"I'm not a kid, you know."

"Yeah, I do." He reaches for his jacket. "You're worse."

I scoff.

"I mean it. Get some rest," Noah says from the doorway. I hold on to my bathrobe like a lifeline. "You look like shit."

"Gee, thanks, brother." I frown, but he smiles.

He doesn't say anything else, just steps forward to press a kiss on my forehead before making his way out. On one hand, I'm grateful to him for giving me a new purpose in life: to kick his ass. On the other hand, I'm sad—sad that he has to do this, checking in on me, making sure I'm still breathing.

Sad that I'm such a burden to everyone.

I make myself a cup of tea and sit by the window, staring out at the yellow moon, shining just bright enough to catch bats fluttering from tree to tree, stealing whatever fruits like thieves.

At some point, I close my eyes for a moment, and the moon is no longer gold when I open them again.

It's bleeding—crimson at the edges, partly swallowed by shadow.

I jump up from my chair.

Holy shit.

The seer didn't lie.

She just never specified it was going to be a lunar eclipse.

Chapter 2

Shit, what do I do?

How does this work?

I grab my coat and bolt outside, scanning the night sky like the answers I'm looking for might be written in the stars. I spin, desperate to catch the rare sight of the Court of the Fallen revealing itself to me. It's happened only three times in my lifetime, and each time, I was either too young and had no idea what was going on, or I was doing something else and missed it entirely.

How much time do I have?

Barefoot, I sprint uphill to where the trees thin out. The ground is still damp and freezing under my feet, but I don't have time for shoes, unless I want to miss the only opportunity to change my life forever.

The moon looks massive from where I stand, looming like an omen. The sky feels heavier, darker than any other autumn night I have ever experienced, and the stars seem to pulse.

Then—

From the shadows, something begins to form. Like smoke curling into shape. Like a mirage summoned by starlight and the night sky.

The Court of the Fallen rises into existence right before my eyes.

A luminous city stitched into the sky, suspended in bright moonlight.

Too beautiful to trust.

Like a bouquet of roses—dazzling, but dripping with thorns.

The city glows with lights that don't belong in this world—soft gold, dusky violets, silver that shimmers like it's been dipped in a river of stars—if such a place existed. I fear it might up there. Towers twist like spirals of clouds. Bridges arc between floating spires, lit by enchanted lanterns. Street after street winds through it, connecting the city like passageways to heaven.

And there are people—Fae, in various shapes and forms. Wings. Furs. Fangs. They glance down at us in their glamorous glowing gowns and wickedly sharp suits, like they've been waiting for us, too.

Gods, I've never seen anything like this in my life.

I just stand there, stunned, and suddenly, I understand why sailors would follow sirens to their deaths—how something so beautiful could drag you under.

Around me, people gather. Some gasp, others murmur, a few scream.

All of us are caught between awe and terror, mesmerised and utterly terrified.

One of the female Fae with blond hair rises from a floating platform, her midnight-blue gown sparkling like the dark, starry sky around her. She graciously descends, wings barely stirring the air, every movement precise, like the Queen of the Night.

"Good evening," she says with a smile that could have all men falling to their knees. "It's been so long since we last hosted your visit to our city."

Visit?

Is that what they think this is?

I thought a visit implied a return.

Unfortunately, most of us never make that journey.

"I trust you all remember the rules, but in case you weren't born the last time we did this, let me remind you." She jokes as if she's hosting a game show—technically, I suppose she is. "They're simple. Seven lucky humans will be selected to compete in our trials. With each round, at least one contestant will be eliminated." She pauses, then winks. "Only one will remain. And that lucky winner will be granted a single wish by the Court."

The crowd goes wild.

Chanting. Shouting. Praying.

Some cry. Others beam with excitement.

All of us drunk on desperation and temptation.

As if fuelled by the chaos, the Fae smiles—the kind of smile that makes my stomach twist.

"Simmer down, people ... it's not like we force you to do anything," she says, voice sweet as sugar. "Those who don't feel like taking a trip to the moon, by all means, please go back to your homes." She flutters her bright-green eyes. "Those who feel like playing—just close your eyes and make a wish."

"And how do we know who gets picked?" a voice shouts.

The Fae arches a brow. "Now, where's the fun in giving everything away?" Then another smile. "Trust me, if you're selected, you'll know."

I blink, again and again.

Then I take a deep breath, only just realising I've been holding it.

For the briefest moment, Noah's face flashes in my mind. His sad eyes and those quiet, heavy words ... they almost make me hesitate.

But when I close my eyes, I see Declan.

He's there, like he's always been.

So close.

Yet impossibly far.

And I know it in my bones, in every breath I take, that I have to do this.

If I don't take this once-in-a-lifetime chance, I will regret it for the rest of my life.

I'd rather break my own heart trying than spend forever haunted by the what-ifs.

So, I squeeze my eyes tighter, wishing in my head, begging, and praying to be picked, over and over again.

The Fae has already vanished when I open my eyes. Some of the people have cleared out. The rest are still wishing at the night sky, some even on their knees.

And I just wait there, for something,

Anything.

A sign.

A miracle.

A chance.

I brace myself in the cold wind. My feet have lost all feeling, and I'll probably wake up with blisters, but that's a problem for tomorrow.

I wait and wait some more.

Five, ten, twenty minutes pass.

Still, nothing.

And then—a gust of wind blasts from the dense lines of pines.

I turn.

And freeze.

A glowing figure stands in the dark. A male Fae spreads his dark wings wide, etched with blue constellations as if they were tattoos.

He's just standing there, arms crossed, a brow raised, waiting.

I swear I can see the vicious curl of his smile from here.

I look around, but nobody else moves. No heads turn.

It's as if I'm the only one seeing him.

Oh, Gods.

I *am* the only one seeing him.

I stumble back, my feet cold like ice.

He steps forward, emerging from the shadows into the moonlight like a dream carved out of a star.

Or a nightmare.

He moves like smoke, graceful, slow, unbothered—then he stops a few steps before me, and still, everyone else seems to be cursed with blindness—a shame, really, because they've all missed a chance to witness the most gorgeous being I've ever seen.

My throat is suddenly dry.

His face is sharp, perfectly and carefully sculpted by the Gods of stars and moons, all clean lines and cruel beauty. A mouth like his was made for lies—and for tracing fire across skin and lips. His honeyed skin glows faintly, like he's been bathed in starlight, and I am now convinced there must be a river of stars up there. His hair is as dark as a midnight storm, strands falling over his brow in just the right way to make it unfair to the rest of the men I've ever laid eyes on.

And his eyes.

Gods.

They're different colours.

One glows like liquid gold, the other like shattered pieces of twilight sky—deep blue, way too deep. Way too easy to drown in.

One glance at him, and I forget the world around me in a blink of an eye.

He is very much *not* human.

"Interesting choice of outfit," he says, his grin matching his voice—smooth, sharp, and far too pleased with itself.

It's exactly the kind of thing I'd expect from someone who looks like a dream and a nightmare had a baby. An angel with the devil's wings.

I glance down at myself. A bathrobe, mismatched coat, and bare feet.

"I—" I start, but words escape me. I clear my throat, then try again. "It's not like there's a dress code."

He seems amused. "My sincerest apologies. I'll be sure to send out a memo next time."

Interesting sense of humour.

I stare at him.

Now what?

As if reading my mind, he extends a hand.

I hesitate.

"Now or never, Cassandra," he murmurs. "Your brother is almost here."

What?

Noah—oh, Gods. *Noah.*

"Cass!"

I make a terrible mistake of turning. Noah is bracing his knees, panting hard, like he's been running since the second he realised what had appeared in the sky.

I don't think Noah can see the Fae.

But maybe my face is enough for him to understand what's happening.

An invisible hand squeezes my heart.

My breath catches, and I try not to cry again.

"I'm sorry, Noah," I whisper. "Please forgive me. I love you."

His eyes widen. He leaps forward—but it's too late.

"Cass, what are you doing?!"

I place my hand in the Fae's.

And we vanish into thin air.

Leaving my brother with the ghost of where I once stood.

Chapter 3

I wake up on a massive bed, so soft it feels like it was stitched together from layers of clouds. It's no longer dark, no stars above, just daylight pouring in through silk curtains that sway in a lazy breeze.

It's the morning.

For a second, I wonder if I dreamed it all. The Fae, the Court, and the hand I took.

But then I look around.

This place ... it doesn't exist in my tiny little house. The ceilings are too high. The scent too pure. The silence too complete.

Strange.

I'm still wearing my bathrobe, but my feet are warm, not a single blister in sight.

Did I die and go to heaven?

Eh.

Who am I kidding?

With all the suicidal thoughts I've had lately, and the way I've treated everyone, especially my own brother, heaven would probably slam its doors in my face.

Or maybe this is hell.

A version of hell appearing as heaven just to mess with me. A place where I wake up every day, convinced I'll find Declan—only to fail because he's in actual heaven, and I'm not.

Now that would be hilarious.

I get up and survey the room, the carpet soft, delicate, and stupidly luxurious beneath my feet. This is the kind of room you'd find in a palace, designed to cradle royalty and all their expensive jewels and crowns.

A massive mirror stretches across half a wall, framed in silver so ornate it probably costs more than my entire house. The kind of mirror you'd expect to show your soul or summon a demon if you stare at it too long. Across from it sits a built-in bathtub, sunken into gleaming marble like a decadent little pond. I wouldn't be surprised if it fills itself and sings when you dip your feet in.

There's a wardrobe on the other side of the room—so big like it expects to house clothes of a permanent resident, not a contestant who'd stay for a few weeks ... or a day, if I'm unlucky and die in the first trial. It's made out of glossy, ancient wood with handles shaped like crescent moons.

I know it in my bones—I'm at the Court of the Fallen.

But nothing is how I imagined it.

Is this how they treat all of the contestants?

I am a contestant, right?

Maybe the Fae are merciful enough to grant us comfort before our deaths, like how prisoners are offered one final meal before execution day.

I open the wardrobe, expecting maybe a few clothes or something mildly threatening for the trials, since I came empty-handed. Instead, it's packed with dresses, shirts, trousers, fighting leathers, even glamorous evening gowns that sparkle in the sunlight.

Huh.

Maybe I really am expected to dance my ass off to win.

My confusion only grows the more I explore the room—there are books, playing cards, jewellery, even a map of the Court.

Am I in a competition or on a bloody field trip?

A knock interrupts my train of thought and almost makes me jump.

I tighten my bathrobe and attempt to tame my wild hair as I walk to the door.

Should have gotten changed first thing—*for fuck's sake, Cassandra.*

Before me stands a slim Fae with high cheekbones. Although all Fae are immortal, she still looks young, her posture soft, shy, like a young girl who lacks confidence or life experience. Her braided hair reaches her hips, and she doesn't smile as she politely greets me.

"Miss Thorne," she says, and I immediately wonder if all the Fae know my full life history, or the colour of my underwear. The handsome one last night even knew my name and my brother. "I'm here to collect you."

"To where?" I ask, and more importantly ... "Now?"

"Well ..." She glances down at my very inappropriate attire. She's already taller than me—all Fae are—but now I feel even more pathetic. "I suppose we can take ten minutes."

"Be right back," I mutter before slamming the door shut and sprinting back to the wardrobe.

Oh, Gods, what do I wear?

I run back and open the door again. I poke my head out.

"Sorry"—I clear my throat—"where exactly are we going?"

"To Orientation, where you'll meet the rest of the contestants," she says with a hint of annoyance ... I should probably have not slammed the door. "A dress will do."

"Thank you," I say apologetically, before shutting the door slowly this time.

Orientation.

A dress.

These people take formality so seriously.

I don't really care about what I have to wear, as long as I get what I came for. If this is how the Fae prefer it, then I'll do it. I pick a soft pink dress that flows nicely past my knees, the fabric delicate and light on my skin.

I consider wearing a pair of sandals that would match the dress perfectly but choose boots for practicality—because what if I have to run?

Everything fits me too well, like it was made specially for me.

Must be nice having magic.

I yank the door open again right when the Fae is about to knock. She lowers her hand, then her gaze, eyeing me from head to toe like she's mentally scoring my outfit.

Then she gives me a subtle nod—I take it my choice of dress is acceptable.

She doesn't talk much—doesn't even bother to introduce herself. She just turns and starts leading me down the corridor in silence. Meanwhile, my heart is trying to leap out of my chest as I scan the surroundings.

The corridor stretches endlessly ahead, soaked in soft golden sunlight that seems to glow from everywhere at once. The marble floor echoes our footsteps. To the left, I assume, are the living quarters, the contestants' chambers. To the right, massive archways open into views of the outside world, framed by twisting columns carved with stars and strange symbols I can't read. Through them, I see rows of trees.

I'm not sure how seasons work up here. In fact, I don't think I ever imagined trees in the Court of the Fallen before—but there're tons of them, and their leaves are turning colours, mimicking the reds and golds of autumn in the human world.

Their scent is so crisp, so rich. The breeze carries it in, warm and spiced, like cinnamon and campfire.

Everything here feels how I imagine heaven would be like.

But when it's too good to be true, it's most likely a trap.

The Fae leads me downstairs and down another corridor until we finally stop at a set of tall arched doors. They open into a massive hall, drenched in gold and black like they're the Court's official theme colours. All eyes turn to us—Fae, humans, other creatures I didn't even know existed.

I press my lips together to keep me from gasping—and to ground myself from bolting.

The choices were between showing up in my bathrobe ... or showing up late.

At least this one is only mildly humiliating.

I think.

"Welcome," a voice says from inside—the terrifyingly beautiful female Fae from last night. "Cassandra Thorne, is it?"

I nod, stepping inside and trying very hard not to trip as I walk towards the group of humans standing in the middle of the hall.

A girl about my age—I've seen her in town a few times. A very chatty girl.

A guy a few years older than me who's staring at my breasts and whistles as if saying hi—definitely a prick.

A lady whose eyes are locked to the floor like it's talking to her.

A boy who looks about seventeen.

A middle-aged man, dressed sharply in a suit ...

And then—

Shit.

Lucas.

Declan's best friend.

"Cassandra," he murmurs. His eyes widen in surprise and something like dread. "You shouldn't be here."

My breath catches. For a second, I can see Declan standing right beside him, just like old days, when we'd all go the beach, lie in the sun, and drink from midday until the stars came out.

I hadn't seen Lucas since Declan's funeral.

"Neither should you," I whisper. "But here we are."

"Shit, you really shouldn't be here," he repeats like he's still stuck between disbelief and reality. "Please tell me you didn't come here to do what I think you're doing."

"I could ask you the same thing."

Lucas doesn't reply. He looks like he's choking on fear and confusion.

The dark rings beneath his eyes tell me sadness has its grip on him, too.

I just hope we don't have to kill each other at some point, because I'm not sure which one of us would survive, or if my soul's already dark enough for me to drive a dagger into him when it comes to it.

But if we both want the same wish, then the odds are stacked.

Only one of us needs to survive.

Explaining to Declan how his girlfriend or his best friend died to bring him back is going to be one hell of a conversation.

But there's no point going there just yet.

"I hope you are all well rested," the beautiful Fae starts, gracing us with her pretty smile yet again. "My name is Aurora. I am the host of these trials."

Aurora.

Gods, she really sounds like the Queen of Night or the Queen of Stars.

Or even both.

"It's an honour to meet you, Aurora," the guy who stared at my boobs says with a slight bow, like admiring some divine queen—I guess he doesn't care what he flirts with, as long as it has breasts and two legs he can get between.

I don't even want to know what his wish would be.

Aurora just blinks at him. I can feel the hall getting a little colder with that lethal stare.

"There will be three trials," she continues, gaze sweeping over us. "To give you time to prepare, and you know, calm down, and mourn"—Aurora pauses, voice dipped in syrup as if she didn't just hint a *death* between trials—"you'll have two weeks before each trial—except the final one. For that, you'll get a full month."

"A month?" The young boy gasps.

Aurora turns to him with something like amusement in her eyes. "Don't worry, dear. Time moves differently here. It might be a month for us, but down there, it'll only be four or five days."

That means a week in the Court is a day in the human world.

Oh, Gods.

I didn't realise how long I'd be stuck here. If I'm lucky enough to make it to the final round, I'll be here for two months.

"Some of you might notice the map we provided in your chambers. You're free to wander the Court as much as you like, visit our markets, museums, libraries ... even our brothels, if you wish. Though, I do have to warn you." Aurora's green eyes narrow slightly. "We cannot guarantee your safety should you wander down the wrong street. Not all Fae are friendly to humans."

I'm surprised there're some who are friendly at all.

But to be allowed to explore this place freely? That's something totally unexpected.

I already know who's on his way to the brothels the moment Orientation ends.

"Your chambers are your safe places. They're warded against any human sneaking in, hoping to slit your throat between trials ... I say this every time: we don't appreciate dirty players, but still, at least one will find a way to cheat, every single time." She exhales but doesn't look as bothered as she sounds. "So, do be careful at all times."

The fact that they haven't enforced a "no killings between trials" rule tells me they might actually prefer the chaos.

"The first trial starts in two weeks," Aurora says, a flicker of excitement lighting her eyes. "Tonight, there will be an opening ceremony. I expect you all to arrive in your best evening gowns and suits—and prepare a few interesting sentences to introduce yourselves." She winks. "For now, please make yourselves comfortable. Breakfast will be served in half an hour. I'll see you all tonight."

I'm sorry—what did she just say?

Opening ceremony?

Evening gowns?

This is ... what?

I thought I'd be locked in a room, depressed and terrified.

Instead, I get a massive chamber with a private bath, warded for my own safety, then a breakfast invitation, and now—apparently—a ball.

Am I in a magical death tournament or a fucking royal debut?

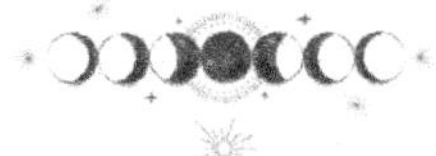

Lucas pulls me aside after Orientation, his grip tight enough on my arm that I wince.

"You need to leave," he says, his eyes sharp. "I'm being serious."

"Leave and go where?" I ask, twisting my arm out of his grasp. Only then does he seem to notice his grip.

He murmurs, "Sorry."

I let out a huff. "In case you haven't noticed, we are in a magical Court set in the stars."

Lucas rubs a hand over his face. "Gods, this is a mistake."

"Oh, don't be a hypocrite, Lucas." I cross my arms. "You can't seriously tell me to go when you're here trying to do the exact same thing."

"Yes, but only one of us can win this thing, Cassandra."

I shrug. "So, we'll be a team, slaughter everyone else until it's just you and me left."

Lucas frowns, his eyes scanning me like he's never seen me before. "Have you always been this ruthless?"

I scratch my arm—good question.

"It's what you have to do to survive," I mutter. "Don't tell me you didn't already know that when you made a wish last night?"

"Well, yeah," he says, his face grim. "I was willing to do whatever it takes, but I didn't factor in that I might have to kill my best friend's girlfriend to bring him back."

I flinch.

"Don't worry. The others might do that for you," I say, half joking, half serious. "I didn't know you wanted Declan back that badly ... everyone seems to think I'm crazy for not letting go."

Lucas sighs, running a hand through his hair. "He came to me that night he died."

I freeze.

"Declan asked if I'd go drinking with him, but I was tired, so I said no."

Fuck.

The next sentence comes out of his lips like a whisper. "And for the past month and a half, I keep playing that night in my head. If only I had gone out with him, things might have turned out differently." He pauses, his voice cracking slightly.

I see my own sorrow reflected in those blue eyes.

"If I had been there, he would still be alive, Cassandra," Lucas admits, his gaze lowering to the ground.

I have seen this shame before.

This kind of hurt.

This same kind of guilt.

It pierces through me, pinning me to the ground, forcing me to relive our argument over and over.

Lucas blames himself, the same way I do myself.

My breaths come out shallow. I want to tell him it's not his fault. I want to reach for him, say something to comfort him.

But that would mean it's also not my fault.

And I just can't accept that.

"We're both here now," I manage at last. "Let's just try to help each other."

He exhales, slow and reluctant, but eventually nods.

It's not like he has any better options.

Neither do I.

If anything, I should be grateful there's someone here to save my arrogant, emotionally constipated ass.

We make our way to the dining hall where the rest of the contestants are already seated. The table is long, laid with all kinds of breakfasts known to man: pancakes, eggs, ham, toast, bacon, hummus, pastries, rice soup, even some sort of noodle stir-fry, and many, many more.

Like overfeeding pigs before the slaughter.

"So, you two know each other?" the girl I've seen in town asks as I sit down next to her, tilting her head towards Lucas. "I'm Tessa, by the way."

"Cassandra," I say, as if Aurora hadn't already introduced me to the entire hall. "And yes, he's a friend."

"Oh." She winces, already piecing together what that entails. "I'm sorry."

Yeah, well.

We could team up to get rid of you. Who knows.

"Hey, Cassie." The flirty prick waves at me, grinning like we're old friends. "Name's Jordan—but you can call me *baby* if you like."

The young boy almost chokes. "Fuck me. You're disgusting."

Agreed.

"Shut up, boy," Jordan snaps, pointing his fork at him. "This is an adult conversation."

"I'm not a boy," the kid snarls. "I'm nineteen."

Jordan frowns. "You're underdeveloped, then. Poor thing."

"Hey, leave him alone, mate," Lucas says, shooting Jordan a warning look. "And I'm going to say this once: don't ever talk to Cassandra like that again, or I'll poke your eyes out."

Whilst I appreciate Lucas trying to protect me, I just now realise that announcing we know each other might not be the smartest move. Who knows; they might all gang up on us first.

But the kid?

Oh, he's furious.

"I don't need you to fight my battles for me," he snaps at Lucas.

Well.

This is going great so far.

Jordan smirks, then turns to his right to harass the quiet woman who was talking to the floor earlier. "What's your deal, lady? Why are you here?"

She looks up from her plate, blinks, then goes right back to eating.

A lot of personalities here, huh?

"You don't have to be nice, but at least be respectful," the middle-aged man finally says, his voice calm and warm, like he could whisper you into believing you're a butterfly because of how kind he sounds. "Nice to meet you, Cassandra. My name is Oliver."

"Nice to meet you," I murmur.

Hope you're easy to kill, since you're old.

It's a stupid thing to introduce ourselves.

I don't want to make friends, know their history, or reasons they're here.

I only have one thing to achieve, and I can't fail because I let my stupid emotions get the better of me by being soft.

That's not why I'm here.

No one here is my friend, not really.

Lucas might be now, but there's no telling what's going to happen when survival instincts kick in and he has to pick who lives and who dies.

He sure as hell isn't going to pick me.

I know I wouldn't.

Chapter 4

This is so stupid.

A fucking ball.

Mother of the stars, save me.

I expected death, screams, a bloodbath—but somehow, I have ended up in a gown long enough to hang myself with, glittery shoes so high I could stab someone with them, and jewellery so sparkly it might blind me in daylight.

It's all for the trials, I tell myself as I take a deep breath.

It's been a long time since I bothered to look nice in front of a mirror. I barely recognise the dark-haired woman staring back at me. My soft curls almost reach my waist, as I haven't found the energy to sort it out for months. My grey eyes have only looked lively in the past hours because I'm too alert and don't know what the hell is going on. I glance down at my golden gown—bright as the moon, shimmering like the stars.

Gods, I hate how beautiful it is, how perfectly it hugs my curves, and how effortlessly it fits me.

This is so wrong.

This should not be how I get Declan back.

But unfortunately, it's the only way.

Let's get this shit over with.

I open the door to find Lucas waiting for me. He's in a navy three-piece suit, as sharp as I've ever seen him. It complements his light brown hair and tanned skin nicely. And Gods—he's tall. Six foot something, maybe? I've always thought he's good-looking, but I've never really *looked* at him until tonight.

Since we might die any day now, I hope this man hooks up with some hot Fae.

I might have considered it myself, if he weren't Declan's best friend—but let's not go there.

"How long have you been standing here?" I ask.

"Not long." He shrugs. "Fifteen minutes or so."

"Why didn't you knock?"

"Didn't want to rush you," he simply says. "I came because I don't trust that guy Jordan."

"I think there's a chance he's out at some brothel."

"Best not leave things to chance around here."

Fair enough.

"Shall we?" he asks, nodding towards the endless corridor. We're left to find our own way back to the hall this time.

I've never really spent time alone with Lucas before. There're friends who belong to both Declan and me, but Lucas was one of his. They basically grew up together.

Now, I'm not sure what to talk to him about without Declan in the picture, and the way Lucas keeps both of his hands stuffed in his pockets and quietly sighs tells me he feels the same way.

"Don't you think it's ridiculous, this opening ceremony?" I try to break the ice first.

"Tell me about it." He scoffs. "And the fact that they're giving us two weeks between trials—treating us like kings and queens, letting us wander outside. Feels like a trap to me."

"Maybe it's just a fun game to them. Something to watch."

"I still don't get it." Lucas exhales, shaking his head. "They could have easily just thrown us all into a cell."

"I know," I murmur. "Though I'm glad they didn't."

He stops walking, turning to me. "I know you know this, but don't trust anyone."

"Not even you?"

His jaw tenses. "They've got magic here, Cassandra. You'd never know how they could use me ... or any of us."

I suppose that's true.

"Same goes for you."

"I'll try." Lucas nods, a faint smile tugging at his lips.

We reach the hall a few minutes later, the sound of music seeping through the arched doors. Laughter and conversation echo down the corridor, rich and alive. This time, the doors swing open on their own—and I'm almost blinded by glitter, candlelight, and gowns so glamourous they look like they're made of stardust.

Good lord.

All the Fae are masked.

It's a masquerade for them—but not for us.

The Fae part like the tide, eyes locking on both of us as we walk in. Some grin underneath their masks.

I scan the hall—not all contestants are here yet. Only the quiet woman whose name I still don't know, the nineteen-year-old, and Oliver.

They all look absolutely petrified.

"I hope they've got strong wine," I mutter. "I'm going to need it."

"That makes two of us."

We join the little circle of no-magic people, completely surrounded by a group of wings, claws, and unsettling beauty. Even with the masks, I can practically feel them radiating. If they weren't so terrifying, this masquerade might almost trick me into thinking they were angels.

None of us knows what to do with ourselves, or even where to look. The same young Fae walks by with a tray of drinks, and Lucas and I immediately grab one each.

"I wouldn't drink that," Oliver warns. "Who knows what Fae wine would do to a human body."

"Yeah, well." Lucas clicks his tongue. "We're going to die sooner or later, anyway."

He chugs the wine.

I do the same.

Oliver underestimates what two depressed people, bonding over the same grief, are willing to drink just to forget the pain.

Oh, that's punchy.

The wine is stronger than I expected. The first sip is almost divine, sweet and dry with a little hint of something unfamiliar, but it leaves a lovely taste lingering on my tongue.

Tessa arrives in a light blue gown a few minutes later, her jaw dropping to the ground after realising it's a masquerade party. She sprints to us, eyes wide.

Still no signs of Jordan.

I hope a Fae suffocated him in the brothel with a silk pillow and zero regrets—it would save us all the trouble.

But a cockroach like him doesn't die easily. Cut off his head and he'd probably live another week.

He finally graces us with his arrogance half an hour later, all grinning like a champion who just fucked a Fae for the first time. It's written all over his face.

I knew he wouldn't miss the chance.

He grabs a glass of Fae wine as he walks over to us, instantly bragging. "I don't know about you guys, but I had a rather interesting afternoon with a Fae."

"What the fuck did you use to pay at the brothel?" Lucas frowns. "You *did* pay, right? Because these Fae will cut off your head if you didn't."

"Why, asking for a tip for yourself?" Jordan lifts a brow.

Lucas rolls his eyes. "Please, I'm not so desperate I need to pay for sex."

I grin.

That must have hurt.

But of course, a guy like Jordan doesn't give a shit.

"You should," he says, grabbing a drink before sipping it. "These things feed on promises, if you don't have money. All you've got to do is offer them one, and make sure you keep it."

What?

Promises are a currency around here?

Lucas narrows his eyes at him. "So, what sick thing did you promise the Fae?"

Jordan smirks now. "That she'd come before me."

Of course he did.

His arrogance is truly staggering.

I wouldn't be surprised if his wish was to sleep with a Fae and remain alive just long enough to tell the tale.

I'd be lying if I said the idea isn't tempting. Sleeping with a magical, gracious Fae—a gorgeous one like the one who came to me the other night.

I wonder how different it would be compared to a human...

There's a ninety-percent chance I'll die in one of the trials, anyway.

The thought of shagging one before I kick the bucket doesn't sound half bad.

Declan is dead. It's not like I've been touched much these days.

I sip my wine in silence, half embarrassed, half thirsty from the thought. Guilt creeps in, like it always does every time I let myself feel anything that resembles happiness or excitement.

Letting go of Declan, even for a moment, feels like a betrayal.

My eyes scan the hall once more, trying to shake off this guilt that's eating me alive.

And then I see him.

Standing at the far end in a black suit, wings tucked tight, hands in his pockets.

His eyes are already on me.

Two different eye colours—one gold, one deep blue. Like he was born from an eclipse storm. I see them, even with his mask on, even from distance.

Just when I was tempted to climb that body for fun before I say goodbye to this earth.

Or maybe these shameful thoughts will be the death of me.

Sure, I'm still mourning over Declan—doesn't mean I'm blind to a smoking hot, dangerous Fae.

"Wow, what a sight!"

I'd recognise that voice anywhere.

All eyes turn to the platform where Aurora stands in a scarlet gown slashed down to her chest, her full, perfect cleavage on display. A gold mask rims her eyes, the edges dusted in red to match her dress and her crimson lips curved with delight.

She looks radiant. Ethereal.

Such beauty doesn't belong in this world.

Even I might not pass on a chance to sleep with her.

If there is ever a time to try everything before I die, this is it.

Gods, what the fuck did they put in the wine in this place?

I glance back at the hot Fae—but he's gone, completely vanished.

Huh.

"Contestants." Aurora's green eyes drop to us, her voice so smooth like her velvet gown. "You all look dashing tonight. Please come forward and introduce yourselves and give us one promise … just one you'll keep throughout this competition. It doesn't have to be related to your wish." She smiles. "There'll be side quests between the trials, granting various prizes. This will help us design the games."

Oh, Gods.

They really love to play.

Jordan is the first to dare stalking towards Aurora, probably wishing he could get close enough to charm her into bed, too. The rest of us follow reluctantly.

"You look beautiful tonight, Aurora," he says, bowing like he's at her altar.

Aurora doesn't react, or smile. She keeps her chin high, her spine straight.

"Hello, my name is Jordan," he announces to the room, no glimpse of fear in his eyes, only delight.

I wonder if he made a bet with his mates and genuinely believes he could win it all. He's vibrating with excitement, probably imagining how he'll brag about all this later.

"I'm twenty-seven and an artist," he continues. "I draw great nudes and would consider sitting as a nude model—so, if anyone's interested ... well, you know where to find me." Then he winks. "My promise is that it will be worth your while."

Oh. My. Gods.

What is this man made of?

Is this really all his tiny little brain could come up with?

Laughter echoes through the hall, but Jordan's confidence doesn't seem to falter for a second. He just grins and waves like he's finished a royal performance, sauntering back to the group with the pride of someone who just announced he's a manwhore to a room full of immortals.

"Gods, he's unbearable," Tessa mutters beside me.

Yes, and most likely will get himself killed trying to bone the wrong Fae.

Oliver is next.

"I'm Oliver," he says, his voice so low you can smell fear radiating off him.

"Louder! What are you whispering about!?" some Fae in the audience heckles.

I think he's about to shit himself.

Bless him.

"I'm Oliver," he repeats, louder this time, voice trembling. "I used to be a teacher, but now I'm a gardener." He clears his throat. "I promise to take care of your gardens—for a small fee."

Oh.

That's clever.

Secured himself a little hobby and some pocket money to enjoy the city later.

Shit, I don't have a clue what to promise.

Next, it's the nineteen-year-old's turn—finally I'll find out his name and stop calling him by his age.

"Name's Leon," he says, tucking both hands in his pockets, his tone bored like he can't be bothered. "Just finished school. Nothing to do with my life. And promise not to touch alcohol while I'm here—it tastes like shit."

Ah yes, a young adult who isn't self-destructive enough to start liking the bitter taste of alcohol.

We all hated it the first time, but it didn't stop any of us.

The crowd gasps like he just insulted their gods.

I'm willing to bet half of them will try and temp Leon with wine by the end of the night just to prove a point.

"My name is Tessa," Tessa says with a polite, slightly forced smile, eyes darting nervously around the hall. "I'm twenty-two, and I'm a cook. I promise to try as much food here as I can."

So soft. So naïve.

Meanwhile, my mind is a damn void, failing to come up with even a half-decent promise.

The shy woman whose best friend is the floor steps forward, head finally lifting as she opens her mouth. "I'm Daisy. Thirty-five, and a librarian."

Yeah.

No shit.

"My promise is to sort out every book I read alphabetically."

Bloody hell.

Even a stupid one counts.

Come on, Cass. Just make up some bullshit and say it with confidence.

It's only Lucas and I left. He glances at me as if asking who's going first, but I shake my head—*just give me another damn minute.*

"Hi, I'm Lucas."

There he goes, beginning his endless mission to save my ass.

"I'm twenty-three. Still studying to be a vet," Lucas pauses. The Fae purr "Awww" like they'll be queueing up to see the soon-to-be veterinarian with fake pets that probably just have allergies. "I promise ... to win at least a trial whilst I'm here."

Risky move.

But from the chants and cheers, it sounds like he's just become the Fae's favourite.

My heels somehow don't betray me as I step forward.

"My name is Cassandra," I say, swallowing my fear, ripping it apart in my head.

I want to be here.

I know why I'm here.

I breathe.

"I'm twenty-three, and I work at a coffee shop in town." I blink.

I mean, I just quit, but who cares.

The weight of every Fae's gaze settles on me, heavy like a stack of a thousand ancient books. I try to stand tall, reminding myself I have to survive amongst them for two months—if I'm lucky.

And there he is again.

The eclipse storm of a Fae.

I tilt my head, and I could swear the corners of his lips twitch up into a grin.

"My promise ..." I pause, letting the silence stretch just long enough to drag out the suspense. My lips curve upwards slightly. "Is to have fun, and only punch those who deserve it."

For a second, the entire hall holds still.

Then, a few Fae chuckle.

And the room erupts with laughter and thunderous applause.

I exhale.

Thank Gods.

That marks the beginning of the trials. Aurora steps forward again, beaming as she invites everyone to celebrate this joyous occasion (for them, at least). Food appearing out of nowhere—plates of the finest meat, glowing vegetables in impossible colours, and wine that refills itself.

It's a feast fitting of royalty.

The worst thing is all of it tastes like a piece of heaven.

I catch a glimpse of Jordan roaming around, trying to mingle with the Fae, whilst Daisy just eats quietly, and Oliver is already negotiating a price for his gardening services with a Fae who looks like he's never seen dirt before.

It seems some of us are already starting to lose sight of what we're here for.

Good for me, I guess.

"I'm putting a bet on you winning."

I turn and almost startle. A male Fae stands beside me, silver haired, his brown eyes glinting with something unreadable underneath his white mask.

"Pardon?"

"You seem to be the most ambitious of them all," he says, grinning. "So, I'm putting a huge bet on you."

I should've guessed there would be gambling.

Of course there is.

What a life they have up here.

Glamourous balls, grand feasts, gambling, drinking, tormenting humans, and probably a whole lot of fucking behind velvet curtains.

We've all heard the stories.

Fallen Fae banished from the stars—what else would they do to kill eternity?

"Well, you're about to lose a whole lot of money." I chuckle, clink my glass against his, and down the rest of my wine. "Disappointing people is my hobby."

"You don't even know what the trials are yet."

"Results will be the same."

Amusement flashes in his eyes, and for whatever reason, he extends a hand. "Name's Gideon."

"Cassandra," I say, taking his hand. "Is this what you all do, Gideon? Party, gamble, drink?"

"Believe it or not, we all have jobs."

I tilt my head, catching a glimpse of Lucas staring at us from the corner of my eye. "Why would Fae need jobs?"

"How do you think we run this Court?" He gestures broadly. "Magic alone doesn't power all of this, you know."

Well, obviously, I don't.

"So, what do you do then?"

He straightens, pride flickering in his eyes. "I'm a warrior."

That would mean there are others ... other Fae Courts. Ones that might not be so friendly to this one.

Interesting.

"Is Aurora the Queen of the Court, then?"

Being a warrior means he serves someone. If there's a chain of command, I need to know who sits at the top, so I know who to befriend ... or who to fear.

Gideon chuckles softly. "You can say she's a noble. But no, Aurora is not our Queen. She's a High Fae."

She sure looks the part and is important enough to command a room full of wings and fangs.

"There's no Queen in this Court." He arches a brow. "Not yet, anyway."

I frown. "There's a king, then?"

Gideon sips his wine. "There is," he says. "But the bastard doesn't give a damn about titles. Wouldn't be King, High Lord, Prince—whatever the hell we tried to call him. Said we're all outcasts here."

I blink.

The way he talks about this king—or whatever he is—makes me think that they're either best friends, or lifelong enemies.

"So why not give the crown to someone who wants it?"

"No one is half as powerful as him." Gideon rolls his eyes, but a hint of admiration glints in them—definitely best friends, then. "And no one dares. A lot of what you see here is running on his magic. Who wants to rule a court when one of your subjects could bring down a city because they felt like it?"

That's ... terrifying.

"Who is this Fae, then?"

"I heard he's a prick," a voice replies behind me.

I turn around to meet a golden eye and a shade of storm blue staring back at me, drenched in starlight and deep sea.

Gideon scoffs. "Agreed, but don't say it too loud. His ego hears everything."

"Yes, it's huge," the hot Fae adds, unfurling his gorgeous, dark wings with lines of constellations like a smug display.

What an interesting way to describe your King—boss—or whatever.

And, Gods—those wings.

Tessa lets out a scream before throwing a hand over her mouth. Daisy's face drains of colour. Lucas mutters a sharp curse under his breath.

And I just stand there, stunned and utterly in awe.

Same as I was last night.

"Cassandra," he says, folding his wings away, not giving a damn who he just unsettled. His eyes lower to the golden gown I'm wearing. He grins. "Now that's a proper outfit."

Thanks for reminding me I met you in a bloody bathrobe.

"It's been two nights, and you still haven't told me your name."

That grin of his curves wider. "Wasn't sure you cared."

"Two nights?" Gideon crosses his arms. "Don't tell me you collected her yourself?"

I raise an eyebrow.

Wasn't that what happened with the others?

"Yes," he replies simply. "And?"

Gideon just shakes his head, grabbing another glass of wine. "Whatever, mate."

"Don't mind him. He's just cranky," he whispers, offering me a hand, exactly like last night. "Kieran."

Kieran.

I place my hand in his, and he lifts it to his lips, brushing a soft, gentle kiss across my skin.

Just for a breath. Just enough for me to feel my own heartbeat.

I blink, unsure if it's the wine or him making my heart stutter.

"May I have this dance?" Kieran asks, nodding to the dance floor. Only then does my brain register the music that's been playing for a while.

I don't know what interest he's taken in me. But I'm willing to do whatever it takes to win, even if it means charming a few powerful Fae into liking me.

Worshipping me like Jordan worships Aurora.

So, I nod.

Kieran smiles, his fingers curling gently around mine as he leads me away from the others, towards the centre of the floor where shadows stretch and gold light spills like liquid.

I had a few lessons in school, but mostly I just jump around when I dance. Never once have I ever slow-danced like this before.

"May I?" Kieran asks as if noticing how nervous I am. I nod again, and he places a hand on my waist. His other hand catches mine, gentle but certain, and we begin to move. I'm stiff at first, unsure where to put either of my feet, but he guides me like he's been doing this for a hundred years—which he probably has.

The music wraps around us, slow and angelic. Fae voices singing in a language I don't understand.

I glance up, and he's already looking at me.

"So ..." I dare to speak, not knowing where this insane courage comes from. "Tell me, Kieran, do you always hit on human contestants?"

He lets out a soft laugh. "Only the pretty ones."

Heat coils low in my stomach. Dangerous. Charming. Probably fatal.

"Why, thank you," I say anyway. "Gideon was telling me about his role in the Court. What is your role?" Besides being hot and flirty.

"Oh, I'm an executioner."

I tense in his arms. My steps falter. His grip doesn't.

He grins. "In a way."

Great. That makes me feel so much better.

And yet, I don't pull away.

"The question is, why are you here, Cassandra?" Kieran tightens his grip, pulling me a little closer. I can feel the tight, hard muscles of his stomach beneath the sharp suit.

And I hate how I don't feel the urge to push him away.

How I let myself forget Declan for a second.

I lick my suddenly dry lips. "You picked me."

"Yes." He leans in, his breath brushing my ear. "But you were practically begging for it—why?"

"Will you help me win the wish if I tell you?"

I can feel his wicked smile curl against my skin.

"There're other ways to get a wish. Winning the trial is only one of them."

I pull away, just enough to meet those impossible eyes. Whatever game he wants to play, whatever it is he wants from me …

I'm in.

Anything it takes to bring Declan back.

"Like what?"

"Like—" Kieran pauses mid-sentence, head snapping towards the arched doors.

A moment later, they slam open. A female Fae strides in, dragging Jordan behind her—half naked and grinning like an idiot.

Oh, Gods.

It's barely been a night. What the fuck has he done?

Everyone parts as the female storms through, dragging Jordan behind her. She stops in front of Kieran and shoves him forward.

The prick stumbles.

"This one doesn't understand that no means no."

Kieran rips off his mask and rubs a hand over his face.

I clamp my lips shut.

Fucking idiot.

Don't tell me he was trying to—shit.

"There's always one." Kieran shakes his head, turning to the female. "You okay?"

"Yes, but this piece of shit won't be."

Kieran's gaze returns to Jordan, and something shifts behind those mismatched eyes. "What do you want me to do?" he asks, his tone sending chills down my spine.

He did say he was an executioner.

Above us, the starry ceiling darkens. Clouds roll in where there were none—and then lightning starts cracking.

Oh, this is not good.

"Just a warning is fine," she says, crossing her arms.

"What are you talking about?" Jordan slurs, swaying as he tries to stand. "We were having fun, weren't we?"

His breath reeks of alcohol. His eyes are barely open.

Kieran lifts a hand.

And Jordan lifts with it—his feet dangling above the floor, magic coiling around his throat like smoke.

He chokes.

I gasp.

Lightning flashes overhead, then a sickening sound—a wet snap, a sharp cry.

A crimson line blooms across Jordan's left eye.

Blood spills.

Kieran took his eye in an instant, without so much as moving a step, without lifting a blade.

Every hair in my body rises.

"Next time, the cut goes on your neck," he growls, low and furious, then releases the magic.

Jordan collapses, screaming, clutching his face, writhing in blood and agony.

An arm wraps around my waist, pulling me back—Lucas.

His eyes stay fixed on Kieran, wide, shaken, his mouth unable to utter a word.

Kieran flicks his fingers. A few Fae step forward without a word and drag Jordan out, leaving only the echoes of his cry behind.

Then, Kieran turns back to me.

"Sorry about the mess," he says, eyeing the blood still on the floor. He flicks his fingers again—just like that, it's gone. "Didn't mean to scare you."

The ceiling calms again, the clouds fade, and lightning curls into smoke and vanishes.

And clear as the night sky, I know.

Kieran isn't just some pretty Fae with power and charm.

He's the King.

The one Gideon was talking about.

Chapter 5

"What was that all about?"

Aurora rushes in, pulling off her gold mask, revealing her beautiful face as she demands an answer from Kieran. All whilst I'm still unable to move, Lucas's grip tightening around me.

"He was asking for it." Kieran shrugs. "Luckily, Laia feels incredibly forgiving today."

Funny.

"Asking for it" is exactly the kind of thing Jordan would have slapped the female Fae in the face with if she were a human and didn't know how to kick his ass.

"I knew that guy was bad news." Aurora shakes her head, stepping closer to Laia and gently rubbing her arm.

These Fae are—

... emotional?

I glance between the three of them. As cruel as Kieran was, he's visibly upset. It's obvious he cares about Laia. And so does Aurora.

Interesting.

I wonder how I can take advantage of this.

Kieran glances at me, at Lucas's arm around my waist. He opens his mouth, but Aurora reaches out, her fingers brushing his neck.

"You've got blood on you," she murmurs, wiping it with the kind of closeness that makes me look twice. Her eyes soften as he leans into her touch, only for a second—before he pulls away.

Her eyes then flick to me.

Too quickly.

Too deliberate

A display of possession.

Basically, a silent warning.

He's hers.

Got it.

"Let me make it clear," Kieran calls out, his eyes darting to us humans—not me, but the rest of us. The entire hall freezes like it's holding its breath. "You are welcome to stay here, do as you please ... but if harm comes to any one of us ..." He pauses, just long enough to make sure that we're carefully listening to every word. "You'll wish you'd never been born."

I stop breathing.

Kieran smirks.

"I wish I could promise no harm will come to you, but I can't help it if you're all reckless fools," he drawls, his voice almost bored. "Now that that's clear, please ... enjoy yourselves. The night is still young."

And just like that, the music swells again. Conversation and laughter fill the room in an instant like nothing happened—like this is just another night in paradise for them.

"We should go," Lucas mutters, gently pulling me back.

I hesitate.

Kieran was about to tell me how to get a wish without winning the trials.

On one hand, he scares the absolute hell out of me.

But on the other ... I didn't come here to play it safe. And to be fair, Jordan did deserve to be punished.

So, I slip out of Lucas's grasp.

"I want to stay," I tell him, and I can see on his face how much he dislikes it.

"Cassandra, you saw what he just did."

"Yes, but Jordan assaulted Laia."

I don't even know why he would think it was a good idea, but with the insane amount of Fae wine he consumed, he probably didn't think at all.

"It doesn't matter," Lucas protests, his voice low, his eyes narrowing like he's looking at a stranger. "You can't seriously want to keep dancing with him."

But that's the problem.

He doesn't know me.

Not anymore.

"I'll be fine," I say. "Don't worry about me."

I have to do this on my own—win these trials, these twisted games. Lucas will try to save me, but he won't be able to follow me everywhere.

"You're my best friend's girlfriend. Of course I bloody worry about you," he snaps, his words piercing through me like a blade.

I step back anyway.

"As long as I don't do anything stupid, they're not going to hurt me."

Those are my final words before I turn my back on Lucas. I don't want to see those eyes. Don't want to know I've disappointed yet another one of my friends.

Now facing Kieran, with Aurora still behind him, I feel the weight of the room shift onto me.

But Kieran tilts his head, and his lips curl into a grin. Something like surprise and admiration flashes in his eyes.

Aurora is going to kill me.

But if her boyfriend humiliates her in front of the whole Court by flirting with me, then I'm not the problem.

"Will you give me a tour of the Court?" I ask Kieran sweetly.

His grin sharpens.

He extends me a hand in answer.

Maybe Kieran isn't hers, after all.

Maybe she just wants to be his.

"Can you warn me next time you do that?" I clutch my chest, heart pounding, stumbling slightly as the world shifts around us—we vanished again, just like last night.

"Next time?" Kieran raises an eyebrow. "Sounds like you're hoping this becomes a habit."

Staring at his beautiful face before Aurora slices off my head is a great way to go.

I shove down my fear and ask, "Is that a problem?"

That I want to befriend the King of the Fallen.

What's the worst that could happen?

I suppose I could die.

And I will die.

"I can smell your fear from here, Cassandra," he says gently, both hands tucked behind his back, leaning in just a little to make my breath stutter.

I frown. "Can you blame me?"

"No." Kieran shakes his head. "But most humans—if not all of them—usually run away at the sight of something like that."

"I'm not most humans." I shrug. "Or are you going to hurt me?"

He crosses his arms, stretching his wings as if to scare me. A blast of wind hits my face.

But I don't flinch.

I narrow my eyes at him.

"Don't flex. I already know your wings are gorgeous."

That gets a laugh out of the man—Fae—who just took another man's eye in cold blood.

A laugh.

Kieran shakes his head like he can't quite believe he's encountered a mortal girl with a death wish who dares to challenge him.

"I like you, Cassandra."

A pause.

"Though that mouth is going to get you into trouble."

Only if I let it land on his.

I smirk. "Or out of it."

Implications hang in the thick air around us. Kieran's storm-blue eye flashes like lightning, but I pretend I don't see it and turn to scan the surroundings instead.

We are in a dark room, lit only by a single enchanted orb, a vast open window before us. I step closer, leaning out. The damp, autumn breeze kisses my skin—it's a tower. And beyond it, the sky stretches endlessly. Streaks of violet and rose stain the heavens, stars scattered like glittering dust across a canvas of night sky.

Gods ...

I wish I could sleep under this starry sky.

"You did ask for a tour," Kieran whispers from behind me. "This is the Tower of Stars."

To my surprise, he doesn't step closer. Doesn't try to take advantage.

He's probably a few hundred years old—he must know I want something from him, and he could easily twist that, make the most out of it.

He took a man's eye without blinking.

But somehow, he's a gentleman?

"Gideon seemed surprised that you collected me yourself last night." I turn back to him. "Why?"

"It's not exactly in my job description."

I exhale, a slow breath pushing past my lips. "So why'd you do it?"

"It's rare I get to leave the Court," he replies, a faint smile brushing his lips—but not the same wicked one he's worn all night. "I fancied a trip to the human world."

I tilt my head. "Maybe you should get out more."

He scoffs, gaze drifting to the night sky. "Just because I have wings doesn't mean I can go anywhere I want. The Court only appears during celestial events. You know that."

I blink.

Once.

Twice.

A shooting star slices across the sky.

Then it hits me.

"Don't tell me ..." I breathe. "You can only leave when the Court appears?"

"The others leave when they feel like it," Kieran says softly, the shadows softening the edges of his face. "I can only do so when the Court is visible to your world."

I press my lips into a thin line.

Two starry nights with him and somehow, he already trusts me with this.

The Fallen King.

Cursed and caged in the Court built by his very own magic.

Fuck.

I thought it would be impossible to find a version of me in this place.

But here we are.

Both trapped in the ruins we made ourselves.

"Why are you telling me this?" I murmur.

"Because, Little Star," he says, meeting my eyes at last. "You won't remember any of this when everything is over."

"What?"

"You'll remember the trials," Kieran adds. "But all the tiny details like this will slip your mind completely."

That's why no one ever talks about the Court once they're back.

It must be nice—being able to just curse yourself into oblivion.

If I could do that, I'd have forgotten Declan by now.

That horrible fight. The awful things I said.

All of it.

I'm tempted to ask Kieran to take it from me—to wipe my memories of Declan.

But I'm not done punishing myself just yet.

Far from it.

Chapter 6

The next morning, all the contestants stare at me like I've grown three heads. Even Jordan, who's now wearing an eyepatch and lost about half of his ego. He doesn't speak, but his one functioning eye is quietly judging me.

They probably think I crawled into Kieran's bed to get ahead of the game.

They can think whatever they want.

I don't give a shit.

"Cassandra!"

Only Tessa greets me with that bright smile like flowers bloomed from her pillow. Everything's sunshine and sparkles in her world. I don't even know what she could possibly want from here.

Maybe she's just trying to get close to me because she stupidly believes I've got the upper hand.

"Good morning," I say, slicing my bacon in silence.

"Where did you vanish to last night?" Lucas asks.

The Tower of Stars, the botanical garden with glowing plants, and the River of Vows—a famous spot for weddings, apparently. It binds the couple's souls together for eternity.

Ancient belief, according to Kieran.

Ironic how even Fae believe in soulmates.

Not that it'd work on me—can't bind what isn't there.

"Here and there," is what I reply to Lucas.

It was just a midnight stroll.

With surprisingly great company.

Maybe it's easier to walk beside someone when neither of you has a soul left.

I don't really care why he's interested in me, or if he just flirts with humans for fun. I'm on the King's good side, and that's everything I need.

But of course, that answer isn't good enough for Lucas.

"Cassandra, what are you doing?"

Here we go, another person disappointed in me.

"I'm eating, Lucas." I sigh. "And I'm safe and sound. He didn't hurt me."

Jordan scoffs from his seat. "Not yet, anyway."

"Oh, please," I hiss. "You assaulted one of his people."

"You don't even know what happened. We're just having fun." He flushes red—then winces, clutching his side like the memory of pain is suddenly real again.

Sure, Jordan. Just having fun.

"I swear to Gods, that fucking Fae will pay," Jordan growls, whilst the rest of us exchange looks. Thank the stars there is no one in this room but us, otherwise we'd have Jordan's head on a spike by sunset.

I shake my head. "He's got magic and can vanish into thin air. How are you ever going to hurt Kieran?"

"Iron, obviously. Everyone knows that's their weakness."

"Right, because they would let anyone smuggle iron up here." Oliver lets out a loud, heavy sigh. "I think it'd be wise for you not to go around announcing you're plotting to kill the Fae King, who—from what I gathered—is probably the one granting the wish at the end of this whole thing."

"King?" Jordan's head snaps to him.

Leon blinks at the idiot in the group. "I'd say try opening your eyes next time, but—well, you've only got the one."

"You think you're so funny, huh, kid?" Jordan spits. "Let's see how long you last."

"I'm not a kid," Leon grunts. "And are you kidding me? It's barely been two days and you've already lost an eye. Pretty sure everyone here will last longer than you."

"At least we all know who will last the longest," Daisy murmurs, voice quiet but soaked in envy. It hits me like a slap. "Right, Cassandra?"

Ah.

So, this is what we're doing now.

I liked her better when the floor was her only friend.

I grin. "Maybe if you looked as sharp as you sound right now, he would have asked you for a dance. But—oh well."

Daisy's face turns red.

Jaws drop.

Tessa tries to bite back a laugh before slapping a hand on her mouth.

I take another bite of my bacon.

Did she think I was just going to sit there, then run and cry and tell Kieran? Please. Don't go throwing punches expecting to go home without a scratch.

"There you are!"

Aurora bursts into the room with two other Fae, cutting the tension like a knife. She's draped in a blue dress, a fluffy white scarf on her neck. Her gracious smile dims slightly when her eyes meet mine—only for a second.

"I hope you all enjoyed last night," she says, voice turning cold as her eyes settle on Jordan, but her smile never wavers. "Especially you."

Jordan says nothing. He keeps his gaze fixed on the floor.

A sign of someone who's either guilty or scared.

In this case, probably both.

"As I said yesterday, the first trial starts in two weeks," Aurora continues, gesturing at both Fae behind her. They begin giving out golden envelopes to each of us. "In the letters, you'll find the clues to the trial. I suggest you use this time wisely. Gideon and Atticus, our High Commanders, are running a training session every morning should you wish to join. There're always classes to attend, both educational and recreational. In a meantime, you can also help around the Court for some pocket money."

I blink.

I can't, for the of life of me, comprehend this generous hospitality.

Weren't we meant to be just some sport for them to watch?

Well, I'm not complaining.

"Pocket money?" Tessa's eyes gleam with excitement. "What kind of jobs are there?"

"Cleaning, cooking, personal assistance, helping around the library or the garden." Aurora shrugs, then flashes a grin. "Or ... you can sign up to be a temporary resident at one of the brothels. I hear the pay's excellent. It's not like we get humans to taste all year round."

Oh, great.

You can even be a whore.

"Yeah ... no, thanks." Tessa laughs awkwardly, shifting in her seat.

Aurora rolls her eyes. "That's what they all say at first." She turns to Jordan. "There're also brothels for females, too, if you're interested. Might be the only place where someone actually wants to fuck you."

Oh, that's a low blow, and I'm absolutely here for it.

"Although, I do have to say," she adds, dragging her gaze down to Jordan's trousers with mock interest. "Male humans don't tend to please us much. They're just ... a little underwhelming, you know?"

I snort before I can stop myself.

Apart from the fact that she probably wants to stab me for what I did last night, I actually think Aurora's kind of savage.

"That's because they haven't met me yet." Jordan smirks. "The female I visited at a brothel yesterday sure seemed pretty satisfied."

This is way too much sex talk for breakfast.

I exhale, lowering my gaze to the golden envelope. Inside is nothing but a single sheet of parchment. On it, the letter reads:

Dearest Cassandra,

What's keeping you up at night?
Careful, for it might come back and haunt you.

Love,
The Trial Committee

What a disturbing letter.

How is this meant to be my clue?

And they have a *committee* for these trials? Aurora must be the chairwoman—chairfae, or whatever.

I glance at Tessa, whose brows are twisted into a knot.

"Yours creepy too?" I ask.

She just nods, still staring at the page like it might bite.

I'm guessing all the letters are different, then.

"What does yours say?" Lucas turns to me. I show him the letter. "Lovely. Look at mine."

He hands it over, and I read.

Dear handsome Lucas,

Where does one go when they die?
Shall we follow and see?

Love,
The Trial Committee

Our eyes meet in silence. My stomach twists like it's trying to squeeze my breakfast back up. Whatever this first trial is ... it might be about Declan.

They know us.

And they know how to use our weaknesses, too.

Aside from the ominous letters, Aurora also leaves us with a list of classes and jobs we can sign up to. I flip through the pages.

Gods, maybe they're short-staffed and we're here to be their slaves.

"Are you going to sign up for something?" Tessa asks as we leave the dining hall. For whatever reason, she's decided to stick with me—must be the Kieran effect.

"I don't know yet, but I'm thinking about it."

"I think I might join the training," Lucas says from beside me.

And he has a good point. Now that we're outside in the corridor, bathed in daylight, I can see how many eyes are on us. Some curious. Some grinning. And some just want to scare.

"Yeah, good idea," I murmur.

I haven't gotten a clue how I'm going to spend the next two weeks in this Court, but I hate this hopeless feeling like I have to rely on the ward in my room to protect me, or stay in a group to be safe.

I didn't sore my arm hurling knives for nothing.

"I'm going to the market," I say.

"How?" Daisy crosses her arms. "Vanishing?"

"There's a map in our rooms, but you might not have seen it, since you barely lift your head off the floor." I exhale loudly, already walking away before she can throw another ridiculous accusation my way.

It's been two days and Daisy's already showing her true colours.

Good.

I won't feel too bad if I have to drive a knife through her.

"Cassandra, wait!" Tessa runs after me. I already know what she's going to say before she opens her mouth. Lucas is right behind her. "Can I come with you?"

I hesitate—but Lucas isn't having any of it.

"We're coming with you."

Yep. Not a question.

Chapter 7

Maybe this was a dumb idea.

Now even more eyes are on us. Curious, glowing, hungry.

I can't tell if they're fascinated because a group of humans only visit the Court once in a blood moon, or just debating which one of us they would like to taste first.

"Tell me again why we're here?" Tessa rubs her arms, eyes darting nervously around.

"I want to buy some weapons," I answer truthfully. "I don't know why you both followed me."

"Are you kidding me? Did you think I wanted to be left with Daisy and Jordan? And as if Leon is going to talk to me." She exhales, pointing at herself as if saying I should take a long, hard look at her. "The only one I can tolerate is Oliver, but out of all the contestants, you two are the most normal."

Lucas and I look at each other and agree silently.

Tessa has no idea how awfully disturbed we both are.

"I think we should stick together, at least as long as we can, because I sure as hell don't want to fight the others alone." She winces, like the idea makes her physically sick. "Yesterday, I thought Daisy was just a shy nerd. Today, she turned out to be a jealous bitch."

"So, you don't think me spending time with Kieran is cheating?"

"Please." She scoffs, grinning like a cat who just found a treat. "Sure, he's terrifying, and I'm probably never going to be brave enough to come within five feet of him ... but that face? And those wings? I'm already writing books about him in my head."

I snort.

So, she's the type that likes to fantasise but doesn't act on it.

"We're talking about the same Fae that just lifted his hand and took someone's eye, right?" Lucas is very much not amused. "You both need to stay away from him."

"This is his Court, Lucas," I say, lowering my voice as I look around. "There's no escaping him, or any of these Fae."

"And that's why we need weapons?" he asks, just as a male Fae with glimmering butterfly wings brushes far too close, almost like it's on purpose. Lucas throws an arm over my shoulder, gently pulling me towards him. "What are weapons going to do? They all have magic."

"Yes, but not all of them are powerful," I say, keeping my gaze locked on the butterfly-winged Fae, who turns to laugh like what he did was some kind of joke. "Pretty sure some have lesser magic. Why else would there be servants, if all of them have the same kind of magic?"

"That's a good point." Tessa's eyes widen.

"Besides, Gideon said that no one is half as powerful as Kieran. And considering they're all fallen starbeings ... they might not be as strong as they once were. Who knows?"

"So, the weapons are to protect yourself from Kieran?" Lucas arches a brow.

This feels like a test—to see if I'd admit I'm afraid of Kieran.

"Don't be silly." I chuckle. "They're to protect ourselves from the rest of the contestants."

The ward will keep them out of my room, but two-thirds of our days are spent outside. I can't be sure that Daisy isn't planning on assassinating me when I'm reading alone in the library.

"Clever." Lucas grins, straightening the map in his hand. "There's a blacksmith two streets down."

"Lead the way."

It's a sunny autumn day, the kind that shouldn't exist in a place like this. The shops and stalls around here look both haunting and dreamlike. They're either cloaked in black, or glowing faintly. Orbs containing bones, shimmering liquid, and things I don't want to know line a shelf in front of one shop. The smell of something buttery kisses my nose, and it gets stronger the further down the street we go.

It's a bakery, right across the blacksmith shop.

Problem is, we don't have any money, and I'm not about to waste two promises today.

"We do need a job, don't we?" Tessa swallows, like she can taste the pastries in her mouth.

"Afraid so," I mutter. "Which job are you thinking about?"

"I'm thinking ... I really hope that bakery is hiring."

"Sure." Lucas snorts "Maybe I'll sign up to be a guard—keep tabs on all the lunatics."

"Hey, that's not a bad idea, actually," I say. "I'm thinking about the assistant position. You spy on the Court, and I'll get close enough to dig up dirt on the Fae."

Tessa points at herself again. "And I'm just supposed to ... eat?"

"You should join the kitchen, since you're already a cook," I say, winking. "And in case we need to poison someone."

She blinks.

I brace myself for her voice going high-pitched as she says it's a barbaric idea.

But Tessa just nods.

"Got it. And I can make sure that no one is poisoning our food, too."

Oh, yes. That too.

But when it's just the three of us left, I'm never taking anything she cooks again.

For now, let's just hope this temporary alliance consisting of sunshine, grey clouds, and a dark storm actually holds.

We turn our backs to the bakery, practically dragging Tessa away, and finally step into the blacksmith's shop.

From outside, I expected something grim and shadowed, like the other eerie stalls we passed, but it's bright and colourful, almost like a summer garden in here. The shop owner—to my surprise—is a female Fae, dressed elegantly in a flowing coral gown, black leather gloves snug over her hands.

She looks less like a blacksmith and more a lady of the Court.

"You must be the new contestants," she says with a smile, glancing over at us. "How can I help?"

Should I be worried that the friendliest place in this entire market seems to be the one that sells weapons?

"I was wondering if we could have a look at some weapons," I say, keeping my tone polite as I step closer. "We don't have any money—yet—but I heard some shops take promises as payment?"

"Well, you heard right, my dear." She grins, tugging a strand of gorgeous red hair behind her pointed ear. "However, the weight of your promise depends entirely on what you're asking for. Can't just promise to bring me flowers and expect to walk out with a hefty sword—you know what I mean?"

I press my lips together. Fair enough.

"If you don't know what to offer me, you could always promise to work here for a few days. It'll be unpaid, of course." The Fae shrugs. "Why don't you have a look around first and decide?"

I nod. "Thank you."

"I don't know about this, Cassandra," Lucas whispers to me as we step deeper inside the shop. "It sounds like a trick."

"The trick is that you have to keep your promise," I murmur, dragging my eyes from shelf to shelf, looking for anything that fits easily in my grip—anything I can hide under my dress.

"Don't you think it's weird that you can pay for anything with promises?" Tessa pipes up, picking up a sword she can barely lift. It tips dangerously low, and Lucas snatches it before it hits the ground. "Shit, sorry! I didn't think it'd be that heavy."

"Be careful, or you might find yourself spending a year here trying to pay off damages." Lucas exhales, carefully returning the sword to its place.

Considering they were made for the Fae who are slightly taller than us, she was lucky she could even pick it up in the first place.

"Sorry," Tessa calls out again, this time to the shop owner, who's watching her with sharp eyes. "Gods, that was terrifying."

I glide my fingers across a row of short knives and daggers on display. They look similar at a glance, but the price tags say otherwise.

"What's the difference between these two?" I ask, carrying them back to the counter.

"The blades are made with different materials," the shop owner says smoothly, taking one in each hand. "This one is moonstone blade—strong, balanced, reliable. Good for killing, better for surviving." She lifts the other one, tilting it so the edge catches the light. It shimmers faintly, like every other thing in this damn Court. "This is forged with twilight glass, sharp enough to slice through silk and bone alike, but it breaks if you don't treat it right. More ... well, you could say temperamental."

Sounds like me—moody, breakable, unpredictable.

But something else catches my eye from the cabinet behind the counter.

A dagger—small, elegant. Its hilt gleams gold beneath the glass, almost too polished to belong in a place like this.

"What about that one?" I point.

The Fae turns, blinks once, then shakes her head. "Sorry, I'm afraid that one's not for sale."

I tilt my head. "But there's price tag on it."

"Yes, but you need a permit. It's made of iron."

Oh.

I stare at it a second longer.

"You sell the only weapon that can actually hurt you?"

"Only to the High Commanders and authorised guards, which is why you need a permit," she replies. "You'd be better off with these two."

I frown.

So, Oliver's guess was wrong—you *can* actually buy iron here, assuming you have the right connections. I mean, there're bad people everywhere—there probably are bad Fae, too. And the guards need something strong enough to keep them in line.

Even if she did sell it to me, I doubt it'd be worth any of my empty promises.

But here's the thing: I might die in two weeks, and a dead girl can't pay her debts.

So, what do I offer her for these two daggers?

As I'm carefully considering my promise, Lucas dumps a short knife and another dagger onto the counter.

"I promise to owe you a favour for all four of these," he blurts out before I can say anything. "Send me to do your dirty work—whatever you need. That pays for them."

My eyes snap to him.

What the actual hell?

"Lucas, I—"

"Deal," the Fae interrupts, not even pretending to care what I have to say. She extends a gloved hand, all teeth and delight.

And Lucas grabs it without a second of hesitation.

Magic pulses in the air, a sharp pressure that makes my skin prickle. They hold hands for a moment longer than necessary, and when they let go, Lucas stares at his wrist like something's supposed to be there.

"Felt like something just wrapped around my arm," he murmurs.

The shop owner smirks. "Something is. You just can't see it."

"Why the hell did you just do that?"

It takes everything in me not to shout at him. From the look on Tessa's face, one of these daggers is probably hers.

Lucas paid for them all.

"Because we can't all be in debt," he simply says, giving me my two. "And a thank you would have sufficed."

I take the daggers, jaw clenched.

I don't thank him.

I just shake my head and walk away, the weight of the blades anchoring my fury.

"Come again." The Fae's voice trails after us, following my anger like a shadow.

I don't speak to Lucas all the way back to the Court. What he did was unimaginably stupid. And to say that he would even do her dirty work—Gods, this could go very, very wrong.

When we arrive back, I'm ready to storm off, but Lucas gently catches my hand, a silent plea in his eyes.

Tessa, sensing the mood, immediately says, "Erm, I'm going to sign up for that job. See you guys later."

Lucas nods. I wait until she's out of sight before I whisper-shout at him.

"Have you lost your mind? How could you do that?"

"What? Protect you?" His brow arches, defiant. "I know what I'm doing, all right?"

"Yes, but whatever it is is stupid, Lucas. And I didn't ask you to."

His jaw tightens. "Well, you wouldn't have had to, if I'd gone out with Declan that night." He pauses, looking away. "But I didn't, so here we are. I owed you at least that."

The garden breeze is cool, but it doesn't quite fill my lungs. Dry leaves scatter across the marble floor—like this pain neither of us can shake.

"Nobody is blaming you," I whisper, swallowing my sadness—just enough to not break down in front of him, because if I do, we'll both drown in our own tears.

It wouldn't have happened at all, if I hadn't said those things.

If it's anyone's fault, it's mine.

And mine alone.

"Thanks for the daggers," I manage at last. "But don't you pull that shit with me again, or I'll stab you with one of them."

Lucas chuckles, shaking his head as he throws up both hands like he's surrendering.

He's not supposed to be here.

I'm not supposed to care about anyone.

But now he's acting like my guardian angel.

My head hurts.

We finally catch up with Tessa at Aurora's office. Aurora's perched in a chair that looks more like a throne fit for a queen, her long legs crossed. She switches them slowly as Lucas walks closer, like she's trying to seduce him.

Lucas stiffens beside me.

Okay—are Fae sex addicts?

Wasn't she marking her territory with Kieran only last night?

Maybe she just likes the attention.

"A guard?" she says sweetly after Lucas finishes signing up. "Good choice."

I take the pen from Lucas, but before I can write my name next to "assistant," Aurora cuts in.

"No."

I blink. "What do you mean, no?"

She pulls the sheet from under my hand. “That position is no longer open.”

“But it’s still empty—”

“You can’t be an assistant,” she says, like she invented the rules.

I frown. “Just like that?”

“Yes.” Aurora doesn’t even blink. She throws both legs on the table and smiles.

Oh, great.

Now I’m blacklisted from working?

Was that a position for *her* assistant or something?

Yeah, whatever.

“Fine.” I roll my eyes, drop the pen onto the table, and just storm out.

Bitch.

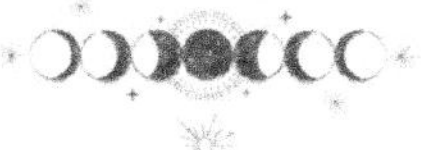

I imagine the target is Aurora’s face and keep throwing my dagger at it.

Turns out, the Court’s facilities are pretty spectacular. There’s a sparring ring, a training ground with proper targets, and even a meditation area.

I don’t know about the others, but I could never meditate and close my eyes just to risk opening them to some fangs when I’m surrounded by the Fae in this place.

Besides, throwing blades is much more fun, and I can be as petty as I want.

Here, eat this, you freak Fae.

Just a High Fae but acts like she owns the damn palace.

I'll find my own way.

She'll see.

Stars don't bend for her.

"Oh, you're cloaked in anger today," a voice offers from behind. I spin so fast I nearly throw a dagger at him.

Kieran.

"I'm—" I'm about to say I'm fine, but wait—

Oh, I know how to make Aurora angry.

Very, very angry.

I school my expression, let my shoulders drop, and make sure the next words come out sounding devastated. "Thanks to your Aurora, I can't even get a job."

"What do you mean?" Kieran stalks closer, tilting his heads. His mismatched eyes follow the dagger I just threw aimlessly.

"Well, I was trying to sign up for the personal assistant position," I start, already walking towards the target to retrieve my dagger. "You know, something low-profile to do, so I won't bore myself to death."

Just as I reach for the dagger, it yanks free and sails into Kieran's waiting hand.

"Could you not have done that before making me walk all the way over here?"

He grins, throwing it in the air and catching it with minimal effort. "I see you bought a toy today."

Then he throws it—and hits the target dead centre.

My jaw drops.

He didn't even use magic.

"You've got to be kidding me," I mutter. "You've got magic *and* can do that? Unfair."

"I've been alive for three hundred and sixty years, Little Star." Kieran winks. "If I hadn't learned to at least throw a dagger in all that time, I might as well just eat iron dust and die."

I snort. "Fair enough."

"About the job," he presses, his eyes narrowing. "Tell me."

I drop my gaze. "It's not important. I don't want Aurora thinking I run to you when something doesn't go my way."

"Well, good news: she's immortal, and I'm not going to kill her, so stop worrying about her punishments." Kieran places his hands on his hips. "What the bloody hell did she do?"

"Maybe it's just my own incompetence ..."

"For fuck's sake, Cassandra." He exhales sharply, like he's already done with my dramatics. "Out with it."

"She said I couldn't be an assistant. Wouldn't let me sign up."

Kieran blinks, running a hand through his hair.

"Aurora," he mutters, shaking his head. "Don't worry about it. You can have the job."

"Really?"

My embarrassingly bad acting skills actually worked?

"Yes."

"Won't she object to it?"

He scoffs, leaning closer. "You'll soon find that in this Court, no one really objects me, Little Star."

I grin.

I guess I do have a friend in high places.

"You didn't have to do it, you know."

"Yes, but since you gave me that sad little puppy face"—he grins—"how could I possibly do nothing?"

"You Fae do like to flirt, don't you?" I try not to roll my eyes. Or maybe it's not flirting. Maybe they just like to toy with us humans. We're basically helpless here.

"Only as much as we like breathing."

Now I actually roll my eyes.

"I knew it. All you want from me is sex," I joke.

Kieran laughs—again.

Just like last night.

He's so ... unpredictable.

"Everyone here wants sex from you. Trust me," he says, tone brutally honest, like he was cursed to never lie. But I doubt he cares enough to lie about something like that.

"Well, may the hottest one win."

At least someone will please me before I die.

"Why only the hottest one"—the corner of Kieran's mouth curves up—"when you can have them all?"

"Oh, Gods." I wince. "You're unbelievable."

"Yes. In bed, too."

I growl.

Kieran just laughs. Again.

I haven't the faintest clue what this is between us.

And I can't believe I'm smiling with him.

Declan is probably rolling in his grave.

My smile dims slightly, but I hide it from Kieran and steer the conversation elsewhere.

"Can I really have the job?"

"I already said yes."

"Thank you," I say, then freeze—I don't even know whose assistant I'll be. "Please don't tell me I'll be Aurora's assistant."

"Did she not say?"

I shake my head.

Kieran arches a brow.

"It's for me, Cassandra."

"Oh?"

"You'll be my personal assistant."

Shit.

Oh, shit.

I'm so fucked.

Now I understand.

It wasn't about the job.

It was about who I'd be working for.

I stare at Kieran, pressing my lips together.

Sure, this gives me countless advantages in the trials, but Daisy is going to be on my case like I personally stabbed her with a fork.

I know I said I'd do anything to win.

But holy hell.

I'm never going to survive this.

I'm never going to survive *him*.

Chapter 8

"So, what are you going to do today?" Tessa asks me at breakfast the next morning, chewing her grapes like we're on a holiday and not about to start killing each other in two weeks.

I haven't told anyone I'll be working for Kieran.

I know they'll find out eventually, but I just want a few more minutes of peace before the others carve their bloody targets on my back, accusing me of sleeping with the King to get ahead of the game. Again.

"The same as you—working." I leave it there.

"Oh, really?" A bright smile paints across her face. "Did Aurora change her mind?"

"Something like that."

It seems most of us have landed a side gig somewhere. Tessa has to report to the head chef of the Court today. I'm pretty sure Oliver has about two gardens waiting for him to work his magic. Meanwhile, Daisy, as expected, is helping out in the library.

As for Lucas, he is currently on a training session with the High Commander Atticus. We only saw him briefly when we came down. By that time, Lucas had already finished his breakfast and was ready for the training—which was great, because he would have asked what my job was.

I'm not sure if Leon signed up for anything, but Oliver has been trying to convince him to be his right-hand man in this grand gardening project. As he's the oldest among us, he probably feels it's his responsibility to take care of the youngest.

And Jordan? I haven't gotten a clue what he's doing. But if he goes out every day from now on, it's probably safe to assume he's either visiting a brothel, or working at one.

"Good morning, lovelies."

Ugh, is annoying us every morning part of Aurora's job?

"I'd like to wish you all the best of luck with whatever it is you're doing today," she says with the sweetest tone. I look down at my food and keep eating. "I would like to introduce you all to Laia. She's part of the Trial Committee. Her job is to make sure you've got everything you need and that all your questions are answered."

Jordan's face turns pale, like he's seen a ghost.

We all remember the Fae who dragged him across the hall to Kieran.

I hope she rigs the trials and makes sure he loses, since he tried to force himself on her the other night.

"Nice to meet you, Laia." Tessa gives her a small, polite smile. Laia returns the gesture.

"When a person speaks," Aurora says cooly, "it's polite to stop eating and listen."

It takes me a few seconds to register that the shot was aimed at me. I look up, putting my spoon down—and all eyes are on me.

Well, isn't this just great?

"I'm listening." I shrug. "You said Laia is here to assist us."

And now she gives me a big smile that doesn't reach her eyes. Her tone is all sugar and challenge. "Have you found a job yet, Cassandra? There're plenty of toilets waiting to be cleaned, if you're still unsure."

Wow, talk about double standards. She offered everyone a nice little job of their choice, but apparently, I should be grateful to clean their toilets.

Aurora really is this bitchy because of Kieran.

I tilt my head, keep my tone neutral. "It's polite not to talk about toilets at the breakfast table, you know."

A beat.

All eyes widen. A fork clinks against a plate. Tessa's biting the inside of her cheek to stop from laughing.

And Aurora's gaze could slice me in half.

But before she can drop her fake friendliness and launch herself at me like I know she's been dying to since that night, the dining hall's doors swing open.

Kieran walks in.

I can practically feel how every human in the room stops breathing.

"Crowded in here this morning," he says casually, his gaze briefly dropping to Jordan, who immediately looks down.

"Kieran," Aurora purrs, tone a drop of syrup. Her eyes gleam like a puppy handed a new toy. "Is there anything you need?"

"Yes." He nods, his eyes flicking to mine.

Oh, no.

No, no, no.

I send him the most desperate look I can manage—*don't you dare.*

It's like he knows but decides that tormenting me is his idea of a perfect morning.

"You ready, Cassandra?" Kieran asks, grinning whilst I'm sweating through every single piece of clothing I'm wearing. Then he adds, "Don't worry if you haven't finished your breakfast. I'll wait."

I'm tempted to stab myself with the dagger I so carefully hid under my dress right about now.

Aurora looks at me, then glances back at Kieran.

I'm going to choke on my food.

I shoot to my feet, smoothing my dress with sweaty hands. "I'm ready," I say, clearing my throat. "Let's go."

"You don't even know where we're going."

"Does it matter? Just do your thing. Vanishing or whatever."

Because I practically feel Aurora's eyes burning into my back, not to mention the rest of the contestants'. Someone scoffs—probably Daisy. Someone else murmurs something.

Pretty sure I'm going to be the talk of the Court within an hour.

But Kieran is so calm and cool this morning. He places his hand on the small of my back and nudges me forward gently.

"No vanishing today. You've got to learn where things are in the Court."

Of course.

Just when I wish I could disappear, he makes me walk.

"You're enjoying this, aren't you?" I whisper under my breath, glancing at the tall, very handsome Fae beside me, wishing I could pinch his perfect face.

Kieran glances back, eyes flashing in delight. "Oh, yes."

"You're going to get me into trouble."

"Why don't you use your mouth to get out of it?" he mutters, quoting my own words from that night.

I groan quietly.

"Plus, you might want to behave," he adds, all faux-innocent charm, "and speak to your boss nicely, hm?"

I blink at him. "You're insufferable."

He whistles, amused. "Yes, and you'll suffer for it."

I fear that has already started.

I don't dare look back at the breakfast table. I just exhale and accept my inevitable fate. The slamming of the closing doors sounds like a snapping of whatever faint bond I had with the others.

They won't believe it if I tell them I know nothing about the trials after this.

Whatever I win will be branded undeserving. They'll shout that I sleep with the one controlling the games.

For a second, I consider taking it all back—not taking this job.

But realistically, who's going to be left to criticise me at the end?

And I can't exactly hear them if I'm dead.

"Where're we going?" I ask, swallowing what's left of my decent side of humanity.

"To the Council Hall," Kieran says, leading me down the corridor. "Unfortunately, being my personal assistant comes with boring meetings you'll have to attend. And more importantly, you'll need to be introduced to everyone, so they're made aware of your role."

My stomach churns. *Introduced to everyone?* Fan-freaking-tastic. Public humiliation and death threats, all before noon.

"And you had to pick me up yourself?" I could have gone and died internally. Quietly.

"If I had told you come meet me at the Council Hall, would you have known where to go?"

Point taken.

I follow Kieran in silence, making notes and mapping every turn and hallway in my head.

The architecture is absolutely spectacular—impossibly tall arches, glided trim, and stained glass that catches the light like spellwork. Who was the architect? Was this all built on Kieran's magic?

We eventually reach another set of tall, arched doors. They swing open without Kieran even lifting his fingers. Inside, half a dozen Fae, draped in silk and subtle elegance, are seated around a long dark wood table. The chair at the head of the table looks the same as every chair in the room.

No throne, no crown.

Yet all rise at his presence and bow.

Gods help me.

What the hell have I got myself into?

Kieran walks in and takes the seat at the top of the table. That's when the others sit back down. I hold my breath, shrinking to two feet tall behind his chair, which looks more like a throne every passing second.

Help.

What do I do?

As if hearing my silent plea, Kieran waves a hand once, and a small, human-sized chair materialises beside him.

I immediately take the seat. The wood groans, like even it knows I don't belong here.

"I trust you all know Cassandra," he starts. All heads snap in my direction. I stiffen. "She'll be my assistant."

I brace for complaints, protest, my knuckles clenching under the table.

Nothing.

Mother of the stars.

They really don't object to him. At all.

"Next?"

I can't see his face from here, but I can practically hear the grin in his voice.

"Come on, now, Kieran," the male Fae to his left says with a joking tone. "Are you really going to let the poor girl guess who we all are?"

It takes me a second to place him without his fancy mask from the first night—but that voice, the silver hair, brown eyes—

Gideon.

"Silly me." Kieran exhales, shaking his head as he glances in my direction. "I think you know this fool—Gideon. He's one of the High Commanders."

I offer Gideon an awkward smile.

"That's Daphne, our Sigil Master. She handles the wards, the Court's glamour, and all those promises you people toss around like candy," Kieran continues, tilting his head to the female Fae on Gideon's left. She's got a head of inky curls and eyes so silver they look carved from ice. "Next to Daphne is Octavia, the Court's advisor."

His advisor is a woman—how modern.

Octavia just blinks at me, arms crossed, watching me sweat, as if trying to assess whether my suicidal mortal husk is a threat to their invisible throne.

"Then there's Felix," Kieran adds, tipping his head towards the next Fae down. "The Oath Recorder—the pain in everyone's ass, since he insists on recording the hell out of everything."

Felix scoffs. "One day, when I'm gone, it gives me peace to know just how hard it'll be for you to replace me."

Kieran rolls his eyes. "We've only got eternity to find the next idiot, brother."

Kieran sure does have a signature way of running his Court and addressing his people.

"And that's Skylar, our High Archivist." He points to the female Fae next to Felix. "She runs the library. All of our scribes report to her."

I wish I had a pen and paper.

By lunch, I'll inevitably have forgotten all their names.

"Then the last one is Virgil." Kieran nods towards the dark-skinned Fae who hasn't so much as glanced my way. There's something eerie, haunting about him. "He's our Night Blade Commander. In charge of our ... well, non-Fae army."

I freeze.

What kind of claws and fangs of an army do they have lurking in the dark?

"Usually, Atticus and Aurora will be here as well, but they have some business elsewhere today," he explains. "Atticus works alongside Gideon, and you already know Aurora. She's the High Curator of Ceremonies."

That's the fanciest title for possibly the most exquisite, yet annoying, Fae I've met thus far.

"And what is your title?" I can't help but ask Kieran.

Kieran exhales loudly, whilst Gideon chuckles.

"Gods, not you, too."

"Well." I shrug. I don't think it's such an outrageous thing to be curious about. "I'm your assistant, but assistant to what?"

Kieran leans back in his chair as if this question personally pains him. In the decades—or centuries—that they have been here, I wonder how many have asked the same.

"Must you ruin the mystery?"

"You mean the egotism?"

Felix snorts. Octavia's eyes are pinned on me, like I have just spat on her crown. Daphne's lips twitch with a glimpse of amusement.

"You and your mouth." Kieran clicks his tongue, his gaze dropping to my lips. The golden and storm-blue eyes flare faintly—and for a second there, I imagine what I could do to him with my mouth.

But only a second.

Because guilt strikes me down like lightning.

Kieran smirks, like he knows exactly what shameful thought just crossed my mind—like he's thinking about it, too.

I narrow my eyes at him.

"I don't need a title," Kieran says at last, licking his lip as he turns away. "I built this Court. What more do you want?"

I blink. "So ... King of Brooding it is."

Gideon wheezes. "Oh, you picked the right one for the job, Kieran."

"Yeah, well, got to pick the one that can handle you lot, too," Kieran says, once again rolling his eyes like life itself is boring. "Now, do any of you have anything actually important to say, or can I go take a nap?"

"Hold on, how can we trust that she won't discuss the Court's matters with her friends?" Octavia cuts in.

I keep my mouth shut. Truth is, I have no idea how deep I'll be dragged into whatever it is Kieran does all day—assuming he even includes me. For all I know, he'll just hand me errands he can't be bothered to run himself and leave me out of anything remotely important.

"I can't believe you actually had to ask that," Kieran murmurs, his eyes flicking to me. "I'll handle her."

I swallow, trying very hard not to think what "handle" might mean.

"Make her swear an oath," Felix suggests. "And I'll need to record that, of course."

"Stars." Kieran scoffs, shooting me a look that says: *Do you see what I have to deal with?* "I said I'll handle it. Now, unless someone says something useful in the next five seconds, I'm leaving."

"The newcomers are getting increasingly aggressive," Gideon says first, glancing at me like I'm part of the cause of his headache. "Ever since—the contestants arrived."

Newcomers?

And they're upset ... because of us?

I tilt my head. Gods, I really wish I had something to write with. Does being Kieran's assistant mean I'm supposed to pay attention to what's being said at these meetings and take notes, too?

"They know the rules," Kieran replies. "If they don't follow them, they can leave."

"That's a death sentence." Daphne sighs, but Kieran just shrugs.

"I don't know what you want me to do. If they want to kill humans, they'll find a way—here, or in the human world."

I tense, shifting in my seat.

I see now why Octavia thinks I'm a liability. I have no idea what half of what they are discussing means—who these newcomers are, what exactly the death sentence Daphne mentioned entails, or why the talk of killing is so casual.

This is all confidential information that will likely never leave this room.

And here I am, listening to all of it.

Whether I understand them or not, I now have an expensive front-row ticket to their secrets.

They continue discussing it for another fifteen minutes before moving on to the next topics: a scribe was assaulted somewhere in town, a shipment of illegal weapons—iron, no less—being smuggled in, a group of Fae demanding a raise, to name a few.

By the end of the meeting, one thing becomes painfully clear: even with magic, the Fae aren't immune to corruption.

Like humans, they're never satisfied with what they already have.

I don't know if that fact makes them more human, or hell of a lot scarier than before.

After the meeting, I eat lunch in silence whilst Kieran sorts through a stack of documents that need his attention. I'm trying to digest more of the gruesome information from the meeting than my actual food.

"Can you bring this to Atticus when you're done?" he asks from his desk, handing out an envelope.

"I have no idea what he looks like."

And honestly, wouldn't it be faster if he just vanished to wherever Atticus is?

"I know what you're thinking." Kieran arches a brow. "I've got other things to do. Besides, you could probably use a walk after that meeting. Just ask around—he's probably at the sparring ring."

"Okay." I take the envelope. Not like I have a choice.

And a walk does sound nice.

"I'll be back in a few hours," he adds without any further explanation. "Feel free to do whatever you want in the meantime."

I nod.

It's probably something secretive—whatever he's off to do.

Or maybe he's just spending the afternoon with some Fae beauty in a sunlit garden somewhere.

I watch Kieran grab his coat. He steps closer and casually curls a strand of my dark hair around his fingers, grinning as he says, "Don't miss me too much."

I roll my eyes in response.

Kieran vanishes right before my eyes, sending loose papers fluttering into the air, his laugh echoing off the walls like a curse that will follow me into my dreams.

Bloody hell.

I gather the scattered papers and drop them back onto Kieran's desk, tempting to peek through them, but after hours of listening to his Court dissect every problem under the stars, I decide against ruining my afternoon any further and instead set off on my task.

Finding Atticus is easier than finding the way from Kieran's office to the sparring ring.

I don't even have to ask, because Lucas is already there, mid-training with him, soaked in sweat and entirely shirtless. Even a few passing by Fae can't resist biting their lips and silently tasting—and teasing—him with their gazes.

Has he always been this hot? Did I just never notice because he's Declan's friend?

I lift a hand in a lazy wave. Lucas nods back. Meanwhile, Atticus is deep in conversation—with Aurora.

She's everywhere.

Here to flirt with Atticus, too, or with Lucas?

Ugh, I'd flirt with every living thing too, if I looked like that.

"Yes?" Aurora turns to speak to me like my very presence agitates her.

"I'm here to see Atticus," I say, stepping closer.

Atticus tilts his head, his green eyes darting to mine. Only now do I realise how dangerously good looking both of Kieran's High Commanders are—good lord. Look at those eyelashes.

I wonder if stunning an enemy with that face before striking is part of his tactics.

"How can I help?"

I hand him the envelope. "Kieran said to give this to you."

Atticus takes it, opens the envelope, and spends a minute reading. He's smiling when he's done. "Thank you."

Huh. Now I'm curious what's in that letter.

Aurora, on the other hand, turns fully to me, arms crossed. "So, what did you do to get the job?"

I know exactly what she's implying. It's the same thing everyone's been thinking.

"Nothing," I say truthfully, not that I owe her an explanation. "I just told Kieran I couldn't sign up for the job, and he gave it to me. I didn't even know I'd be working with him."

Aurora snorts, shaking her head like she can't believe what she's hearing.

It doesn't matter whether she believes it or not.

"Really? Kieran did that?" Atticus asks.

"Yep."

"Interesting."

Yes, sure. I'm a human entertainer. A humiliation. An experiment. What else is new?

He doesn't say anything else, and Aurora is still frozen in disbelief, so I just slip away quietly, the same way I arrived.

What a day.

I don't really know where to go after this. I'm too mentally exhausted to wander the Court and risk giving anyone a fresh shot at me. So, I just retreat to my room—the only place left that resembles peace.

I don't know how much time passes, but I wake up with a book still open beside me and the kind of hunger that could make me eat a unicorn.

Oh, great. It's dark out.

I stretch, fix the curtains, try to smooth out my wrinkled clothes—then notice a piece of paper slid beneath the door.

It reads: "Die, slut."

And so, it begins.

I'm a walking enemy of most of the contestants.

I pack both of my daggers before making my way to the dining hall—which is completely empty.

No food and not a soul to be found.

What time is it? Midnight?

Gods, I slept through my job?

I don't even know when I last had a nap in the middle of the day like that.

What the hell do I do now?

I really hope Kieran is not mad at me.

"Oh, you're finally awake." A voice startles me from behind—again.

Talk of the devil.

"Kieran, I'm sorry. I don't—"

"It's fine," he cuts in, his voice smooth and kind. I have to blink twice to make sure I'm not dreaming this. "Was the meeting so much that you had to retreat into dreamland?"

"No." I shake my head. "I mean, it was stressful, but I haven't been sleeping much since ..." *Declan died.* I don't complete the sentence. "You could've woken me."

"I could have, but since it's your first day, I thought I'd let you off the hook." He grins.

I honestly don't know what to say.

"So, do you think you can still handle the job?" Kieran asks, tucking both hands behind his back.

I think about it for a moment. Working with him, the weight that come with it.

The stare. The gossip.

Even if I want to back out, it's too late now. Might as well just embrace the whole damn thing.

"Yes, I do."

Those words crack a smile from him. "Good, because you passed the test."

"The test?" I frown.

"Come on, Little Star." Kieran says, amusement flickering in those storm-lit eyes. "I left you alone in my office, full of important things, and you didn't so much as peek. You didn't pry open Atticus's letter. And you didn't tell anyone about the meeting this morning."

That was all a test?

But ... "How did you know about any of that?"

He winks. “Magic, of course.”

How convenient.

“You see, one of the qualities you need as my assistant is the ability to shut up and keep my secrets—even from your own kind,” Kieran says, stepping a little closer. “If you hadn’t passed, I’d have had to let you go.”

Does that mean I’ve earned a little of his trust?

“Now, to make it official.” He holds out a hand, like the first night—like the other night he asked me to dance.

And I place mine in his.

Every damn time.

This time, magic ripples through us, cool and powerful. I feel a pressure on my wrist, like something is creeping up my arm, coiling around it.

But when Kieran lets go, there’s nothing on my skin.

And I know what it was.

An oath.

A promise that I won’t break this secrecy and will do my best as Kieran’s assistant—or something awful will happen.

There goes my chance of even telling Tessa.

“What was that?” I ask, glancing at my arm. The skin feels slightly warm, sensitive, like I’ve just gotten a tattoo.

“A promise, of course,” Kieran says cooly, taking my hand in his again.

Then, without a warning, he vanishes us both.

Disorientated and dying of hunger, I take a moment to realise where we are.

The Tower of Stars.

“Gods.” I clutch his hand, trying not to fall. “Did I not tell you to warn me?”

He laughs. “Where’s the fun in that?”

I sigh. "Why are we even here?"

"Because, Little Star." Kieran gently tugs me towards the open window. The nickname is starting to grow on me a little. "You can only see it under the moonlight."

Kieran rolls up his sleeve, holding out his arm.

And there it is.

A tattoo written in the stars.

Faint, shimmering, beautiful. Magic and promise entwined.

I slowly fold up my sleeve and do the same.

And there it is on mine.

Exactly the same.

A mirrored vow, painted in starlight.

I glance at the male next to me, heart skipping a beat for no reason at all. "I don't remember signing up for a matching tattoo."

"Yet, here we are."

I lick my lips, trying hard not to smile.

This is wrong. So wrong.

Like a storm, Kieran struck me from out of nowhere.

It's all for Declan, I remind myself.

Then, my damn stomach betrays me and groans like a war horn.

Kieran laughs.

I look up at him, pleading with my eyes. "You don't think you can magically give me food, do you?"

"What do you think I am? A wizard?"

"A very hot Fae who will feed his assistant?"

Kieran narrows his eyes—then throws his head back and laughs. "Gods, here I thought I was the manipulative one. Fine—

but I can't promise it will taste decent. Pulling food out of thin air can be tricky."

Now I'm the one smirking. "Then don't forget seasoning."

With a flick of his wrist, a table materialises—glowing candlelight, warm dishes, and enough food to distract even my twisted thoughts. And of course ... salt and pepper.

Dinner for two, beneath the stars and moonlight.

"Did not ask for a date." I cross my arms.

Kieran drops into his seat with a smug grin. "Well, then, try not to kiss me and you should be fine."

I groan. Loudly.

Chapter 9

"I'm getting anxious, Cassie," Tessa murmurs, clutching her stomach beside me in a quiet corner of the library. "The first trial is in three days, and we still have no idea what it is."

Only she and Lucas still talk to me—though Lucas, as you can imagine, wasn't exactly thrilled when he found out what my job was.

The others keep their distance. Daisy doesn't hide the hatred in her eyes every time I walk into a room. Oliver said he didn't want to get involved—he's wary of Kieran. And Jordan never liked Kieran to begin with, so he steers clear of me.

As for Leon—well, the man barely speaks. He only helps Oliver in the garden and sits in silence amongst flowers.

We have stared at our creepy letters—the ones that are supposed to be our clues—until they're crumpled, soaked in sweat, and probably a few of Tessa's tears. If anything, they gave us more questions than answers.

"Kieran really didn't tell you anything?"

"For a hundredth time, no," I grumble, flopping my head onto the pile of books.

Working for Kieran is ... well, calling it "interesting" would be an understatement of the century.

I am now part of the trusted inner circle, ever since Kieran officially swore me in that night—much to Felix's delight. They speak freely around me now, which makes me think breaking the promise would either kill me, or earn me a lifetime in magical jail. Either that, or they'll kill me and *then* lock my soul in the magical jail.

The only meeting that I'm not allowed to sit in is the meeting about the trials. Aurora lives for the moment she gets to kick me out of that room.

It's fine, really.

I don't want to be in the same room with her, anyway.

"I still don't understand what the deal is between you and him," Tessa says, closing the book she hasn't managed to get past the first page of.

Yeah, well, everyone wonders.

Get in line.

"Pretty sure he's just toying with me," I drawl, flipping aimlessly through the pages of my own book. "To them, we're exotic, and you know—they're interested in trying the fruit they rarely have ... just like how Virgil's been eyeing you every time he walks past."

Tessa's face turns the same shade as the autumn leaves outside.

Please. Did she really think I didn't notice her and the Night Blade Commander exchanging suspicious, loaded glances?

"I don't know what you're talking about." Tessa opens her book again, turning the pages like she already knows every word.

"Hey, I get it." I grin. "He's hot. All of them are. And we both might die in a few days—might as well have fun before we go."

"Is that what you plan to do with Kieran?"

I've considered it since we first got here.

Do I want to win? Sure.

Do I think I will? Not a chance.

And if I die—me, and this ghost of a girl I've been dragging around for two months—without at least one last wild, most-likely-regrettable night with the hottest Fae I've ever seen ... you can bet your ass I'll throw myself head-first into the thorn-lined walls of Hell the second I arrive.

Declan would never find out, because he's lying comfortably on a cloud bed in heaven.

"Maybe if I'm drunk enough," I lie, sipping my tea.

I'd undress the mystery that is Kieran in a heartbeat—probably surrendering what's left of my humanity in the process.

Now, if by some massively stupid stroke of luck, I win the trials and wish for Declan back—well, I guess I'll cross that bridge when it comes to it. I'll give it my best, but I'm ninety-nine percent certain the bridge doesn't even need building. I won't survive long enough to reach it.

Before we can continue our shameless conversation, something slams into a bookcase on the other side of the room, knocking a book onto the floor with a heavy thud.

Tessa and I glance at each other.

The movement doesn't stop.

Another slam.

Followed by a moan—and the unmistakably filthy sound of kissing.

Oh, Gods.

Quiet as a mouse, Tessa springs on her feet, tiptoeing towards the noise for a peek at whoever's going at it in the library at nine in the evening.

She runs back a second later, jaw dropped and eyes wide.

"It's Daisy!"

"What!?" I whisper-shout. "And who!?"

"Pretty sure he's one of Atticus's guards. I've seen him train with Lucas a few times."

"Oh, my Gods," I slap a hand over my mouth. "She saw us when we came in, right? She *knows* we're here."

"Maybe she just doesn't care." Tessa giggles.

The moans are getting louder.

I wince, covering my ears.

"That bitch is a fucking hypocrite."

"Yes." Tessa smirks. "But she couldn't get the King, so she settled for a guard instead."

I almost laugh, clapping a hand over my mouth to muffle it. Then, I hear the moans again.

Fuck me.

"I'm done. Let's get out of here." I start gathering my things. I've been scarred enough for the night.

Lucky for us, Daisy and the guard are tangled up in each other enough that we manage to slip out without seeing anything that will probably haunt me for the rest of the night. The second the library door swings shut behind us, Tessa and I look at each other—before bursting out laughing.

"Gods, that was—" she starts, shaking her head. "I don't even know what that was."

"It's a little hot tonight." I chuckle, fanning my face with a hand.

"Because it's a full moon," a voice says behind us. We turn to see Lucas, looking obscenely good in the Court's midnight-blue uniform. "Atticus warned me earlier. I swear every Fae is fucking tonight."

"What?" I wheeze. "You're telling me Fae get extra horny when the moon's full?"

"Either that, or I'm just super hot today." He grins, glancing down at his uniform. "You wouldn't believe how many Fae invited me to their beds on the way over here—female and male."

"Oh, dear Gods." Tessa can't stop laughing.

"And you said no?"

"Did you think I was going to sleep with just anyone?" Lucas arches a brow. "I'm waiting for an invite from the right one. Ask me again when Aurora walks by—no offense, Cass."

"Oh, no worries. I hate her but wouldn't say no to that either." It's a love-hate situation.

"Hate to disappoint you, but she's probably in Kieran's bed tonight." My amusement dips a little.

Over the past week and a half, I've learned so much about the court and its people.

For example, Aurora and Atticus are siblings. Should have seen that coming, really. They've got the same eye colour, same out-of-this-world kind of beauty, and same radiating grace that practically spills from both of them.

And another fun fact: Aurora is Kieran's ex.

Apparently, they were together for a decade. That sounds like a lifetime for humans. Most of us would have gotten married and had kids by then.

But for Fae? That probably felt like a month.

I can't stop wondering how good they must've looked together. How many fancy dances there were. How he took her hand in his. How many nights they spent side by side.

I bet they made the stars burst every time they took each other to bed.

Then again, Leon refuses to talk about anything.

Even if they broke up over a year ago, who's to say they haven't had a few meaningless nights since?

"That's fine, as long as you're not in his." Lucas narrows his eyes at me, playing the overprotective guardian angel role yet again. "Plus, this isn't the only full moon we'll get. Who knows, I might get lucky next time."

"Or we'll die in the next three days."

"Shit," he mutters. "Is it bad that I sometimes forget what the hell we're actually doing here? I didn't expect them to feed us and give us jobs—or invite us to what I can only assume is an orgy."

"I know what you mean," I murmur.

Because what cruel joke is this?

I'm laughing—with the people I swore I wouldn't care about.

But maybe this is how they get us, tricking us into thinking it's not so bad here—then they'll start taking it all away.

Taking everyone away.

One by one.

On second thought ...

"You should probably say yes to the next Fae who invites you to bed, Lucas." I sigh. "Then, after you're done with her, go find another one. Fucking your way through this shit isn't a bad idea."

Lucas looks mildly terrified but still laughs. "True."

I glance at Tessa. "And you should probably take a long walk until the Night Blade Commander notices you."

Tessa presses her lips into a thin line.

"And what are you going to do?" Lucas asks.

"Why?" I give him a half-smile. "Worried I'm going to cheat on your dead best friend?"

Lucas flinches. He runs a hand over his face. "You can do whatever you want, but I'd appreciate not hearing about it."

I grin and simply say. "Goodnight then, Lucas—and have fun."

With that, I wink at Tessa, then I turn and walk away.

Lucas didn't lie when he said every Fae is fucking tonight. It takes less than fifteen minutes to walk back to my room from the library—but in that short time, two males smile at me, one bumps into me on purpose, and another literally stops me mid-step.

When I stare at him, he just says, "Have you tried a Fae's cock yet?"

"I beg your pardon?"

What happened to romance and actual courting?

"I'm just saying—you could try one tonight."

And here I thought humans were the worst at this.

He doesn't look half bad, probably a bit drunk—but with that ego, I'd bet the only thing he's going to satisfy tonight is himself. He looks like the kind of popular boy in school who gets a girl on pure looks and can't give her an orgasm to save his life.

"No, thank you." *If I do try one, it won't be yours.*

I start to walk away, but the Fae gently pulls me back.

"Oh, come on. I promise you won't be disappointed."

"I doubt that." I exhale, twisting my arm, but he refuses to let go.

Is he seriously doing this?

"You don't need to play hard to get, you know," he slurs, leaning in closer. "Everyone does it. It's not a big deal."

"The big deal is I don't want to do it with you," I say, my voice low, hand slipping towards the dagger tucked beneath my coat. "Let me go. Now. Or I swear to Gods—"

"Is there a problem here?"

A voice cuts in, sharp, authoritative. The Fae immediately stiffens.

I know that voice all too well after spending every day with him for almost two weeks.

Kieran.

"I—I was just ..." the Fae stutters, eyes darting around like he's looking for a hole to vanish into, but all the other Fae nearby only lower their heads and walk on.

"You were just leaving," Kieran says, his voice cold like ice. "Right about now."

That's all it takes. The Fae bolts like he's been lit on fire.

I let out a long breath. No more evening walks on a full moon for me.

"Thank you," I whisper.

He doesn't say a thing. Just offers me a hand.

Like every time, I take it.

The next thing I know, we're in my room.

I've started to learn that if Kieran holds out his hand, it's basically a warning before we vanish.

"Here I thought my room was warded against anyone coming in."

It's probably the wrong thing to say when Kieran is in my room on a night where everyone is horny, but I can't help it.

He raises a brow. "I believe Aurora said the rooms were warded so your *human* contestants can't get in."

Well, shit.

They never said anything about Fae.

"Unbelievable."

Kieran grins, his eyes darker than usual. There's something different about him. I'm fairly convinced the moon's got her claws in every single one of them tonight.

"You shouldn't be out alone on a night like this," he murmurs. "Full moons are—"

"When you guys are especially horny," I cut in, crossing my arm. "Yeah, I heard."

"To be fair, we are always horny, so you can imagine what a full moon does to us," he adds, unbothered.

I lick my lips without thinking—and Kieran's smile fades, his gaze dipping to my mouth, watching the way my tongue swirls on my bottom lip for a split second.

That's how long it takes for my breath to go shallow.

"Kieran," I breathe.

It comes out like a warning dipped in temptation.

He leans in, grinning. "Yes, Little Star?"

I blink, swallowing the lump in my very dry throat. Even the way he smells is different tonight—faintly like cedar and spiced wine and sin.

Like something I know I'll regret in the morning but go right back to the next night.

"You should ..." I pause, changing my mind for a second, but say it anyway. "You should probably leave."

"You sure about that?"

I don't answer.

I can't quite cross that line just yet.

"You're doing exactly the same thing as the Fae you just saved me from, you know."

"No, because I actually know how to take no for an answer." He huffs, his warm breath brushing my skin. "Though I feel you might be interested in something else."

"Will you tell me about the trials if I jump into bed with you?"

Kieran laughs. "Nice try, Cassie."

"Will you?" I arch a brow, daring him.

Kieran blinks, like he wasn't expecting me to be serious. "You know I can't do that."

"So, you get sex, and I get what?"

"Orgasms."

I snort. That confidence. That maddening grin of his.

"What? I only suggest a very effective way to take your mind off things." He smiles, leaning cooly against the wall.

Even the simple gesture makes my face flush.

For fuck's sake.

I seriously won't survive this.

Not tonight.

"I'll let you know when I actually need that." I flick his arm, and Kieran sighs dramatically. I laugh. "Not tonight."

Not yet.

"Fine." He pushes off the wall, still smiling. "Other nights, then."

"Oh, please." I groan, pushing him towards the door before I change my mind.

"Ah, I could listen to you say 'please' all night long."

Gods save me.

"Good night." I bare my teeth at him, shoving him forward, then close the door and lock it behind him.

"Good night, Little Star." His laugh echoes in the corridor like the devil itself.

And I linger, finding myself wanting to open the door and drag him back in.

The moon surely has an effect on us all.

Chapter 10

I can't stomach anything on the day of the first trial. The whole table feels grim, just like the weather outside.

Two days ago, we were laughing, gossiping about who hooked up with who under the full moon. Today, reality strikes as if it's been drawing the bow for weeks, waiting for the perfect moment to loose the arrow.

Living a glamorous life in a Fae Court makes you forget your old life. Here, there's no poverty, barely any hardship. We're dressed in silk, fed like royalty, lulled into thinking we belong.

It's addictive.

But by nightfall ... at least one of us will be gone.

"Uh, sexy," Aurora purrs, biting her lips as she steps into her role as trial host. "I love that you're all wearing matching leathers."

Of course we are—we were told to do so.

Life is a game to her.

But then again, what did I expect?

We gather in the Court's immaculately manicured garden, but it's the woods ahead that draw every eye. Dense. Shadowed. Massive.

Behind us, the Fae lounge in gilded viewing stand—placing bets, chanting, cheering like their favourite sports team is about to win.

"Welcome," Aurora calls out, capturing everyone's attention with a single word. The noises die instantly, like her voice is laced with magic. "The moment we've been waiting for is here. I hope you're well rested, contestants."

Sure. The dark rings under my eyes confirm it.

"In a moment, our attendants will take each of you to different parts of the woods," she continues. "All you have to do is find your way out—easy, right?"

"Yes, but what the hell do they have hiding in those woods, is the question," Lucas mutters, his jaw tightening.

"Agreed. It can't be that easy," I murmur, eyes drifting to the stand.

It doesn't take long to find a familiar silhouette framed by constellation wings.

Kieran sits among his people, arm crossed, deep in conversation with Atticus and Octavia. The Council members are all present: Gideon, Daphne, Virgil, Felix and Skylar—a reminder of just how important these trials are.

The wind shifts, stirring the air with dry leaves. I tighten the braids that took me almost twenty minutes to do.

And when I look up, Kieran's eyes are already on mine.

He didn't say a word about the trials to me. No warning. No good luck. Nothing.

Kieran only has two settings: the ruthless ruler, and the let's-fuck-on-my-desk horny male.

And yet, for the past two weeks, I've somehow let myself believe that he might care, even a little. That the banter, the laughter, the teasing—maybe they meant something.

Maybe they resembled friendship.

Turns out I was right to begin with: there's no point getting involved with anyone.

Now, I'm about to walk into a death trap, and he's busy chatting with his friends.

I can't blame him, really.

"If I don't make it, and somehow one of you guys wins this thing," Tessa says, her voice trembling, "will you go tell my mum that I love her and I'm sorry?"

My heart drops.

Not a goodbye.

Fuck.

It's only been two weeks. She's just a stranger. Why do I even care?

I now realise the past two weeks have been crueller than the actual trials.

I didn't need this.

I didn't need to break my already shattered heart.

"Are you kidding?" I scoff, blinking fast. "Go tell her yourself."

Tessa chuckles, even though her eyes are glassy. "Can I at least get a hug?"

"No, bitch," I yap, and now Tessa looks like a lost puppy. "Let's hug when we're out."

And that does the trick. She's all sunshine and smiling again.

Good.

Don't you fucking dare die.

At least not before me. That would be incredibly rude.

Lucas, on the other hand, just pulls me into a hug without warning, tight enough to crack my ribs.

"I'm going to stab you with my dagger," I groan, but his back rumbles with laughter.

"So you keep saying," he hums, loosening the hug just enough for me to fill my lungs with air. "I'll find you in the woods. We'll both get out, okay?"

"I doubt it'd be that easy."

"I'll find you," he repeats, steady, not an ounce of fear in his eyes. I stare at him when he pulls away, then he turns to Tessa. "I'll find you, too."

Tessa nods, returning to lost-puppy mode, eyes glassy again.

"Ugh." Someone scoffs.

Of course, it's Daisy.

"You people make me sick." She sneers. "What the hell are you going to do if it's just the three of you left and you have to start backstabbing each other?" She rolls her eyes. "Are you going to draw straws to see who dies first?"

"You'd better hope we don't stab you in the woods, Daisy," I say, smiling like it's summer and we're going to a tea party

"Or maybe it'll be you first, Cassie." Jordan snorts. "You have made an enemy of half the group. Do you really think no one's going to take a shot when your precious little King isn't watching?"

I tilt my head, eyes narrowing. "Was that a threat, Jordan?"

He lifts a brow. "Just a friendly reminder."

"Then I would also like to remind you that you've only got one eye," I say cooly, glancing at Kieran. "If I do make it out, maybe I'll ask Kieran nicely to take the other."

I don't think Kieran will just do whatever I ask.

But they don't know that.

They don't know the sex they think we've been having only exists in my head—and Kieran's, I guess.

"You'd better fucking hope I don't catch up to you before Lucas does," Jordan growls, voice low and venom laced.

Lucas steps in front of me, pulling me back by the arm. His eyes lock on Jordan like he's seconds from drawing blood. "Touch her, and you die."

Jordan clicks his tongue, shaking his head. "Didn't realise you sleep with both Kieran and him." His eyes flick between us. "But I guess the odds of surviving are better when you've got them both wrapped around your little finger."

Fucking hell.

He had to go there.

"What did you just—" I'm halfway through the sentence when Aurora's voice cuts through the moment.

"It's time, lovely contestants," she announces. A dozen attendants step out from the tree line like wraiths, all black leather and masked faces.

Oliver gasps. Leon freezes.

"May the best one win," Jordan whispers as he passes me, leaning in just enough to make it personal. Then, with a sharp smile, he drags a finger across his throat in a silent gesture—making sure I know what happen will happen to me if he finds me first.

The woods stretch endlessly—damp from rain, cold as punishment.

Each breath clouds the air in pale mist, and I have no idea where to begin. A Fae vanished me here, then left without so much as glancing at my face.

I don't know if it's the cold sinking into my bones, or the dread.

Think, Cassandra. Think.

I close my eyes for a moment, listening to the noises around me—trees rattling in the wind, birds chirping in the distance, and the frantic pounding of my own heartbeat.

The sun was in front of me before we entered the woods.

If it is at my back now, I'll be moving towards the Fae stands.

Yes, let's do that.

Now I just have to hope that I don't spend hours getting lost in these woods that the damn sun shifts enough to confuse me.

I unsheathe my moonstone dagger and start moving towards what I hope is the entrance of the woods. Each few steps, I mark a tree with a shallow slash, just in case I end up getting lost and circling back.

Apart from a few scurrying animals, there is no one here but me and the faint fog, creeping along like a quiet, eerie companion. The first twenty minutes are easy. Nothing leaps out. Every step I make is careful and calculated—no snakes, no poisonous insects, no traps.

Then—

"Cass! Cassie!"

A voice shouts from behind me. A man's voice. Followed by rattling underbrush and pounding heavy footsteps.

I spin, grip tightening around the dagger.

The man emerges, and my face goes pale.

It's not Lucas, nor Jordan.

It's worse.

It's Noah—my brother.

"How—" I choke. "How the hell did you get here?"

How is this even possible?

Noah's panting like he ran the whole way here. "How the fuck would I know?! I went to sleep normally—you know, not that I get much sleep since you disappeared. And the next thing I knew, I woke up in this bloody Court and got dumped in these woods!"

No.

No, no, no.

He can't be here.

He *can't* be here.

Is this some kind of sick joke?

"No ... Noah, you need to go back. You can't ..." I stutter. Words fail me.

Mum and Dad can't lose us both.

"Did you think I want to be here?" Noah snaps. His voice cracks. "I prayed they'd take me in your place, but you're still here. Gods ... it's not supposed to be like this."

Gods.

Oh, my Gods.

The Fae are twisted, so twisted.

They did this to us?

I was supposed to face some creatures, maybe one of Virgil's monsters. But they decided to mentally fuck us up instead?

Fuck.

Deep breaths, Cassie. Deep breaths.

"We need to get out of here," I manage at last, forcing my voice to steady. "That's the rule. Maybe once we're out, they'll send you back home."

"I'm not leaving without you," Noah says, his voice low. "You vanished right before my eyes, and now that I'm here, I'm never letting you out of my sight again."

"You have to," I snap. "They won't let me leave, so you have to. If you don't ... you might not get that chance again."

"And what am I supposed to tell Mum and Dad? That I found you but let you go?"

"Don't tell them anything. You said it yourself—you went to sleep and woke up here. Time works differently around here. They probably don't even know you're missing."

"For gods' sake, Cass. Do you hear yourself!? That's fucked up!"

"I've got no time for this." I shake my head, starting to walk again. I can't have this fight with Noah. It's pointless.

One of us needs to survive and get out of here. I chose to be here, to do this, but Noah didn't. He has to go.

"Oh, great! Suddenly you have no time? What am I meant to do with that?"

"You need to shut the hell up and not die." I groan. "Don't you get it? They put you here as part of the first trial to try and mess with my head. I need to get out of here to win this, but if you don't shut up, you'll attract unwanted attention and we'll both be dead."

Noah freezes.

For a full minute, he says nothing. Just stands there, like he's trying to calculate exactly how deep in the shit we are. Then, he runs a hand over his face and steps closer.

"Fine. At least let me lead, then."

I nod, pointing him the direction—or what I think is the direction. "That way."

Noah doesn't say anything, just starts moving. I follow closely, watching his back in silence, eyes scanning every detail.

Is this real, or am I hallucinating?

He walks like Noah, talks like Noah, reacts exactly like Noah.

He even knows what happened before I vanished with Kieran.

This is not a trap.

This is my brother.

Right?

"So," Noah murmurs after a while, his voice calm at last. "You look ... okay. They didn't hurt you?"

"No," I reply. "Believe it or not, they've treated me well here. The Fae love to party. So far there's been three. And I even have a job between trials."

"What, all that in two days?"

"For me, it's two weeks. I told you—time moves differently here."

Noah stops mid-step, turning to frown at me. "You're telling me you've been here for two weeks?"

"Yes, and I'm still alive."

My brother exhales, long and hard. "This is ... unbelievable."

"So is you being here," I say softly, meeting his eyes.

Noah doesn't reply. I can tell just how much he's still in shock, trying to make sense of all this.

If this isn't my brother—I don't know what the hell he is.

We keep walking in silence, letting the cool wind and the passing time settle over us like dust, reminding us both of the cruel fact that we're really here, and there's not much we can do about it.

I swear to the stars, if we make it out and Kieran doesn't send Noah home, I'll scream at him until the Court cracks.

I don't see the other contestants. No sign of Lucas or Tessa. Not even Jordan.

What if someone they love got dumped here, too?

What even is the point of this?

There are no monsters, no sharp-toothed beasts lurking in the dark. If anything, having Noah here might even help me get out faster—two people are always better than one.

So, what's the catch?

There has to be something.

We stop for a break after an hour. Noah settles on a rock, while I hike up a hill to get a better view.

Still no one.

Only trees, dense and vibrant in autumnal crimson.

It's a good sign, I guess.

But when I turn around—Noah isn't there.

I sprint back to the rock, heart in my throat, praying he just wandered off to check something. But there's nothing. No sound. No footprints.

Just fog and trees.

Shit.

"Noah!" I call out, panic tightening my chest. "Noah, this is not funny!"

I circle the area, hoping to find something—anything. How can he be gone? He was just right here!

"Cass ..."

Wait.

I freeze. That wasn't the wind, was it?

"Noah?"

"Cass, I'm down here. Shit ..."

Down?

I walk towards the noise, eyes scanning the ground, watching every step.

Then I see it.

A hole—wide, jagged, and perfectly camouflaged. A massive trap carved into the earth—and Noah is at the bottom, hand holding one ankle.

"Gods, are you all right?"

"Yeah, but I think I twisted my ankle."

I exhale, relief flooding over me. It's not great, but at least it's better than him being mauled by some creature. "Hold on. I'm going to get you out of there."

I spin around, eyes sweeping the thick brush. There has to be something I can use as rope. A vine, a low-hanging branch, anything.

It'd be ugly if I fall in, too. Then we can forget about leaving here alive.

"You need to leave him," a voice whispers behind me—too familiar, too calm. It sends a chill straight down my spine.

I know that voice.

No.

It can't be.

"Cassie, do you hear me? You need to leave him. That's not your brother."

I stop breathing.

Every fibre of my being screams "don't turn around." This is another trap. It can't be him.

It's impossible.

But I make the mistake of turning.

The colour drains from my body like I'm seeing a ghost—because I am.

Declan.

In the flesh.

Standing right in front of me.

"You—you're not real," I whisper, choking on the very air I'm breathing. My head spins. "How ... how can you be here? You're dead ..."

I squeeze my eyes shut for a moment, but when I open them, he's still there.

"I am, and so will you be," he warns, his jaw ticking. "Don't save him. If you do, he'll pull you in, too. He's a shapeshifter."

What—

Oh, Gods.

I glance at the trap barely ten metres away, then back at the man in front of me.

He looks the same. His eyes. His face. I've seen him wearing that shirt a hundred times.

But—

How is Declan real ... and Noah isn't?

"I—I don't understand."

My whole body trembles. My knees buckle, and I hit the ground hard. The cold seeps through my skin like poison, curling around my ankles and creeping up my body, perfectly wrapping me until I can't move. I hear Noah calling from the pit behind me—if that is even Noah.

But what the hell is Declan?

"You're not real," I whisper again, dragging in a shaky breath. "You can't be real."

"This is the Court of the Fallen, Cassandra," Declan murmurs. "The Fae manipulate things. It doesn't matter how I'm here. You just need to wake up and believe me ... that isn't your brother."

"But how can I be sure? What if it's you who's trying to trick me? What if you're the shapeshifter?" I snap, rising to my feet.

For months, I wished for this—for him. For just one more minute with Declan. One more chance to see his face, to hear his voice. I used to close my eyes, praying that it was all a dream and when I opened them, Declan would still be beside me.

And now that's right in front of me ... I'm terrified.

Terrified to touch him.

To believe him.

I want to run to him. To throw myself at him and tell him how sorry I am about that night.

Tell him I miss him so much it's rotted a hole in my chest.

That I haven't stopped replaying the terrible things I said.

The guilt is crushing my insides, slowly and painfully.

But I don't move.

Because he's gone.

And this ... this can't be real.

None of this is real.

Wait. The clue—

Dearest Cassandra,

What's keeping you up at night?
Careful, for it might come back and haunt you.

Love,
The Trial Committee

Come back and haunt you.

Careful ...

None of this is real.

This is what the Fae want—for us to get tangled up in our messy past, for grief and confusion and guilt to drag us under.

To watch us unravel until we slit our own throats with memory.

They're all shapeshifters.

I step closer to Declan. He doesn't move. The man truly looks exactly like him, but his scent is off. Off enough to twist my stomach.

Still, I raise a hand, hesitant, brushing my thumb against his cheek.

Declan closes his eyes to the touch. He feels real, warm even.

His breath clouds the air.

It's the only proof I need before I drive the dagger straight through his heart.

The man—shapeshifter—jerks back, eyes wide with horror, lips parted in a silent scream, gasping for air that won't fill his lungs.

And then he drops, limp and twitching, back to whatever hell spawned him.

Dead people aren't warm and don't breathe, you sick fuck.

I almost believed him.

Almost.

I pant, silver blood dripping from the tip of my dagger. My hand shakes, but there's no time to feel sympathy for something that would have killed me if I hadn't struck first.

Noah's been quiet.

Too quiet.

I look up from the shapeshifter.

And there Noah is—standing beside the hole, perfectly upright. No limp. No scratches. No twisted ankle.

He bares his teeth at me, eyes flicking to his fallen mate, still bleeding out in the dirt.

And I fucking run.

Chapter 11

Splinters on my face. Splinters on my arms. Splinters everywhere.

But they're nothing compared to what the shapeshifter wearing my brother's face will do to me if he catches me.

The only thing I'm focusing on is the sun at my back and making sure not to trip. Because if I do, that's it for me. I'll join Declan and the other shapeshifter I just killed.

How big are these damn woods?

I walked with fake Noah for over an hour, and I'm nowhere near getting the hell out. The trees are so damn thick, the fog too heavy. Everything feels like it's closing in, swallowing the path behind me as quickly as I clear it.

Then—

Somewhere to my right, someone screams.

My heart sinks.

Tessa.

Gods, please don't let it be Tessa.

But I can't stop. If I do, this shapeshifter will kill us both.

I have to believe that wasn't her.

And if it was, I have to believe she made it out somehow.

"Come on, Cassie. Are you seriously running away from your own brother again?" The shapeshifter whistles, almost amused as he chases me through the trees relentlessly. I don't look back, but the words chase me faster than the shifter himself.

I left him.

I left Noah.

No.

I can't think about this. Can't let guilt sink its claws in.

He's fast. Too fast. Inhuman.

Every step he takes is two steps of mine. If I keep running, he'll catch me, probably pin me to the ground and tear me apart

There's only one way to stop him.

I skid to a halt, drawing my twilight glass dagger in one hand, the moonstone dagger in the other.

Fighting gives me more chance of surviving.

"Oh, look who's finally stopped running," the shifter drawls, grinning as he closes in on me like an animal stalking its prey, unhurried and sure of the kill.

He's still wearing Noah's face, but the voice isn't his anymore.

I'm going to be sick.

"You can shift back now," I demand, twirling one dagger in my hand.

I may have not been training everyday like Lucas, but he still taught me and Tessa some basics. And I throw knives for fun.

"Why? Don't like this one?" He cocks an eyebrow. His features ripple, shift—until he's Declan. "How about this?"

I curse under my breath, circling slowly, scanning for a weakness, for a chance to strike.

"Pity," I breathe, trying to steady my shaky hands. "It seems I'll have to kill my boyfriend twice."

The corner of his mouth curves into a grin. "Are you sure this isn't your third time?"

I flinch.

He knows about that night.

He knows it's my fault.

And that's all it takes.

He surges forward—and I stumble, just slightly, just enough to lose rhythm.

I lunge with my moonstone dagger, but he's so much faster, ducking the strike like he's dancing—like this is his idea of fun. His grin widens as he grabs my wrist mid-swing and twists hard, forcing me to drop the dagger. Pain shoots up my arm. I let out a sharp cry, but I hold on to my twilight glass dagger tight.

Then, for a split second, I see an opening, and I use the momentum to plunge the dagger towards his ribs without hesitation.

Miraculously, it lands.

Silver blood hisses out, splattering across my leathers. His eyes widen—I think more in surprise than pain—but I'm not dumb enough to wait and see what he does next. I wrench free, pivot, and slash again, this time aiming for the neck.

He shifts again, right in front of me.

Declan's face turns into Tessa's—her glassy, terrified eyes. Then Lucas's.

I freeze for a blink too long, and that's all he needs.

Before I know it, his long, sharp claws slash my side. Pain blooms like fire, spreading slowly until red is all I see. I scream. I don't need to look to know that the cut tore through my clothes. Crimson blood drips on the forest floor.

Fuck.

"You're sloppy," he sneers, stepping closer, silver blood still leaking down, but somehow, I'm the only one in pain. "New boyfriend of yours?"

"Shut your filthy mouth," I groan, clutching my side.

The shapeshifter chuckles. "Come on, even the Fae have a crush on him. If you want ... I could wear his face while you ride me."

Is he fucking serious?

"You're sick," I breathe through the pain. "Just kill me already."

He hums, tapping a finger to his chin like he's deciding which outfit to wear, whose face he's picking to haunt me next. "Ah ... wait, I should have known." He pauses, then he shifts again.

Not into Noah. Not Declan.

But Kieran.

Dark wings with lines of constellations shimmer behind him. That beautiful smirk. Those impossible eyes.

My breath catches in my throat like a hook.

"Hm, does your dead boyfriend know you fancy the King of the Fallen?" he muses, savouring every bit of stupid emotion I show. "Oh, wait—he's dead."

"Why don't you ask him yourself, seeing as you'll be joining him soon?" I tighten the dagger in my grip.

The shifter doesn't flinch. He just laughs.

Big mistake.

I hurl the blade straight at his left wing.

Let's see if the bastard remembered he has those.

It lands. He stumbles back, eyes wide. I don't hesitate—I dive, snatch the moonstone dagger from the dirt, and launch it at the other wing, pinning him to the tree behind.

He screeches, the sound shrill and inhuman, ripping through the trees like a siren.

Pain sears down my side, but I don't stop. I spot a thick branch nearby, a little heavy but manageable.

Ignoring the pain in my wrist, I grab it and run before slamming it into him as hard as my broken body allows me to. He crashes to the ground, the weight of the blow tearing his pinned wing as he hits the dirt, silver blood splashing across the leaves.

Desperate to clutch his wound, the shifter rolls onto his side.

I leap up, snatch the dagger on the tree—

And drive it through his skull with all my weight.

Silence.

Utter silence.

Silver bleeds into the forest floor.

I collapse next to the body, a ringing sound echoing in my head.

Then slowly, the woods come back to life again. The sounds returns—wind in the trees, birdsong, the thud of my own pounding heart.

Still breathing.

I'm still breathing.

And it's not over yet.

I swallow the pain and drag myself up, using the branch as a crutch. I pick up both daggers, wiping silver blood on my leathers, and start moving again.

Only death awaits me here.

I walk and I walk.

Minutes pass, hours—who knows.

Then I see it—light.

I don't hear footsteps. No one in sight.

Until—something slams into me from behind, knocking me flat.

I scream as pain flares in my side, fresh blood blooming again.

And Lucas has a knife to my throat.

"Who are you!?" he demands, wild eyes, shaking hands, blood trailing down his temple.

I freeze.

Oh, Gods.

He thinks I'm a shapeshifter.

"It's me, Cassandra!" I yell, even though it hurts. "What the hell is wrong with you!?"

"You think I'm going to fall for that the second time?" He growls, hand still trembling, the blade poised like he's a split second from driving it into me.

"My blood is red! I'm not a shifter!" I scream, eyes squeezed shut, bracing myself for the blow.

But it doesn't come.

Lucas freezes. Then, he lowers his eyes to my side. They widen. The wild panic fades, replaced by something softer—before it's swallowed by horror.

"Shit, Cass ... I'm so sorry," he breathes, dropping his knife. "Oh Gods, you're hurt."

"Well." I exhale, blinking through the pain. "You should see the other guys."

Lucas doesn't laugh. He sheathes the blade and slips an arm around me, gently pulling me upright. I wince, lightheaded from blood loss, from the fight, from everything.

We're so close.

So close.

"You look like paper," he whispers, holding me tighter.

"I'll be fine," I lie. "Let's get out of here."

We keep walking, every step harder than the last. The light draws closer. A warm wind flushes in—and then we emerge exactly where we started this morning.

The Fae cheer. The noise crashes around us, echoing in my head. It's all I can hear before I collapse to the damp ground.

Lucas catches me just in time—his arms strong, grounding—and that's when I see it.

Blood.

Smeared on his fighting leathers. Some of it even on his neck.

But he's not hurt, no open wound that I can see.

"Whose ..." I whimper, voice drowned out by the chanting. "Whose blood is that?"

Lucas glances down, his face grim.

He hesitates.

And I know.

I just know.

"No ..."

"Cass, I tried—" He swallows, voice breaking. One arm cradles my head, keeps me from touching the cold, filthy ground. "I tried to save her—"

"No, Lucas ..."

"I'm sorry," he murmurs, still not meeting my eyes. Pain blooms across his face. "I was too late."

Tessa.

It's Tessa's blood.

She's gone.

That scream I heard was hers.

And I didn't help.

I didn't help.

I let her die.

Chapter 12

I wake up a day later, still reeling from the pain that is now nothing more than dull, aching bruises. Fae medicine is quite literally magical.

If only it could heal my broken heart from losing a friend.

As annoying as she was, and as much as I hate to admit it—Tessa was that.

A friend.

Everybody else made it out.

Bruised, broken, shaken—but still breathing.

A funeral will be held tonight in honour of Tessa—ironic, really, considering it's the Court's shapeshifters that killed her.

And all I can think of is how I never gave her that hug.

How I should have.

I never fucking learn.

Now I understand why they give us two weeks between the trials.

"How do you feel?" Lucas checks on me every two hours, like he's trying to make sure I haven't slit my own throat.

It's like the blind leading the blind.

Now two of the people we cared about are dead. And we're outnumbered by the rest of the contestants.

"Splendid," I say, picking sarcasm over screaming. I've been in bed all day, reading and resting, trying not to get in my own head. Only now do I notice he's in his guard uniform. "You went to work?"

"Yeah, well," he replies, sinking into the chair next to my bed. Lucas explained to me this morning that he basically begged Daphne to lift the ward so he could be the only one allowed to visit me. "Needed something to distract me."

That's not a bad idea, actually.

Kieran hasn't been by.

And I'm not sure how I feel about seeing him.

This is his Court.

His shapeshifters.

He might as well have driven a knife into her himself.

"You coming out for the funeral?"

That word hits me like a blow to the head. I can't even bring myself to speak, so I just nod.

I won't miss it.

Not when I already missed our last hug.

Lucas seem to understand exactly how I'm feeling. He just gives my arm a gentle squeeze and rises to his feet, even though it's barely been five minutes since he sat down. "I'll let you get ready."

"Thanks."

I lie there for another ten minutes after Lucas closes the door behind him. Part of me refuses to move—to get up, to pick a suitable dress and attend this funeral.

I can't quite wrap my head around what happened.

It might have only been two weeks, but in that short time, we shared something that I haven't with anyone else.

And I failed her.

Like I failed everyone I care about.

I manage to get up at last. I don't know what a Fae funeral is like, but black is a universal colour of grief.

Lucas picks me up twenty minutes later, now dressed in a sharp black suit. We walk in silence, sadness clinging to us like ghosts. In a span of two months, we've attended two of our loved ones' funerals. How do you even deal with something like that?

The funeral is held in the garden. The sky is clear, and the stars have risen, brighter than any other nights since I arrived. Seats are arranged in neat rows, and at the front, on a flower-laced dais, lies Tessa's lifeless body.

So many flowers. Too many.

The Fae wear black. Some have already taken their seats. In the front row sit Oliver, Leon, and Daisy. No sign of Jordan.

I didn't expect this.

Not any of it.

I thought only Lucas and I would show up—maybe Oliver and Leon, since Oliver is the only other normal one of us, and if he did, he would convince Leon to come, too. They've become a weird uncle–nephew duo.

But this?

I don't understand.

They kill us off, then host our funerals?

"I guess we should be glad that at least Tessa is getting a proper send-off?" Lucas mutters in confusion.

I guess so.

We walk up to the dais. I don't know the details of how she died. I don't want to. All I know is that her version of twisted shapeshifter got to her. I assume there're injuries, but the Fae must have used magic to make her look untouched.

She looks so young.

Now that she's lying in front of me, not breathing, it finally feels real.

Tessa is dead.

I lean in, gently giving her the last hug she asked for, wishing she could still feel it, somehow. I let my tears fall, just for a moment, then I pull back.

I watch as Lucas kisses her forehead goodbye. Then we both turn to take our seats next to the other contestants.

"Why are you even here?" I ask Daisy before I can stop myself.

She glances at me. "How heartless do you think I am? I want to win, but that doesn't mean I enjoy watching someone die."

I don't know if I believe her. She could be trying to get on my good side, since the position for my friend is now open.

But I let it go. No point arguing at a funeral. Lucas rests his hand on the back of my chair and pulls me closer gently, as if to both comfort and calm me down.

"It's okay. Tessa wouldn't mind," he whispers.

No, she wouldn't. She had a big heart like that.

But good doesn't defeat evil in real life, and nice people die young.

The wretched ones?

They sit amongst us.

Immortal.

"Good evening, lovelies." Aurora steps onto the dais after everyone has taken their seats. She's wearing a long-sleeve black gown and veiled hat, crimson paint on her lips—but tonight, there is no smile, no inappropriate jokes. Her tone is crisp, solemn. "This is my least favourite part of the trials."

Least favourite?

Then why put shapeshifters in there?

Why not just send whoever loses home?

"I think I speak for everyone that Tessa was one of the brightest ones here, and I'm not going to dishonour her by pretending I knew her well, or by saying something pretty just for the sake of it. But a life has been lost. And tonight, we honour that life before we give her back to the stars." She glances up at the sky. "Would anyone like to say a few words?"

That question is for me and Lucas.

But I don't move.

This is wrong.

They killed her.

Lucas doesn't move either, guilt hanging over us both like we're doomed to carry it for eternity. I just rest my head on his shoulder and close my eyes.

"Very well, then," Aurora says quietly.

The music begins—low, haunting. One by one, the Fae leaders step up to place a black rose on the dais—Kieran is the first. He lingers afterwards, standing off to the side as the others follow.

Lucas and I are the last. His arm hasn't left my shoulder all night.

I meet Kieran's eyes as we step down from the dais.

It's been a few days since we last spoke.

I don't know if he's my friend, just a Fae I'm trying to use—one who's also using me—or just someone I'm about to turn into a rebound when grief and alcohol swallow me whole.

I don't know anything anymore.

Everybody stands once the last flowers are laid. Kieran steps forward again. He raises a hand, and slowly, fireflies rise from Tessa's body. Hundreds of them, glowing soft and gold, spiralling up into the starry sky, leaving only the flowers behind.

How can something so beautiful be so heart-breaking at the same time?

The crowd leaves not long after that, but Lucas and I linger.

Kieran still stands there, giving us a moment before stalking closer.

"I'm sorry," he offers softly. I can feel Lucas's arm tighten around me.

"Cry me a river." Lucas snorts. "Your shapeshifters killed her."

"I know."

His words are unexpected, heavy. Acceptance without any excuse. He doesn't say anything else, just glances up at the sky, his jaw tense.

And I don't understand any of this at all.

"What's going to happen to her family?" I ask. "Will they ever find out?"

"No," Kieran murmurs, direct and cruel. "Their memories of her will be erased. Anyone who knew Tessa won't remember she existed. Except us."

My breath catches in my throat. Lucas is still as a rock.

"That's too cruel."

"Maybe," he whispers, letting a soft sigh. "But never getting closure is worse."

"Why?" I demand, pulling away from Lucas to face Kieran fully. "Why can't you just tell them?"

“That’s the rule. No one learns what goes on in this Court,” Kieran says, frowning. “You already know that.”

“But that’s not fair! You need to do something—change the bloody rule!” I shout.

Heads turn in our direction.

It’s not very wise to raise my voice at the King of the Court, and I doubt many ever have.

But I don’t care if he hurts me.

Let him.

Let him take my eye like he did Jordan’s.

Let him snap his fingers and erase me from existence.

I probably fucking deserve it.

“Would you rather her family grieve forever?” Kieran narrows his eyes at me. “Do you know she came here because her mum is ill, and she wanted the wish to save her?”

What—

Tessa’s mum is sick?

“She’s been bedridden for months. Do you know she lies there, blaming herself for Tessa’s disappearance?”

His jaw tightens. His words land like thunder.

“Would you rather the poor woman die of heartbreak and guilt?”

I press my lips into a thin line, refusing to break eye contact. Never once did Tessa mention that to me, or Lucas. She was always light and sunshine.

And this?

This is Kieran’s version of kindness?

Fuck.

The worst part is—I get it.

Somewhere deep down, in the ugliest, most broken part of me ... I find myself agreeing with him.

Kieran's eyes soften, like he sees it, too.

Somehow, we understand each other, as twisted as it is.

"Come on." He offers me a hand again. A truce.

Lucas immediately pulls me back by the arm. A silent no from him.

I open my mouth, then close it, finding myself hesitating.

My hands are shaking.

"Where are we going?" I whisper, my voice hoarse, even though Lucas is still holding me.

"To get drunk."

And that's enough for me. I hear Lucas calling my name, trying to stop me, but I place my hand in Kieran's.

Not once—not ever—have I said no to this hand.

I'm beyond hopeless.

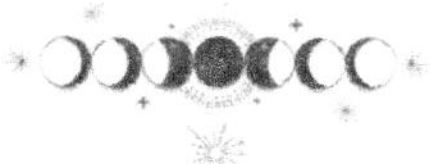

It's not the Tower of Stars we vanish to. This time, it's the River of Vows.

Under the gazebo, a carafe of Fae wine waits on the table. Two glasses. Set like it knew sadness would make us find our way to it eventually.

I don't care how dark, or how cold it is.

I sit, pour myself a glass, and start drinking, the wine bitter on my tongue, stronger than the usual Fae wine I'm used to. It's exactly what I want.

The darkest of the darkness stands before me—wings and all.

"Do you truly know why everyone's here?" All their wishes?

My wish?

Kieran sighs, rolls up his sleeves, then pours himself a glass and settles beside me. "Why? Was I not meant to know you're doing all this for your dead boyfriend?"

I swallow.

"Is that all you know?" I lick my lips. A test.

Kieran grins. "You're going to have to be more specific than that."

What's the point?

His sentence already says enough.

I exhale, shaking my head. "I don't understand you people. First you feed us, give us jobs, then toss us into a deadly trial, and throw a funeral when we die—what the hell is this place trying to be?"

Kieran hums, low and amused. "You might hate me even more if I told you what this is really for."

"Oh, I'm far from hating you." And I'm pretty sure he already knows that.

I don't hate him.

I hate myself for not hating him.

I thought I would when I saw him at the funeral.

But I didn't.

I still don't.

He bursts out laughing this time. "Sorry, I forget—my charm is irresistible, even with the dead boyfriend."

I roll my eyes. "Says the one who keeps vanishing me from place to place and clearly wants sex."

"I know." His grin deepens, shameless. "How fitting. We could fall in love and doom each other to death."

"What a brilliant idea." I smirk. "Then what do we do when I grow old and cranky, but you're still young and pretty?"

"If the sex is that good, I might even curse myself human for you."

"Go to hell, Kieran."

And another laugh, loud, echoing, bright as the stars, coming from the darkness himself.

Once again, I find myself smiling.

He turns to me, eyes flaring in the dark. I blink as Kieran twirls the end of my hair between his fingers. He really likes doing that.

Gods, he's so beautiful.

"My dear," he whispers, "I'm already in hell."

Those words hit me, hard.

I suppose this gilded cage is a version of it.

"Why can't you ever leave?"

He lets out a breath, not meeting my eyes. "Let's just say my family and I ... we don't get along."

"Tell me," I say. "All of it."

The storm-lit eyes meet mine again—golden, dark, like lightning at midnight.

Kieran hesitates. Our invisible tattoos shimmer faintly in the moonlight—a promise of our shared secret, binding and unspoken.

"All right," he says at last, sipping his wine like he needs it. "When a human is born, a Fae is bound to them. We don't interfere directly and can only influence your life choices—like a whisper in your ear. A nudge."

I gasp. "What—like a guardian angel?"

"Something like that." Kieran nods. "As humans grow, some turn bad. They break promises. Again and again ... until there's no going back. That's when their Fae fall from the stars."

I blink.

Once.

Twice.

We are the reason they fall?

No wonder they hate us.

"For thousands of years, those fallen Fae scattered the earth. The thing is—we don't last long down there without magic. And I—" Kieran pauses, like the words seem to weigh something in him. "You could say I was born with a gift. Powerful enough to create all this—a shelter for the Fallen."

I bury my face in one hand.

This—

Gods. This is so fucked up.

"My family's something like royalty. They were furious. So, they cursed me."

And that's why he's trapped.

Kieran built a home for the fallen—Fae cast down, punished, purely because of the failures of the humans they were bound to, through no fault of their own.

And he was cursed for it.

Mother of the stars.

"That's ..." I start but shut my mouth again. I'm utterly speechless.

"I know," he murmurs. "I know."

I drink.

It's the only thing I can do.

And Kieran drinks beside me.

After a long silence, I say, quietly, "I'm sorry."

"Why?" he asks, brow raised. "Your Fae hasn't fallen yet."

Well, isn't that a surprise?

With everything I have done, you would have thought that Fae would be kissing the dust on the street in front of my house by now.

"How come we never know about this? Humans, I mean."

"Because we don't want you to," Kieran simply says. "But if you look hard enough, our library's full of it. Though, no one ever does, especially when they're busy chasing a wish."

"So it's not exactly a secret."

"Oh, it is." He smirks. "You just won't remember any of it when you leave."

"*If* I leave," I correct, crossing my arm. "Will I remember you?"

Kieran pauses as he lifts the glass to his lips, a smile blooming from him. "That depends entirely on whether I want you to or not."

"Hm."

"But why would you?" he asks, settling down his glass. "If you manage to leave, you'd be leaving with your boyfriend. No need to remember whatever fling you had trying to bring him back—although I do imagine sex with me would be ... unforgettable."

I snort my wine.

Unbelievable.

"Fling? You seem awfully confident we'll end up in bed."

Kieran licks his wine-stained lips, his smile wicked. "Won't we?"

I meet his gaze, heart thudding like a warning in my chest.

"Doesn't seem worth it," I mutter, eyeing him. "You won't help me with the trials, anyway."

Kieran laughs, low and dangerous, and then he leans in. His breath brushes mine, smiling against my ear as he whispers—

"Wouldn't be so sure about that, Little Star."

I hold my breath, daring to glance up to meet those magnificent eyes up close. I know Kieran can hear my racing heart, but I don't bother hiding it. I want him to know how much he affects me.

Whether it's grief, lust, or just pure insanity we both share—

Who the fuck cares?

He's a great distraction. A dangerous, beautiful, and most likely addictive one.

His shapeshifters killed my friend, and I still want to be near him.

Kieran might be fucked up.

But so am I.

So am I.

"You know," I murmur, painting him the picture, "you could make it easy. Tell me something about the trials ... and we could fuck—right here. Right now."

For someone who's aware he's being used, Kieran seems far too amused.

His lips graze the shell of my ear, trailing slowly—*painfully*—down the line of my cheek.

"Or," he whispers, "you could stop wasting time, because we're going to do it eventually—then we can fuck. Right here. Right now."

I purr, sweetly, right into his ear—giving him another vivid taste of the noises I'd make with him between my legs.

Kieran growls. "You absolute evil."

And I burst out laughing.

This is fun.

For a moment, I forget the sadness. Forget that my friend just died. That Kieran might even be the cause of it. Even the reason I'm even here at all.

There's something about Kieran.

I always thought that if I ever survived Declan's death and fell in love again, it'd be with someone who could pull me from the dark.

But Kieran is the darkness.

And somehow, I like staying in it.

For a moment—just a moment—I tuck that enormous, aching guilt into a locked room.

And then it's just us.

Us, and the stars.

Chapter 13

I wake up with my head pounding, a punishment from the Fae wine.

The stars outside my window have vanished, replaced by streaks of white clouds and blue sky.

A sign that today, we start again.

That a new trial awaits.

A note sits neatly on my nightstand. I unfold it.

Rest another day.
Don't worry about work.
— K

Is this kindness? Or guilt about Tessa?

Or another way of luring me to his bed?

Maybe all of the above.

Nothing happened last night, just a whole lot of flirting and drinking. The wine kept pouring itself as we talked absolute nonsense, silly topics that meant fuck all.

I laughed, I cried, then I got angry, and then I wanted to climb Kieran like a tree.

Me and the oh-I'm-so-cranky-I-brood-for-a-living King.

One minute, I hate him.

And the next, I want to drag him into bed and bite those dangerous, arrogant lips until he begs.

Kieran is going to be the death of me.

If not, Declan will kill me himself once I revive him.

"To lift your moods, today we'll start our mini-game," Aurora announces at breakfast.

If you really wanted to lift my mood, Aurora, all you'd have to do is not show your face for one bloody day.

Laia is also with her today. They're both wearing fur and long coats. The autumn breeze grows colder by the day. I wonder if, by the end of it all, we'd be in the dead of winter.

Who knows how time works around here.

"What mini-game?" Leon asks.

The man speaks today.

"I'm glad you asked." Aurora beams, the kind of smile that says our curiosity just made her morning. "Around the Court, we have hidden eclipsed coins—hundreds of them. The one who finds most of them will be given a small advantage in the next trial."

I suddenly feel alive.

Lucas shifts beside me. "What kind of advantage?"

"Well, you'll have to win to find out."

Of course, secrecy is Aurora's specialty.

"You have one week."

"But before we officially begin"—Laia steps forward, all smiling—"we would like to offer the winner of the first trial their prize."

That gets everyone's attention. I cross my legs. Who even won the first trial? I was so out of it I could barely keep my head up.

"Now, there's various prizes to choose from," Laia says, dragging out the suspense. "Money. Fancy dinner. Pick a Fae to sleep with. Even borrow magic for a day."

Gods.

The Fae are very on brand, aren't they?

Greed. Lust. Power.

That about sums up the entire Court.

"Any Fae?" Jordan's only eye flares with amusement. He turns to Aurora. "Even you?"

Aurora scoffs. "Keep dreaming, Jordan. You're not the winner."

"Finishing first only secured you some points, but thirty percent of the vote came from us," Laia continues, grinning as she lets us in on the secret. "One of you performed particularly well ... very entertaining."

Every member of this Court is twisted beyond saving.

I imagine they've got criteria and proper guidelines for this popular vote, handed out like flyers on sports day. Meanwhile, we're being chased to our deaths and mind-fucked in the middle of the woods.

"Cassandra." My name spills from Aurora's mouth like a surprise no one saw coming, not even me. I straighten my spine. "Not only were you the quickest to realise your brother was a shifter, but you also managed to kill both of them—even while injured, I might add. The audience couldn't quite believe what happened."

Oh, Gods.

I wonder if it physically pains her to say all this.

I wince—internally, at least.

"The prize is yours."

I don't know how I feel about this.

My survival earns me a reward, whilst my friend was left dead in the dirt.

I can feel the tension thickening between the other contestants—so heavy it barely fits in this massive hall. As if having Kieran on my side hasn't already made me an enemy of half the Court.

"Which prize would you like?" Laia asks. "Or would you like some time to think about it?"

"Come on, you're a fool if you don't pick having magic for a day." Daisy offers her unwanted opinions, as usual.

"What about money?" Oliver chimes in. "How much are we talking?"

"Enough to buy diamonds."

Oliver swallows.

That's useless.

I'm fed. I've got no need for jewellery, or any luxurious crap. Plus, I'm probably going to die before I get a chance to spend it all.

"I—I'm not sure," I murmur.

"At least you don't need a Fae to sleep with." Jordan whistles, his only remaining eye begging to be taken again.

I exhale.

This again.

Aurora's jaw tics. Her voice drops. "That's a serious accusation—one that could cost you another part of your body if the Court finds you guilty."

"Maybe I'll get magic for a day just to shut you the fuck up." I hum.

Aurora's head snap towards me. "Using magic on the other contestants is off limits."

Ugh.

What's the point of having power if I can't be petty about it?

I click my tongue. "In that case, I'll think about it."

Aurora nods, her pretty face showing no emotion, but it's fairly obvious being nice to me takes great deal of effort. "You have until the day before the trial, or you will automatically forfeit the prize."

Right, can't use magic in the trial—got it.

"Now, I will give you each an eclipsed coin each, so you know what to look for," Laia adds, starting to hand them out.

It's bronze and has a half-moon engraved on it, small enough that it could be hidden anywhere.

"Have fun, my lovelies."

With that, Aurora sweeps out of the room. I spin the coin in my hand as Laia stalks closer and stops in front of me and Lucas.

"I wanted to say I'm sorry." She glances at the empty chair that used to be Tessa's. I swallow another hard lump in my throat. "I help in the kitchen sometimes and got to talk to her. Tessa was a lovely person."

It was such a short time, but Tessa touched so many lives.

The kind of person I could never be.

I nod. "Thank you."

Laia hesitates, then lowers her voice. "You know, I don't always agree with everything we do. If there's any support you both need, just let me know."

I know it's part of her job to ensure we have everything. Still, she didn't have to offer a damn thing.

"Also, you two should be careful. After the first trial is when contestants usually turn on each other," she adds. "Especially you, Cassandra. Kieran can't protect you forever."

"He hasn't been protecting me."

If anything, Kieran has left me to fend for myself.

"It doesn't matter." Laia sighs, voice barely a whisper. "Who do you think they'll turn on first, if not the strongest candidate?"

"She's right, Cassandra." Lucas agrees. "I told you—you should've stayed away from him."

"Or you people should stop telling me what the hell I'm supposed to do," I snap, rising to my feet and shoving my chair back a little too hard.

I storm out, not looking back.

Gods.

Can't a girl catch a break for a day?

My head still pounds—now more from rage than the wine—as I wander beyond the Court and into the market. I have been back here a couple of times with Tessa, and sometimes Lucas. The first place we went, after making handsome money from our side jobs, was the bakery.

I still remember the taste of their pastries on my tongue. It's exactly how I imagined heaven would taste like.

Today, I buy one of Tessa's favourites—a chocolate-filled butter bun.

And I eat it for her.

Then, I cross the street to the blacksmith. The shop owner is draped in silk, just as elegant as the first time I saw her. But this time, she's not alone.

Atticus stands in front of the counter.

Their conversation dies the moment I step inside.

"Look who it is," he greets, then turns back to the shop owner. "You should know, Florence. Cassandra slayed two shapeshifters with your daggers."

Is there anything people don't know about me?

"Really?" Florence looks surprised. "Happy to hear my craft landed with someone who's worthy."

Yeah, well.

Tessa also had one of your daggers. Look how it turned out for her.

"Anyway, I should go." Atticus straightens, sliding a small box towards Florence. She covers it quickly with a gloved hand.

I tilt my head.

Huh.

Atticus is a High Commander—he probably has the license to buy prohibited weapons. I wonder what else they've got hidden behind the cabinet, apart from the iron daggers.

"You know, we could use you in the army, judging by the first trial," Atticus says, turning back to me with one hand on the door handle. "Maybe show up to training sometime. Gideon and I would be happy to work with you."

I just don't know if I can be bothered. Training with Lucas is good enough for me.

But I say, "I'll think about it."

If even he and Gideon start favouring me, and people notice, Jordan will probably wait outside my room all night just to take me out the second he sees me.

"How can I help?" Florence asks as I step closer.

I glance around and say at last, "Got anything that's not blades?"

Anything small. Easy to carry. I will even consider poison—classic, most effective, delightfully feminine.

"Well, that depends on your budget."

I grin, not hesitating for a second. "Put it on Kieran's tab."

Chapter 14

"We haven't even kissed and apparently, you've already gone shopping with my money," is the first thing Kieran says after vanishing into my room without permission—not that I'm upset about that.

I smirk, turning the page of the book I'm currently reading—as I'm peacefully enjoying my bubble bath.

The sight shuts Kieran up instantly.

He arches an eyebrow. "I suppose this alone almost pays off the debt you owe me."

I laugh. "Almost?"

"I've got ideas for how you can repay the rest." Now he's the one grinning. Surprisingly, he hasn't moved any closer. "But for the sake of being a gentlefae—would you like me to come back later?"

"Would *you* like to?"

"Oh, what I'd *like* to do is ... tricky," Kieran mutters, arms crossing, wings tucked in tight. "But I will leave you alone if you prefer."

I think about it for a moment.

Kieran's kindness is complicated ... and utterly attractive.

"Stay," I muse, flipping the page slowly. "Tell me about your day."

Kieran sinks into the armchair only a few feet away. "I can tell you now—my day didn't involve buying tiny, deadly weapons."

"How boring." I chuckle.

With a flick of Kieran's finger, a piece of paper appears before him. "Stinger ring, charm hairpin, stardust perfume, enchanted lip tint ..." he reads aloud. "Who exactly are you planning to use these on?"

Ah. Florence sent him the receipt.

I shrug, turning another page. "Whoever deserves it."

There's no rule regarding the use of weapons in the trials, but since they haven't supplied us with any, nor have they taken away my daggers, I'm going to assume everything is allowed ... until told otherwise.

And honestly, I can think of a handful of people who'd love to kill me and dump my body in the forest.

No one is going to take care of me but me.

"Those won't work on me, nor can they keep me away—I hope you know," Kieran says, grinning.

No, of course not. Trying to scare him off with these would be like waving a twig at an elephant.

"And who says I want to keep you away?" I smile, eyes still on the page. "I just asked you to stay."

A beat.

Kieran doesn't reply right away. For the first time ever, he takes his time and doesn't jump at the first chance of throwing a dirty joke at me.

"My day was fine," he says at last. "Though I missed you."

Oh.

That's—

It takes me a minute to register what he has just said. I look up from my book, meeting his eyes—surprised to find how genuine they are.

Like he actually meant it.

I bite my bottom lip to keep from smiling.

"You did?"

He rolls his eyes. "Believe it or not, spending hours discussing politics isn't quite as entertaining as listening to your sharp little mouth talk nonsense whilst you seduce me from the bathtub."

Okay.

This is—

Kieran is—

Adorable.

I blink at the unexpected warmth pooling in my chest—delicious, surprising, and absolutely terrifying.

"That still won't get you in my bed, you know." I grin, glancing at the massive bed that could easily fit both me and him, and those stunning wings.

"Yeah, I know," he drawls. "No sex until I give up clues."

He sounds almost bored.

Yet, he's still here.

Kieran rubs his chin, eyes flickering with mischief. "Maybe it's time I start seducing you."

I hum, turning another page of the book I have barely read. "If that's your plan, you might have to take your shirt off. For starters."

Another flick of his fingers, and his shirt vanishes—leaving nothing but bare, tight muscle and sinful confidence in its wake.

I lick my lips. "Must be nice. Getting naked that easily."

"Not what I plan to do with you, though," Kieran whispers, drumming his fingers on the armrest. "When you decide you're done with this game, I'm going to take my time—dragging every bit of clothing off that precious little body I plan to savour. Slowly. Completely."

Good Gods.

No man has ever said anything like that to me.

Then again, he's not a man.

My stomach knots. My face flushes. And my mind is trying very hard to suppress the urge to rub this wet, naked body all over him in that damn armchair.

Who the fuck is this Fae turning me into?

I dip half of my face beneath the water—hiding, surrendering, letting him win this time.

Kieran chuckles, low, pleased, and utterly satisfied at the sight of me unravelling.

"I can't share any information about the trials," Kieran says, waving a hand casually, "but I can give you a head start on the mini-game."

A soft clinking sound follows—

Eclipsed coins begin dropping into the bathtub like it's his personal wishing well.

My eyes widen.

"There are ten of them in there," he adds.

I set my book aside and pluck one from the water, watching the light catch its edge.

This is my kind of foreplay.

"Now, I'm not saying you have to." Kieran raises an eyebrow. "But does that earn me anything?"

Oh, Kieran.

Kieran.

Kieran.

I don't reply.

I just slowly begin rinsing bubbles off my skin—unhurried. Precise.

Then ... I rise.

Water runs in trails down my body as I squeeze it from my hair, every drop catching the candlelight.

Our eyes lock.

Kieran curses under his breath, storm-lit eyes scanning every inch of my wet body.

Drip. Drip. Drip.

I step out of the bath, taking my time before I reach for the bath robe.

Kieran slides lower in the armchair as I wrap it around myself—slow, deliberate, in full control.

I step closer.

And it's all Kieran can do before he drops to his knees.

He groans, head tipped back. "I swear to the stars—this is where you'll find me when you're done teasing. Kneeling in front of you. Tasting that fucking body."

The King of the Fallen.

On his knees.

Losing control.

Gods, I don't care how it came to this, but this insane fire—it's been crackling since the first night I placed my hand in his.

Unstoppable.

Irrational.

Burning.

So bright it's starting to melt the ice of the guilt about Declan that I froze in my own heart.

I reach down, lifting Kieran's face. He rises to his feet.

I trail a single finger down that perfect body ... then I lean in, pressing a soft kiss to his cheek.

"Good night, Kieran."

He exhales, long and hard, his hand holding mine on his chest. "One of these days, you'll stop kicking me out."

I smile, gently nudging him forward, and Kieran has no choice but to slowly back towards the door.

He opens it, steps out, but lingers in the doorway.

"I hope you know what I'll be thinking about tonight," he murmurs, dragging those storm-lit eyes down my body.

The moon does nothing to hide the heat rising in my cheeks.

I cross my arms, leaning against the doorframe.

"Why is it that you always vanish in, but never out?"

"I vanish in, Little Star, because it's the fastest way to see you," Kieran whispers, leaning closer enough to steal the air from my lungs. "And I don't vanish when I leave ... so I can linger at the door like this."

"That almost sounds like you have feelings for me."

"I'd say it's too soon to tell, but the concept of time is fucked up around here."

I smile. "You're doomed if you think this could ever work out."

"I'm a prisoner of the Court. I was sentenced to die here anyway." Kieran smiles. "What's the worst that could happen?"

Well, I could love him.

Then I would forget him.

But if I'll forget it all anyway, then there's no point in playing it safe.

"I missed you, too, today," I purr, leaning into his palm as Kieran reaches up to brush my cheek. I could swear he stills for a second. Then I tease, soft and wicked. "But my friends want me to stay away."

"I think they're wise," he says, thumb grazing over my skin. "We're just in denial."

I laugh.

"Maybe."

"Maybe," Kieran echoes, his maddening smile landing on my forehead in a kiss so gentle everything else in the world fades into dull, grey colour.

Then he pulls away.

"Good night, Cassandra."

Chapter 15

Lucas has been ignoring me—like, actively ignoring me—during breakfast.

Eyes on his food. Speaks to everyone but me.

Last I checked, I was mad at him, not the other way around.

"Did you fall off the bed or something?" I ask, cracking a boiled egg with my spoon.

"No."

No—?

And that's it?

"Are you seriously angry with me for not listening to you?" I can't believe this. He'd better be joking, because that's just childish.

Lucas sets down his cutlery as his head snaps towards me, jaw clenched. "You want to know why I'm mad at you?"

"I literally just asked."

"I saw him, Cass," he bites out. "Last night. I saw Kieran coming out of your room." His voice drops even lower. "Topless, I might add."

Oh, my Gods.

This is what he's upset about?

"Funny." I scoff. "I seem to remember you saying you didn't care what I did with him, so long as you didn't have to hear about it."

"That was before he killed Tessa."

The words hit me like an arrow to the chest.

I should have known he would judge.

"He didn't," I whisper.

"He might as well have!" Lucas throws up his hands. All heads turn. He lowers his voice again. "Good Gods, Cassandra ... how you don't see Tessa's face when you're in bed with him is beyond me."

Wow.

That's low.

Lucas has taken it too far this time.

"So you're just thinking what everyone is thinking." I snort, shaking my head.

Sure, what I do with Kieran doesn't really help my case.

But I never thought I'd hear something like that coming out of his mouth.

Well, good to know Kieran might be the only friend I have left.

"I don't know what I'm supposed to think." he mutters. "I don't even know what we're here for anymore."

"Well, maybe next time, you might want to ask before assuming."

I don't say anything else. Just stand, pick up my plate, and move to sit at the far end of the table.

No one wants to talk to me, anyway.

I'm a slut, self-destructive, delusional.

I eat in silence, barely looking up from my food, contemplating asking Daphne to ward the room against Lucas again.

I don't want anyone talking to me like that in my safe space.

Then—as if the day hasn't already punched me in the face—Kieran barges in, looking furious, like he's just been stung by a hundred bees.

He's draped in black, wings fluttering behind him. A portrait of power.

No one meets his eyes but me.

Then, with one hand on the table, another on his hip, he says, "You're half an hour late, Miss Thorne."

I almost choke.

"I'm sorry?"

Half an hour late?

But I don't start for another—forty-five minutes?

Did I miss something?

And why the hell is he calling me *Miss Thorne*?

I narrow my eyes at him, sending a thousand question marks his way—but Kieran only arches an eyebrow.

"Well?" he snaps. "Are you going to move your ass, or do I need to take something from you first, like your pal Jordan, here?"

Pal?

What the actual fuck?

Is this the male who said he missed me, wanted to linger at my door, and kissed my forehead goodnight?

"Miss Thorne," Kieran barks again—this time with the tone I've only heard a once, when he was furious at his own people. "Don't make me say it again."

I drop my knife.

It clatters against my plates—and finally, everything clicks.

I told him my friends—who now no longer exist—didn't want me near him last night.

Oh.

My.

Gods.

Kieran.

I shoot to my feet, dropping my gaze and sprinting towards him—playing my part.

"I'm—" I clear my throat, forcing my voice to tremble. "I'm so sorry, Kieran. I lost track of time."

"Yes, and you've also wasted my time," he says, eyes locked on mine. "Don't you dare do that again."

I nod frantically, sniffling like I might actually cry.

Then I bolt out of the room, all but shaking, with Kieran grumbling something about me being irresponsible behind me.

We shut the doors behind us.

Silence.

Then Kieran's whole face softens.

That dangerous smile returns.

His voice drops, gentle and sweet. "Sorry. I didn't scare you, did I?"

I nearly burst out laughing. I slap a hand over my mouth, shaking my head.

"It was brilliant."

Him acting like a scary boss, bullying me into work—just to stop people from whispering about us. Gods. "When did you even come up with that?"

"Last night, but I needed your reaction to be real, so I kept quiet."

This time, I can't hide the smile on my face, no matter how hard I try.

"You think they bought it?" I ask.

"Probably for a while." He nods, grinning now. "Try not to look at me like that, and they won't find out."

I bite my lip. "Look at you like what?"

"Like you're smitten." Kieran hums, gently poking my nose before starting to walk. I hop after him.

"Please ... if I'm smitten, then what are you?"

"Crazy," he whispers, stopping mid-stride. I smack straight into his back. And his wings. Kieran laughs as he turns. "Crazy about you."

"Oh, Gods, I'm going to be sick." I actually burst out laughing.

He's using *lines* on me now?

I'm never surviving this.

"Oh, shut up." Kieran scoffs but once again holds out his hand.

I frown. "But ... we never vanish to work."

"Who says we're going to work?"

I blink at him. "Where are we going, then?"

"For breakfast, of course." Kieran sighs. "Don't think I didn't notice you barely touched the food on your plate."

Kieran noticed.

When did we become like this?

It doesn't matter, really.

Breakfast with him does sound wonderful.

We vanish to a part of the city that I've never been to before. The only thing I recognise is the mountain—though it looked much smaller from my window. Snow already coats its peak whilst dry leaves still scatter every inch of the ground below.

Nestled against its base is a small village, lined with shops and quiet cafés.

"What is this place?" I blink at Kieran.

"Asterhollow," he says, a soft smile gracing his lips. "This is where I live."

"Wait ... you don't live at the Court?"

"Please," Kieran chuckles. "With all those noises? I associate that place with stress. It only takes me a few seconds to vanish here and back."

Well, I suppose that's true.

I glance around. "So ... do you, like, have a house?"

Kieran tilts his head towards one of the houses built into the cliffside—clearly designed for someone with wings. From the outside it looks ... normal. Warm colours. A bench on the porch.

So simple.

Not what I pictured for the King of the Fallen. I guess I expected something darker. Lonelier.

At least inside this cage, he found a home.

"Can I get a tour?"

Kieran smiles. "Yes, but after breakfast." Then, he waves a hand in front of my face. I arch a brow. "Since we just put on a dramatic show, I figured it'd all be a waste if someone sees us having breakfast together—so I just glamoured you to look like a Fae."

"Really?" I don't feel a thing. I raise a hand to my face.

"Here." Another flick of his fingers, and an object materialises in his hand—a mirror.

Holy shit.

The girl in my reflection looks like me, but she isn't me.

She has my grey eyes—but they glow faintly, like they've been kissed by starlight the same way most Fae in this Court have. My skin, usually pale but soft with human warmth, now shimmers like moonlit quartz. Even my ears taper into elegant points, peeking out from my freshly dried hair that curls just a little more perfectly than mine ever does on its own, especially in this chilled autumn wind.

Beautiful. Ethereal.

I could challenge Aurora for the position of queen with the right gown.

Gods, I hate how much I like it.

"Now I know why you like flirting with me," I murmur, still staring.

Kieran grins. "I barely changed much. You're already beautiful."

I look up from the mirror, biting my lip.

Barely twelve hours ago, he was on his knees for me. And now this.

"Are you okay, Kieran?"

"Why? Do you really believe anyone who finds you attractive must have lost their minds?" he drawls, tucking both hands in his pockets. "Give yourself a little more credit. Half the Court would have launched themselves at you if you didn't work for me."

I bite my lip harder now.

"They should. You need a little competition."

Kieran scoffs, practically puffing himself up to look taller. "Not to brag, but I can turn them into frogs with a flick of my fingers—there's no competition to begin with. Certainly not a close one."

The moon save me.

"I need a giant cup of coffee to deal with this version of you."

"I know you like it," he says, smug, "so stop the bullshit and let me hold your hand."

I massage my temples ... then burst out laughing.

"You're unbearable." I'm wheezing now.

What have we turned each other into in the past few weeks?

"Sure." He smirks. "You'll bear me anyway."

This is crazy.

So crazy.

Let me hold your hand.

Gods, it's also kind of cute.

"It must be because you're old," I mutter, dragging out the game just a little longer. Kieran frowns, arms crossed, tapping one boot against the ground like a warning that I should pick my next words wisely. "When older people fall for someone, they don't waste time; they just get married in a month."

"Sure, we can go back to the River of Vows and do that, too. I just think it might be a little awkward when your boyfriend comes back to life and you have to introduce him to your husband."

I don't know whether to laugh or cry.

I came here for Declan, but all I'm doing is betraying him.

"Will that make me a queen?" I ask softly.

Once again, I shove Declan aside.

"Considering I don't even have a title, that would be difficult."

I click my tongue. "Then no. No title. No ring. What's the point?"

"First, you'll only sleep with me to learn about the trials. And now you won't marry me unless you get a title and, apparently, a giant rock."

I find myself grinning from ear to ear. "You still want to hold my hand?"

Kieran groans, but he grabs my hand—and squeezes it gently.

Smiling feels like a sin.

But I'm going to hell anyway.

Kieran takes me to one of the cafés near the foot of the mountain. Funny enough, its name is Cassiopeia—not far from mine. The staff here greet him with easy smiles, no trace of fear in their eyes, and no flicker of curiosity about who I am.

"This looks lovely." I hum, reading the menu. Suddenly, it feels like I'm on holiday—tucked away in a tiny café at the base of a mountain on a crisp autumn morning.

Sometimes I wonder if I'm still asleep in my own bed back home, and this is just another wild dream I'll wake from.

And I'm trying very hard not to think about everyone I left behind.

Noah, my parents, Susan ...

Every time my mind drifts there—to the deepest, darkest thoughts—I shove them all back into a locked room inside my head.

I won't survive this if I let myself think about them.

This time, I reach for Kieran's hand and squeeze it.

He squeezes back.

"What's wrong?" he whispers, tilting his head.

"Nothing," I lie, biting down the pain and forcing smile. "Thank you for bringing me here."

Kieran stares at me for one second too long—almost as if he can tell I'm lying—then the corner of his mouth curves into a grin.

"You can thank me later," he says, voice laced with mischief.

"You said I only want to sleep with you if you tell me about the trials ... and then you go and do all this just to get something in return, too?"

Kieran throws his head back, laughing. "People would say we were made for each other."

Yes, we would make one hell of a couple—dark, twisted, toxic, and stupidly in love.

The kind of couple that breaks up five times and still finds their way back to each other, over and over again.

But beneath all the chaos, I know that he cares.

I wasn't sure if he did a few days ago, but something changed last night.

Somehow, it's different.

Still, who knows if we'll have changed our minds again in three days.

Let's enjoy it while it lasts.

I order a huge cup of coffee, and pancakes with strawberries, cream and caramel. Meanwhile, Kieran opts for a glass of orange juice and a full breakfast. The food arrives barely ten minutes later. I let out a quiet purr of pure bliss at the first bite.

Gods, everything tastes amazing in this Court, but this place is truly something else.

"This is bad." I point at the food. "If I want to enjoy this on my day off, how am I meant to walk here from the Court?"

It must take at least a few hours, if not longer.

Kieran rests his chin on his palm, blinking at me with those long lashes and magnificent eyes that show nothing but fake innocence. "Guess you'll just have to stay over at my place."

I narrow my eyes at him.

But before I can deliver a comeback, his gaze shifts past my shoulder.

"I sense we're about to cancel the house tour." Kieran exhales—just as Gideon stops at our table.

Oh.

I settle down my knife and fork.

"Sorry to interrupt, but you know I wouldn't come here if it wasn't important." The High Commander's voice is sharp, serious. His eyes land on me, narrowing at the sight of my pointed ears. He blinks and hesitates. "Cassandra?"

I offer an awkward smile, guilty as sin. "Good morning, Gideon."

He gives me a polite nod, then throws a look at his friend, who doesn't flinch. Gideon clears his throat. "Virgil's spies captured a few members of the faction group this morning. One of them serves in our Court."

A faction group? I thought they lived in paradise up here …

What could they possibly rebel for?

Kieran's jaw tenses. "You're saying we have a rat?"

"Either that, or a whole damn nest."

I swallow hard and take a slow sip of coffee.

So much for a peaceful morning.

"Give us ten minutes," is all Kieran says. Gideon nods, then offers me a brief smile and simply walks away without another word.

Kieran exhales, low and tense, then quietly picks up his cutlery again.

I hesitate, unsure if I should ask.

Any Court business they discuss is safe behind my sealed lips and the oath we made, but I don't want to pry, if Kieran doesn't want to talk.

"Remember when I told you no one objects to me in this Court?" Kieran says at last. For the first time, he sounds exhausted. I nod. "Well, no one does, but they form rebellions instead."

Shit.

"I built the whole damn Court. Made my vision and purposes clear. Put rules in place. Sit through these headaches of meetings, since they want me to be the ruler so bad," he mutters, frustration gleaming in his eyes. "And now they disagree with how I lead. I've got the angry newcomers to my right, the rebels on my left. Some of them have probably even joined forces, and all I wanted was a quiet breakfast."

Gods.

What do I even say to that?

I don't know what this whole thing means to us humans, or to the Fae, but the thought of someone hurting Kieran twists something sharp in my chest, something I didn't even know was there. My stomach clenches with both guilt and worry. Guilt for Declan—and immense worry for Kieran. He seems so invincible to most people, so powerful and untouchable.

They don't see what I see—the King of the Fallen, imprisoned by this family in the very Court he built to save others—only to be punished by the ones he tried to save.

I glance at the mountain in front of us—gorgeous and towering, dusted with snow. All the café chairs are neatly positioned towards the view, designed so guests can eat while soaking it in.

I move mine closer to Kieran's.

Then I reach up, bringing his face closer to mine, and press my lips on his—slow, gentle.

There's a flicker of surprise—just for a heartbeat, before his lips move against mine—and that's all it takes for these warm embers around us to ignite into blazing flames. Kieran slides a hand on the back of my neck, fingers tangling in my hair, as he gently pulls me closer into a kiss so intense I can barely breathe.

But fuck breathing.

A soft moan slips from me as his tongue brushes mine, tasting the lingering sweetness of caramel on the tip of my tongue.

I know there's no going back, not after this, but I kiss him back with the same intensity.

Guilt be damned.

Maybe this is my punishment—maybe the Gods sent me this dangerous, addictive male to play with my heart, only to make me forget him later when the trials end.

When we finally pull apart, I lick my lips, tasting the ghost of him still clinging there. My breath comes shallow.

Kieran's eyes drop to my mouth, hungry and feral. They are so raw, expressive, basically whispering into my ear what else he's planning to do to me with those lips. Kieran's practically undressing me with his storm-lit eyes, and honestly, all I can think about is how close his house—his bedroom—is.

One flick of those fingers, and we could be tangled up in that bed.

"Didn't know talk of the rebellion would turn you on." He hums, thumb brushing my bottom lip. "What was that for?"

Because I couldn't stand seeing you like that.

Because I didn't know how else to comfort you.

Because I'm falling for you and I hate it, but also want to drown in your eyes.

But I say, "In case they manage to kill you before I got to do that."

"In that case, we should probably do more," Kieran says, grinning, eyes flashing as he leans closer again. "The rebellion can wait another ten minutes."

I want to ask, *What about our breakfast?*

But his lips find mine again, and all the words fall away like autumn leaves in the wind.

Chapter 16

I find Lucas waiting in front of my room when I come back in the evening.

His face is half swallowed by the dark, eyes downcast.

And that's when I know he's snapped out of whatever mood he was in this morning.

"I'm sorry," he says as I unlock the door. "I thought you and Kieran were ... I didn't know he treated you like that."

He doesn't.

And Lucas isn't wrong—not entirely.

I didn't agree with his choice of words this morning, but I understand where he was coming from.

I open my door wider, a silent invitation for him to come in.

"Look," I start, taking off my coat and scarf, before closing the door once Lucas steps in. "You're my friend, and I don't want to lie to you, so I'm just going to tell you whether you like it or not ... this morning was an act. Kieran put on a show because I told him last night that you guys wanted me to stay away from him."

"What?" Lucas frowns, sinking into the armchair.

I nod. "He doesn't treat me like that, and before you get mad again—I'm not sleeping with him."

Yet.

Lucas keeps his mouth shut, blinking at me like he's waiting for me to continue.

"I know you don't like him, and I don't expect you to, but ... just know that he isn't hurting me," I say, setting down onto my bed. "Kieran is ... not like what people think."

"He killed Tessa, Cass."

Anything I say after that will sound like I'm trying to make an excuse for Kieran, I realise that.

And maybe it is true.

I don't even fully understand what the trials were actually designed for. It contradicts his whole "no one kills humans in this Court" rule.

Then there're the thing about us being bound to them.

Maybe I'm that naïve or blinded by whatever charm he's got over me.

"He's my friend," I mutter, voice barely a whisper.

Even I know that's not true.

We don't kiss our friends.

We don't think about taking them to bed.

"Tessa was our friend." Lucas groans, his voice cracking as he looks at me like he doesn't even recognise me anymore. "What the hell is going on with you, Cassandra?"

I scoff, bitter and empty.

Where do I even start?

A shit ton is wrong with me.

"Can we please not?" I exhale, burying my face in my hand. "I'm exhausted."

"But this isn't you," he says, rising to his feet and stalking closer. "I want to help because it's killing me seeing you like this."

"Like what, Lucas?" I glance up at the man standing before me. "Just because I spend some time with Kieran, that means I've lost myself? You do realise I'm also using him, right?"

"So you keep saying," he snaps. "But it looks like there's something else."

I don't say anything.

I don't know what to say, because it's true.

"For fuck's sake, Cass," Lucas growls, dragging a hand through his hair like he can't believe we've become this.

And honestly, neither can I.

A few weeks at the Court and we can barely remember who we were, or why we even came here.

"Are you angry because I got too close to him, or are you angry for your best friend?" I ask quietly.

He shakes his head, fury still flickering in those eyes, but his worry seems to win out. "I just don't understand ... and I don't want you to get hurt."

"Look around, Lucas. We are participating in deadly trials."

Getting hurt is a guarantee.

He exhales and turns away. For a moment, I think he's about to leave—but instead, he grabs the coat that I just hung up and throws it next to me.

"Get up," he says, firm, tense, unlike him. "We're getting a drink. And one way or another, we're going to sort this shit out."

I doubt it.

It's not like Lucas can will me to stop being attracted to Kieran.

But I put the coat on anyway.

Lucas doesn't say where we're going, and I don't ask. I just follow him quietly. I have never left the Court after dark before, but clearly, he has. He moves with certainty, turning down alleys and side streets like he's walked them a hundred times.

Ten minutes later, we reach a tavern with glowing amber lights and pulsing with live music. Laughter spills into the street like it's Solstice night.

"The guards come here after shift sometimes," he explains like he can read my mind.

I didn't know he was that close with them.

But I guess we all cope with this madness in different ways.

I've been tangled up with Kieran.

He does it with company and alcohol.

I don't realise how much of Lucas's life I've missed until we step inside and one of the Fae at a nearby table immediately turns to greet him. In fact, the whole table seems to know him, and not just one table—several.

And strangely enough, no one looks at us like we don't belong because we're humans. No stare. No side-eyes. This tavern might be the most human-friendly place I've ever seen since arriving here.

I'm not sure if it's because of Lucas ... or they're just too drunk to care.

And he thought he didn't know me anymore?

We've both changed.

We find a quiet table at the far end, and I stare at Lucas in confusion.

"I didn't know you were that familiar with them." I blink.

"When you spend all day and all night with the same group of people, you do get to know them." He shrugs. "Wait here. I'll go and get us some drinks."

I nod.

I glance around the tavern, full of different kinds of Fae, and realise that I'm not scared of them like the first days anymore. Somehow, in such a short amount of time, we've grown used to this place. And bit by bit, we've become part of this Court.

Like it or not, the Court of the Fallen is our home. For now.

We haven't just waited around to compete in the trials. We've all taken jobs, involved ourselves in a whole new community, and even made friends with the Fae.

This isn't just a place we're passing through.

This is a part of our lives.

Lucas comes back with two giant mugs of golden liquid. It smells slightly of honey and something else I can't quite put my finger on.

He sets one in front of me with a small nod.

"Cheers," he says, clinking his mug with mine.

Well, if everyone is drinking it, it's probably not poisonous.

I take a careful sip—and immediately cough in regret. It's sweet at first, then hits the back of my throat like fire.

"Fucking hell," I wheeze. "That's ... intense."

He chuckles into his mug, drinking like it's nothing. We went out drinking a few times when Declan was still alive, but I don't remember him being *this* good at it.

Lucas asked what was going on with me—I think maybe the real question is *what's going on with him?*

"Now, tell me." He pauses, settling down his mug. "What is it with you and ... you know who."

Great pivot.

I'm eternally grateful that he's still not insane enough to accuse me of sleeping with the Fae King in the middle of the tavern. These Fae might not be looking, but who knows what those pointed ears will catch.

"I'm trying to get him to tell me about the trials," I say, lowering my voice.

It's the truth.

Does he need to know the rest?

If Kieran were a human, I wouldn't go around announcing that I've been making out with him.

That part's mine, private.

I don't need to tell him anything.

"But so far he hasn't given anything up?" he asks, brow raised.

"No, and I would've told you if he did."

Lucas drums his fingers against the wooden table, then takes another sip of the horrible golden liquid. "Anything else you want to tell me?"

I take another sip too, bracing myself.

Huh.

Actually, the second one tastes a bit better.

"Why?" I ask, narrowing my eyes. "You know I swore an oath with him and can't tell you anything about the Court business."

"No, it's not about that. I just—" He exhales, rubbing his face like he doesn't know how to explain. "I feel like you constantly choose him over us."

I pick my next words carefully. "Over *you*, you mean?"

There's no "us" anymore.

Tessa is dead, and I don't consider the rest of the contestants my friends.

A pause.

"Come on, you know what I mean," he mutters, crossing his arms. "Tessa used to warn you. And Laia?"

"Tessa also thought he's incredibly hot." I roll my eyes. "And Laia doesn't know me."

And now Lucas is shaking his head, jaw tight. "Sounds like whatever I say, you won't stop seeing him."

"You can't tell me what to do, Lucas."

Friend or no friend, that's a line we don't cross. I don't force him not to spend time with the Fae guards I know nothing about. Sure, I might warn him if I think someone's dangerous, but whether he listens or not is entirely up to him.

That's what I do as a friend.

We're all adults. We're free to do whatever we want.

"I'm not trying to tell you what to do. I'm just worried."

I know he is.

I can see it in his eyes, and I understand it.

"You don't have to take care of me because you think it's your fault Declan died," I whisper. Lucas looks away, shifting in his seat. "It's my fault, not yours."

"How?" he snaps. "I'm the one who wouldn't go out with him. How is it your fault?"

I take another sip of the drink.

Then another.

And another.

Because I need it.

I need the bitterness of the liquid to drown the guilt. I need the alcohol to make me brave enough to admit the thing I haven't been able say to since it all happened—not even to myself.

"Because ..." I swallow, eyes lowering to my mug as I finally let the truth rise for the first time. "I ... tried to break up with Declan that night."

Lucas doesn't say anything.

He just sits there, the silence growing heavier with each breath, until he finally downs his drink in one long gulp. Then he sets the mug down—too hard—and presses his hands to his temples, like he's trying to keep his head from exploding.

"Fuck," he curses. "Fuck, Cass. That's—"

I know.

I know.

It's ugly.

It's unforgiveable.

And the guilt is mine to carry—mine alone.

"I didn't—" He pauses, a long breath shaking through him. "I didn't know."

I shake my head. "I never told anyone ... not until now."

In the beginning, I thought maybe Declan might have told Lucas when he went to see him that night, but Lucas never said anything about it.

And I was too much of a coward to bring it up—even just to comfort Lucas that it wasn't his fault.

For a while, we both just sit there in silence, drowning in the guilt we share.

Lucas is the first to speak.

"Why?" he asks quietly.

Good question.

One I only have cruel answers for.

Declan was kind, smart, and good-looking. And more than anything—he loved me. Completely, deeply. We had our whole lives ahead of us. He always included me in his passions and dreams—whatever they were and however far they'd take him. Declan talked about the future like my name was written at the end of it.

He saw it all. Us.

The problem is, I didn't.

Somewhere along the line, I just ... stopped.

I fell out of love.

Just like that.

Everyone would think I'm out of my mind. And maybe I am.

It was easy and safe with Declan. He was good to me, and I think I liked that—having someone to take care of me. I cared for him deeply, but I was never that in love with him.

I'm a wreck. I never deserved him in the first place.

So, I decided to tell him the truth.

I wanted to be honest. To let him go.

Because he deserved so much more than me.

But we never had a chance to discuss what was going to happen to us before he was murdered.

I should have been more grateful for the love he gave me. Should have just snapped out of whatever blind hole I was in, and maybe, someday, it might have all been okay ... maybe I might have started loving him more, the way he deserved. The way he wanted.

Plenty of people fall in love after they're already tied together.

Who was I to deny him that future?

Who was I to take Declan from this world?

From everyone that loved him?

"Does it matter?" I reply, my voice breaking.

Lucas might hate me for breaking his best friend's heart. For coming here to bring him back, only to jump at the first chance to betray him with Kieran.

He *should* hate me.

I never planned for this to happen.

And I don't even know what I'd say to Declan if we win.

'Hey, sorry for trying to break up with you. Welcome back to earth. By the way, I might've fucked a Fae King.'

I haven't.

But I wouldn't put it past me—to ruin everything, to destroy myself and follow Kieran into the darkness, even after all this.

I don't know anything.

I don't trust myself.

I just know that Declan would still be alive if it weren't for me.

Even if it kills me, I want to save him.

"So ... what now?" Lucas asks after a while. "It's kind of awkward to bring him back just to break his heart, don't you think?"

I chuckle, even though I'm in tears. "I honestly don't know ... but he didn't deserve to die."

A beat.

"Yes, but you also shouldn't be with him just because you feel guilty about what happened," Lucas mutters, his eyes dark. "It's not fair to you, or Declan."

I was expecting some insults and judgement.

But they don't come.

Lucas doesn't call me a monster, or selfish.

He just meets my eyes, exhales, and reaches for my hand.

"I know the guilt you've been carrying, Cass, because I'm carrying it myself," he admits, and my heart breaks into pieces. "And I know saying that it's not your fault doesn't make you feel any better. I just hope you know that I'm still your friend ... no matter what."

I'm not sure I deserve this either, but I nod. "Thank you."

"Let's just take a step back," Lucas offers, gently brushing a tear from my face. "I won't cross a line about Kieran. If you tell me there's nothing to worry about, then I'll trust you. And we'll focus on bringing Declan back."

Gods.

There's a reason this man is Declan's best friend.

He's also good and kind—the same kind of people I hope to be—but never will be.

Why people like them are cursed to care for someone like me, I'll never know.

I don't know what to say, so I just bite my lip and nod, trying not to break down completely.

And Lucas doesn't say anything else. He just leans in to kiss my forehead and murmurs, "I'm going to get us another drink."

I think I need that, too.

It takes me a minute to calm down. I survey the tavern again to pass the time. There are new faces at the table across from ours, but I recognise a couple of them.

Jordan.

And ... Florence?

I tilt my head. What a strange combination.

Jordan is rarely at the Court. I've never been sure if he actually works at one of the brothels, or somewhere else entirely, but I definitely never pictured him and Florence, the blacksmith, sharing a drink with a few other Fae I don't recognise.

Whatever they're talking about, it's nothing fun.

They drink, but there's no laughter, no smiles.

Just hushed voices and grim expressions—locked in a conversation that looks far too serious.

"Don't look," a voice murmurs beside me. "Look at me."

Oh Gods, Atticus.

I blink at him as the High Commander slides into Lucas's seat like it's his own.

"Where did you come from?" I whisper, eyes darting back toward the table.

And what does he mean, *don't look*?

"I should be flattered that I can still slip into places unnoticed." He smiles, not really answering my question. "I've been following a lead about the rat." Atticus lowers his voice, leaning in closer. "And I think that group might have something to do with it."

A cold ripple runs down my spines.

"You're serious?" I whisper. "Jordan and Florence?"

"I don't have any proof—yet," he adds, voice low and sharp. "But Jordan's a contestant, which means you and Lucas are close enough to keep an eye on him. You two are the only ones I trust. If anything seems off—anything at all—you come to me. First thing."

I clamp my lips together, tight.

Way too much is going on tonight.

"Atticus?" Lucas appears behind him, brow raised at the unexpected guest in his seat.

Atticus rises smoothly. "She'll fill you in."

Oh, great.

I'm a spy now?

"On what?" Lucas frowns, gaze flicking between me the High Commander.

"Ask Cassandra," is all he says before disappearing in the crowd, then out the door a few seconds later. Lucas turns to me, still holding the drinks. His confusion mirrors mine. “What’s he talking about?”

I swallow hard.

Lucas isn’t ready for this.

Chapter 17

"Can't believe you kissed me then went out drinking with another man," Kieran says after vanishing into my room as I'm getting ready for breakfast.

"Good morning to you, too, Kieran," I reply, trying not smile as I run the brush through my hair in front of the mirror.

"Good morning, gorgeous." He stalks closer behind me and leans in to give me a brief kiss on the cheek. I lean into his touch. "Look at you and your beautiful hair—you must be kidding me. How am I ever going to get anything done?"

Ugh, so dramatic.

So affectionate.

I love it.

Gods, it's hard for me to accept, but I want more of this.

Whatever this is.

"Hm, is this how we start our morning now?" I murmur, still not looking at him directly, because his reflection in the mirror is already too much. All sleepy smirk and bedroom eyes.

"It could be," he says, voice amused as his fingers twirl the ends of my hair. "Unless your other man objects."

"My other man is my friend."

"Have you seen how he looks at you?" Kieran rolls his eyes. "That bastard Lucas clearly has a thing for you."

"Oh, he does not." I gently smack Kieran with the hairbrush. "We've known each other for ages."

He hums like he doesn't believe me. "So? I've known you for three weeks and still want to lick every inch of you every time I see you."

"Gods." I laugh, but Kieran catches the brush before I can smack him again. "You Fae are just way too horny."

"Thank Gods we are." He lets the brush drop and slides his arms around my waist instead, lips grazing the back of my neck. "I know we can come on a little strong, but I hope you know I'd never do anything you didn't want."

Hmm, it's difficult to think about all the things I *don't* want him to do when his lips are doing exactly what they are ... I meet his eyes in the mirror, those wicked, storm-lit eyes—and breathe.

"The question is," I murmur, turning in his arms and tracing my finger along the buttons of his shirt. "Will you do *everything* I want you to?"

Kieran pulls me to my feet in one smooth motion, bodies nearly touching, a breath between us.

"Anything," he mutters, his voice low, dangerous.

I lick my lips, and his gaze drops to them—but just as he leans in and our mouths almost touch, I say sweetly, "Then tell me about the trials."

Kieran groans, burying his face against my neck.

"Vicious." He growls into my skin, teeth gently grazing the curve of it, wings tucked in tight dramatically. "Absolutely vicious little human."

"That's the rule," I whisper into his ear, trailing my fingers along the sharp line of his jaw.

Kieran responds by sucking on the tender spot on my neck. I gasp—a sweet, startled moan slipping out before I can stop it.

He chuckles, low and wicked.

And he doesn't stop.

"The rule is no sex unless I tell you about the trials," Kieran whispers into my skin, one hand tracing down my spine, the other tightening around my waist as he slowly guides me back towards the bed. "Luckily for us, there're plenty of things we can do without technically breaking it."

Oh, Gods.

Loopholes.

I don't know if I'm annoyed ... or thrilled that there are loopholes in my one golden rule.

"Are you sure this won't make it worse for you?" I ask, my voice a drop of sugar as the backs of my knees hit the edge of the bed. "Seeing me like this. Hearing me. And not being able to do more?"

Kieran just grins, dark and dangerous, his brow lifting like a challenge.

"Oh, it will either kill me," he says, voice thick with dark promise, "or you'll beg me to fuck you. And I swear to Gods, Little Star—when I do, I'll take my sweetest time."

His lips crash into mine—and the stars might as well detonate overhead, even in goddamn daylight.

My heart races, then my back hits the bed the next second.

And we're all over each other.

All the hair-brushing was a complete waste—Kieran's fingers are already tangled in it. I wrap my arms around his neck, desperate to feel him on me, against me. His other hand fists the fabric of my dress like he's debating whether to pull it off, or rip it apart—whatever the hell is faster at this second.

The kiss deepens, hungry and reckless. Kieran gently nips at my lower lip, and I let out another moan—only for him to swallow the sound with another devouring kiss, harder this time, stealing the air from my lungs. And I never knew I needed this kiss more than I needed to breathe until this very moment.

Gods, I really want more of this.

More of him.

Kieran pulls away, dragging his lips down my neck, licking it as he moves lower.

Heat coils in my chest, sharp and aching. I arch to his touch, silently begging for more.

Kieran growls low in his throat, slipping a hand beneath my dress, fingers gliding up my thigh, each inch he climbs setting my skin on fire.

My breath stutters as his fingers find the thin layer of fabric separating him from the pleasure I so painfully need to feel.

He waits, staring into my eyes like he's looking for a quiet permission. Fire burns in his eyes, his kiss, his touch—and I am desperate for whatever it is he wants to give me.

"Touch me," I whisper, pulling Kieran into another kiss. Then, breathless, eyes glazed with want, I beg, "Kieran ... touch me."

And that's all it takes.

"Fuck." Kieran growls, yanking the fabric aside the second he has that permission he was seeking. And I couldn't care less where it lands.

He drags my hips to the edge of the bed, kneeling before me, then pushing my dress up to my stomach. His hands tremble slightly, like he can't get it done fast enough. I brace on my elbows, face flushed, heart hammering like crazy. Our eyes lock—and Kieran lowers his head to my core slowly, storm-lit eyes flaring like lighting before impact.

I watch as he kisses me, soft reverent ... then his tongue flicks—finding that aching spot—and circles it, again, and again, harder.

I collapse on to the bed, breathless and burning. Kieran takes his time kissing, sucking, devouring me like a starved male—and I'm utterly undone. Moaning like it hurts, chasing every flick of his tongue, every graze of his teeth.

Then he slips a finger inside. One. Two. Three.

And that ruins me.

His mouth never falters, and his fingers thrust into me in a hard, punishing rhythm—until nothing exists but him. Until his name tears from my throat, louder and louder.

Mother of the stars.

I beg. I break.

I can't deal with this.

I can't have enough, either.

It's too much.

He's too much.

And when I finally shatter, it's with a cry sharp enough to split the stars.

But Kieran doesn't stop.

He keeps going—driving me past the edge again, and again—until I'm wrecked. Legs shaking. Breath lost. Words gone.

Kieran tastes every last drop of me like a reward he's earned.

And it's safe to say that he bloody has.

When he finally rises, there's a wicked smile on his lips. Then he leans in and kisses me—deep—letting me taste myself on his tongue. I purr into the kiss, drunk on pleasure and still aching for more.

His hardness presses against my skin, and I grin.

Oh, Kieran.

"I could get used to that before breakfast," I murmur.

He hums. "Before. After. With breakfast. Lunch. Dinner. Every hour of the day—I'm there."

I bite my lip to keep from smiling, lacing my fingers with his and pulling him onto the bed—then I flip us, crawling on top, pressing myself against him.

We melt into another hungry kiss. I trace my hand down his muscled body to the hardness straining beneath his trousers, heart pounding at the sheer size of him. Kieran groans into the kiss.

Then, I pull away slowly. "I'm late for breakfast."

Kieran growls like I've just stabbed him in the heart.

"I will remember this," he mutters, sitting up as I adjust my dress. "Mother of the stars, you're so fucking hot."

I smirk, picking up my underwear and tossing it beside him on the bed.

"You're not going to put these on?" Kieran asks, breathless, clutching them like a lifeline.

I brush a thumb over those lips—lips that pleased me barely five minutes ago. "Easy access for later."

That absolutely destroys him.

Kieran collapses back onto the bed, cursing at the ceiling.

I just laugh and walk out the door. "See you after breakfast, handsome."

The autumn walk from my room down to the dining hall helps cool me from the ... *unexpected event* that just happened. I'm the last one to arrive. I look at no one in particular as I slip into a seat beside Lucas.

"You look a little flushed," he says, reaching out to feel my forehead. "Gods, you're warm, too. Are you sick?"

Well, that's—

Lovesick, probably.

"I just came back from a run." *If a run involves an orgasm or two.*

I chug a glass of water like it's holy.

Even that couldn't cleanse me and Kieran of the things we've done. Or the filth we're about to dive into next time we're alone. Because trust me, I know that was just the beginning—my heart is throbbing in dread and excitement just thinking about it.

Gods, I need to stop thinking about him. I'm going to see him for work right after breakfast.

"Have you decided yet?" Lucas ask.

I tilt my head. "About?"

"The prize." He arches a brow. "What will you pick?"

Between making out with Kieran, baring my soul to Lucas, and the rebellion talks—I haven't even thought about it.

And then there's the eclipsed coins. I only have the ones Kieran gave me the other day.

"Probably having magic for a day."

That seems to be the most sensible choice. I don't need money, or a fancy dinner. Definitely don't need a Fae to sleep with—unless I want to make Kieran jealous.

I don't know what I'd even do with magic. I doubt I'd be powerful enough to bring back Declan on my own. Still, I want to use it for something useful rather than just for fun, or just because I can.

Maybe I could enchant my weapons. Give myself an edge in the next trials.

I need to look into it properly.

"Gods, what a beautiful day."

You never know how Aurora is going to greet you. Today, it's all orange silk and white fur, beaming like it's summer and the sun is singing just for her.

For a fleeting, wicked second, I consider telling her whose head was between my thighs a few minutes ago, just to wipe that smug smile off her flawless face.

"The second trial will begin in two weeks," Aurora announces, like we didn't know that already. "Now that you've had a few days to rest and grieve"—her gaze lands on me and Lucas—"we can properly celebrate the upcoming trial."

Yes, because we need an excuse to throw another fancy party.

"There will be no clues this time," she adds, voice syrup sweet. "Only the person winning the mini-game will receive an advantage. All I'm going to say is, the second trial will be completed in teams. Two people will go home. Or, you know ..." She blinks, unfazed. "In a coffin."

Two people.

Not a team, but two *people*.

I've made it a habit to listen very carefully to everything the Fae say, ever since Aurora said the rooms were warded against contestants and mentioned nothing about the Fae.

Lucas and I look at each other.

"Oh, great." Daisy throws her hands up. "Cassandra and Lucas will pair up, Oliver and Leon are thick as thieves—so what, I'm stuck with a one-eyed sex addict?"

"I'd rather go solo than have you as my partner," Jordan snarls. "It's not my fault you've been such a bitch that no one wants you."

"Says you. At least I'm—"

"Simmer down, both of you," Aurora cuts in, her voice sharp enough to take both their heads off. Then she bares her teeth, wicked and absolutely terrifying. "I said the trial will be completed in teams. I didn't say anything about team members helping each other."

Oh, here we go.

They're trying to mess with our heads again.

"Are we not?" Oliver asks, brows drawn tight.

"I didn't say that either."

Lucas sighs beside me, low and weary.

Do we pair up ... just to kill each other?

"You have until the day before the trial to choose your partners," Aurora says, her smile bright as day, her eyes sparkling at the sight of us slowly unravelling. "Tonight, there will be a ball—and you are all invited. Bring a plus-one, or two." Her smile sharpens. "Whatever you're into these days."

The Fae are unbelievable.

They feel like partying, so they are throwing a ball—tonight.

"Attendants will stop by with a few outfits for you to choose from. I look forward to seeing you all tonight."

With that, she blows us a kiss and sweeps from the hall, her gown whispering across the marble floor. She barely does much, hips swaying naturally, but all eyes follow her like we are all enchanted to do so.

I'm trying very hard not to imagine Kieran between those legs.

"Guess I've got to find a plus-one," Jordan murmurs as he stands.

Daisy barks a laugh. "Please, who would want to dance with you?"

Jordan just stalks out of the hall, slamming the door like he's aiming for Daisy's face.

I exhale.

It's not mandatory to bring a plus-one ... is it?

Because if I asked who I'm actually thinking of, Aurora might just combust on the spot.

"Well, I guess we'll just be each other's plus-one," Lucas drawls, biting into an apple like it's no big deal.

"I don't think it's mandatory," I say carefully, keeping my tone light and reaching for a slice of bread and butter. "Besides, this is your time to bring a hot Fae—or whoever you ended up with last full moon."

Lucas almost chokes on his apple.

I grin.

Tessa and I had been trying to find out which lucky Fae he hooked up with that night, but Lucas never let on. Only kept saying, "A gentleman never tells."

"It was a one-time thing," he mutters, flushing slightly. "Just drop it already."

"Oh, come on," I say sweetly. "Give me a name. If it's just a one-time thing then it shouldn't matter, right?"

He glares. "You're relentless."

"And you're cute when you're flustered." I laugh, squeezing his cheek gently.

Lucas is very much not amused, his face turning even redder now. "For Gods' sake, can't a man have some peace at breakfast?"

Peace?

Next to me?

That's never been an option.

Especially after breakfast—when I have to see Kieran again.

I take a deep breath before I step into the Council Hall. Sometimes Kieran works elsewhere—but today we have an important meeting. Updates about the rebellion, and of course, the rat in the Court.

Not everyone has arrived yet—thank the stars. Only Gideon, Octavia, and Skylar.

Kieran is already in his usual seat, eyes tracking my every move like a hawk stalking its prey—though the handsome face gives nothing away.

A face that was between my thighs, kissing, licking—

I clear my throat and make a beeline for the furthest seat.

The golden and deep blue eyes narrow, like he's asking "Really? You really think you can escape me?"

Gods save me.

"I never got to thank you." Gideon turns to speak to me. I blink. "Because of you, I won a handsome sum in the last trial."

Oh, right. He said he was betting on me.

"Maybe we should strike a deal," I say with a grin. "I try my very best to entertain—and you share a slice of your winnings."

Gideon laughs, a sunshine-on-an-autumn-day sort of laugh. "Always so witty. How about five percent?"

"Ten." I cross my arms.

He raises a brow. "Seven."

"Come on, it has to be at least eight."

The High Commander shakes his head, though his smile never leaves that angelic face. Gideon runs a hand through his silver hair. "You're robbing me blind."

"Well, it's my life on the line." I shrug.

"Fine," Gideon says at last, extending me a hand. "Deal."

I take his hand, shaking it firmly. "Deal."

"Pretty sure that's against the rules ..." Octavia mutters, yawning like she's about to fall asleep. "But whatever. Aurora isn't here, so I'm going to pretend I didn't see it."

"You both done flirting yet?" Kieran cuts in, voice sharp with that commanding edge he only uses in this room.

I straighten in my chair like I've just been caught committing a crime.

"Why?" Gideon teases, glancing at me, then back at Kieran. "I haven't had a chance to ask her to the ball tonight yet."

Kieran doesn't say a word, but his eyes shoot straight through Gideon's skull like a golden, storm-lit arrow.

"Sorry I'm late," Virgil announces as he strides through the door, then pauses, surveying the room. "Never mind. I'm not even close to being the last one."

"You'd think people would learn to be on time after all these years." Kieran groans, frustration lacing every word.

I doubt it's really about his Council's tardiness.

I open my notebook and dip my head to hide a smile

Aurora, Atticus, Daphne, and Felix arrive not long after—and the King of the Fallen barks at them like he's ready to bite their heads off ... even though they're just less than five minutes late.

Oh, Kieran.

The meeting begins with a stressful conversation about the rat. Most of the time, I only listen, jot down anything important, and keep my mouth shut, unless anyone asks me something—which they rarely do.

Today is the same.

But also ... not quite.

"I have a reason to believe Florence, the blacksmith, might be involved with the rebellion," Atticus reports to Kieran. "I don't have any proof yet, but my people are tracking her and her suppliers."

Kieran nods.

But his eyes are on me.

I scratch my arm, glance around, pretend to listen to the others, and note nonsense down on my notebook, because I can't properly concentrate with Kieran's eyes burning into me.

But every time I look back, he's still watching me.

Shit.

"I'll post more guards at the ball tonight, just in case." Virgil offers a very reasonable solution.

Kieran just hums.

Then he grins.

Right at me.

I swallow—hard and slow.

That mouth was on me barely two hours ago, kissing almost every inch of my body. His tongue and the things he did—

Gods, dirty images explode through my mind like fireworks.

I cross my legs, trying to steady my breath.

The gesture earns a brow raise from him, like he knows. Like he remembers how I'm not actually wearing anything under this dress—for "easy access."

It doesn't take long for someone to notice.

For *everyone* to notice, actually.

Their eyes start darting between us.

"Kieran, are you even listening?" Aurora snaps, her voice more upset than it probably should be. "This is a matter of life and death—*your* life and death."

"Yes, I'm listening," Kieran mutters, eyes still glued to me, voice flat and completely unamused. "And you are all boring."

"I'm sorry?" she asks, like she can't believe what he just said.

My heart skips a beat, then slams into a sprint.

"Get out," Kieran demands, calm, but deadly.

Everyone stares at him like he's lost his mind.

"Kieran, this is ridiculous." Skylar frowns.

"I said *out*."

Oh, fuck.

I shoot to my feet, ready to bolt—

But then Kieran stops me. "Not you."

I freeze. Swallow hard. Another lump caught in my throat.

"The rest of you—out," he repeats, his voice sharper now. Urgent, like there's fire in the building. "Now."

And I think there is.

It's him.

His people have no choice but to obey. They shuffle out, mumbling as they go. But from the look in Kieran's eyes, he couldn't care less.

The doors shut.

Silence falls.

Then he rises, both hands bracing on the edge of the dark wood table. His eyes never leave mine.

And with a wicked, wolfish smile, Kieran says, "Get on the table, Little Star."

Chapter 18

I'm going to combust into stardust.

I lick my suddenly dry lips, kicking off my boots one by one.

Slowly, I climb onto the table, and I don't stop there—I crawl across the polished surface towards Kieran, never breaking eye contact, behaving like the good girl he wants me to be.

The good girl he's about to unleash.

Kieran curses under his breath.

"Can't believe you kicked everyone out for this," I whisper. "You couldn't even get past the life-and-death topic they're trying to raise."

"Trust me," he says, low and dangerous, hands reaching for my hips—then he grips, hard, and drags me closer. "Those who want to kill me can wait in line. I'm going to die first if I don't touch you. Now."

"So needy," I murmur, throwing my legs on his waist. "You just touched me a few hours ago ..."

"Not enough." He groans, staring at me like he can't decide whether to worship me, or ruin me—or both. "Fuck, you're driving me insane."

I muse. "All I did was just sit there."

"Exactly."

His voice breaks on the word, hoarse and undone. His eyes flash with something dangerous. And then his mouth crashes into mine. There's nothing soft about it.

This kiss is a claiming. A punishment. A goddamn prayer.

A fucking redemption.

I gasp into it, fingers threading through his dark hair as his hand roams—rough and reverent, like he's trying to memorise every inch of me with touch alone.

Kieran parts my legs wider with his knee, dragging me to the very edge of the table, my dress bunched around my waist.

"I can still taste you," he growls against my lips. "Still feel you pulsing around my fingers."

I moan, shameless, desperate.

"You gonna be good for me now?" Kieran asks, one hand slipping lower, trailing over my inner thigh. "Or are you going to keep teasing me until I break you on this table?"

"Can I be a good girl," I whisper, sweet as the darkest sin, breath absolutely stolen, "and you break me as a reward?"

That earns me a low, wicked groan.

The storm-lit eyes let me know how absolutely, deliciously torturous this next moment is going to be as Kieran drops to his knees.

Right there, in front of the chair that's more or less his throne.

In the fucking Council Hall.

Kieran's hands wrap around my thighs like shackles, and he yanks me closer until I'm right at the edge, teetering on the precipice of madness.

He kisses the inside of one thigh, then the other.

Fingers trail down, and down—one slipping inside.

I gasp, a quiet moan slipping from my lips.

Kieran purrs, "You're so fucking wet."

And then he devours.

His mouth finds me with a hunger that makes my spine arch off the table. His tongue moves like he's trying to unmake me. My head spins. Shameful noises tear from my throat.

Every flick, every circle, every press—he's spelling something in a language only my body can understand. I cry out. One hand claws at the table, the other tangles in his hair as my hips buck shamelessly.

"Fuck—Kieran—"

He hums against me, then slips another finger inside. Then a third—exactly like he did a few hours ago—but this time rougher, harder.

They move in a cruel rhythm, curling just right, thrusting deeper—driving me higher until I'm seeing stars, floating amongst them.

The table creaks beneath us.

Fuck.

Fuck.

I come undone with a scream that echoes off the ceiling.

And Kieran is nowhere near being done.

He never has enough, never wants to stop. He licks me through the aftershocks, mouth relentless, finger dragging me towards a second climax so fast I don't even have time to beg.

My voice breaks.

My body trembles.

And I shatter all over again, this time gasping his name like a curse and a prayer.

When he finally pulls away, his mouth is wet with me, eyes raging like fire.

He stands. Leans over me. His smile a promise that he already plans to do it again.

"So beautiful," Kieran murmurs, brushing a thumb across my thigh.

I'm breathless, seeing stars.

My head can't process how many orgasms I've had in one morning.

Kieran is exactly how I thought he'd be, and then some.

"Come here," I whisper, pulling him by the collar. He obeys instantly. Our mouths crash together again. His hardness presses between my thighs—still clothed, still straining.

Gods.

I'm the one being touched, tasted. Worshipped like a goddess.

But it's not enough.

It's not enough.

I want him undone.

I want to make a mess of him like he did me.

I shift, pushing Kieran back towards his not-throne chair. He lands on it with a grunt, laughing low and dark as I climb onto his lap.

"Tell me the rule is off now," he says, voice husky, hands gripping my thighs. "Please?"

I laugh in my throat. "Did you really think saying please would make me change my mind?"

"Can't blame a male for trying."

I shake my head, then I kiss him—hard—biting his lips until he groans into my mouth. My hands trail down, unbuttoning his shirt one by one, slow and cruel.

"You're so fucking smug," I whisper. "Thought you could ruin me and get away with it?"

He smirks. "I was actually counting on you ruining me, too."

In that case ... I drag my lips down his neck, sucking gently at the soft skin near his collarbone, marking him as mine, like he did to me before breakfast. Then I go lower, over his chest—each kiss harder than the last.

And I don't stop there. I drop to my knees.

I reach his stomach—then the waistband of his trousers.

Kieran's breath catches.

I don't break eye contact. Kieran lifts his hips in anticipation, but I take my sweet time, fingers brushing the edge—tracing, teasing.

"Maybe I should leave you like this," I murmur. "Hard. Desperate."

"You already did earlier." His laugh is breathless now. "Do it again and I'll bend you over the goddamn table."

"Hm," I muse. "You say like that's supposed to be a punishment."

Then, I lean in. My breath brushes over the hard line of him through his trousers, and Kieran hisses a sharp, ragged sound, like he's losing composure one heartbeat at a time, even though I haven't done anything yet.

Gods, I love seeing him like this.

I drag my tongue slowly over the fabric, never breaking eye contact. His hands clench the arms of the chairs like he might break if he doesn't.

"Fuck, Cass—"

I undo the button. Unzip. Tug his trousers down just enough. Kieran groans as I finally lay eyes on him.

Big. Hard. Beautiful.

I take him in my hand, wrapping my fingers around the base, and then I stroke—once, twice, slow enough to drive him insane.

Kieran's breath punches out of him. His head tips back for a second, then snaps forward again, watching me like I'm both his salvation and his absolute undoing.

I lick my lips, then kiss the tip—a soft brush.

His whole body jerks.

"Fuck," he rasps. "You're such a tease."

I smile, satisfied with how unravelled I've made the King of the Fallen, and then I take him into my mouth.

Slowly. Deeply.

Kieran chokes on a moan, hips twitching, hands fisting the arms of the chair like he's using every last ounce of strength he has not to thrust into my mouth, or pull me up and bend me over the table. Every lick, every stroke of my tongue has him falling apart, muttering curses under his breath.

"I knew you and that goddamn mouth were going to ruin me," he groans.

I pull back just enough to say, "I take that as a compliment."

Then, I suck him deeper. His hips buck and he swears, voice strangled.

I bob my head, faster now, hand working in tandem, and it's not long before I feel him tremble—so close, so wrecked, a mess of want and wildness.

"Cassandra—fuck—I swear to the stars, if you stop—"

I absolutely do not stop.

And Kieran shatters. With a growl so guttural it echoes off the walls, he comes, hips stuttering, fingers digging into the arms of the chair like he's been struck by lightning.

I swallow every last drop—and that has Kieran growl like a wounded animal.

And when I pull back, I wipe the corner of my mouth with my thumb—then lick it clean. Kieran's chest heaves. His eyes are still glazed, wild.

"Beautiful." I copy his own word, settling back into his lap, smug as sin.

With the underwear that I left in bed and his trousers undone, our bare skin brushes. I deliberately rub myself against him, wet, and full of need that we both can't seem to get enough of. I grin as I feel him harden again.

One move, and he could be inside me.

"Mother of the stars," he rasps, grabbing my hips in place—tight—like he's *this close* to thrusting into me. "Yesterday it was a kiss. Today it's this. I can't wait to see what tomorrow holds."

"Tomorrow?" I lick my lips. "It's not even noon yet."

Kieran laughs, breathless and broken, then he pulls me into another longing kiss—so deep I purr into it. By the time we break apart, he's so damn hard beneath me I'm tempted to just sink down and ride him until we both forget our own names.

But no.

Not yet.

"Shit, I might actually be in love with you," Kieran bursts out.

I throw my head back laughing, even though my heart is about to explode. "Tell me again when you're not drunk on lust and I might believe you."

"I'll fucking tattoo it on your skin."

Then he bites my neck, again and again, leaving red marks like he's branding me.

And I love them—every single one of them.

But ...

"You're limiting my dress options for tonight," I mutter, breathless. My face flushed.

"Doesn't matter." He laughs into my skin. "Any one you pick will be on the floor by the end of the night, anyway."

Oh Gods.

How much of Kieran can I even take in a single day?

I guess we're about to find out.

Chapter 19

It took me a long time to convince Kieran to glamour the bite marks he left on me—even if just for tonight.

But I finally managed to do it. The question is: at what cost?

My head's a battlefield as I replay everything that happened in the Council Room.

Every kiss. Every flick of his tongue. Every little filthy, beautiful thing he did to me—and let me do to him.

My cheeks flush again, like maroon is my permanent colour.

Now I'm standing in front of a mirror, trying not to look like I didn't just get ruined by the King of the Fallen on the very table where they plan to pass judgement on rebels and debate which laws to bring into effect.

Breathe, Cassandra. Breathe.

I pick a heavenly dress from a few options the Court's attendant left for me. It was an obvious choice. The rest were dull as a paper. This dress, on the other hand, clings and floats like its thread was spun from moonlight. Pastel silk layers melt from rose to sky, wrapping me in weightless magic. The bodice dips scandalously, and the sleeves hang off my shoulders so perfectly.

Lucas stares at me, blinking, when I meet him outside my door.

"You look ..." And then he shuts his mouth.

Speechless.

Good. That's what I was going for.

"Thank you." I wink, looping my arm through his. "Let's go."

The ballroom hushes the moment we step in. Someone gasps. Another whistles.

My eyes scan the room—then land on Kieran. He looks unbelievably sharp and wicked, in a tailored three-piece suit. Even from across the room, I can still feel his gaze on me, like back in the Council Room, in front of his Council.

Kieran looks like he's choking on the very air we're breathing in.

His jaw clenches. His drink is still halfway to his mouth. Those gold and storm eyes rake over me as he mutters a curse under his breath, like the sight of me undoes him in the best possible way.

He wears his bite marks with pride.

But his fingers curl around his glass, like he's imagining it's my waist.

I smirk and keep walking, hips swaying just a little more than necessary, drawing attention from every direction, but I move like I don't see all eyes on me. My dress is the only one bright as daylight in a Court that favours black and gold. It was truly made to be seen—designed to haunt those who lay eyes on it.

"I hope they don't lick you with their eyes like this all night, because I can't be bothered to throw punches in formalwear," Lucas mutters.

I chuckle. "Maybe I want to be licked."

"Good Gods, Cass." He groans, scrubbing a hand down his face. "You're enjoying this way too much."

"Shut up and go get us some drinks."

"I would," Lucas says, glancing around like he doesn't trust even his own shadow, "but I'm afraid someone will snatch you while I'm gone."

"With a gown this bright in a room full of darkness, I'm sure you'll spot me in a second." I gently nudge him on the back.

"Fine." He frowns. "I'd say try not to get into trouble, but it's probably impossible when you look like that."

I don't know whether to roll my eyes, kill him, or blush.

"Go."

He hesitates, then sighs and disappears into the crowd—completely unaware of how many female Fae are already eyeing him like a main course they can't wait to devour.

"You clean up nice," a female voice says behind me.

Daisy.

I'm not sure if that was an insult or sarcasm. Daisy is dressed in gold gown tonight, sparkling like sunlight. A golden armband gleams on her bicep, catching the chandelier light.

I don't smile. "What do you want?"

"I have a proposition for you," she offers, taking a sip of Fae wine in her hand. "It's about the next trial."

I tilt my head. "What about it?"

"We should team up," she replies, all sugar and no sincerity. "Think about it. You don't want to get stuck with Lucas if the pairing twist ends in betrayal. If it's a trap, you'd have to fight him. Do you really want that?"

I narrow my eyes.

"If you partner with me, there's no emotional strings. No tragic heartbreak. You can swing a blade at me guilt free, and as much as I hate to admit, I'd probably never stand a chance." Daisy shrugs. "Lucas? He can finally beat the crap out of that one-eyed jerk, Jordan."

"You're only saying that because you don't want to partner with the one-eyed jerk."

Daisy doesn't even blink. "Can you blame me?"

I suppose not.

She does have a point. I'm ninety percent certain that if I end up fighting her, a librarian like Daisy will probably just run. But there're still two weeks until the trial.

Who knows what twisted little skill she'll master by then.

In this Court, if you are smart enough, you can probably learn how to kill someone with a bookmark.

"I don't know." I shake my head. "I need to think about this."

"Fine." She huffs, clearly annoyed. "Don't take too long. In case you haven't noticed, it's just us girls against them now. If we don't stick together and start thinning out the competition, they'll eat us alive." Then she lowers her voice. "Let me know if you want to get rid of Jordan before the trial. I'm down for that."

Absolutely ruthless.

Even I haven't thought about taking out competitors between trials.

"How do I know you haven't gone to Jordan and said the same about me?"

Daisy arches a brow, downing the rest of her Fae wine. "You don't."

I exhale.

That's what I thought.

Daisy walks away without looking back.

"Why is it that every time I leave you alone for two seconds, I always come back to you talking to the last person I'd ever expect?" Lucas asks as he returns, handing me a glass of Fae wine.

"What can I say—everyone wants a piece of this." I grin.

"More like want to slice a piece of you, in Daisy's case," Lucas mutters, deadpan. "What did she want?"

"To see if I'd pair up with her for the next trial."

"Yeah, right." He scoffs. "And I want to go on a date with Jordan."

I snort. "She did have a point, you know. What happens if we partner up and they order us to take each other out?"

"Then I'll just let you kill me," Lucas says, completely unfazed, no hesitation. "No way in hell I'll fight you."

"You don't mean that."

He shrugs. "You're the only person here smart enough to win the whole thing. And if I go down, I'd prefer it to be on my own terms."

My chest tightens. I've been trying not to think about this for the entire time we've been here—the fact that we might end up hurting each other.

How could I ever hurt him?

"So what? I'm supposed to be remembered as the heartless bitch who killed her friend?"

Lucas laughs, then winks. "Just make it quick. It'll earn you another popular vote."

I just shake my head and drink. Lucas has been spending too much time with me—he's starting to sound just as twisted.

"Have you two found anything yet?"

Atticus appears out of nowhere again, like a damn ghost.

I nearly choke. What is his power? Turning into smoke?

"It's barely been a day since we saw you at the tavern," Lucas says flatly. "And it's not like we spend every waking minute with Jordan."

"So that's a no." The High Commander narrows his eyes at us like he's looking at two underperforming apprentices whose hobby is to disappoint him. "You're a trained guard, Lucas. Can't believe you came up empty handed."

"Are you kidding me?" Lucas clicks his tongue. "I should be getting paid for this."

"For what? Nothing?" Atticus shakes his head. "You should be honoured I even asked."

I raise my eyebrows. Watching the two of them bicker is more entertaining than half the performances this Court puts on. Even a few nearby Fae glance over and chuckle, biting their lips like they're imagining what it would be like to take both of the smoking-hot idiots to bed.

I'm just about to chime in when someone grabs my waist from behind.

I turn and meet the storm-lit eyes.

And just like that, all the noises fade from the world.

"Oh, hello, handsome." I smile like I haven't spent the entire morning tangled up in him, gloriously undone by him. My stupid heart flutters like it's the first time I'm seeing him today.

Kieran leans in, close enough to brush a kiss to my cheek—but instead, he whispers into my ear, voice low and sinful, "You are"—a pause, a soft inhale—"taking-off-clothes gorgeous."

A shiver dances down my spine.

"Do you ever think about anything else?" I murmur, thumb brushing a bite mark on his neck—all these marks he didn't care to glamour, like he's so proud to let the world know he's taken ...

He's not really mine, but he doesn't know I'm already secretly, hopelessly his.

"With you?" he whispers, eyes flaring like twin suns under the starry ceiling. "How the hell am I supposed to think about anything else?"

I try not to blush, but it's damn near impossible when Kieran's been like this all day—when the memories of what went down in the Council Hall are still imprinted in my brain. I glance over my shoulder, hoping that Lucas isn't watching.

It's right then he notices Kieran.

"Let's dance," Kieran says, offering a hand. "Show our faces, then we can vanish the hell away from here."

Yes, because slipping away with the King of the Fallen while dressed like a star-kissed fever dream won't be noticeable at all.

But before I can place my hand in his ...

"Kieran." A voice cuts in behind him—Aurora.

She stands there like a queen in gold, expression carved from ice. "A word?"

"What is it, Aurora?" Kieran sighs, not even bothering to turn to her.

The beautiful face goes a faint shade of red. Public humiliation from her ex yet again. "It's important."

This time he glances at her, then turns back to me and lets out a soft breath.

"Hold that thought. I'll be right back."

I nod, trying not to look too disappointed. Gods, I hope this is actual Court business, and not Aurora dragging Kieran away purely because she can't stand the sight of me within two feet of him.

She had him for a decade.

Those lips. Those hands. Probably pleasing her the same way they pleased me. How many times have they done it in ten years? Thousands?

I clutch my stomach, tasting the bitterness in my mouth.

Why do I feel so small all of a sudden?

I've got nothing on Aurora—nothing but stolen moments and bite marks I begged him to glamour.

I'll be gone in the next few weeks.

Aurora will still be here for eternity, looking down at me the next time the Court reveals itself, smiling because she knows I won't even remember her.

That is, if I'm lucky enough to get to leave at all.

"Wow, your dress is gorgeous!"

The voice pulls me out of the pit in my head.

A female Fae has stopped mid-stride, one hand wrapped around a glowing drink, the other gently curled around my arm. Her wide, beautiful eyes rake over my gown like I'm something she wants to hang in a gallery. I don't remember seeing her in the Court before.

"Oh." I blink. "Thank you."

"Where did you get it from?" she asks.

"Wish I could tell you, but it was one of the options I was given by the Court." I glance down at myself. I'd wondered the same. It's not exactly on theme with the usual doom-and-gloom aesthetic, but it's so beautiful that I couldn't resist.

Once in a blue moon, I get to wear something like this here.

"Guess I'll have to ask Aurora." She chuckles. "You do look fantastic."

"You're too kind." I offer her a genuine smile, then reach out a hand. "I'm Cassandra."

"Oh, Gods, I know!" She laughs, then leans in to kiss both my cheeks like one of the highborn girls I've seen back home. It's strange, a little too familiar for a Fae. "Too bad I'm going to have to stain that pretty dress ..."

"I'm sorry—"

I haven't finished the sentence before pain explodes in my side.

Something sharp—piercing through the left of my ribs, just below my heart.

I gasp, choking as my brain tries to catch up.

Searing agony blooms up my arm, spreading slowly down my body. My vision swims as crimson blossoms on my dress.

The Fae pulls back, still smiling.

A second later, she's gone.

Just—gone.

Cold creeps in. The world tilts around me. It all happens so fast I don't have time to utter a word before I collapse to the marble floor.

I hear screams. Panic rips through the hall like wildfire.

Someone shouts my name.

Footsteps thunder towards me.

The light fractures.

And everything turns pitch black.

Chapter 20

It was part of a plot, that dress.

That beautiful, stardust-bright dress in a room draped in black and gold.

I see it now for what it was—

A beacon.

A target.

The thoughts echo in my mind again and again, like a nightmare I'm trapped in. No way out. No way forward. No way back ... I try to open my eyes, but they refuse. My ears strain, trying to make sense of the chaos around me. I don't know what's happening.

Something is going on.

All I hear is shouting.

Lucas. Atticus. Kieran.

Others.

Too many voices. Too far away. Too close.

But my eyes are heavy. My limbs heavier, paralyzed.

Then slowly, everything starts to feel lighter—the pain, the noises, even my own body.

Like floating.

It's nice.

Peaceful.

I'm just going to sleep ... just for a while.

"Cass! Cassandra!" someone shouts, shaking me, causing my pain to roar back. "You need to stay awake!"

Why can't they just let me be?

It's nice over here.

"Move!" another voice barks, urgent, commanding—followed by chaos, other voices clashing like waves I don't understand.

I feel light as feather.

Like someone's carrying me through a meadow—warm, dreamy, bright as day.

"Kieran, what are you—"

A swoosh.

Then a cold gust slams into me. The air is damp. My stomach flips. I try to open my eyes, but all I see is a blur—lights, darkness, figures.

Something slams.

More panic. More shouting.

"Save her!" a voice yells. "I said, save her!"

Gods ... they're so loud.

Too loud.

I need to sleep.

I just ... need to rest.

Just for a little while ...

Chapter 21

Pain.

Agony, really.

It licks through my side like fire, sharp and blinding.

I'm trying to blink, but all I'm seeing is bright red because of the pain at my side. So, I just lie there, unable to move, wincing in pain, breathing shallow.

"Cass?"

A voice.

Familiar. Strained.

I breathe in ... slowly ... then try to open my eyes again.

And then I see—a face I know, two different eye colours, a pair of wings behind him, vast and dark, like a night sky painted with stars.

Constellations.

"Kieran?" I rasp.

Kieran exhales, long and sharp, like he's been holding his breath for hours. Relief crashes over his face like a wave slamming into shore.

"Gods, I really thought I lost you," he breathes, his voice hoarse, fingers brushing my cheeks. He's trembling, like he's not sure I'm actually alive. Like touching me might somehow wake him from a nightmare.

I try to reach up to him, but I wince instead.

"Easy," Kieran whispers, catching my hand and gently squeezing it.

"It hurts," I whisper, biting my lip to try and keep it together and not burst out crying.

Kieran flinches, like my words physically pierce him.

Then, soft as a feather, he places a hand above my ribs—and slowly, the pain begins to fade.

A shaky sigh escapes me. Thank Gods for magic. I'd never recover soon enough to participate in the next trial otherwise. I'm about to thank Kieran, too—

But then I see his face.

He drops his head onto my arm with a groan, low and guttural.

That's when it hits me.

He's taking the pain from me.

"Oh, Gods, Kieran!" I nearly scream. "Stop! Stop it!"

He doesn't.

Instead, he groans softly into my arm again, like he's trying to muffle it. Horror slams into me. My hands shake, my heart in bits, trying to make sense of what's going on.

"Kieran," I whisper, voice trembling. "You can't just—you can't just do that."

"Too late," he rasps, his voice cracked at the edges. "Already did."

I stare at him, horrified and absolutely shattered all at once.

"Are you mad?" My breath catches. I clutch his hand, begging. "Stop it ... please, stop it."

"I'm immortal. I heal quicker than you."

"Why are you—" I choke, unable to even finish the sentence. Tears sting my eyes, hot and sudden. Kieran lifts his head, and I nearly break at the look in his eyes.

Somehow, this hurts more than the blade did.

Kieran is fucking stubborn, and a fool.

And all I can do is pulling myself upright, ignoring the fire in my ribs, and wrap my arms around him, tight enough to feel the pain. Tight enough to keep him from drowning in the pain that should have been mine.

Kieran hisses—but I don't let go.

I won't let him feel this pain alone.

I refuse to.

"For fuck's sake." He curses into my hair, finally giving in. "You're unbearable."

"And you're crazy." I pull away just to slap him on the arm. "What did you do that for?"

A lazy grin tugs at his lips. "Maybe I just enjoy the pain."

"Well, good," I snap. "Because I'm going to beat the crap out of you for that."

Kieran sighs dramatically before leaning in to wipe the tears from my cheeks. His eyes soften, thumb brushing over my skin. I rest my face in his palm. "You're loud—that's good. Means you're not dead."

"You're about to be."

He smiles, beautiful as ever, but he looks exhausted in a way I've never seen him before. Usually, Kieran buzzes with restless energy. Now it looks like he hasn't slept all night.

I shouldn't feel so happy about that, but my stupid heart dances at the thought of him sitting by the bed, worrying himself sick.

"What happened?" I murmur, glancing around for the first time.

This isn't my room.

I'm in a bedroom—but someone else's. It's massive and sunlit, the sheets soft as clouds, and the air smells faintly of cedar and sandalwood. Across from the bed, two tall glass doors open onto a balcony with a view of snow-dusted mountains.

I blink.

I've seen that mountain before—and this place, too. The house carved into the cliff.

It's Kieran's house.

"I don't think I need to remind you of this part, but you were stabbed," Kieran says as he carefully eases himself into the bed beside me. "By the time I got to you, it was almost too late ... I couldn't heal you fast enough, so I took you to our healer. A few minutes later, you would've been—"

He stops, swallowing the word. His jaw tightens, like the memory still haunts him.

"You're okay now," he whispers, leaning in until his head rests gently against my shoulder. "That's all that matters."

I breathe, deep and shaky, trying not to get emotional.

We haven't known each other long, but I've spent almost every day with him—at work, sometimes before, and even after. Somewhere along the way, we've become part of each other's day, and now seeing him like this ...

It's killing me.

I am completely confused, and surprised by how much Kieran affects me.

One minute I was using him.

The next, I'm blinking back tears because he looks like an apocalypse just tore through him.

It was supposed to be fun.

I was supposed to forget him.

"So ..." I swallow, trying not to give in to pain—though this time it's no longer physical. "You decided to take me here?"

"It's the safest place. The wards are so thick you can't go through them unless I let you in."

"My room is warded." I lift my chin. Kieran pulls back just enough to narrow his eyes at me.

"Yes, against humans," he says, voice low like it's a reminder. "A Fae stabbed you."

I wince, my wound flaring like the blade is piercing me all over again.

"I've never seen that Fae before, and I can't think of any reason why she'd do something like that."

It's clearly not part of the trials—because what did she have to gain? Unless she bet on someone else to win the first trial, so she decided to take her loss out on me.

"It's not about you," Kieran mutters, shifting as he leans back against the headboard. "It's about me."

I frown. "What do you mean?"

"I think it was a test ... just to see if hurting you would affect me." His jaw tics. "It's not exactly a secret we've been ... fooling around. And I won't lie and say I've never been this public with anyone before—because I have."

I press my lips together.

I'm not naïve enough to believe I'm the only one who's ever mattered to him. In fact—until now, I never thought I mattered to him that much at all. But when you have lived a couple hundred years, you are bound to break your heart at least a dozen times, maybe more.

"But ... it really got to me this time. I fucking lost it."

Gods.

"Please tell me you didn't do anything stupid," I murmur.

Kieran licks his bottom lip, grinning like a mad Fae that he is. "Depends on how you define stupid."

"Kieran ..."

"I may have killed her ... that Fae," he admits, eyes shutting as he lets out a long, frayed breath. "And honestly? The worst part wasn't even that ... it was the fact that I let my emotions get the better of me, and now the whole damn Court probably thinks I'm in love with you."

A breath.

A beat.

And I laugh, even though I shouldn't.

I should be terrified. I should run to the edge of the earth and never look back.

I still remember what he did to Jordan—how cruel and merciless he could be. And I can only imagine what went down when I was unconscious.

But none of that makes me flinch.

All I want ... is to be closer to him.

"Stupid fucking mistake," Kieran mutters. "Now the rebellion will keep using you against me."

"I see." I tilt my head. "Everyone thinking you're in love with me is a mistake?"

"I couldn't care less what people think—you, of all people, should know that," Kieran drawls, his tone almost bored. "I only care about keeping you safe, but I instead, I put you in danger."

My breath catches.

Gods—Kieran needs to stop being so blunt like that.

Or else I'll madly fall in love, and we can drag each other to hell together.

"I've always been in danger," I quietly say. "I'm in the trials."

"This is not the same," he counters, voice rough. "Yes, you could die in the trials, but now you have to be paranoid. You have to question if your water is poisoned. If someone's going to slit your throat on a walk. If your friends are still yours."

"And that's why you brought me here."

"I wasn't going to wait for them to finish the job." He scoffs. "And if that Fae wanted to kill you, she could have. But she didn't. The whole thing was a message for me."

"I understand that." I sigh, the weight of it all pressing down on me. "But Kieran ... you've put me in a difficult position. It's even more obvious now that you favour me. The others already think that I'm cheating. And you know you can't keep me here forever."

He smirks like it's a challenge. "Try me."

I stare at him, blinking.

For a moment, I let myself imagine it—staying here, wrapped in his starlit world, far from trials and chaos and the weight of what I came here to do. How easy it would be to lose myself in him.

But I'm still human.

He's Fae.

I didn't come here for this.

I came here for a ghost.

"Don't be ridiculous," I mutter, looking away.

"Ugh, you always have to ruin the fun." He groans, leaning in to nip at my shoulder like he's famished. "Can't we just fuck and forget about the world?"

A chill threads through me, even as my skin burns beneath his mouth.

Is this all he wants?

Is it his solution to everything?

"Here I thought kings were supposed to be responsible."

"Good thing I'm not a king." Kieran raises his brow, then glances at the time. "You've been out for over a day—are you hungry?"

"A day?" I wince. "Oh Gods, that means I don't have much time to look for the eclipsed coins!"

He blinks. "Is that seriously what you're thinking about right now?"

"Is having sex with a wounded person seriously what *you're* thinking?"

A pause.

We stare at each other.

Then burst out laughing.

I'm wheezing, clutching at my side.

Kieran rubs a hand over his face, shaking his head like he can't believe this is what we've become.

I take a deep breath, unable to stop smiling. "If I say I'm hungry, are you going to cook for me, or just conjure something out of thin air with magic?"

"Magic doesn't work like that," he says, chuckling. "I could pull a soup out of thin air for you, but it'd taste like garbage. It's difficult to get the ingredients right. That night at the Tower of the Stars was a fluke."

I bite my lip.

Now I can't stop picturing him frowning over a pot of magically tasteless soup—and Gods, that's too cute.

"So, I'll have to do it the old-fashioned way," Kieran adds, rolling up his sleeves and starting to climb out of bed.

But I tug him back by the arm.

Kieran pauses, brow arching ... and I answer by sliding closer, tucking myself into his side and closing my eyes.

I just want to stay like this.

Just for a minute.

Kieran's breath brushes my skin.

"Or, we can just do this for a while," he murmurs, arms wrapping around me, pulling me in until my back rests against his chest.

And I let him hold me.

In his arms. Under his wings.

The safest place in the world.

Chapter 22

"What's that?" I ask, pointing at a small jar of seasoning Kieran just sprinkled into whatever it is he's whipping up. It looks like salt, but it's pink and gold. He glances back, a smile gracing his beautiful face. His mismatched eyes soften, like he's looking at a naughty, curious girl who's getting on his nerves as he tries to cook but can't help adoring her silly little questions.

"That," Kieran says, "is stardust salt."

He must be joking.

"Stardust as in ...?"

"Stardust," he repeats, as if he's talking about just another spice they imported from the East ... or in this case, the skies. "Honestly, there's so much of the market you haven't seen yet. I'd say you should go there more often, but then again, with everything that's been going on, I'm not sure it's a good idea."

I hum, resting my chin on my palm, smiling even though his back is to me. "Maybe you can take me one day."

Kieran swings a tea towel over his shoulder, turning to me, a gorgeous smile already on those perfect lips as he leans in and whispers, "Only if you ask nicely."

I lick my lips.

There's something about when a man—a Fae King—cooks for you in his kitchen, the tea towel on his shoulder, the veins on his arms as he braces the edge of the counter, and those impossible wings. His honeyed skin is so beautiful, and Gods, I haven't even mentioned those eyes yet.

Lord save me.

If all Kieran had going for him was his looks, things would have been so much easier, but I find his kindness and our nonsense conversations utterly charming.

Like that night at the River of Vows. We could talk about anything and everything.

"I would love to see more of the Court, you know," I reply, trying not to drag my eyes all over him. It's an effort, especially just less than an hour after he took the pain from me. "I used to go out with Tessa and Lucas ... but, well, Tessa is gone, and Lucas works in shifts, so he's rarely around. And I don't always want to wander out by myself."

The golden and deep-blue eyes flick to the floor for a brief second, before they meet my eyes again. There's something in them—guilt or sadness. I can't quite tell. It fades away in a heartbeat.

"There's street called Moonlight Walk at the market. You can find all these home-made spices there."

I blink. "Can we go?"

"Focus on recovering first." He brushes a thumb cross my cheek. "Then we can talk about it."

I suppose that's fair.

I watch as Kieran returns to cooking. I've followed him around everywhere nearly every day, and I've seen him put on the

King of the Fallen mask when he works. He's ruthless, dangerous, yet ... so gentle and thoughtful.

And I just want ... more.

I want to learn everything about him.

Not that I have a lot of time left to do so.

I sit there, in awe of how elegantly he moves. How he crafts those ingredients into a meal. Every move is precise and without hesitation, like he knows exactly what he's doing.

I'm an all-right cook, but I don't even have to taste Kieran's food to know it's probably a work of art.

Does he do this a lot—cook for someone?

There's a hole in my chest. It swallows all my words because I'm scared to hear the answer.

And I don't want to think about anyone, or anything else right now.

Kieran sets the table on the balcony. I'm not sure I want to catch a cold when I'm already injured ... but he offers me a hand, and I take it without question.

He gently helps me to my seat. I'm about to make a joke about the cold ... then I feel the heat radiating from the chair, pulling me in a like warm hug.

This is—

I glance up at Kieran, who leans in to place a blanket on my lap.

"I thought you might want some fresh air."

"You heated the chair up," I murmur, surprised, clutching the blanket.

"What's magic good for if not to impress a lady, eh?" He winks and sits down next to me. I throw my head back laughing.

Kieran's made it insanely difficult not to adore him.

"Thank you." I can barely hold back a smile. Guilt and shame manage to snatch me back every time I feel slight happiness ... but not this time. "The food smells lovely. What is it?"

"Pork rib stew with root vegetables. You can say it's my comfort food."

"I have so many questions." I tilt my head. "Where do you get meat? Where are the animals? Do you have farms?"

Kieran laughs, sinking into his own seat. "Yes, we do have farms. Like I said, there's so much of the Court you haven't seen. When you entered, you practically stepped into a portal. Usually, contestants only stay at the Court and the city outside it, but even the wine we drink has to come from somewhere."

"And you have resources to produce all this?"

"We do steal some from your world when you're not looking."

My jaw drops. "Well, that explains it."

He chuckles, nodding at the stew. "I hope you like it, because if you don't, the only other option left is eggs and toast."

He doesn't know I already love it.

I pick up a spoon and try it carefully. The fragrance of herbs and spices reminds me of something familiar, but the stew tastes like nothing I've ever tried before. The broth is rich with flavours, warm and delightfully spicy, and the pork is so tender it melts in one bite.

"Oh, my Gods." I purr. "This is gorgeous! Is there anything you can't do?"

"Keep you tame, I believe."

I grin, reaching to squeeze Kieran's cheek gently. "You like me messy and wild, I know."

He scoffs. "A normal woman couldn't deal with me anyway."

I giggle before stopping mid-laugh because the damn pain decides to become my reward for being cheeky. Kieran immediately frowns.

"You okay?"

"Yeah, I'm fine." I nod, trying to change the subject because of the look in his eyes. "Where did you learn to cook like this?"

He sighs. "Again, if I can't make a decent meal after living for centuries, I might as well stab myself with an iron blade."

I get the joke, but this time I don't laugh.

Hearing him say that after what happened ... I just ...

"Please don't," I whisper, but it sounds like a plea. Kieran lowers his spoon, blinking at me, like he's wondering if his ears are playing tricks on him. "Don't die ... okay?"

And I don't really know what's gotten into me.

Or why my chest is so tight at the thought of Kieran doing that to himself.

I know he wouldn't ... but that doesn't change how I feel.

Kieran presses his lips together, and for a beat, he doesn't say a thing.

Then, his hand finds mine, fingers intertwined.

"If I die, it won't be by suicide." The corner of his mouth curves into a grin. "Besides, you said you were going to beat the crap out of me earlier."

And it works—one line and I'm laughing again.

I shake my head, but I can't shake the smile on my face.

"Tell me more about you," he says, letting go of my hand and starting to eat. I do the same.

And suddenly it feels like we've shared this moment every evening.

This thing we have is so familiar and comfortable.

And no matter how hard I try, I just know nothing will prepare me for the day it ends.

"I think it's possible you know more about me than I do myself."

"So?"

I bite my lip. "Fine. I'm twenty-three."

Kieran rolls his eyes. "Why do I even try to be romantic? Mother of the stars. You know exactly what I mean."

I do. Kieran wants to learn more about me like I do him, and it's cute and romantic.

But it wouldn't be me if I didn't try to tease him a little.

"Well, I'm a caffeine addict," I start, and Kieran scoffs. "I did all right in school, but I've never been a scholar. All I ever wanted to do was own a café—and I know, you probably think 'If all women's dreams came true, we'd probably have a million cafes,' but that's genuinely the only thing I want to do."

"I didn't think anything." He smiles. "Apart from the obvious fact that you're adorable."

Gods, I can't do anything around him.

It's so hard to focus. Every damn second I'm not touching him is harder than the last.

"I grew up in a loving family, and I was fortunate enough to have a small house of my own. I don't have that many friends, but every single one I do have is a friend for life."

My voice is barely a whisper. I haven't allowed myself to think about everyone I left behind—Scarlett, my best friend. Joanna, Devon—they must be worried sick. I wonder what Noah told them about me.

I abandoned them all after Declan died. In my grief-stricken state, I pushed everyone away.

Kieran seems to sense my sadness. He says, "Well, you probably have more best friends than me, because I only have Gideon."

I offer a faint smile. "What about Atticus?"

"We used to be closer, but let's just say he's not entirely happy I broke his little sister's heart." He winces.

"Yeah … I can imagine."

"Did you have any pets growing up?"

I'm pleasantly surprised by that question—a very common one, but from the mouth of the King of the Fallen, it's unexpected.

"We had a dog, but he died when I was fourteen. I cried for days."

"Maybe I should get a dog." He taps on his chin.

"Did you not hear the part when I said I cried for days?"

"I did, but would a puppy not make you feel better?"

I frown. "Yes. Until it dies."

"We'll make him immortal. I can do that."

And now I'm laughing again, the pain be damned. Our nonsense conversation has started, and I know damn well it won't stop anytime soon. The stew is probably cold. The moon is casting a soft light over us, and Kieran looks too perfect, and all I want to do is sit on his lap and kiss him until we're breathless after drinking too much for our own good …

Mother of the stars.

There is no way out of this grave I've dug myself into.

"Come on, how many dogs should we get?" he presses. "What about cats? Horses? Goats? Hairy little fluffy cows? You fancy those too? I'll buy them all."

My laughter spills out, loud and careless until my chest aches.

But the pain fades into nothing with Kieran in front of me.

I am drowning, but for the first time in a long time, I've never felt more alive.

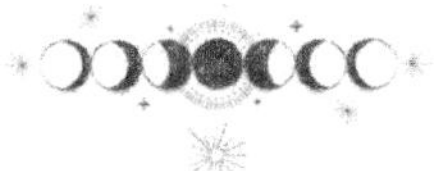

I wake in an empty bed, blinking at the sunlight spilling through silk curtains, the sheets still warm beside me. The bed smells faintly of Kieran, like cedar and something delightfully earthly. A scent which has become far too familiar to me.

Last night lingers like traces of stardust—beautiful, glittering, and impossible to forget. It's sprinkled everywhere in this house, on this bed, and in my ruined heart. Our laughter blurred into something real.

Something I don't want to admit.

We spent hours on the balcony as the stars rose. The moon hung over us like it was eavesdropping, full and silver, casting a soft glow as our tattoos shimmered in the cold.

And we sat there—talking, drinking, and laughing.

Until the wine blurred into warmth, and the night turned still.

Until three in the morning crept up on us, and the line between "just fun" and something more started to disappear and we spent ages tangled up in each other, lips brushing skin, hands wandering, hearts racing.

Kieran kept muttering, *"This is not good for your injury."*

But he couldn't stop kissing me. And I didn't want him to.

We were so drunk—on wine, on adrenaline, but mostly on each other.

And if it weren't for the ache in my ribs, we might have gone further, but Kieran was too careful, too gentle, like touching me too roughly might turn me to dust.

Like I was something breakable, something he held precious.

Gods, I'm in big trouble.

When I finally sit up, I spot a note on the nightstand.

Left you some food in the kitchen.
Will be back later with Lucas.
The bastard hasn't stopped harassing me about you.

— K.

Oh, Gods.

Lucas.

He must be worried sick.

I hope he doesn't do anything stupid.

I exhale, swinging my legs over the side of the bed. The wound doesn't hurt as much as it did yesterday. Kieran gave me some potions to ease the pain—ones I couldn't take when I was unconscious, which is probably why I didn't heal as quickly as I did after the first trial.

I'm not sure what I'm supposed to do now.

I finally had a tour of the house last night, before all the kissing and making out. It's massive. Three storeys, three bedrooms, a study, a library, a kitchen big enough to feed a village, and a living room that could host a royal banquet.

And it's bright and warm—homely, even.

But my favourite thing about this place is the bath. It's sunken into the far end of the bathroom, right in front of a wall of glass that frames the mountains like a painting.

I might spend a little too long in it.

After that, I eat, then I wander into Kieran's massive library and pick a book at random and devour it in one sitting.

I never pegged Kieran as a fantasy fiction fan, but here we are.

I barely notice the time, when I hear noises from downstairs—footsteps and voices. I bolt from the couch, my ribs flaring in protest, but I don't care. I'm already running down the stairs before my head can stop me.

And there he is.

Kieran, standing in the entryway with Lucas beside him.

I haven't seen my friend in days, but all I want to do is throw myself at Kieran.

"Cass, you're okay." Lucas pulls me into a hug so tight I wince. "Oh, shit, sorry!" he blurts, pulling back immediately.

"Yeah ... I was okay until just now," I mutter, rubbing my ribs.

"Sorry," he says again, eyeing Kieran warily. "Last I saw you, you were soaked in blood. And he just took you and vanished. I had to see for myself."

Kieran rolls his eyes.

Gods, I want to squeeze him. Why is everything he does so bloody adorable?

"I'm okay," I murmur.

"So why haven't you been back?"

My eyes flick to Kieran.

That's a tricky question.

One that Kieran clearly has no intention of answering. He exhales and says, "I'll let you two talk. I've got things to handle back at Court."

"You're leaving again?" I frown.

But ... he just got back.

Kieran nods. "I might be back late. Someone will bring food by later." Then he turns to talk to Lucas. "You can leave then."

"So now you're timing how long I get with my friend?" Lucas snaps, shaking his head. "She should be back at the Court."

"No, she shouldn't," Kieran says, narrowing his eyes at Lucas, his tone low and sharp. A warning. "And if you'd rather spend hours walking back in the dark, be my guest."

Lucas doesn't say anything, but I can tell from his face how much he hates Kieran's guts.

Well, what else is new?

"I'll see you later," Kieran mutters. He doesn't even meet my eyes. He looks like he's about to vanish any second.

I push past Lucas and catch him before he disappears.

"Wait," I whisper.

Just wait.

What's the rush?

I haven't seen him all day.

Kieran looks at me. His eyes soften, but he still doesn't say anything.

Something is ... off.

Last night was different.

This seems ... cold, distant, coming from someone who spent hours drinking, laughing, kissing me. I fell asleep in his arms.

And now the same person who kissed every inch of me last night won't look me in the eye.

Is he just stressed from whatever happened at the Court today?

"Kieran." I tilt my head, frowning. "What's wrong?"

"Nothing," he replies—almost too fast. "I just have a lot to do."

"When will you be back?"

"I'm not sure. But don't wait up, okay?" he says, squeezing the hand still clutching his arm. His eyes never quite meet mine. "I'll see you later."

Then he presses a quick kiss to my hand—and vanishes into thin air.

And I just stand here, confused, wondering what the hell I did wrong.

I want to believe that it's all in my head. I'm just overthinking it. But I know in my heart something's off.

"You're living with him now?" Lucas's voice cuts through the silence behind me. I stiffen before turning to face him.

He's standing with his arms crossed, jaw tight, eyes sharp with disapproval. Sometimes, he reminds me of Noah—the way he looks at me like a big brother watching his sister commit a crime.

"It's not like that."

"Then please, enlighten me."

I shake my head and lead him into the living room. I'm very much not in the mood to have this conversation again, because I know exactly how it's going to end—another blown-out-of-proportion fight, where I'll get mad, Lucas will be judgy. Then, he'll apologise, and I'll forgive him.

Same song, different verse.

And I'm tired of it.

"Did you come here to visit me, or grill me?" I ask quietly. "You promised you wouldn't cross the line about Kieran."

Lucas takes a deep breath, like he needs it to take one step back. His shoulders ease slightly as he follows me into the living room and sinks into the armchair.

"I'm sorry," he says. "But I find it hard to believe that someone like him is ... good to you."

"Kieran would never hurt me."

He's never said it aloud.

But I know.

Somehow, I know.

"Don't get me wrong. I know he cares about you—you should have seen him that night." Lucas pauses, his face grim as if he's sorting through a nightmare in his head. "Gods, I thought he was going burn the whole damn Court down. And I don't know if you know ... but he killed the Fae who stabbed you."

"He told me," I whisper.

"No, Cass." Lucas stares at me—really stares at me. His voice hardens. "Killed. As in, turned her into dust."

I freeze.

Kieran did that?

Oh, Gods ...

But then—what the hell was that about just now?

I rub my arm, unable to meet Lucas's gaze. In his eyes, Kieran must be something monstrous. Terrifying beyond reason. And maybe he is—but that's just one side of him.

I don't agree with killing. Unless it's the bitch who tried to kill me first—then maybe I do.

But if I let even a flicker of emotion show—if Lucas so much as suspects that the idea of Kieran losing control for me makes my heart flutter—he'll probably lock me up in an asylum and throw the key away.

I clear my throat. "I don't know what you want me to say."

And there it is again, that look in his eyes—the one that seems unsure whether he still knows me.

"Honestly?" Lucas exhales, long and hard, like he's given up. "I really don't know." He leans back in the armchair, running a hand down his face. "Look, I'm sure you already know this but ... you're only going to get yourself hurt if you actually fall for him."

I keep my mouth shut.

I think it's a little late for that.

"Who knows if we'll still be alive next week," he adds with a shrug. "So yeah, I get it—if this is just a fling. I just wish you'd help me understand, because I don't get how you, of all people, came to like him."

I glance down at my hand, picking off invisible fluff on my shirt—Kieran's shirt—the one I put on because he refused to take five minutes and vanish to my room to get me fresh clothes.

He likes me in his clothes, he said.

And I was all soft because of that one sentence.

"I don't know what this is," I answer truthfully. If this is going to help ease his stress and his worry, then I'll tell him. "If I'm honest, I haven't allowed myself to think about it. Because it's like you said—who knows if we'll still be alive next week."

A pause.

I swallow the lump in my throat, but my chest tightens.

"And I don't know what it is for Kieran, either. We've just ... been having a good time together," I say, smiling as I think about it. "And you might not believe this, but Kieran makes me laugh. A lot. I really like being with him."

Lucas frowns like he can't imagine it—Kieran laughing, making me laugh.

"Sure, he has that darkness about him. He's the King of the Court, for Gods' sake." I let out a soft breath. "But when he's with me, he's something else completely." I glance up and meet Lucas's eyes. "And despite what the whole Court thinks ... we haven't even slept together."

For whatever reason, Lucas's eyes soften at my words ... relief, sadness—I can't quite tell.

"That last part is actually unbelievable."

I grin. "I know."

He huffs a short laugh, then winces, rubbing the back of his neck. "Though ... you might want to come up with an excuse when we bring Declan back."

My smile falters. "I can't think about that yet." I shake my head. "Not now."

I can't do it. I refuse to worry about things that may never come to pass, because what are the chances of that ever happening? What if someone like Jordan wins the trials instead?

I need to take every day as it comes.

And right now, it's with Kieran, as irresponsible as it sounds.

"Fair enough." Lucas lets out a soft breath and lets the subject go. "I'm glad you're okay."

"Yeah, sorry if I scared you." My voice drops. "I woke up yesterday and could barely move. I would've asked Kieran to take me to you, too."

"And now I've got a timed visit." Lucas snorts.

I laugh. "To be honest, I'm surprised he even let you in at all."

He shakes his head. "So, when are you coming back?"

"I don't really know." I shrug. "I mean, I'm off work for obvious reasons, but Kieran brought me here because it's safer than the Court. He said the attack was a test to see how much I mattered to him. And now he's convinced the rebellion is going to use me against him."

"Gods, this is more complicated than I thought." Lucas exhales. "Can't he just post guards outside your door? I know a few people who can be trusted with that."

Look at him. Knowing people now.

"You should tell that to Kieran. See what he says."

I get another exhale in response—we both already know the answer.

Talking to Kieran is like talking to a wall. If he doesn't want to do something, then he doesn't want to do something. I think the best solution is to stop pushing and see how things go.

Lucas stays for a few more hours. We sprawl across the oversized living room, talking about everything and nothing. He tells me what he was up to today, then I give him a dramatic tour of the house like I actually own the place.

Around seven, Gideon arrives with carefully packed dinner, and Lucas leaves with him.

Yes, Kieran sent one of his High Commanders to deliver me food. I'm pretty sure that doesn't fall under Gideon's duties, but here we are.

I know Kieran said I shouldn't wait—but I do anyway.

I tell myself I'm not tired because we went to bed so late. I haven't just been waiting. I've been reading. Snacking. Reading again.

Hours tick by.

Kieran still isn't home.

By two in the morning, I finally crawl into bed alone.

The sheets still smell like Kieran, but they're cold now.

The next morning, I wake up with nothing but myself—and the growing questions in my chest.

Chapter 23

This must be a joke.

Kieran has been avoiding me.

He comes home after I've fallen asleep and leaves before I wake up. He'll have someone deliver me food, snacks, and medicine—usually Gideon, but Virgil did arrive to surprise me last night.

No more notes. No kisses. No explanation.

For five days in a row.

My wound is nearly fully healed. There's been no talk about getting back to work or moving back to the Court. And Gideon, of course, has no idea about it.

I'm bored out of my mind.

I've finished three books. I've cooked, baked, cleaned, drank every tea, and tasted every alcohol to ever exist in this house. Today, I started talking to the wine bottles to keep me company, like they're guests at a dinner party.

This silence is screamingly loud.

When Gideon comes by this evening, I am ready to go to war.

"Hello, Cass—woah." He stops mid-sentence, eyes wide, nearly dropping whatever precious dinner he was sent to deliver

I grip the knife in my hand, and without explanation, I demand, "Take me to him."

Gideon blinks. His lips twitch like he's trying not to laugh. "You seriously think you could threaten me with that tiny little kitchen knife?"

"Of course not," I reply, baring my teeth. Then slowly, I bring the blade closer to my skin. Just a few centimetres more, and it'll draw blood. "It would be stupid to threaten you," I add. "Much smarter to threaten myself."

Gideon flinches.

He sets the food down fast and lifts both hands like I'm a cornered animal and he doesn't want to spook me.

"All right, all right," he says. "Let's not do anything dramatic."

"Dramatic?" I snort. "You should save that line for your King. Maybe remind him before he leaves someone alone in this massive house for nearly a week. Tell me, Gideon ... did a war break out? Is the Court in flames? Did someone assassinate a Council member? Or has he just been hiding from me?" I take a step forward, my voice dropping, low and sharp. "Because six-hour ghost shifts don't exactly scream busy. They scream avoidant."

It takes Gideon a full minute for all of that to sink in.

I realise I've just blurted out a very personal crisis at his feet, but I don't care.

Kieran doesn't get to do this to me.

If he freaked out—if he decided this, us, was a mistake, all he has to do is tell me.

Not vanish into thin air, cutting me off from the world whilst still pretending to care by sending me food and medicine like I'm a pet he forgot to rehome.

If he's done, he needs to say it.

I can't, for the life of me, think of a reason why, since everything about that night was genuinely amazing. But whatever has changed, he needs to just make it clear.

Because it's killing me.

Gods, it's really killing me.

"First of all, I'm sorry," Gideon says carefully, stepping forward. "I didn't realise what was going on. Kieran's been in an impossible mood, so I figured you two had a fight."

"A fight would have been better than this!" I throw my hand in the air. "I haven't seen him in five days! He's given me no explanation. Nothing! I'm the one who should be upset, not him!"

"Yeah ... I can see that," he mutters, edging closer. "Why don't you put the knife down and I'll get a message to him?"

"No." I lower the blade closer to my skin. "Either bring me to him, or go get him. Now."

"Cassandra, Kieran's in a meeting. Why don't we—"

"Now."

The knife presses, just enough to kiss my arm. Gideon's eyes widen, but he doesn't move—so I cut.

A sharp sting. A thread of red.

I hate using this tactic—being this pathetic to get attention.

But this is the Fae.

I need to speak their language.

"Gods, Cass—please. Let's talk about this. Kieran's going to kill me if I interrupt him," Gideon begs, panic rising in his eyes as I lower the blade again, steady as ever, without even wincing.

"Tell me, Gideon." I hum, tilting my head. "Are you sure he won't kill you for this?"

A pause.

It's a dangerous game I'm playing, but I'm willing to bet that whatever meetings Kieran seems to always be stuck in lately aren't half as important as me—considering he basically turned a Fae into dust for laying a hand on me

"Well?" I arch a brow, waiting.

Gideon curses under his breath. I don't know what kind of magic the High Commander possesses, but the knife hasn't vanished from my hand, so I'm guessing he can't magic it away.

Instead, he takes another step towards me.

"Don't you even think about it," I hiss, lowering the blade from my arm to my wrist. "Or I swear to Gods—you'll regret it."

"You're not going to kill yourself, Cassandra."

I smile, slow and wolfish. "See, this is where you're wrong," I mutter, eyes narrowing. "I haven't got much to live for these days. I entered this Court—do you think I'm scared of dying?"

That hits him, right where it's supposed to. Gideon goes still, the blood draining from his face.

Did he think I believed I could win the wish? Because I didn't. There's no way, and I already knew that.

I know exactly what's waiting for me at the end of the trials, and it's not a wish.

"So, go ahead." I scoff, tipping the blade just a little closer. "Let's see if I'll do it."

Gideon takes a deep breath, then slowly steps back.

"Fine. I'm going," he says at last, voice rough. "Just please ... don't do anything stupid. I'll be right back."

"Make it quick."

Gideon doesn't reply. Just nods—then vanishes with a swoosh of wind.

I drop the knife with a huge sigh, blood dripping onto the hardwood floor.

Then I sink into the sofa, not bothering to tend to the cut on my arm. It's not deep, and one drop of Fae medicine will cure it in the blink of an eye.

Wish I could say the same about the stupid wound in my heart.

Barely three minutes later, Kieran appears right in front of me, jaw tight, panting.

No sign of Gideon.

"Have you lost your mind?"

"Have I lost my mind?" I shoot up to my feet, pushing him in the chest. "Have *you* lost your mind?! Where the hell have you been? Why are you avoiding me?"

Kieran barely moves. He doesn't answer but instead grabs my arm to look at the cut. "Please tell me you didn't do this just to get my attention."

"How else am I meant to? Considering you act like a guest in your own home, sneaking in and out every damn day just so you don't have to see me!"

"It's not like that. I—"

"Oh, it's exactly like that," I cut in, staring him in the eyes. "Don't give me that crap. At least have the decency to tell me the truth. Why else have you been coming in so late and leaving so early when you were practically all over me the other night?"

Kieran's jaw clenches. His gaze drops to my arm again, then he hovers a hand over it.

I feel a slight cold, then the cut is gone when he lifts the hand.

If Kieran thinks that makes up for everything ... well, I've got bad news for him.

"Oh, good." I twist my arm from his grasp. "Next time I can do more."

"Fucking hell, Cass," he growls.

"What? Are you saying I'm the unreasonable one?" I raise my voice. "Am I supposed to be reasonable when you left me here all by myself for almost a week with nothing but books to entertain myself with? I can't even go to the cafés because I'd have to climb up a mountain to come back here. Gods, Kieran. What is wrong with you!?"

Kieran runs a hand through his hair, then exhales, long and sharp, like he's trying to steady himself to go to war.

"What's wrong with me?" he mutters. "Everything, apparently. You scared the shit out of me that night at the ball, and I'm the idiot who let things get too far." He looks at me, something fragile cracking through the mask. "I had no idea I was going to feel this much. And that ... gods, that night was the first time in a long time I've actually felt something real."

My breath catches. I blink, trying to make sense of him unravelling in front of me.

Kieran swallows. "How can you not get it, Cass? I realised that night that I wanted this," he adds, his voice cracking. And for the first time ever, those beautiful eyes are full of fear. "And I can protect you from whatever the rebellion throws at me. But you're in the trials, and I can't get involved with that. I swore an oath centuries ago."

His voice turns ragged.

"So, tell me—how am I supposed to stand there and watch you die?"

The words hit me like a dagger to the heart. I'm trying to breathe—to steady myself.

But it hurts.

Gods, it hurts.

Here we are, screaming at each other because we want the same thing—the very thing we can't have.

"You really have no faith in me, do you?" I whisper, but my voice breaks at the end. "What if I win?"

Kieran lets out a bitter laugh. "Then you go home with your boyfriend."

"But I don't love him."

Silence.

Utter, crushing silence.

I step closer, and Kieran doesn't move.

I know telling him I don't love Declan doesn't mean much, not when there're still other unresolved issues—because still human. He's still Fae. Will I just forget the life I left behind and stay in this Court forever?

And to do what, exactly? Continue to be his assistant?

Gods, the problems are endless.

But in case I don't make it ... "I only came here to save Declan. I wasn't going to get back together with him."

Kieran shuts his eyes, only for a brief moment. "No, Cass—you came here to die."

The breath in my lungs turns sharp, piercing me like a blade. I can't meet his eyes because I know ... I know it's true.

"Why do you think I freaked out so much when you were stabbed? I knew you came here to punish yourself," he continues, his voice rising, each word sharper than the last. "Fuck—I was terrified you were going to give up on me that night. And then you went and hurt yourself just so I'd come and see you."

I brace myself and glance up, a useless attempt to hide the tears.

I came here to die.

I knew I would.

But I couldn't live with myself, not after what I did to Declan. Dark clouds had their claws in me for months. And I let them pull me under—to the dark hole of my own sadness, my grief, my guilt.

Nothing made it better.

Nothing.

Until him.

I told myself Kieran was it—my punishment. The darkness inside my heart in a shape of a Fae. A mistake I could cling to. I convince myself he was bad for me. That he's another fucked-up thing I chose to ruin my life with.

Because I had to go there. I had to betray Declan.

Because I deserve to suffer.

But the truth is ...

Kieran was never the punishment.

He became my redemption.

The one who pulled me from the pit.

He gave me back myself.

The me I lost in those months of complete darkness.

"It's not that I don't have faith in you," Kieran whispers, his voice cracking. "I'm scared you wouldn't even try ... because what if this—what if us—still isn't enough for you to want to stay?"

My knees sink to the floor, hot, endless tears running free.

Why does he have to be like this?

Why does he have to care?

How am I supposed to pretend I'm not madly, blindly in love with him now?

Four weeks shouldn't be enough to ruin me, but they have.

The worst part is we barely have time left.

It terrifies me to my core that I might never find out what we could've been.

"I want to stay," I manage through the tears. Kieran kneels beside me, and my whole body trembles. The next words come out like a confession. "But I'm scared I won't get to be with you."

"Oh, love," he whispers softly, wiping the tears from my cheeks. "You say it like that, and you can bet your pretty ass I'm going to burn down the whole damn library just to find a way."

I laugh through my tears. "Let's just hope I survive the next trial first."

Kieran's smile fades. He sighs and gently pulls me into his arms. "I'm sorry I handled it badly."

"Wow," I murmur against his shoulder. "He apologises."

That earns me a low, surprised laugh. "Look at me. Mature and everything."

"It's about damn time, Grandpa."

He groans. "You'd be surprised what a grumpy, old male like me can do in bed."

And now we're back to being horny.

Gods, I hate how much I love us.

"Do you have to go back to the Court—or can you cook for me?" I glide a hand along his neckline, looping my arm around it as he pulls me up from the floor.

"Gideon just brought you food."

"Yes, but I miss your cooking," I purr into his skin, resting my chin on his chest as I look up and sweetly ask, "Please?"

Kieran exhales sharply. "It's infuriating how you can ask for just about anything with that voice and those eyes."

I smirk, brushing a kiss over his collarbone. "So ... is that a yes?"

"Yes."

The word ends on my lips, hard. I hum into the kiss as one of Kieran's hands touches my cheek, other sliding behind my neck. I burn beneath his touch, sparks skittering under my skin.

It's been five days without this.

I didn't realise how much I needed it until now.

I press my body to his, wrapping my legs on his hips as Kieran picks me up, hands gripping hard on my ass.

A groan tears from my throat.

There's nothing like a kiss after an emotional fight. A touch after the storm. Yearning, longing, burning. My ass hits the top of a cabinet. Something rolls off and shatters on floor. But Kieran's mouth never leaves mine.

More.

I want more.

It's like Kieran is reading my mind. He walks us to the bedroom, my back slamming into the wall, then something else along the way. The kiss is too much, too consuming, that we need to feel each other against something solid.

I break the kiss just long enough to gasp, "Gods, I really wish you'd vanish us to the bedroom right about now."

Kieran laughs in his throat, lips crashing on mine again. "I need to treasure every second of this. And besides, I thought you were hungry."

"I am," I breathe, yanking at his shirt and wanting to rip it off because unbuttoning it is not fast enough. "But for something else now."

"I swear to the stars, if you do this and say no sex until I tell you about the trials one more time—"

"That depends," I tease, a wicked smile tugging at my lips. "Will you behave?"

The storm-lit eyes flash, full of sin and mischief. "You really don't want me to behave for this part, my dear."

I throw my head back, laughing.

The next kiss we share is much gentler. Slower. Kieran pulls back just to look into my eyes, like I'm the most beautiful thing he's ever seen. His eyes are warm, his kiss sweet, lips brushing mine like a vow.

And somehow, I burn even more.

Our clothes scatter along the way to the bedroom, piece by piece. My hands shake as I fumble with his shirt, then his belt, my breath coming shallow. Even those few seconds apart—when my back hits the bed and he hasn't yet followed—feels like torture ... especially when he climbs in like that, like he has all the time in the world just to worship me.

Kieran pulls me closer. His shirt that I'm wearing still clings to my body, though his hands already unbuttoned it halfway down. I breathe as he unbuttons the rest, never breaking eye contact.

"You drive me mad," he whispers, voice rough against my neck. "I can't focus when you're around because this—having you naked in front of me—is all I can think of when I see that beautiful face."

I gasp when his lips finds that sensitive spot just below my jaw. My hand runs through his hair, heart pounding. I let the shirt fall past my shoulder onto the mattress, just for Kieran to throw in on the floor like he doesn't want a single thing to disturb us tonight.

His hands trail down, slow and steady, tracing down the swell of my breasts. That dangerous mouth follows a second later, nipping, tasting me like I'm something sacred he can't get enough of. I arch into his touch, head thrown back, biting my lips as his tongue flicks over the tip—and Gods, I want that tongue everywhere.

"I want you," I whisper, dragging my nails down his back as his mouth continues its descent to my stomach—then lower. "Kieran—"

He hums softly against my skin, fingers trailing down my thighs. "Patience."

Kieran said that he was going to take his sweetest time once I was done teasing—and that's exactly what he's doing.

His lips find the inside of my thigh, and I tremble, aching as he rips the underwear off me. He teases me with a single, maddening stroke of his tongue. I nearly crumble. I groan.

For fuck's sake.

Slowly, painfully, he tastes me like he's never done before, like we have all the time in the world. My mind is a blank page. Kieran is writing filthy words that only exist in my imagination all over it. He knows exactly where to touch—where to kiss—how to drive me hopelessly insane. I grip the bedsheets like a lifeline. Every flick of his tongue and every thrust of his fingers sends an uncontrollable wave of sparks through me.

But just when I'm gasping for the waves of pleasure to crash over me—Kieran just stops.

"Kieran," I growl, damning him with my eyes as he pulls away, only to wipe my wetness off his smug face and crawl up to kiss me again, deep, breathless, making me want him even more. I'm drowning in desperation.

"I want to be inside you," he whispers, dragging his mouth to my ear. "I want to feel you come on my cock—unless you change your mind again."

I lick my lips, slipping a hand down my body. My fingers come back gleaming in the wet, hot mess he's made of me. Kieran's eyes flare fiery.

"Does it look like I want to change my mind?"

He laughs, leaning in to flick his tongue across my fingers. The sight alone almost sends me over the edge.

Good fucking Gods.

"You're so sexy." He hums the exact same words I'm calling him in my head, then straightens himself, spreading my legs wider with his knees. I push myself up on my shoulders, heart hammering in anticipation, as he moves closer to my entrance. And with one slow, delicious movement, he pushes inside me, steady, gently, until he's buried deep in me. My lips part, and I gasp for air, feeling myself embracing him. A loud moan slips from me.

Kieran groans as I adjust to him, his hand gripping my hips like it takes all the willpower he can muster not to thrust into me before I'm ready. I breathe, heavily now, biting my lips at the pleasure rippling through me.

"Stop being so gentle," I murmur, voice hoarse, "and fuck me already."

Kieran arches a brow, like he's taking it as a challenge. "Careful what you wish for."

He pulls out just enough for me to let another shameless moan slip free, and then he moves—a hard, grinding thrust that has me dying for more.

Then another.

And another.

Again.

And again.

Every stroke sends a delicious ache spiralling through me, until I'm arching off the mattress, desperate to feel him deeper inside me.

"Don't stop," I choke out, nails digging into his back. "Fuck—please don't stop."

"Wasn't planning on it," he growls against my neck, lips dragging down, teeth grazing the sensitive spot as his pace quickens. One hand slides up and wraps around my throat—not tight, just enough to make my head spin with how much I need him.

It's rough. It's hot. It should never end.

Whatever he wants, he can have. I give it all.

I want him unleashed, undone, again and again.

When I finally lose it, a scream rips from my throat as I shatter beneath him, my body trembles, stars exploding behind my eyes.

But Kieran is nowhere near being done.

He slams into me, giving me the pleasure I didn't know I need. I throw my head back against the pillows, chasing another climax so fast my head can't catch up. I cry out, clenching hard around him.

That's what undoes him.

Kieran growls, and curses slip from his mouth. He buries deep inside me, shattering as he trembles with release.

Our lips find each other again like they were cursed to do so. His fingers gently brush my cheek, and my heart dances at his touch—at everything about him.

Mother of the stars.

I love him.

I love him.

Fuck, I really love him.

"Gods," Kieran murmurs against my lips, nipping it softly. "I missed you so bad. Those five days were horrible."

"I missed you, too," I reply, kissing him again sweetly. "Please don't do that again."

"Never," he promises, fingers lacing with mine. A soft cold rush of magic ripples through us, binding us in an invisible bond.

I burst out laughing. "Did you just give me another one of those magical tattoos?"

"Yes." Kieran chuckles. "A promise does mean something around here, you know."

I brush my thumb over that beautiful face, still covered in sweat, but I reach up to press a kiss on his cheek anyway. "You're mine, Kieran."

"Oh, proudly," he teases, dragging his mouth down the side of my face. I tense as I feel him harden again inside me. "And you're mine."

In one smooth move, Kieran rolls us over so I'm straddling him, our bodies still connected. I gasp, startling as he thrusts up in painful, teasing strokes.

"And since I'm yours ... you can do absolutely anything you want with me," he whispers, his voice wrecked, hands squeezing tight on my thighs. "Anything at all."

I swallow.

My thighs are sore. My body still aches.

But I move anyway.

Chapter 24

I wake up and the sun is already high. I panic, thinking I've overslept and Kieran has once again left me alone, slipping out like smoke while I was dreaming of him.

But I turn and find him sleeping soundly next to me, arms dragging me back into his hold without even opening his eyes, like the sound of me turning stirred him up but he refuses to move just yet.

He's still here.

Still mine.

Still naked.

I can't resist the urge to curl up against him, our skin brushing, his breath ghosting over my forehead, warm and steady like my own beating heart.

As much as I would like to stay like this all day ... "Gorgeous," I whisper, gently tapping his cheek. "I think you may have skipped work today."

Kieran hums, tucking his face in my dark hair sprawling on the pillow. "Let's just call in sick."

I chuckle.

Right, because the three-hundred-and-sixty-year-old King of the Fallen is lovesick in bed after a long night with his girlfriend.

Girlfriend.

Am I his girlfriend?

I don't even care, as long as I have him.

"You seemed so busy all week, and now you can suddenly be free," I say—meant to sound casual, but it lands with an edge. Kieran's eyes flutter open. He blinks slowly.

"Don't do that, please," he murmurs. "Let's not fight first thing in the morning. I already promised you I wouldn't do it again."

I sigh.

"I'm sorry. But you should still get up."

"Why?" Kieran drawls, tucking me into his chest even tighter now.

"Because you've got work, and I don't want your Court to hate me more than they already do."

"Come on, nobody hates you," he mumbles into my hair, stroking it as if to say I'm silly.

"Aurora does."

His hand stops mid-stroke. "Aurora is ... Aurora."

I've never heard of a better description of the High Curator of Ceremonies.

She's definitely special—not just because of her beautiful face or gracious walk, but the respect and attention she commands. The kind of Fae who makes you feel like the dress you wear because you think it's beautiful was made from threads of muddy hay just by standing next to her.

"I don't think she likes me very much."

"Well, she can get ... possessive, when it comes to me."

I frown. “Does she still love you?”

“Who knows?” Kieran throws one arm up in the air, then runs a hand through his hair. “I’m sorry if she’s been unpleasant to you. The truth is, she’s rarely ever nice to other females.”

While that might be true, I still think she hates me.

I look up at Kieran, curiosity getting the better of me. “You were with her for a decade. Why did you split up?”

Kieran sighs. “On second thought, I think I prefer fighting to talking about my ex.”

Of course he does.

“Why? Did she break your heart?” I press. They seem to still be civil, or at least professional at work—most of the time.

“I understand why you want to know, but can we please not talk about other people in bed?”

I clamp my mouth shut.

Fair enough.

“All I’m going to say is ... we broke up because Aurora wanted more. She wanted me to become King,” he admits at last. My eyes widen. “And she’d be Queen. But I didn’t want it—becoming King or marrying her—so I ended it.”

Damn.

That’s ... unexpected.

But Aurora as Queen would have been stunning. I picture a shimmering crown on her head as she wears one of those pretty gowns she wears everyday—she’d make a star look dull like a rock.

Thank Gods he said no.

“Since I’ve already started answering questions, anything else you want to know?”

I arch a brow, then roll on top of him.

His hands immediately wander like they know every bit of my body—which they probably do, considering how he basically mapped me out with them last night.

I can't stop the stupid smile trying to escape me. "I want breakfast at Cassiopeia. Then, I want to go back to the Court, and before you say no, just remember what leaving me here for a week did to me. I need to see people. I need to go outside and have some normality."

Kieran blinks at me, quiet for a minute, then exhales like he's surrendered. "Fine. you can go back to the Court, but you're not staying there. We come back here at night. And my people will keep an eye on you when I'm not around ... well, from a distance at least."

"Fine." That's a compromise I'm willing to take.

Besides, who'd say no to sleeping in the same bed with him, especially when you never know which night will be your last.

"As for breakfast, I have a better idea ..." His hands find my hips, sliding down to cup my ass, and he squeezes it, firm, greedy. I bite my lip, feeling him grow rock solid beneath me. "Something you can eat before we go down to the café."

I tilt my head. "Is that so?"

The corner of his mouth curves up to a smirk. "Only if you want to."

It's so attractive every time Kieran puts me first, not the aching want burning hot and obvious between us. Some men try to persuade you even though you have already said no. But not Kieran. He could easily press, and I would crumble like I'm made of sand.

But he respectfully waits.

Consent is so damn hot.

And it makes me want to do more than just *eat* him.

So, I lean down, brushing my lips on his, soft and gentle.

"Lie back," I whisper.

Kieran obeys, his face amused. He tucks both arms underneath his head, anticipation flashing through his storm-lit eyes. Slowly, I trail a finger down his chest, feeling the shiver running through him.

Gods, he looks so fucking perfect, especially with those bedroom eyes and majestic wings spread lazily behind him.

Oh, the things I want to do to him.

I slide down his body, lips kissing, sucking a path across his warm, honeyed skin, as I listen to the quiet surrender in every breath he draws. Kieran's hand tangles in my hair—the hair he pulled last night. The sensations, the images of it all are still burning in my mind. I can feel the heat coiling in my own body.

I press a kiss to the sharp cut of his hip, then I move lower ... kissing the tip and swirling my tongue just enough to make him growl. Then I take him in a slow, teasing stroke.

Kieran groans, head dropping back against the pillow, the same hand in my hair now burying deep in it.

"Cass," he chokes out. "Fuck, you're going to kill me."

I pull back, licking my lips, wicked smile blooming. "I'm just getting started, my love."

I don't give him time to recover. I drag my tongue along the underside of him before taking him back into my mouth in one slick, hungry motion. Kieran swears viciously—a curse or a prayer? I have no idea, only wish he stayed vocal, because it's so fucking hot I might actually explode.

His wings twitch, half unfurled now, tension rippling through every inch of him. I grip his thighs, holding him still, working him deeper, hollowing my cheeks as I suck harder.

Meaner.

Messier.

"Mother of the stars," he rasps, voice hoarse. "Keep going like that and I will—"

I moan around him.

That's his last straw.

Kieran's grip on my hair tightens and his wings fully flare out behind him, casting shadows across the bed like he's something divine unravelling at the seams.

"Go on," I pull off just to whisper. "Come for me." Then I take him back, sucking, devouring him, deeper and harder.

And Gods, Kieran shatters—hard, broken, his jaw clenched and muscles drawn tight, his whole body trembling as I finish him off with cruel, punishing strokes of my tongue, and I'm already thinking of committing this vicious crime again just to see him come undone in the most beautiful way like that.

I don't know what he did to me.

But this—seeing him lose control and cursing my name like a prayer—is all I'll live for from now on.

"Holy fuck," he breathes. "You're never leaving this bed."

I grin. "Is that a promise?"

Kieran pulls me up into a hungry, devouring kiss like he need to taste me just to breathe. One hand grabs my ass, the other sliding between my thighs ... I let out a soft moan, sharp and needy, as his fingers slip inside me. Slow. Deep. Curling into that slick, aching spot already throbbing for release.

"Get on your knees," he demands.

Gods—that voice.

Give Kieran consent, and he'll give me exactly what I need.

I obey.

I shift, turning over, baring myself to him—my palms sinking into the mattress, thighs parted, heart pounding.

Behind me, I hear a low, reverent curse under his breath.

Then his hands are on me, spreading me open, gripping me so mean I sigh into the pillow. His fingers return, slipping back inside me, slower this time, teasing me, savouring me. He fucks me with them for a few more strokes before pulling away completely.

The loss has me whimpering.

But then he replaces it with something much bigger—hot and heavy, his cock slides into me in one hard, unforgiving stroke.

And I scream.

My hands clutch the sheets. My body tenses around him, clutching him like it's been holding its breath for this. He's so deep inside me I can barely breathe from the need.

"Kieran," I groan, my voice ragged.

"Yes, my love?" He presses his lips on my ear, purring softly. A hand slips between my legs, flicking over that sensitive bundle of nerves. I fall forward, moaning shamelessly into the pillow. "Tell me, what do you want me to do?"

Before I can answer, he pulls back—just to slam into me again so hard I'm seeing stars.

"I want you to do that again," I whimper. "But faster—and don't stop. Please, please, don't stop."

I can feel Kieran grinning behind me. He presses a kiss to the side of my neck. "Good girl."

And the whole world fades away.

He grabs my hips, hard enough to bruise, and fucks me like his life depends on it. His cock pounds into me over and over, each thrust harder, hungrier, better than the last. I choke, screaming, crying in pleasure and pain, already chasing my climax, even though I don't want to just yet.

"You like that?" he pants, fingers brushing my sensitive part again.

"Yes," I sob, clenching the sheets, drowning in desperation. "Yes—Kieran."

He growls, rubbing my clit in hard, ruthless circles whilst he keeps thrusting, deep and brutal.

My thighs are shaking. Everything is blurry. I'm an absolute wreck.

And then I'm gone.

It hits me like a storm, violent and blinding, tearing through every inch of me as I scream into the pillow, convulsing around him.

Holy fuck.

I don't know what day it is.

Where I am.

Or how to speak.

I lose the ability to breathe. To make sense of things.

And Kieran is still chasing his own climax—his rhythm turns wild, erratic.

And then—

A fucking knock on the door.

"Kieran," a voice calls through.

Kieran groans like he's about to bite someone's head off—and I think he is.

"Whatever the fuck it is, come back in five minutes," he shouts, still buried deep, still thrusting—I scream before I can stop myself.

Holy shit.

"Sorry, but we've been waiting for you for an hour," the voice says—sharp and clearly annoyed.

My brain lags for a second, still catching up to reality. Then the voice clicks.

Gods—that's Virgil.

I don't have time to think before another moan tears out of me because Kieran refuses to stop.

Kieran growls, voice feral. "The wait won't kill you, but I swear to Gods, I fucking will."

I don't hear anything else but the filthy sound of Kieran pounding into me, skin on skin. My breath hitches. I try to stifle the scream building in my throat, but Kieran slides a hand to my neck, holding me upright. His other hand cups my breast, rough and possessive.

I'm gone again.

My sensible thoughts vanish beneath a cry I can't contain. I collapse forward onto the bed. Kieran snarls behind me, driving in deep one last time, and shatters with a broken, raw groan, spilling inside me, hot and thick, pulsing in waves that drip down my thighs.

I can't move. I can't think.

Kieran slumps over me, panting against my back, fingers digging into my hips like he's holding on to dear life.

Oh. My. Fucking. Gods.

When he finally pulls out, Kieran presses a kiss on my shoulder and whispers, "As much as I would like to stay in bed forever, I need to go take care of that."

I roll over, running a hand down my face. "Gods—and now Virgil knows."

"So?" He grins, unbothered. "Why don't you get ready? I'll pick you up in an hour, then we can go to Cassiopeia."

I bite my lip, so in love with him it might actually kill me. "What about work?"

"I gave them everything for centuries. They can last one afternoon without me," Kieran says, kissing me softly, lingering. "It's a date."

A smile blooms from me, my heart fluttering like he just said he loved me. "Promise?"

"Always," he replies.

Always.

Forever.

As short as that may be.

Chapter 25

"You're still ... alive?" Daisy looks at me like she has just seen a ghost the next morning when I walk into the hall for breakfast as if I slept here last night—when I just woke up in Kieran's arms for two mornings in a row.

"Unfortunately, for you." I smile sweetly, dropping into the nearest chair with grace.

"Where have you been?" Leon asks, frowning at me.

In short—heaven.

Full story?

On a deathbed. Then on a love bed. Under Kieran. On top of him. In front of him. Up in the moon, as he carried me in his arms and flew around the mountain last night just to make me laugh.

One human.

A Fae King.

Two extremely horny, hopeless, can't-keep-hands-off-each-other, doomed romantics.

I simply sip my tea and say, "Recovering."

Lucas huffs a laugh—then immediately chokes.

Karma travels faster than the speed of light in this Court.

I roll my eyes behind my teacup, then pause, realising I never even checked if my tea was poisoned. Kieran would be annoyed, since he gave me this magical potion. One drop of it turns any poisoned drink or food red like a warning flare.

Technically, it doesn't break any rules, since this is about the rebellion, not the trials.

Kieran argued that point with his Council yesterday. That's what the meeting was about.

Now, if anyone in the trials tries to poison me and the potion catches it—well, unlucky for them.

So far, I haven't choked yet, no blood dripping from my ears, so I'm going to assume the tea is safe to drink.

"Hello, my lovely participants."

Why is it that Aurora always has to interrupt my happiness? She glides in, draped in black today, gown sweeping the marble floor, looking elegant like she's hosting a masquerade the rest of the Court hasn't been invited to. Laia trails behind her like an underpaid apprentice whose only job is to keep the hem from catching anything unfortunate.

Her eyes drop to mine.

"Good to have you back, Cassandra."

I'm surprised she didn't clench her teeth when she said it.

"Good to be back," I say sweetly—a little too sweet, because I'm in a rather good mood, and if Aurora can see through Kieran's glamour, she's going to love how he's repeatedly branded me across my neck.

Her eyes narrow, gaze dragging pointedly to my neck.

Okay, that's a little creepy.

"You look like you enjoyed your time away, Miss Thorne." Aurora blinks, a cold, deliberate smile brushing her mouth.

Oh, she really can see through glamour.

I grin like a cat. "Yes, I did. A lot."

Her smile widens, but it doesn't reach her pretty eyes. "Perhaps you should get stabbed more often."

Lucas chokes on his drink—again.

My smile falters, but I hold her gaze. The whole room is quiet like everyone is holding their breath. With a neutral tone, I ask, "Why? Did you plan the first one?"

Aurora laughs, light, airy—perfectly performed. Her expression remains unreadable, her smile bright as day.

"I didn't," she says sweetly. "Though I wish I did."

And how can I be so sure that it really wasn't her?

She called Kieran away right before that Fae came up to me.

"Didn't know the trial host can be involved in plotting to remove a contestant," I drawl. I'm tired of the fakeness. Perhaps it's a good thing Aurora admitted she wishes she was the one holding the knife.

"This is a rather heavy topic for breakfast, don't you think?" Oliver laughs awkwardly.

Aurora doesn't even turn to him.

"It's not usually on our to-do list, but I might consider it ... if a contestant is a threat to the Court," she says, voice still laced with syrup, like she's inviting me to an afternoon tea.

I frown. "How exactly, am I a threat to the Court?"

She scoffs, shaking her head like she can't believe I even ask. "You know what, Oliver is right—I can't be bothered to discuss this in the morning. How about we keep it professional, and you stay out of the Court's business?"

"I work with Kieran. I can't stay out of the Court's business."

"Well, some things are simply none of your business. So, it'd be wise for you to know your place," she says flatly. Then, with a bright smile, she turns to the rest of the table. "I do apologise for my behaviour, lovelies. Now, shall we move on and announce the winner of the mini-game?"

Just like that?

I blink in confusion.

Was she talking about my involvement with Kieran? How is that the court's business?

But Aurora doesn't seem interested in explaining anything further. She just takes a golden envelope from Laia, who's been so quiet I almost forgot she existed.

"Oliver," Aurora calls, finally turning to meet his eyes. "You found most of the eclipsed coins—congratulations!"

Jordan snarls. "How couldn't he? He's been digging around the Court like a deranged landscraper with all those gardening tools of his."

So, that's what people have been doing while I was gone for a week?

They must be pretty happy the Fae almost did their job for them.

"Yes, when you were busy plotting to take me out," Leon says from the end of the table. "If Lucas hadn't saved me, I'd be dead. So, shut the fuck up and be very scared of everything edible from now on."

Woah.

Jordan tried to kill Leon?

And Lucas saved him?

My head snaps to Lucas, who shrugs like he's saying, "Well, you weren't here."

Jordan doesn't even bother to deny it. He just laughs. "Poison? Really? That's a girl's weapon. I could snap your neck with one hand."

"All right, all right," Oliver cuts in, his voice a little too high-pitched for comfort. "There's no need to be this violent. You mind your business. We'll mind ours. End of."

I almost laugh.

Oliver still lives in that cute little world where he believes good will defeat evil, doesn't he?

In this Court, if you don't strike first, you're dead meat.

I know Jordan will never stop. And if they don't do something, sooner or later, Leon's going to end up floating belly-up like some overfed goldfish in a tank.

Aurora takes a deep breath, still all smiles as she says, "Anyway."

She gets off on this, doesn't she?

"Here's your prize." She hands Oliver the golden envelope. "A little advantage for the next trial. It's enchanted so that only you can read it. But I do have to warn you—it catches fire the moment you do. So ... maybe don't read it in bed."

"That's ... good to know. Thank you." Oliver takes it from her and carefully puts it down on the table like it might explode.

"Now, I hope you all have a wonderful day," Aurora says. "The second trial starts in a few days. I can't wait to find out who teams up with who."

There's a chance Aurora might be a sociopath.

Or she's just cold-blooded.

And Kieran loved her for a decade.

Ugh.

"I have decided on my prize," I chime in before she can turn. Aurora doesn't even bother pretending my voice isn't an offence to her ears.

"And?"

"I'd like to have magic for a day."

Her face doesn't flicker. She's already halfway out the door the next second. "Go to Kieran. He'll give you a ring. Once you put it on, the power will hold for twenty-four hours."

Kieran and ring in the same sentence?

Jordan bursts out laughing like the air itself tickles him. All heads whip towards him.

"That's hilarious." He shakes his head, wheezing. "It's like these trials are made for you, Cassie. Everything always goes your way. Now you're getting magic and a ring from your beloved."

I raise a brow. "Jealous much?"

"Yeah ... whatever," Aurora murmurs, then just walks away, footsteps echoing louder than they're supposed to on the marble floor.

Lucas massages his temples, exhaling sharply.

"This is all ridiculous." Daisy stands, her chair squeaking on the floor. "She's going to win it all, and you are all sitting there, doing nothing."

Ah. Here we go again.

"How exactly am I supposed to win it all?" I gesture to myself. "Believe it or not, Kieran isn't helping me with any of this. He swore an oath centuries ago not to interfere with the trials."

"Oh, please. It's his Court. His rules."

"Well, it would be good if that was the case." I blink at the delusional group of people in front of me.

Yes, not a lot of people dare to object to Kieran, but their oaths are sacred. I don't think even he could break one.

"You know, I actually respect you." Jordan offers an opinion no one's asked for. "I mean, sure, it's fucking annoying. But this is a game. You do what you have to do to survive. At first, I thought of getting rid of you—but maybe it's smarter to be your ally."

And now I'm the one laughing. Everyone seems to want something from me.

First, Daisy wanted to team up with me. Now, Jordan wants to be my ally.

"You've got nothing to offer but annoyance," I say. "So, no."

Daisy exhales like she's lost faith in humanity, then leaves without so much as a goodbye.

Oliver and Leon leave a moment later—probably off to tend to someone's garden. Sounds like their side business is thriving. I wonder what Leon would have been like had Oliver not taken him under his wing.

"I need to meet with Atticus," Lucas says, nodding his head to the last person left in the room. "Are you going to be okay with him?"

I glance at Jordan, who's chewing his toast. My daggers are strapped on my thigh and my ankle. Stinger ring on my right hand. Charm hairpin blade nestled in my curls.

If he does attack me, I won't go down without a fight.

I nod. "Don't worry. I'll be fine."

"You sure?" he asks again.

"Brother," Jordan says. "I'm sitting right here. Besides, I want to be friends with your girlfriend now." Then he pauses, correcting himself. "Oh, wait—is she your girlfriend if she also has another boyfriend?"

Lucas sighs, loud and sharp. "Shut up, Jordan. Touch her, and I don't care what anyone says, I'm going to convince one of Virgil's creatures to eat you from the inside out in your sleep."

I really hope they don't actually have that kind of monster in their army.

Gods, what the hell is in Virgil's army anyway?

"And I'm not your brother," Lucas adds as he walks towards the door, stopping just long enough to place a hand on Jordan's shoulder—then squeezes. A little too hard.

Jordan curses, twisting himself out of Lucas's grasp.

Lucas just glances back at me and offers me a smile before disappearing through the door.

"Your friend has changed a lot. Have you noticed?" Jordan mutters, rolling his shoulder like it's still in pain.

"Or maybe he's always been like that with dickheads." I return to my own breakfast. I don't want to be alone with him longer than I have to.

"I know I haven't exactly act like a saint, but I didn't try to kill that Leon kid," Jordan says, tone shifting slightly. "Someone knocked him on the head. I found him in the corridor, but Oliver and your friend saw me there and assumed it was me."

I narrow my eyes at him. "Sure, whatever you say."

"This is exactly why I don't bother being nice." He scoffs. "You guys won't believe me anyway, so what's the point?"

"You're telling me this whole time you've been acting like a jerk on purpose?" Because that's not pathetic at all.

"No, I didn't say that. But we all came here for the trials. Why bother making friends?" Jordan replies, sipping his juice.

Honestly, I think this is the first time I've talked to him for longer than a minute since we arrived.

"You have no idea what fucked-up shit I've been put through since your precious King took my eye. And yeah, fine. I probably deserved it. I was drunk, and I already apologised to Laia. But this"—his voice sharpens—"this double-standard treatment and the hell you and the whole Court put me through after that is just bullshit."

Is that how he sees it?

Because I think it's rather deserving.

"You can't exactly expect me and the others to treat you nicely, Jordan. I seem to remember you threatening me just before we went into the woods during the first trial."

He scoffs but doesn't deny it.

"Still, it's not me. I didn't hurt Leon."

I don't reply right away.

This is interesting. A man like Jordan likes to brag. And for him to keep denying something that sounds exactly like the kind of thing he'd do is a bit weird.

Either he's scared shitless of Lucas, or he's telling the truth.

But Atticus thinks he's working with Florence and the rebellion.

"I'm telling you, dodgy stuff is going on in this Court," he says, leaning back in his chair, arms folded. "If I were you, I wouldn't trust anyone. Not even Lucas."

Chapter 26

I didn't expect this much headache on my first day back.

I took whatever Jordan said with a pinch of salt. In a way, he's right. You can't trust anyone here, and that's exactly why my opinion of him hasn't changed.

It would make a lot of sense if he's working with the rebellion. He hates Kieran for taking his eye, for humiliating him. And now he's trying to cozy up to me, hoping I'll let my guard down long enough for him to stick a knife in my back.

Because why would he want to befriend someone who's clearly involved with the person responsible for taking his eye?

I'm not taking any chances.

With Kieran off doing some business with Atticus and Gideon this morning, I spend my time in the library, browsing books about spellwork and witchcraft.

If I'm going to have magic for a day, I need to make the most of it.

I don't exactly know how Fae magic works, but I hope witchcraft is close enough to count. I find a comfortable seat next to the window and start flipping through the pages of one of the books.

Gods—is there any spell in here that doesn't require ingredients like raven's bone, shapeshifter's hair, or animal blood?

How am I supposed to find any of that?

Maybe witchcraft isn't the way to go after all.

"You should enchant your weapons," a voice whispers behind me. I almost jump.

Laia.

"I'm just saying ... you've got magic for a day, but your weapons will stay enchanted," she says, stepping closer, nodding towards the pile of books. "Isn't that what you're looking at?"

"Yes." I arch a brow. "But why do you want to help?"

"I've been meaning to apologise." She sighs, sinking into the chair beside me. "I was the one who left that dress for you the night you got stabbed. I feel ... somewhat responsible."

I shake my head. "It's not your fault."

"I know." She swallows, eyes dropping to her hands. "But I was in such a hurry that day. Aurora was running me ragged. I didn't even check the pile properly. I just grabbed what was there—I swear, I didn't know."

"It's fine," I mutter, not sure what to say. It isn't really fine because I almost died—but I don't blame her. "Is that why you're helping me?"

She shrugs. "Don't know what you're talking about. I just came here to get some books for Aurora."

I grin.

"In that case, thank you for stopping by," I say, closing the book as Laia stands. "I'll keep your advice in mind."

Laia nods. A small, fleeting smile blooms on her lips as she walks away.

I dump the useless books on the librarian's desk—well, Daisy's desk—just to annoy her and start looking for ones about enchantments instead. I swear Daisy wants to scream at me, and she probably would if this wasn't her working hours.

Oh, well. She was a bitch to me first.

When I return to my seat, Kieran is already there, waiting for me.

I stalk closer, my heart lifting—then sinking at the same time. I want to run into his arms and kiss him like we're the only ones in the world.

But it's a library full of Fae, and I'm not sure how to act around him in public.

"Hey, gorgeous," he says, reaching out a hand. I glance around to make sure no one's watching before slipping mine into his.

"How did you know I was here?"

"I've got eyes and ears everywhere," Kieran says, brushing his thumb over my knuckles. He leans in to kiss my cheek, but I pull back.

"I didn't think we were doing this in public."

He huffs a laugh. "Pretty sure said public suspects we've been fucking for a month."

I tilt my head, blushing like a virgin. Every time I think about the things Kieran and I do in bed—Gods.

"And now you owe me a ring," I murmur.

A magical ring, but a ring regardless.

"Ah, yes." Kieran nods. "I assume you picked magic, then? Is that why you're studying enchantments?" He flicks his fingers on the book's cover.

"Yes."

"You know, I could just help you with that," he says, crossing his arms. "I know a thing or two about magic."

I roll my eyes. "Fine. Teach me, then."

"First, let me get you a ring."

I smirk. "Preferably one with a big rock."

"Of course." He chuckles, offering a hand to help me with the books. "But let's go somewhere private for that part."

That's the first time he's actually warned me before vanishing us. I squeeze my eyes shut—then suddenly we're standing on a wooden bridge, surrounded by crystalline blue water, a giant moon hanging overhead despite the daylight.

The River of Vows.

I spot the gazebo in the distance, the same one where we drank after Tessa's funeral. The first time I really gave in to the temptation that's called Kieran and blamed grief and alcohol for it.

The same spot beloved for Fae weddings.

"Kieran." I tilt my head, joking. "If you were going to propose, at least you should have made sure I was wearing something nice—"

Kieran snaps his fingers—and there I am, in a white gown, soft, lacy, glowing at the hem. A bouquet in one hand. Meanwhile, Kieran is now dressed wickedly sharp in a black suit.

"Kieran." I burst out laughing.

"What?" He chuckles. "I made sure you look exquisite."

"We're not actually getting married." I look at the gorgeous flowers in my hand—white, orange, and red, like the colours of autumn.

I will think about him every time autumn comes around.

Even if I don't remember him, something in my chest will remind me how beautiful this season has been.

"Not legally," Kieran whispers, lifting my hand to his lips. "Doesn't mean we can't make it a special occasion."

I blink, heart skipping a beat as Kieran reaches into his pocket and pulls out a ring—a beautiful pear-shaped obsidian stone with a shimmer of starlight caught inside, like the night sky frozen in glass.

Gods, it's so beautiful I can't take my eyes off it.

"Now, if I put this on you, you'll have magic for twenty-four hours," Kieran says, lacing his finger with mine. "It's enchanted until then, but I wouldn't mind if you never take it off again."

I can't stop smiling.

It's ridiculous, really—how quickly this male undoes me with just a few words and a ring that looks like it holds thousands of stars.

"You've never even told me how you feel, and now you're already giving me a ring?" I mutter, glancing up at those storm-lit eyes. "Don't do this just because you think I might be gone in a few days."

Kieran exhales. His jaw tightens—then he leans in, forehead brushing mine. His other hand cups my face gently, delicate like he's afraid I might disappear right before his eyes.

"Let's not talk about that, Cass," he whispers. "I can't think about it. I pray to the stars nothing will happen to you ... but if they resent me so deeply that they have to take you away from me, at least let me have this."

My breath catches, sharp pain striking through me like lightning.

It has been an emotional week, and seeing Kieran's vulnerable side is worse than being physically stabbed in the rib.

I reach up, brushing his lips with mine, softly at first—but he kisses me back, hard, deep. It steals my breath away. Kieran pulls me closer, his hand sliding to the small of my back like he needs me to anchor him. I tangle my fingers in his hair and let the kiss unravel me, piece by piece, inch by inch, until all I can feel is this moment with him.

When we finally break apart, I'm breathless.

"If we're doing this," I muse, leaning on his chest and glancing up at him, "where's your ring?"

Kieran grins. A hint of excitement and happiness in his eyes. "You can use your magic to give me one later."

"Are you telling me I have twenty-four hours to learn how to do that?"

"Yes." He laughs. So beautiful.

"You got me the most gorgeous ring ever, and I'm afraid you're about to get some cheap-ass metal made of crap in return."

Kieran's shoulders shake with laughter. "I'll treasure your crap metal forever."

I narrow my eyes. "You say that now, but wait until it turns your finger green."

"Even so." He smirks. "Now, can I finally give you the ring?"

"Fine." I bite my lip, placing my hand in his like I've done countless times. I hope to Gods my hand doesn't shake, because Kieran has no idea how dangerously I'm about to have a heart attack right now.

I think this might be the most romantic thing I've ever experienced in my life.

He slides it onto my left ring finger with such deliberate care. The obsidian sparkles as it settles against my skin. It fits perfectly, like it's made only for me. The moment it locks into place, a quiet hum ripples through my bones.

Cold floods my chest, spreading gradually like frost and starlight through my veins. It feels ... strange, overwhelming, but beautiful and terrifying at the same time.

Magic.

It's different.

I'm different.

Alive.

Like I can do anything.

"Is this what you feel all the time?" I murmur, staring at my hand like something's supposed to be there, but it isn't. My power is invisible, yet, fully charged. Electrified.

"Not when I use it daily," he replies. "But for you, it probably feels like you're on drugs." Then Kieran glances up, hand still holding mine. "Especially with that."

The full moon hangs above us, luminous and impossibly close.

Gods, I picked the perfect day for this.

"Go on." Kieran arches a brow. "Let's get high."

Chapter 27

"You have to use your heart, not your head."

Easy for Kieran to say. He's had magic his whole life.

Me?

Three hours in, and I'm already wondering if I should have picked money as my reward instead. Having magic for a day sounds like a grand prize anyone who's not stupid would jump head-first at. But is it, really? According to Kieran, the Fae spend years mastering their magic.

What kind of an arrogant ass am I to think I could do it in a day?

So far, I've tried lifting a twig, materialising a coin out of thin air, and changing the colour of a leaf. The twig wobbled. A quarter of the coin showed. And the leaf was just blown away by the wind.

"Gorgeous, you need to calm down," Kieran says, his voice soft and maddeningly gentle, eyes amused like he wants to mock me but also adores me to bits. He steps closer, fingers brushing mine before taking my hand. "Winding yourself up will only make it harder."

"But I only have a day—no, only twenty-one hours now." I sigh, frowning at Kieran. Still looking as annoyingly dashing as ever, he lifts his other hand to my nose and brushes it with his thumb.

"Are you just going to do this all day and all night without sleeping? Why don't we take a break for a while and get some dinner?"

"But that's more time-wasting."

"You're really incredibly relentless sometimes." Kieran lifts a brow. That word earns a grin from me. "But I adore you for it."

He says a few words, and the ice in my heart melts into a pool of water. Just like that. Kieran once told me I could ask anything of him, but he doesn't realise how he could easily do the same and I'd surrender even whatever tiny piece of my soul I have left.

"You're just trying to distract me."

His smirk confirms it. "Well, it worked. And you're still adorable."

Gods, this is unfair.

He has three-hundred-something years of dating experience. Probably already knows every trick in the book to make a girl smile.

"You're too much." I tug on his delicate suit, pulling him closer—then rise on my toes to press my lips against his, soft and sweet. Kieran blinks at me when I pull away. "But I also can't get enough of you."

That makes him laugh. Kieran isn't the only one with cheesy lines.

I don't remember what I was like when I fell in love with Declan. Was I this crazy? Did I feel like the world spin every time we kiss?

What kind of magic did this Fae cast on me?

With Declan, it was comfort. It was safe and security.

With Kieran, it's fire. Wild and dangerous.

The kind of love that hits you out of nowhere. The one people say is the best kind, but only a rare few ever get to experience it in a lifetime.

Maybe it's the moon.

Maybe the magic.

Or maybe it's just the high.

But I can't help but whisper, "If I only get a few more days with you ... it's enough for this lifetime."

Kieran goes still for a full minute. Then slowly, his hand reaches to brush a strand of loose hair from my face. The autumn breeze is cold and utterly lonely. The sky above turns deep orange and violet. The moon shimmers overhead, swallowing the light as the stars flicker.

Yet, he's the most beautiful thing I see.

"Easy for you to say." Kieran breathes, every word etched with the same pain reflecting in my heart. "If the rebellion doesn't kill me, then I'm cursed to remember you for the rest of my eternal life."

"Don't." I swallow, trying hard not to choke on my own words. "I won't hate you if you forget me."

Kieran exhales, pulling me into such a crushing hug that I can barely breathe. "I will."

For a while, I can't say anything. I'm scared that if I do, it will sound like a goodbye, or I'll break down in tears and spend the next hour uncontrollably sobbing.

I knew what I signed up for.

I knew what the cost of loving him was.

And I don't want to waste what could be our last hours together in pain.

"Let's get dinner," I manage at last. "We can go again later."

"You're not planning on sleeping tonight, are you?" Kieran knows me well.

"It's a full moon," I say, biting my lips. "I thought you Fae get especially ... frisky on nights like this."

"Which is exactly why I'm trying to get you home." He laughs, all sunshine and mischief.

The word *home* sounds lovely from his mouth.

So I lean in and press a kiss on Kieran's neck, painting him the picture. "I don't think we need to be home for that."

"Oh, Little Star," he murmurs, tucking a strand of hair behind my ear as his lips graze my cheek. "You're in for a wild ride—pun absolutely intended."

One minute, my heart is splintering. The next, Kieran has me laughing like crazy, and all the ache fades away like it was never there.

I squeeze his cheek, the obsidian ring on my left hand glowing faintly in the moonlight. "Let's get food first."

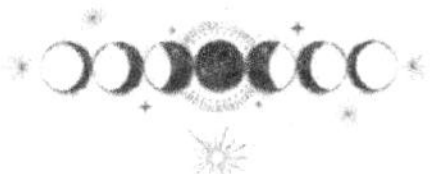

Dinner didn't take long.

I can't say the same about dessert. That got ... deliciously out of hand.

By the time we returned to the River of Vows, the moon has risen high above us. Wine stains our blood. Laughter echoes in the air. Our hands haven't left one another once. Kieran had to fix my gorgeous fake wedding dress—ripped when he sprawled me across the desk in his office. His jacket is now wrinkled and hanging on my shoulders, his shirt mostly unbuttoned, giving him that even more dangerous, undone look.

"Could we not have done this inside?" I ask between laughs.

"You know damn well what we'd be doing inside." Kieran chuckles. "And I'm not about to let an amateur with magic blow up my bedroom."

"Okay, fine." I roll my eyes but smile anyway.

We move from the bridge to the gazebo. Kieran clearly did something to it, because I don't feel even an ounce of the cold—or perhaps it's the alcohol that keeps us warm on this autumn night. I take my daggers out and try to concentrate.

"Remember, you have to feel it to wield it," Kieran reminds me before stepping away to give me some space—or maybe he doesn't trust me not set the gazebo on fire.

I close my eyes for a moment and let my mind wander to what my heart desires the most. It should be easy to say that my biggest desire is to enchant my daggers—but when Kieran is standing less than a metre away, it's hard to think of anything else.

I breathe in deep, focusing on the weight of both daggers in my hands.

The magic is there—I've felt it all night. It flows slowly through my vein, hums quietly under my skin, and pulses in my chest.

I can do this.

I can do this.

I can do this.

And then—I feel it. A rush. Something deep inside me rises like a beast awakened by moonlight. And when I open my eyes again, my hands are glowing—golden and violet. My breath catches.

The glow fades a few second later, but not without leaving its mark—two faint traces of light, one on each dagger.

"Wow," I whisper, turning to Kieran, who's already watching me like a proud boyfriend. "That was awesome!"

"You did it." A gorgeous smile paints across his lips.

I drop both daggers and throw myself at him, pulling him into a kiss until we're both breathless—Gods, it must be the moon. The reason for this relentless yearning for something that's already mine—something that's standing right in front of me.

"I did it!" I laugh.

"Now," Kieran says, glancing at the daggers on the ground. "What exactly did you do?"

Hmm. "That's a good question."

"What?" He laughs, breathless. "Please tell me you know."

"Well ..." I pause, pulling away to pick them up. "I sort of ... just asked for them both to have powers that might give me an edge in the trials."

"Oh, dear Gods." Kieran drags a hand over his face, even though he can't seem to stop laughing. "I should have known giving you magic would be dangerous. My love, you can't just wish for vague power. You have to be specific, otherwise it could backfire spectacularly."

I swallow, pressing my lips together tight.

Well, he should have warned me, in that case. He knew I was a walking red flag.

"Let me see." Kieran holds out his hands for the daggers. I pass them over. He flips them around a few times, storm-lit eyes narrowing, studying them carefully. "Don't be alarmed. I'm just going to test them."

"How?"

Kieran answers by slicing a shallow cut across his finger with the moonstone blade. Just a tiny thread of blood. Then he does the same with the twilight glass.

I gasp, instinctively grabbing his hand, and without intending to, something in me flares. The magic rushes out. And in the blink of an eye, the cuts are gone.

"Oh, look at that." He blinks. "You just healed me."

"You cut yourself!"

"Just a tiny bit," he says softly, hand rubbing my back like that's supposed to make me feel better. "Did you think I'd let you walk into the next trial, not knowing when your daggers will play a trick on you?"

I exhale sharply, arms crossed. "Well?"

"This one will flare when you're in danger," he says, handing back the moonstone dagger, then holds up the twilight glass one, inspecting the blade "And this one is ... actually quite impressive. It draws energy from anyone it cuts."

My brows hit the gazebo roof. "Like their strength?"

"Or maybe even their magic." He shrugs, smirking like it's not even a big deal that I now have another tiny deadly weapon.

"Oh, that's fun." I glance at them both in my hands, eyes flaring in amusement.

"You know what else is fun?"

"What?"

"Sleeping," Kieran says, rolling his neck. "I'm exhausted. Can we please go home now?"

My heart flutters every time he says *home.*

Damn it, I'm in love with my fake husband.

"One more thing," I say, sheathing the daggers back onto my thigh and ankle. Kieran frowns, but I don't give anything away, only offer him a hand and lead him back to the bridge.

We're standing out in the cold. Bats flutter in the nearby trees. Stars flicker above, thousands of them.

Yet something in my chest is tight and warm.

"What are we doing here?" Kieran asks, glancing around. His wings look insanely beautiful in the bright moonlight.

"Close your eyes."

He arches a brow. "You'd better be naked when I open them."

I hiss. "You just said you were exhausted."

"It's an expression." He laughs, eyes squeezing shut, fingers lacing with mine. "I can be wildly awake when you're in my bed."

"Shhh!"

Kieran sighs, finally shutting up.

Now, I pray that I'm not too nervous to ruin this —I close my eyes, reaching inward, searching for that source of power again. This time, I focus only on him.

I breathe.

And I concentrate on the one thing I want to give.

When I open my eyes, a cold, metal object sits in my palm—an obsidian ring, shimmering like the one he gave me. Matching. Equal.

Entirely ours.

I slide it onto Kieran's finger. He frowns as he opens his eyes.

Then his smile turns bright as moonlight.

"Hey, it's the crap you promised to give me," he says, holding up his hand. I punch him gently on the arm.

"It's not crap! I concentrated very hard, you know."

"I know. I know." He laughs, pulling me into an embrace, wings folding around us like a cocoon. "I love it. Thank you."

"You're welcome," I murmur, trying not to blush but probably failing miserably.

How did I go from having a dead boyfriend to exchanging rings with a fake husband?

"Now we have to kiss to make it official." He says that as if we haven't been kissing all evening.

But do I object?

Heck, no.

Kieran officiates our fake wedding with a kiss so hard my knees go weak. I hold on to his wrinkled shirt with one hand, the other on the back of his neck, kissing him back like it's some competition I refuse to lose.

I love him.

I love him.

Gods, I really love him.

When we finally break apart, a cold wave of magic pulses through my chest. My fingertips crackle like lightning. Kieran tilts his head, eyes glancing down at himself, then back to me like he feels something, too.

Something just ... shifted.

And I have no idea what.

"Did you just shoot me with your weird power?" he asks.

My eyes widened. "I hope not."

"Huh," Kieran murmurs.

We both stare at each other, confused. The cold in my chest already fades away. Kieran scratches his head like he's just been handed a riddle he can't solve.

Whatever it was, we're still breathing. That's good enough for me.

"Let's go home."

That pulls Kieran's attention. He nods, wrapping me tight in his arms.

A few seconds later, we're back in the warmth of his house. The same moon hangs in the sky, its silver glow casting shadows across the mountains.

"You know what else people do on their wedding night?" Kieran asks, voice low and teasing.

I already know the answer... especially when he starts unbuttoning the rest of his buttons.

Exhausted, my ass.

Chapter 28

It would be nice to say that after our fake wedding, Kieran and I went on a honeymoon, and we lived happily ever after.

But nothing could be further from the truth.

As the second trial creeps closer, so does the weight pressing down on the both of us. I can feel it in the way Kieran looks at me. In every word he speaks. In every kiss that brushes against my skin.

They are not just touches, but our last goodbyes.

There's a longing in them now. A quiet sadness.

And now that the day is finally here, I can barely chug any food in my stomach. Anxiety coils inside me like a snake crushing its prey.

Kieran hasn't left my side all morning, his brows drawn tight in permanent worry.

"I could just pull you out of the trial," he blurts.

My eyes widen. "You don't mean that. What would we do after?"

"I don't know," he says, frowning. "Live?"

I swallow the hard lump in my throat, letting myself imagine it for the hundredth time this week.

Could I do it? Leave everything behind?

Abandon my family. My friends. My whole life.

Whatever is left of them.

In a way, I already did. I left them all, without so much as a goodbye.

But I was prepared to die, not to live.

And I know. I know it in my heart that if I threw everything away and chose Kieran—whatever that may entail—I would never be able to forgive myself for abandoning Declan again.

Not if there's still a chance. Not if I could still try.

Could I ask Kieran for a wish even if I don't win this?

Would he do that for me?

Would he love me enough to bring back my dead boyfriend?

The snake in my stomach crushes around me even tighter. All I'd have to do is ask. One sentence is all it takes.

But I'm terrified of the answer.

So we let everything hang in the air between us.

The dread. The tension. The unspoken love.

Unsaid and unbearable.

"I can do whatever I want," Kieran says, frustration echoing in the corridor. His hand tightens around mine. "I'm the King of the Court."

"I thought you didn't want to be King."

"I don't." He groans, voice fraying at the next words. "But I want you."

My heart skips a beat. It blooms with happiness and hopeless dreams that break into shards of sharp pain the next second.

Did he just say that because he's upset, or he meant it and would burn down the entire Court just for me? He broke up with Aurora because he didn't want the crown.

I can't be the reason he takes it.

Kieran is clearly blinded by whatever spell I have over him. Sooner or later, he would regret it. I can't force him into something he never wanted, just because he wants to save me.

I'm not worth it.

And Kieran will be doomed for eternity—long after my fragile mortal body is still and buried in the ground.

"Kieran, I'll be fine," I say, forcing a smile even though my voice trembles.

"Even *you* don't believe that." He scoffs. "I can smell your fear."

"I'm scared. I don't know what's waiting for me," I snap back. "But I've got my weapons—*enchanted* weapons. Only Oliver has the advantage, and you know Lucas will die before he lets anyone lay a finger on me."

"Yes, I have a bone to pick with him," Kieran mutters under his breath.

I blink. "You can't seriously be jealous."

"I can," he says, completely unfazed. "He should stop acting like a guard dog around something that's not his."

And just like that, my anxiety turns into a smile that sneaks up on me before I can stop it. "You should be glad someone's there to protect me when you can't interfere with the trials."

"That fucking oath," Kieran mutters. "I should've never taken it."

"What would happen if you broke it?"

He lets out a sharp breath, his jaw tight. "I'd be stripped of my powers."

The blood drains from my face. I thought at most, maybe a punishment, or an injury.

But if Kieran lost his powers, the entire Court would crumble.

"It's not like this for every oath," he adds as if he's reading my frantic thoughts. "The one I made is binding. It's deep magic. Now you know why I couldn't tell you about the trials."

"Are they stupid?" I snap. "If you lost your powers, the rest of this Court would die."

"Yes, well ... Fae can be quite intense." He flinches. "Even when it means burning everything down just to prove a point."

Oh, Gods.

I hope I can hide the terror in my face, but I doubt it.

Before we can continue our walk to the courtyard, Aurora finds us. She turns on her heels, white gown sweeping the floor like falling snow, all smiles like it's her wedding day—when she knows we're about to have another funeral ... or two.

Maybe that's the point. Maybe she wants me to see it. To imagine her in a white dress next to Kieran. The last thing I see before stepping into whatever twisted, fucked-up mind games the Trial Committee has cooked up next.

"You're late," she says, shooting me a look. Then she turns to Kieran, softer this time. "And you shouldn't be here."

"I can be anywhere in a matter of seconds," he drawls.

I keep my mouth shut.

Aurora ignores Kieran and presses me instead. "Everybody is waiting. Lucas is looking for you."

Fair enough.

I sigh and glance back at Kieran. I'm about to let go of his hand—when he pulls me in, tucking me into a hug, tight. I gasp. "Kieran—"

"You're going to be okay," he whispers, wings folding around me, blocking out Aurora's cold gaze. "Please be okay."

I've been dreading this moment ever since the day he took my pain from me and made it his own—the day I could no longer pretend this was just a fun game. A harmless flirt. A distraction.

Everything changed after that day, and I've spent every waking minute since savouring it, soaking in everything about him. And even then, I was secretly hoping that maybe Kieran would grow bored of me. That once he actually had me, the spell would fade.

But it only grew, and grew.

Into this wild, soul-crushing love I can no longer deny.

And I want to tell him.

Gods, I want to.

But what if he doesn't feel the same?

And worse—

What if he does?

"It'll be over before you know it," I whisper, anything to comfort him, because I can't bear the look in Kieran's eyes. I can't walk away whilst he looks at me like that.

I can't say goodbye like this.

"I'll be waiting for you," he murmurs, fingers brushing my cheeks as he leans in—and kisses me like he's trying to memorise this feeling we share for eternity.

Aurora coughs behind us.

But Kieran and I don't break apart until a moment later. I cup his gorgeous face in both hands. I no longer have magic, but the ring has never left my finger since he put it on, still burning with a promise neither of us has spoken out loud.

I want to memorise this face, in case I don't make it.

I want to stare into those eyes, just a little while longer.

"Cass, I—" Kieran starts, but he stops, glancing away like the words suddenly escape him. There's conflict in the storm-lit eyes. The same one in mine. When Kieran finally speaks again, his voice is hoarse. Frayed. "Fuck, I really need you to come back."

I bite my lip, trying not to cry when every part of me is crumpling like torn paper.

"Please ... I need you to come back to me," he says again, begging this time.

And I nod.

I nod, even though I can't promise.

"I'll try," is all I manage to say.

Then I turn before the tears can fall. Aurora waits with that frozen gaze of hers—but I don't look back.

I can't.

If I do, I'll break

I'll beg for him to take that crown, burn everything down, just so we could be together.

Aurora walks alongside me down the corridor, her white gown trailing. I'm swallowing the tears threatening to fall. Every step I take is a battle. It takes everything in me not to turn.

After a long silence, Aurora says, "You don't need to wear the ring anymore. It doesn't give you power."

I stay silent, head held high.

She scoffs. "Did Kieran secretly marry you? Why does *he* have a ring?"

I don't answer.

I don't fucking care what she thinks.

But then, she stops walking.

"You love him."

The word slices through me like a blade. And even though she's the one saying it, I swear it cuts her, too.

"Oh, Gods." Her voice is quieter now. "You really love him."

"Shut up," I snap, my voice trembling. "Just shut the fuck up for once, Aurora."

And surprisingly, she does.

I don't want to think anything of it. The only thing in my mind is Kieran's words. His voice. His hug.

Gods.

He was trying to say something.

And I didn't say anything.

Fuck.

Why didn't say anything?

I didn't give Tessa the hug she asked for.

And now this.

When will I ever learn?

It's too late now. I can't go back. Kieran isn't there when I look back over my shoulder. He'll never know how I feel—never know how much I love him.

And I hate that this is what I'm carrying into the trial, but I can't undo it.

We arrive in the courtyard without exchanging another word. The gilded stands circle us like a circus, the sun shining bright above. The others are already there, dressed in fighting leathers. Lucas spots me and heads straight over.

"There you are! Where have you been?"

Emotional hell.

"Nowhere," I lie, not meeting his eyes.

I scan the crowd, desperate for a glimpse of Kieran. Just one last look. One silent goodbye. One moment where he knows all the things I didn't say.

I spot Gideon first, then Octavia, then Skylar.

But no Kieran.

No sight. No shadow. Nothing.

Aurora steps onto the platform, already shaking off whatever that awkward walk stirred in her, then she smiles like she was born exactly to do this.

I don't like the bitch. But Gods, I admire her.

"Good morning. It's my absolute pleasure to welcome you all—"

I don't bother listening to the rest. My heart is pounding, aching, punishing me for not doing anything until it's too late.

Kieran isn't here.

He isn't here.

What if I never get to say it?

What if I don't make it?

Please.

Gods, please.

Where is he?

Then—

A hand grabs me from behind and yanks me back. I stumble—but he catches me like I was made to fall into him.

Oh Gods, how did he—

"Kieran." I breathe.

He's here.

He's here.

Before my eyes. Pulling me into his arms. In front of the eyes of his entire Court. Aurora's voice fades. The whole arena holds its breath.

"I love you." He blurts it out. Raw and unpolished. Then again—louder this time. "Cassandra, I love you."

And I freeze.

Still as a stone in his arms.

I blink.

It's possible everyone heard what he just said. Everyone but me.

It takes me a moment before I realise I didn't dream this up out of desperation.

Kieran is here, and he's saying he loves me.

Oh, Gods.

I throw myself at him, kissing him like the whole world isn't watching—like I'm starved for air. And maybe I am. Lately, it's been hard to breathe without him. Kieran hasn't left my mind when I'm awake. I dream of him in my sleep.

Tears spill down my cheeks, no matter how hard I try to hold them back.

It's no use.

I'm hopeless when it comes to him.

"I love you, too," I whisper, not caring who the hell is listening. "Gods, I thought I'd never get to say it—I love you, Kieran."

He exhales like he's been holding his breath since we said goodbye, then he leans in to rest his forehead on mine.

"Be careful, all right?"

"I promise," I mutter, though my voice wobbles.

Kieran draws a deep breath. His eyes are still filled with fear, but his lips are warm as they press against mine again. A promise sealed with a kiss. "I'll see you later."

And I nod.

Not a goodbye.

It's not a goodbye this time.

Kieran lets go of my hand and watches as I step away. The whole arena is watching us. Even Lucas's jaw is still hanging somewhere near the floor.

Aurora hasn't continued speaking.

But Kieran's eyes stay locked on me.

"Honestly," Lucas murmurs, shaking his head slowly. "I may be a man, but that might've been the most romantic thing I've ever seen."

I chuckle, wiping at my eyes. "Oh, shut up."

"Shut up?" He glances around like I've lost it. The arena erupts again—cheers, shouting, even a few boos. "I don't think the whole Court will shut up for a long time after *that*."

Heat flushes my cheeks, and Kieran is just standing there, arms crossed.

Oh, great.

Aurora clears her throat, voice cutting through the noise. "As I was saying—"

She lifts a hand.

From the ground, a vast mirror maze unfurls like blooming glass—towering walls of silver and light, hundreds of them, gleaming under the bright morning sun. Blinding. Disorienting. *Terrifying*.

"The rules are simple," Aurora continues. "Each pair will enter through separate entrances. Inside, you'll face reflections of you or your teammate. Some will turn on you." She pauses, eyes narrowing. "Find the real one—and walk out together. If you choose the wrong person, you lose. And your teammate wins."

Gasps ripple across the arena.

Lucas stiffens beside me. I stare at the maze, heart sinking to my ankles.

Oliver chose to pair up with Leon, and since he was granted an advantage, Lucas and I figured he might know the twist wouldn't force teammates to turn on each other. So, we teamed up, leaving Jordan and Daisy to end up together.

Oh, they're going to kill each other dead.

"We need a safe word," Lucas murmurs, low enough only I can hear. "So you know it's really me."

"Remember the first time Declan introduced me to you?" I ask.

"Yeah, it was at—"

"Don't say it," I cut in quickly, eyes darting around. "You never know who—or what—is listening."

"Good point."

"That's our safe word," I whisper, and he nods, agreeing in silence.

"Oliver," Aurora calls out. "Since you won the mini-game, you're given another advantage. You get to choose whether you'll go first"—she smiles, winking at the crowd—"or last?"

"I'd like to go first," Oliver replies without hesitation.

"Oh, boy," Daisy mutters. "He's not holding back. Wonder what the hell was in that letter."

"Something useful." Jordan crosses his arms, shooting a disgusted look at his own teammate. "Unlike you."

"I hope my reflections eat your guts."

"Well, I hope mine fuck you to death."

Lucas and I exchange a look.

Oliver and Leon walk forward. They stop in front of an entrance, exchanging a few words. These two have been inseparable since day one, gardening and all that. And I get it—this must be a hell of a situation.

The crowd claps as they hug.

I expect one of them to step back, walk to the opposite entrance.

But then—

Light flashes off something metal. Quick and brutal, a blade plunges into Leon's back.

The clapping dies mid-echo.

The crowd grasps.

I slap both hands over my mouth.

Daisy screams.

Oliver just stabbed Leon in the back—literally—right through the left side of his chest.

No scream escapes from Leon. His eyes are wide as he collapses to the ground, blood spreading dark and fast across the cold dirt.

For what feels like forever, no one moves.

No one breathes.

Then—the crowd erupts again, thunderous and cruel, cheering like they've just witnessed the climax they've been waiting for.

I drop to my knees, clutching my own head.

Leon's eyes are still open.

Lifeless.

Just like that.

And Oliver wipes the blade clean on his leathers, not a trace of remorse on his face. He turns—then bows to the crowd.

The arena explodes.

Who the fuck is that?

Who have we all become?

Oh, Gods.

Aurora's face looks pale, but she smiles. A practised, polished smile that doesn't quite reach her eyes.

"Well," she breathes, voice sweet. "That works, too."

Chapter 29

Brutal.

Absolutely brutal.

With a blink of an eye, we are down to five contestants. Oliver never turns to us, just walks off, waving at the audience like they are his group of personal admirers.

"You know, at first I thought it might have been Lucas who knocked Leon unconscious that day," Jordan mutters, his voice tight. "But after that—pretty sure it was Oliver."

Even he is in disbelief, and that says a lot.

Leon's blood is still staining the dirt. The cheering echoes off the stands. I haven't managed to open my mouth. My head can't comprehend the things my two eyes have just witnessed.

I knew it was a game.

But I never knew how far everyone would go.

"There go the popular votes." Daisy barely manages to speak, her voice still shaky. As disturbing as that statement might be, I fear she might be right.

Nobody laughs. Nobody blinks. Not even Jordan.

Leon is lying on the cold, hard ground. Dead.

Oliver murdered him in front of us all.

And the crowd loved it.

Lucas crouches beside me. His hand finds my arm, gently curling around it like I might shatter. He helps me to my feet, his skin cold, his face pale as paper.

"You okay?" he asks softly.

No. Not even close.

How could I be?

But I nod anyway. Because what else can I do?

I barely even knew Leon. Apart from the occasional *hi* at breakfast, we never really spoke. And it's not like he was the talkative type. The only person he opened up to was Oliver—the very same person who stabbed him in the back.

He was only nineteen.

"All right," Aurora's voice chimes in again. "Who's next?"

The four of us look at each other.

Lucas rubs a hand down his face, exhaling hard.

"What the hell," he murmurs, turning to me. "Should we go now? I'd rather get this over with than watch these two kill each other and feel even more disturbed before stepping into that maze."

Jordan scoffs. Daisy looks like she's about to faint.

I nod. "Let's go."

Lucas raises a hand in response to Aurora. Still shaken, I'm about to step forward—but Daisy tugs on my arm with her trembling hand.

"There's jewellery in my room," she whispers, before taking in a deep breath like she's bracing herself for what's coming next. I arch a brow. "If I don't survive this ... can you ask Kieran to give it to my daughter? At least she'll have something. She can sell it. Be okay for a while."

The words hits me like a slap on the face.

She's desperate.

So desperate, she's asking *me*—the person she can't stand—to look after what little future her child might have.

"I—" I swallow. "I didn't know you had a daughter."

"Will you ask him?" she asks again. "Please?"

Gods, why do people keep handing me their last wishes?

And now I'm carrying this with me into the battlefield.

I nod. "I will."

If I make it.

"Thank you," she says quietly before letting go.

I walk with a heavier heart towards the entrance, where a pair of attendants are already carrying Leon's body away, blood trailing behind them. A path no one wants to follow.

Lucas turns to me once we reach it.

"If anyone can survive this, it's us," he says, rubbing a hand along my back. Then he adds, softer this time, as if he's trying to lighten up the mood, "You've got weapons, and I've got skills."

I'm forcing a smile. "Sure. Whatever you say."

He laughs. "Try not to die—or at least, don't die before me."

"Believe it or not, I would like to avoid dying at all costs," I mutter, glancing back at Kieran. "Otherwise, that'll be the first and last time I ever hear him say 'I love you.'"

Lucas flinches. "Dear lord, Declan might very well want to die again if we bring him back and you're snuggled up with Kieran."

I draw a breath.

Can't think about that right now.

"Let's try to survive this first," I say, unsheathing both of my daggers. The moonstone blade glows faintly, already sensing danger in the maze ahead.

"See you soon," Lucas says before pulling me into a tight hug.

And no, I don't stab him with the blades in my hands—much to the crowd's displeasure.

They boo like they're genuinely disappointed.

I turn—and flip them off.

Somewhere in the chaos, I swear I hear Kieran's laugh from the stands.

Lucas disappears towards the opposite entrance. And I wait—until Aurora lifts her hand to give us a signal.

I meet Kieran's eyes one last time.

Just one last look.

Then I step into the maze.

Instantly, the world fractures.

Light bounces off hundreds of mirrored walls, each one splintering my reflection until I'm surrounded by twisted versions of myself—blurred, confused, some looking at the wrong directions, the others smiling even though disorientation is about to force its way up my guts.

This must be a version of hell.

Who designed this? The Trial Committee?

If I make it out, I'm going to fucking kill Aurora.

I can't tell where the ground ends or where the walls begin. In here, the noises outside are completely blocked out, even though there is no roof. No cheers. No chanting. Like it was warded so no one can shout us a hint from the stand.

My heartbeat is deafening.

I reach both hands out, my grips tightening around the daggers—either the moonstone one glows brighter now, or this blinding light is tricking me.

Either way, I know something is coming.

I turn a corner—

And immediately stop.

Mother of the stars.

Dozens of me, scattered across the mirror maze, each reflection even more disturbing than those first ones I saw at the entrance—slightly off, twisted, broken. One version of me stands with her head tilted too far to the left. One turns her back, but her neck is still facing me. Another smiles too deeply, lips stretched to her ears. Another has blood on her hands.

One is crying. One is laughing. One is wearing the same white wedding dress I wore the other night, but her throat is slit open.

And the worst one of all is one I recognise all too well.

It just stares at me with empty, lifeless eyes.

As if I'm already dead.

I swallow hard. My boots move slowly on the ground. Better to go slow, instead of running and being blinded by the light so I can't see two things in front me.

It's okay, Cassandra.

They haven't leaped out of the mirror—yet.

All the reflections move with me.

All but one.

The one wearing the wedding dress stays still, her expression blank, daggers gleaming in her hands.

I narrow my eyes. "Don't you try anything stupid."

She tilts her head, blood dripping from the cut on her throat.

I wince, touching my own neck with the back of my fist, and can almost feel the pain.

"Why?" she asks softly. "You already did. You fell in love."

Before I can reply, another reflection laughs—this one with hollow cheeks and a crown of bones in her dark hair.

"And who are you supposed to be?" I ask through clenched teeth.

"I'm you, of course," she says, smiling sweetly. "Who you'll become ... if you survive."

"I don't fancy crowns made of bones—no, thanks."

"Please." She huffs. "Do you really think Kieran will let you go home after this? Eventually, he will take the crown. And you? You'll either sit beside him—or die."

Is this supposed to be a prophecy, or a twisted little trick?

"I am no queen." I lift one blade towards her.

"Of course not," another one offers—the one with blood on her hands. "There can be no human queen in the Court of the Fallen. The Fae will riot. And besides ... you came to die, didn't you?"

"I—"

Another cuts in from my right. "Yes, you should die. You let Declan die."

And another to the left. "And Tessa."

My breath catches.

Their voices rise, overlapping, until they drown out the silence.

"You don't belong here."

"You're weak."

"You're selfish."

"You're a disappointment."

"You'll never make it out."

"You don't deserve Kieran."

"SHUT UP!" I scream, slashing the nearest mirror.

Glass explodes—shards falling like autumn leaves—and the reflections scatter, retreating deeper into the maze. I stand there, panting, heart thundering.

I'm not sure what is more disturbing: those reflections, or the fact that I now have none.

Not a single mirror shows me.

Still, I don't stop. I keep walking.

Because the only way out is through.

Before I stepped in, I considered memorising a face in the crowd—Gideon or whoever—so I'd know which direction I was heading if he's at my back. But I can't trust the Fae not to pull some magic trick on me, so like the first trial, the sun is my map.

I stop at a junction, each path veering off in a different direction.

Lovely.

Left. Right. Or straight ahead?

I glance at the sun.

Okay, let's try right.

I turn. My reflections start appearing again, reflecting across the mirrored maze. Keeping one hand in front of me, the other brushing the wall, I continue walking—

—until the tip of my dagger slams into a mirror.

I'm staring straight at it, but there's no reflection.

And my other reflections?

They fucking burst out laughing, wheezing, cackling, like they've been dying for me to walk into it.

Didn't know I could be such a dick.

Shouldn't be surprised, really.

I exhale sharply through my nose, then turn and walk back the same way until I reach the junction again—I pick left this time.

The reflections follow me, whispering between themselves.

Another junction.

Shit.

I honestly have no idea if I'm still heading the way I'm supposed to.

I turn right.

And silence.

The reflections don't follow.

But then a few steps in, something else appears on the mirrors instead.

This time, it's Lucas.

Dozens of him.

Same clothes. Same hair. Same smile.

I freeze, my breath hitching.

Then, from the mirror at the far end, one steps out.

Oh, hell, no.

Chapter 30

"Hey, Cassie," the fake Lucas says, wearing a smile I've seen a hundred times before. But the warmth the real Lucas carries fails to show up on his face.

I guess I should be grateful he's made it obvious.

"Hey, Lucas," I say back, the moonstone dagger glowing too bright and hot in my hand now. "I killed your fake best friend once. So, unless you want matching scars, I'd say back the hell off."

"So aggressive." He chuckles softly, then tilts his head. "I've always found that sexy."

I blink. "What?"

"Oh, don't pretend you didn't know." Lucas—or whatever he is—grins, eyes glittering with amusement. "He's always had a soft spot for you. Some might even call it a crush."

My stomach twists. I know he's trying to mentally break me. It's not the first time the Fae have pulled this kind of shit. They served me Fake Declan on a silver tray during the last trial.

But this time, I feel it in my gut.

And I believe him.

But so what?

It's just a crush.

We all get stupid crushes on our friends sometimes, ones that burn quietly, fade quietly, and mean nothing in the end.

Lucas knows I'm with Kieran.

"Well, the feeling isn't mutual," I mutter. "Now, get the hell out of my way."

But of course, he stalks closer instead.

"You know ..." he says casually. "Sometimes he even wonders if coming here to bring Declan back was a mistake."

My grips tighten around both daggers, but I don't flinch. I keep my eyes locked on him.

For a second, I wonder if he's telling the truth.

But no. I can't let him get into my head.

"And?" I ask. "Everyone doubts themselves sometimes."

"Not the way he does."

It's just a mind game. Just another trick. This is not the real Lucas. No way in hell he could read Lucas's mind. This man is just trying to play with my head.

"You know what, maybe we should stop pretending this conversation is going anywhere. I'll go that way." I point to the direction behind him. "And you—you can go back to whatever hellhole you crawled out of."

But he doesn't stop. He keeps walking towards me.

His hand slips to the hilt of his dagger.

Guess we're getting physical, then.

"Didn't want to ruin my hair today," I say, my voice low, taking a step back and lifting both blades. "But sure. Let's dance."

Without another word, he lunges.

I dodge left, barely missing the arc of his blade as it whistles past my cheek. Only now do I regret turning down

Atticus's offer to train with him. For the past month, Lucas has been training every single day—even on his days off. He's packed tight muscle, fast and brutal.

And although he's taught me some tricks, I doubt they'll work on him.

Good thing I've got a dagger that drains his energy.

My moonstone blade meets his dagger with a clash of metal, and the impact rattles straight through my bones.

Gods, he's fast.

But so am I.

I twist, driving my boot into his knee. He grunts, stumbles—but recovers quickly, slashing again before I could do anything. I duck and strike. My blade slices across his ribs—not deep, but enough to make him hiss.

Good news: I made him bleed.

Bad news: it's with the wrong dagger.

But I'll take that over nothing.

"Not bad," he snarls. "And here I almost thought you fancied me too."

"Well, I've told Lucas this before, but men shouldn't just assume," I spit, kicking off the wall to gain momentum. I strike again, my twilight dagger to his shoulder, but he grabs my wrist mid-air and twists so hard I scream.

Pain erupts through my arm, blinding and raw.

Then he punches me in the stomach—hard.

Air rips my lungs in a choked gasp. I stumble back, hit the ground hard, and before I can recover, he's on me. One hand wraps around my throat, slamming me against the hard ground.

Fuck—

Stars explode behind my eyes.

"Stay still," he growls

Then he drives his dagger through my left hand.

I cry out—pure, raw agony, like nothing I've ever felt before.

The blade pins me to the ground. It hurts so much I can barely move. And now his grip is tightening around my neck. I'm choking, legs kicking, desperate for air. The more I struggle, the wider his smile.

No—

This can't be it.

I will not die here.

I will not—

I slam my knee between his legs. He doubles over with a gasp, and I break free, coughing, trying to remember how to pass the air back into my lungs. My vision swims.

My hand.

Fuck, my hand is pinned.

I need to get out of here.

Just fucking do it, Cassandra!

A scream rips from my throat again as I shove down the pain and rip out the dagger in one quick motion. Lucas turns, furious—but he's a little too late.

I drive the blade into his chest.

He gasps, eyes wide—then drops like a stone.

And I collapse back to the ground, blood dripping from my hand, hot and thick.

Then, I hear footsteps—

"Cass?" the voice calls. "Oh Gods, Cassandra!"

Another Lucas.

Problem is, I don't know if he's the real one or not.

“Get away from me!” I shout, forcing myself upright. Pain sears through my hand, but I grit my teeth and grab both daggers, blood-slick and trembling.

“Woah, woah—it’s me!” he says quickly, stopping in his tracks with both hands raised.

His face is bruised, leathers torn at the arm, like he’s been through the same fucked-up fight I had.

I narrow my eyes. “Lucas?”

“Yeah, it’s me. Gods—don’t tell me that thing did that to you.” He glances at the lifeless version of himself—shapeshifter or whatever it was—then winces. “Sorry.”

He sounds like Lucas. Talks the same way, too.

But I’m not taking any chances.

“Tell me the safe word.”

Lucas frowns. “What about you? You could be an imposter, too.”

I suppose that’s right. I wipe a shaky hand over my forehead, blood sticky on my skin. Can’t really blame him for being paranoid. “Fine. On the count of three?”

“Deal.”

We both inhale at the same time. Eyes lock on each other.

“One,” I start.

“Two,” he says.

“Three,” we finish together.

Then in unison, we say, “Evermere Park.”

I suck in a breath. That’s it. The park where Declan introduced us when he invited me to meet his friends for the first time. It feels like a lifetime ago now.

Only the real Lucas would know.

My knees give out.

"Thank the stars," I whisper, letting him catch me. His arms wrap around me, warm and steady—and for a second, I breathe and let myself believe it's over.

"Gods, that prick got you good, huh?"

"Yep." I wince. "But I got him better."

Lucas lets out a low laugh. "Come on, let's get out of here. It's not over until we're out."

I nod, sheathing my moonstone dagger. My ruined hand is too damn slick with blood to hold anything now.

But before we can go anywhere—

Another set of footsteps.

Then, another Lucas stumbles around the corner, bruised, bleeding, wide-eyed.

"Cass?" he gasps. "Cass, it's me!"

I'm going to lose my mind.

I tear out of the first Lucas's arm so fast I nearly collapse.

"What the—"

My heart pounds like it's trying to break out of my ribs. I look at the one I just hugged, who's staring at the new one with the same wide-eyed confusion I'm wearing.

And then it gets worse.

Another *me* steps out behind us.

The colours drain from my face.

"Fuck," she says, face filled with horror. "Which one of you is real?"

I'm going to throw up.

We're never getting out of here.

"Safe word!" I shout. "Now!"

It's the only way I can think of that can prove to me and Lucas which one of us is real.

Both of them—both *me* and *Lucas*—say it at the same time, "Evermere Park."

My stomach drops.

The first Lucas curses under his breath, his fingers curling into a fist. His gaze darts from me to the fake version behind us. He looks like he's about to be sick. "Gods, it's not going to work, Cass. They heard us when we said it the first time."

Shit.

My breath stutters. I stumble back a step, nearly slipping on blood—maybe mine, maybe his, maybe ours. I can't fucking tell anymore.

My eyes flick between them—between *me* and *me*, *him* and *him*—and the maze spins harder.

This is merciless.

The Fae are truly vicious.

Think, Cassandra. Think.

How the hell are we going to get out of here?

Reflections—

Aurora said they're *reflections*.

I grip the hilt of the twilight dagger and lash out, slashing the nearest mirror I can reach.

Crack.

Then another.

Shatter.

And another.

The other me lets out a sound that doesn't belong to anything human—a shriek so piercing, like a siren's scream.

I fucking got you, bitch.

"Get the mirrors," I snap to the first Lucas. "They don't exist without them."

I see it click on his face.

"Fuck, yeah!" he breathes, already spinning toward the nearest panel.

Glass explodes beside us as Lucas drives his blade through the first mirror.

And that right there. That's it.

The thing that tells me he's the real one.

I don't wait. I lunge for the next one, my hand screaming, my dagger cracking the surface again and again.

Another me screeches, flickering—gone.

"Over there!" Lucas yells, and we split.

Shards crunch beneath our boots. Illusions scream and vanish as fast as we can destroy them. The tide has turned, and suddenly Lucas and I are in hunting mode, pouring our rage into cracking every single glass.

Another fake Lucas lunges at me—but he's slower now, glitching, one limp at a time. I stab the mirror beside him, and he drops to the ground, twitching.

We both tear through the maze like storm winds, smashing reflection after reflection. The more we shatter, the quieter it gets.

Until there's only us.

Bloodied. Bruised. Broken.

Breathing hard, Lucas lowers his daggers, eyes still wide. "Gods, I hope that was the last of them."

I stare at the shards glittering at our feet. "Let's get the hell out of here."

He grabs my hand, and we both run. No hesitation. Our boots slam against glass-slick ground, blood trailing in our wake, the sound of our breath reminding me we're still alive. And we are so close. Gods, we're so close.

We don't stop. The noises from outside start bleeding in.

Louder.

And louder.

We sprint towards it, through another stretch of mirrored hell, shattering glass as we go and cutting a path straight through the chaos.

And then, we burst out into the arena.

The roar of the crowd hits like thunder, deafening me for a beat.

I pant, adrenaline slowly wearing off, pain blooming in its place.

I nearly collapse onto the ground when I see them. Familiar faces, waiting just beyond the chaos.

Gideon, Daphne, Aurora, and—

"Kieran?"

Their expressions are tight, eyes wide and wild.

Without the blinding light in the maze, I can see Kieran clearly now.

My heart drops.

Bruises darken his neck. His clothes are torn. And his hand—his hand is bloody, split open in the same place the fake Lucas stabbed mine.

The same wound.

Like he felt every second of it.

Terror blooms on my face.

"I don't know what the hell you two have done," Daphne says first, her voice sharp, "but we seriously need to talk."

No.

It can't be.

I freeze, still as a rock. But Kieran steps forward, gently pushes Daphne aside, and pulls me into his arms.

And just like that, nothing else matters.

"Kieran," I choke, my voice cracking, everything crashing into me all at once—the fear, the horror, the exhaustion. "I—"

I try to speak, but nothing comes out.

He holds me tighter, tucking me against his chest. "I know, my love. I know—I felt it all."

Those words hit me harder than all the messed-up things the maze threw at me combined. The terror on my face slowly creeps down to sink its icy claws in my chest, one by one.

Gods, no—

How could it be?

"It seems," he breathes, voice rough and ringing in my ears, "the River of Vows gave us something that night after all."

Chapter 31

"Mates?"

The word rolls off my tongue like a foreign language.

Daphne and Skylar just dropped it on me as if it's a weather update.

I don't even know where Lucas is. I haven't seen Daisy or Jordan since the maze. Don't know if they're alive or dead. The second Kieran let go of me, the Council swooped in, dragged me back to the Council Hall, dumped a healing tonic down my throat, wrapped my bleeding hand in bandages ...

And then casually told me that Kieran channels my injuries because we're *mates*.

Mates.

MATES.

"I'm sorry," I say, taking a slow, shaky breath. "Did you just say *mates*?"

"There's no such thing as fated mates in this Court," Kieran says carefully, his bandaged hand a mirror of mine.

"There is now," Octavia chimes in, her eyes narrowing. "Not fated—but chosen."

I'm really going to be sick this time.

"That's not possible." Aurora shakes her head. "There's a reason this Court doesn't have mates, and you're telling me a *human* is Kieran's?"

"Look, I don't have an explanation for this either," Daphne snaps, her voice razor sharp. "These two fooled around on a full moon while she had magic—and whatever the hell they did, it seems the River of Vows apparently decided they're bound. Like they begged for it."

Oh, Gods.

Oh, Gods.

Oh, my fucking Gods.

I remember.

I remember wishing we could be together.

I remember asking the stars for forever.

Did I do this?

"What does that even mean?" I shout, my voice louder than I mean to—my voice cracking on the last word.

Everyone flinches.

Except Kieran.

He's looking at me with the expression in his eyes I can't quite read—like heartbreak, fear, and hope all tangled together.

"Give us a minute." No one moves. Felix looks like he's about to open his mouth to argue, but Kieran cuts him off without even turning around. "I'm not in the mood to ask again."

No one breathes this time.

They all clear out in a minute.

When the doors fall shut, silence crashes over us.

Kieran turns to me, sadness softening every edge of his beautiful face. He reaches for my hand—bandaged like his—and holds it carefully.

"I'm sorry," he says, barely meeting my eyes. "That night, I ..." He pauses, running a hand through his hair, his voice barely a whisper when he continues, "Gods, I think I ... did this."

My chest tightens.

Does he regret it?

Does he regret me?

That I'm bound to him?

That I'm his mate—whatever that entails?

"How ..." I swallow, trying not to choke on the pain in my heart. My stomach clenches. "How can it be your fault, Kieran?"

"I don't know, Cass." His voice cracks, and that scares me more than anything. "But we don't have mates here. Not in this Court. Maybe because I've never believed in that bullshit." He exhales sharply. "I've always believed everyone should have a choice. Sure, fate might bring people together, but it shouldn't bind them. Not for life."

I press my lips together, squeezing his hand.

"But that night—I wished we'd be together," he admits, eyes finally meeting mine, and my heart skips a beat. "I wished you'd stay. That you'd be with me. Forever."

Mother of the stars.

We both wished for the same thing.

Chosen mates.

I don't know whether to cry, scream, or be over the moon.

"You didn't do this."

"Of course I fucking did." He groans. "I was selfish, emotional, and horny. Who knows what fucked-up magic I let—"

"Kieran, you didn't do this," I say again, gentler this time. I reach up to cup his face with my uninjured hand. The storm-lit eyes soften in an instant, like my touch is something sacred and wonderful. "I wished for the exact same thing."

That hits him.

He doesn't speak. Doesn't blink for a full beat.

Then slowly, his mouth curves into a crooked grin. "You did?"

I nod, unable to stop myself from smiling with him. "Yes, I fucking did."

"You really love me," he mutters, eyes wide like it's a surprise, but then he laughs—a gorgeous, constellation-bright laugh. The terror and the fear vanish from his face, chased away by pure happiness blooming like spring flowers in the dead of autumn.

And I forget every second of the pain I endured before.

I'm back in his arms.

And we're mates.

Chosen mates.

"Yes, you idiot," I whisper, tugging on his shirt to pull him into a kiss. I haven't stopped thinking about how he said he loved me in front of the entire Court. Getting back to him was the only thing keeping me going in that mirror hell.

The only thing that pulls me from my own darkness and gives me a reason to live again.

Kieran pulls me onto his lap, kissing me even harder as his hand wanders down my back. I don't know what the future looks like—I haven't thought about it in a long time.

But this.

Right here in his arms.

This is exactly where I want to be.

His happiness mirrors mine.

And my happiness is his.

But when I pull back, just enough to breathe, I catch the look in his eyes. I don't know if it's the bond, but I can feel that something else is still bothering him.

"What is it?" I murmur, resting my forehead against his.

Kieran exhales, his finger brushing my cheek. "You're human. And you don't know what this means." A pause. "Cass, we're not just mates. We channel each other's feelings, and that's ... dangerous."

"I'm sure your Council will find a way."

"I don't mean to ruin the moment—because believe me, I'm over the moon that you're my mate," he mutters, but his eyes are heavy, shadows pooling in their depths. I can feel the weight dragging on him. "But ... you have a family back home. A whole life. Then there's the last trial, and I—"

"Kieran," I cut in softly, pressing a finger to his lips, asking him to stop for a minute. He's still beneath my touch. "We'll talk about this. I'm sure those people outside are dying to voice their opinions." I glance at the door. "But right now—just for a second—can we take this in?" I smile. "My love ... we're mates."

Kieran leans into my touch, eyes fluttering shut as he presses a kiss to my finger. The same bright smile returns to his face. "We are mates."

"And there's never been mates in this Court before." I bite my lower lip. "Does this mean I have you ... forever?"

"Before we fell, that's exactly what it meant. Mates are bound for life. But here? Who knows. I'd like to think it still means the same thing."

"Do you think this is because of our fake wedding?" I laugh. "And the wishes, of course."

"Probably a bit of everything," he replies, nibbling on my fingers. "I don't really care why. You're my mate. I chose you. And you chose me."

"Don't be too happy. I'm sure your Council is about to drag us down from the moon." I tap his chest, flinching when I think about what comes next. "No way in hell they'll let you have a human mate."

"Well, tough luck." Kieran scoffs. "Anyone who's got a problem can pack their bags and fuck off."

I want to believe it's that easy.

But he knows how the rebellion is going to feel about this.

They'll use it against him. Twist it into proof that he's gone soft.

People will turn on Kieran because he allows the very reason they fell to sit beside him as his mate.

Kieran looks at me.

He knows exactly what I'm thinking.

"Okay, on second thought, this whole feeling-each-other thing is kind of creepy," I say, narrowing my eyes.

But Kieran just smirks—and leans in to whisper against my ear. "Just wait until we're in bed and you feel my climax when I feel yours ..."

Oh.

That's—

Um.

Yeah, maybe we should try that.

"You're thinking about it, aren't you?" He laughs.

I groan. He knows damn well I am.

"As much as I would love to test that theory right now ..." Kieran hums, kissing my cheek softly. "You—we—are injured. And I have to take care of that." He looks towards the door. "But why don't I take you home first? There's no need for you to sit through this. You've been through enough today."

"You've been through just about the same." I cross my arms. "And if you're going to talk about me, then I'm staying."

Surprise flickers across Kieran's face. He chuckles softly.

"Fine, if that's what you want," he says, grinning as he brushes a strand of hair from my face. "If I ever take that throne, you'll be a magnificent queen."

"Oh, God." I swallow, clutching my stomach. The image of myself in that bone crown flashes in my mind. "One thing at a time, please."

Kieran laughs. "You should prepare yourself for when I open those doors again." He winks. "Think of it as your first trial as my—hm, what would you be?"

He arches an eyebrow, like he doesn't know the answer himself.

I roll my eyes.

It's difficult when he refuses to pick a title, isn't it?

"Just open the doors," I order. "Let's get this over with."

"See—I might never be a king," he says, stalking towards the door, "but you're still my queen."

"Open the door, my love," I say again, voice sugary sweet, "so, we can finally go home and test that theory of yours."

Lighting flickers in those eyes, and Kieran's smirk deepens. "Your wish is my command."

After two hours of discussions, we still haven't gotten anywhere.

The truth is, the council doesn't know how to handle something that's never happened before either. Every time the conversation veers towards what to do next, it circles right back to how the hell this even happened in the first place.

They don't want to believe it.

And I don't blame them.

It sounds impossible

But Kieran and I are mates now—as much as that still sounds strange to me—but I feel it in every fibre of my being. And nothing is going to change the fact that we're bound.

"We have to sever the channelling link," Virgil says, his voice low and cautious. "If she's hurt, Kieran's hurt. That puts the entire Court in jeopardy."

This is probably the first reasonable thing I've heard in the past two hours.

Sure, the sexy theory Kieran has might be fun, but it's not worth the long-term risk.

I'm too fragile. I stub my toe every time I turn a corner. I fall over air. Trouble finds me all the time.

If the connection sticks, I'm probably going to end up killing Kieran by choking on the food I inhale too fast.

"Agreed, but while we try to find a way to do that, what about the final trial?" Octavia asks, and the whole room goes silent.

I keep my mouth shut.

For a minute, no one says anything.

Tension hangs in the air, so thick I can barely breathe.

Aurora is the first to break the silence. "We have to pull her."

"What?" I shoot up straighter. "You can't do that."

"Yes, I can," she counters, eyes narrowing. "And I am. You can't risk your life when you don't know what'll happen to Kieran. If you die, this whole Court might go with you."

I want to argue. Scream that it's not fair.

But as much as I hate it, Aurora is right.

She's right.

But Declan—

Gods, Declan.

Is this it?

Is this how it ends after everything?

After the hell I've been through?

"I know you want to save Declan," Kieran says quietly beside me. His hand squeezes mine gently, like he feels the sadness crashing over me. "And this isn't just about the you-die-I-die thing—but I was going to pull you out from that trial myself even if this hadn't happened. I can't watch you do this, love. Not anymore."

I glance at Kieran as I feel the gentle brush of his pain through the bond like a bruise beneath my skin—his terror, raw and aching, like he's reliving whatever it was he saw from the stands when I was in the maze.

And it's horrible, the feeling he shares with me.

I don't ever want Kieran to go through that again.

But how can I let go of Declan like this?

"We'll talk about Declan later, all right?" he asks softly.

I have no choice but to nod.

And truthfully, I'm grateful he even wants to talk about it at all.

"Does everyone agree that we should pull Cassandra out of the trial?" Aurora asks, her tone clipped and formal.

One by one, they all nod.

And just like that, I am no longer a contestant.

A hollow ache opens in my chest. Suddenly, I'm floating with nothing to anchor me but Kieran.

"What does that mean for me?" I ask quietly.

"You are our leader's mate," Skylar offers, glancing over at Kieran, her voice gentler than I expect. "It's not traditional, but the stars made their choice. And we'll honour it."

"I get that," Felix mutters. "But she's human."

Here it comes.

I brace myself.

"We might have to ..." Gideon starts, then pauses, then continues carefully. "... turn her Fae."

Oh, Gods.

He did *not* just say that.

"Absolutely not," Kieran snaps. I clutch his hand even harder now. "I'm not turning Cassandra Fae. She's young, and we have years to figure this out. I'm not ripping her from herself." He looks around the room. "If you are worried about appearances, then lie. Tell them we're fated mates, not chosen. Shut them the hell up."

Thank Gods Kieran says that—I wouldn't know what to do if he agreed with Gideon.

Yes, there's still the he's-immortal-but-I'm-human problem, but I'm not ready to talk about that now.

Hell, we just said *I love you* for the first time today.

And now we discovered that we're *chosen mates.*

I don't want my whole life decided for me just yet.

"Fine, we can talk about it over time," Atticus says, his arms crossed. "But do you realise this means Cassandra will have to spend the rest of her life here? She can't go home—because *you* can't leave, Kieran."

Blood drains from my face.

My entire body, actually.

I didn't say goodbye to anyone.

Noah threw the letter I wrote for Mum and Dad in the fire.

I was in such a dark place that I hadn't let myself think about what I'd left behind.

My family. My home.

"Again, we can talk about that. I'm sure we can sort out a few days' visit for Cassandra, and I will just stay behind," Kieran replies, quieter this time. "There's no need to decide everything right now."

The whole room goes silent.

Beside me, Kieran exhales slowly, thumb brushing over mine. He doesn't look at me, but I share every shattering emotion running through his beautiful mind.

"Look, I know this is a lot to take in," he says at last, his voice steady but tired. "Let's take some time. Think this through. There has to be a way to sort it all out."

And he's right.

His people know he's right.

A sleep or two can change the way the stars look. Right now, we're still in shock—or in denial—and none of us can see clearly when we're bleeding emotions. Myself included.

"We've already got enough to deal with. Let's take a step back. Cassandra isn't going anywhere." Kieran finally turns to me, and the smile he offers is soft and grounding. "Neither am I."

That ends the hours' long discussion.

Everyone starts filing out, talking quietly amongst themselves, and I just sit there in silence, too drained to move.

Aurora turns to me as Kieran leaves the room to speak privately with Gideon.

I brace myself for the nastiest comment of the century.

But instead, she just says, "I'm sorry I had to pull you out."

I blink.

Is she serious?

Or did the fake Lucas actually succeed in strangling me, and this is some fever-dream purgatory?

"What?"

"I said what I said." She lifts her chin, cool and regal again. "You understand I had no choice, right?"

"Yes, but—" *You don't have to apologise to me.*

"I knew it was important to you," she mutters, not quite looking at me. Her eyes drop to the ring on my left hand, her words bitter. "I suppose congratulations are in order."

I haven't even registered what she just said, but Aurora's already turning away.

What just happened?

I either need sixteen hours of sleep, or a bottle of extremely illegal Fae wine.

I'm still slumped in my chair, drowning in my own spiralling thoughts, when the door creaks open again. I thought it was Kieran.

Turns out it's Lucas.

"Lucas," I breathe. My chest caves in with relief. "Oh, Gods—you have no idea how happy I am to see you."

He forces a smile—but fails miserably.

My stomach twists.

"What's wrong?" I ask.

"It's the trial," he whispers. Something in his expression makes my heart stop. "Jordan won."

My breath catches. Daisy's last words echo like a curse in my head.

I know before I even ask, "And—and Daisy?"

Lucas looks down, shaking his head.

She's dead.

I know she's dead.

Mother of the stars.

I thought I'd be okay. We weren't exactly kind to each other.

But she begged me.

Gods, she begged me.

"I—" I swallow, steadying my breath. "I'll ask Kieran to honour her wish."

Lucas nods, and he doesn't say it, but I know just how much today has hollowed him out.

And I haven't even told him that it's now entirely down to him.

He's the one who has to bring Declan back.

Chapter 32

Everything has changed.

Two contestants dead. One pulled out. The remaining three can't see eye to eye.

The Council announced our new development to the Court—and it gives a brand-new definition to the chaos of this wild journey I'm current sitting in the front row, strapped to the chair, as I watch it all slowly unfold.

First, I made an enemy of the contestants.

Now, I've made an enemy of the Court.

Forget asking Kieran to bring Declan back to life—people will riot if he grants a wish right after telling the world his mate is human.

Though, the Fae don't know the whole truth.

They believe the reason we fell deeply in love in such short time is because we are *fated* mates who were bound to be together. All the poetic, star-chosen, shit.

They don't know we *chose* to be together, and the stars agreed.

Does that make it better?

Not really.

It just keeps the blame off Kieran and me. People are pissed, but they haven't protested.

Yet.

I have been respectful. I showed my face at Daisy's and Leon's funeral—Gods bless them both. I've kept my head down. Stayed out of trouble. Walked away from any fool who approached me because they felt the need to discuss my relationship with Kieran like it's their business—not because I'm scared of them, but if one of them says the wrong thing, Kieran is going to turn them into dust. And that will only make us look worse.

"This whole mating thing isn't going away easily, huh?" Lucas whispers beside me.

It's been a week since the news came out. We waited until after the funeral to announce it. It even came after the announcement of the second trial winner—Oliver, no less. The Council planned the whole thing, of course. Since the Fae love to dance, they threw another ball—because as you know, there need to be celebrations before and after every trial—and made the announcement there.

They stuffed me into a black and gold gown, the kind Aurora would wear, and planted me next to Kieran like some decorative puppet.

We needed to control the narrative.

To explain why I'd been pulled out of the final trial and make my status official—and get ahead of the whispers before they turned into riots.

Politics makes my head hurt.

The Council doesn't want the public to know about the channelling, especially with the rebels sniffing around the Court like blood hounds. If they find out hurting me means hurting Kieran, they'll stop at nothing to get their hands on me.

And that's why Gideon has been glued to my side like a shadow for the past two weeks.

It's either him or Virgil.

My very own pair of handsome bodyguards.

"You calling it 'mating' makes us sound like animals." I wince.

Although with the channelling, we've been fucking like—

Let's not go there.

"Sorry." Lucas laughs. "I'm not familiar with the term yet."

"You and me both, my friend." I scoff, sipping the bitter coffee slowly. I swear to the stars, once the Fae get used to the idea of me, my first mission as Kieran's—whatever title I get—will be introducing the Court to proper coffee.

Their food and wine might be heavenly, but a dying dog in the dessert would still say no to their coffee.

I mean, I still drink it, because shitty coffee is still better than no coffee at all.

"So," Lucas starts, settling down his own cup. We are at a café in town, one of the few places that serves something resembling drinkable coffee. Gideon's at the next table, eyes darting around like he thinks the old lady behind the counter is a disguised assassin. "How do you feel?"

I have been trying to figure that out for the past two weeks.

"Honestly, I don't know," I say, exhaling. "Kieran said I could visit my family, but it's risky with the channelling link, and it probably won't be anytime soon. I assume Noah told them where I am, but what will I say when I see them again? 'Hey, guess what? I'm alive, but I will spend the rest of my life at the Court?'"

"And that you have found them a son-in-law? Who's a Fae King? Has wings? And is immortal?" Lucas snorts. "I'm sure they'll take that exceptionally well."

"Right?" I flinch. "I don't know what's worse—them not knowing if I'm dead or alive, or them thinking I've completely lost my mind."

"Have you considered asking Kieran to wipe their memories of you?"

"Lucas." My eyes widen.

He shrugs. "What? That might be a kinder option."

I blink at him. "A month ago, you would have said that's cruel."

He sighs, lifting his cup for another slow sip. "A month ago, I was a completely different person. I didn't agree with him when Tessa died ... but now that I think about it, Kieran is probably right. It's better for my parents to forget than spend the rest of their lives wondering what the hell happened to me."

"But you could still win," I mutter, dropping my gaze to the cup, stirring it aimlessly. "You could still go home."

Even if it breaks me.

Although I'd rather him leave and be alone here than watch him die in the final trial.

"Funny ..." Lucas lets out a quiet, heartbreaking laugh. "Home is a strange word for me now. A lot has happened here in such a short time. Sometimes, I don't even know who I am anymore, Cass."

His words hit me hard.

I've been too caught up in my own darkness and this whirlwind romance that I let my only friend drift in the dark alone. Drown in it.

I didn't want anything to do with him in the beginning.

Now I'd do anything to keep him from breaking the way I once did.

I just hope it's not too late.

"I'm sorry I haven't been there for you, Lucas," I say softly, reaching for his hand. "You've always looked out for me. I should've done the same for you. And I'm really sorry that it's all on you to bring Declan back now—I wish I could do something."

It breaks my heart that I can't bring Declan back, that I have put it all on Lucas.

But it hurts me more to see Lucas suffer in silence.

Declan is gone—long gone.

I think... I think a part of me has made peace with that.

But Lucas—Lucas is still here.

"None of it is your fault," he whispers, squeezing my hand gently. "This place changes you. Even you ... you're not the same person you used to be." He smiles, but there's sadness behind it. "I'm just glad you found some happiness here."

For a minute, I think back to what the fake Lucas said to me in the mirrored maze—about how Lucas had a crush on me. And I still don't know if that's true. Maybe it was.

But it doesn't matter.

His friendship is genuine, even when I have been a stubborn bitch.

I'll forever be thankful for that.

"Thank you." I smile.

I hope he finds some happiness, too.

Somehow.

"But does this mean you'll be Queen of the Fallen?" Lucas asks, his sadness morphing into a crooked little grin. I nearly choke on my tasteless coffee.

"Oh, Gods." I wince again. "I doubt the Fae would ever let that happen."

"Yeah, but being mates means you're bound for life, right?" He tilts his head. "That basically guarantees marriage and all that."

"Trust me," I breathe, shaking my head. "No one is rushing into that."

Right now, we just want the chaos to die down. Let people make peace with the fact that this fragile little human is here to stay. Then maybe—*maybe*—we can start thinking about what's next.

"I thought you had an appointment with Aurora and Laia today—what was it? To talk about the image you represent as Kieran's mate?" he says in a mocking tone.

Aurora has been all over me lately, disapproving of every bloody choice I make on a daily basis like it's her favourite hobby. Saying everything I do reflects Kieran as the Court's leader. I'm honestly surprised she hasn't started picking out my underwear.

And now she wants to talk about my *wardrobe*, making changes to fit my status, apparently.

It's annoying.

She's doing this because of Kieran.

For Kieran.

And it's almost admiring that she's willing to do it, even though I'm pretty sure she's still head over heels in love with him.

I've said it before, and I will say it again.

The woman—sorry, the *female*—is a sociopath.

"Don't even get me started on that." I exhale. I would rather sip this shitty coffee all day than deal with Aurora.

But unfortunately, I can't.

Kieran doesn't give a damn about what I wear. His preference tends to lean towards a whole lot of shameless *nothing*. But it can't always be about what he—or I—want when it comes to politics ... as much as he believes it is.

I refuse to cause him any more trouble.

The Fae already have their eyes on me. Let's not give them another reason to hate my guts.

I return to the Court in the afternoon, after Lucas leaves to report to Atticus for his shift. Gideon is still following me like a lost puppy.

"Isn't there anything else that requires your attention as a High Commander?" I finally ask him.

"Yes." He shrugs. "But what else could be more important than protecting the future Queen of the Fallen?"

I get his point, but I flinch at the word. "I'm not a queen ... and Kieran and I aren't married."

That earns a grin from the silver-haired commander. "Yet, you're both wearing rings."

"Gideon," I breathe, trying hard not to flush and look like a total idiot. "As your future queen, kindly shut up."

He bursts out laughing. And all I can do is shake my head.

"But let's be honest here," I murmur. "You people are never going to see me as anything but Kieran's lucked-out human toy. Even if he takes the throne, I wouldn't be queen."

"Do you really believe Kieran would let that happen?" He arches a brow. "He wouldn't do shit unless it meant you were there by his side."

"It's nice of you to say that, but—"

"No buts, Cassandra," Gideon cuts in, his voice soft and gentle. "I accept you as our Queen—or whatever title Kieran ends up with—and those who don't will just have to deal with it."

I'm taken aback by how kind this male is. Kieran once told me that Gideon was his best friend, and now I understand why.

"Even so ... I wouldn't know the first thing about being a queen," I say quietly.

"Please." He scoffs. "You handled those two trials like they're nothing. Smashed every mirror in that maze without hesitation. Most people would have spent days trying to figure it out."

I chuckle. "I pay attention."

"Sometimes that's all your partner needs—someone who sees the things we might miss."

I can't help but smile at how genuine his words are, but before we can continue our conversation, Aurora and Laia appear, flanking a rack full of glittery gowns.

I swallow hard.

"Stars," Gideon mutters. "Are you trying to turn her into you?"

Aurora blinks at him. Her green eyes could cut him in half. "It's not my fault I'm the only one with taste around here."

Easy for her to say.

With that face and the hourglass figure, she could put on a rag and men would still throw themselves at her.

"I can't wear those and walk around the Court," I say, pointing at them. "And in case you haven't noticed, it's still autumn."

"Beauty is pain." She lifts her chin. "It could be a weapon, if you wear it well."

Of course it could. Only Aurora would live her life by a quote like that.

"Let's go. We have a lot to work on," she says, glancing down my body, no doubt making mental notes of every single flaw I didn't even know I had. "You can stay out here, Gideon. No males allowed."

"Wouldn't dream of it," he replies. "Kieran would shred me into pieces, then bring me back, just to slowly shred me again."

Aurora rolls her eyes like the mere mention of his name physically irritates her, then throws open my door and storms inside without so much as an invitation. Laia trails after her, awkwardly wheeling the rack.

"Let me help," Gideon offers, politely taking it from her and steering it in himself.

I catch the glimpse of Laia's pink cheeks as she drops her chin to hide a smile.

I raise an eyebrow behind them.

Oh, I do adore a secret love story between an apprentice and a loyal High Commander—so, please, let there be one.

He says goodbye and heads for the door—but not before giving Laia another irresistible smile as he pulls it shut behind him.

Okay, I'm invested.

"Where are all your clothes?" Aurora's displeased voice snaps me out of my romantic side quest.

"At Kieran's house." I shrug. He finally had people move my things in the other day. "You're welcome to look through the wardrobe."

"Ugh, never mind. I was thinking of throwing them away anyway."

"Then why'd you ask?" I throw both hands up.

She's unbelievable.

And she doesn't even bother to acknowledge me—just plucks a sequined maroon gown from the rack and shoves it into my arms. "Try this on."

"And what occasion would I be wearing this for?"

Aurora's expression doesn't change when she says, "Tuesdays."

"Right," I murmur, blinking at her. "Perfect for a knife-throwing session or a stroll through the fish market."

"Oh, dear," Laia mutters, glancing between me and her boss like she's about to witness two massive storms colliding. "Why don't I help you with that, Cassandra?"

"Yeah, sounds good." Before this turns into a cat fight.

"Oh, please. Can't you dress by yourself now you're Kieran's mate?"

Fine, if a cat fight is what she wants ...

"Well, who knows?" I tilt my head, blinking sweetly. "I figured as the future Queen of the Court I might get used to having a lady-in-waiting. Don't you think?"

Laia swallows an invisible lump. Aurora's jaw tightens, but she smooths a hand down her perfectly tailored dress like I didn't just slap her on the face with those brutal words.

I am getting everything she wanted.

I know she hates that.

But I didn't start this fight.

"That's a lot of big talk coming from you," she says quietly, her green eyes sharp with something bitter. "Especially from someone Kieran only took an interest in to spite his family. Tell me, Cassandra, are you sure this chosen mate thing was really chosen?"

"I beg your pardon?"

What the hell did she just say?

One confused look from me gives Aurora an edge. A slow, gleaming smile spreads across her beautiful face. She arches a brow, full of silent triumph.

"He still hasn't told you, has he?"

"Told me what?"

Now she's crossing her arms, fingers drumming against her bicep like she's holding the winning hand.

She turns to Laia.

"Leave us, please."

Poor, sweet Laia nearly sprints out of the room as fast as my heartbeat. As soon as the door shuts, Aurora drops into the armchair, legs crossed, completely at ease.

"You must be really naïve to believe that Kieran fell stupidly in love with you on night one." She scoffs, her grin deepening. My fingers slowly curl into fists. "Sure, maybe he did fall for you after, but why did you think he picked you? Why do you think he went to get you himself?"

"I don't want to play a guessing game," I grit out. "So just say it."

Aurora's eyes shimmer with cruel amusement. "You were bound to his brother at birth, Cassandra ... the one who hasn't fallen. The golden prince who can do no wrong—who could cause a war and still be cradled like a miracle child by the stars."

I—what?

His what, now?

"Since you're so desperate to become Queen, you'll find out eventually ... but honestly, what do you think we do all of this for, huh?" she asks, gesturing broadly like she's addressing the whole Court. "These trials. The feast. The jobs. The balls. All these temptations—they're not just here to save the Fallen. They're here to prove that we shouldn't be punished for you."

My blood runs cold.

"This whole damn Court was designed to expose your kind. To show the stars that humans are ruled by greed and lust. That every human who steps foot here can be corrupted. So why the hell should we suffer for *your* sins?" she adds, her voice bitter and hands shaking with fury. "We're at war, Cassandra. A war with the very Court we fell from." She leans forward, her voice dropping. "And Kieran? He's determined to win. To show them just how blinded humans are. That's why he took interest in you. Not because you're special, but because if you fall ... his brother falls with you." She pauses, her next words laced with poison. "You stupid, stupid human."

I don't—

Kieran's brother? Bound to me?

This can't be right.

Has all this ... has everything been a lie?

But—

Kieran loves me.

He said he wanted forever.

Is it all just to spite his brother?

To prove a point?

Am I just a pawn? A weapon to stab his brother in the back with?

"Oh dear, look at you," Aurora murmurs, shaking her head, lips curling into a smile. "That look is priceless. It hurts, doesn't it? But what can I say ... you fell in love with the devil. What did you expect?"

My brain can't process any of it.

It refuses to comprehend.

I can't move.

I can't breathe.

My whole body is frozen, suspended in webs of lies I never saw coming.

And then—

The door slams open. It crashes into the wall with a force that rattles the floor.

Kieran stands in the doorway, his jaw clenched, fury burning in those storm-lit eyes.

His voice is a cold, lethal whisper as he turns to Aurora.

"Get the fuck out before I kill you."

Chapter 33

Aurora snorts, then snaps her fingers—and vanishes into thin air.

I blink at Kieran.

Once.

Twice.

His eyes soften and his posture shifts as he walks closer, but he freezes as I let my tears run free.

Again.

And again.

"Oh, no, no—baby, please," he breathes, pain flickering in his face like it physically hurts him to see me like this. "Cassandra, please ... it's not what you think."

"Is it not?" I shout. "Did you not lie to me, Kieran? Am I not bound to your brother? Was I not just a piece in your perfect little plan?"

Kieran chokes. He can't even say it.

And that tells me everything I need to know.

"For fuck's sake; do you even love me?!"

"How can you ask that?!" he blurts. "Of course I love you! I love you so much I can't fucking breathe!"

"Then why didn't you tell me?!"

Kieran opens his mouth—then closes it again. He doesn't step any closer. Instead, he just raises both hands up, drawing in a shaky breath like he's begging me to take a step back with him. I've seen sadness in those eyes, back in the days leading up to the second trial, when we both nearly shattered at the thought of losing one another.

But I've never seen fear in them ... not like this.

"You can feel me, love," he whispers. "You can feel how I feel ... you know I'm not lying to you."

I close my eyes for a moment. And somewhere down bond we share, I can feel the overwhelming despair, the choked panic curling around every inch of him. His heart breaks at the sight of me crying, yelling at him.

And he's scared—terrified—of losing me.

But he can feel it, too.

My sadness. My shock. The betrayal lodged in my chest.

"Why?" I open my eyes, my voice barely above a whisper. "You could have told me."

"I was planning on it," he admits, shame eating him up from the inside—I feel that, too. "I swear I was going to. But I never meant for any of this to happen. I knew you wanted to use me, and I was no better. I played along with it, thinking if I dragged you down with me, my brother would fall, too." He pauses, eyes darting to the floor like he can't bear to face me. "But the more I spent time with you, the harder I fell for you. You smile, and I get nervous. You tease, and I want to drop to my damn knees for you. You kick my ass, and all I can think of is how badly I want to marry you for it. I'm completely insane, love. It's irrational. It's reckless. And it's fucking fantastic."

Through the bond, I can feel it all—every flicker of emotion in his heart.

The peak of his joy.

The pit of his ache.

And I want so badly to hate him for what he did.

Gods.

But I can't

It's impossible.

So fucking impossible.

"I don't want to feel your emotions anymore." I groan, dragging my hands through my hair. "It's not fair! I can't stay angry at you when you're like this!" I shout, my voice cracking into a half-laugh, half sob. "I want to fight! You deserve to sleep in the doghouse tonight, but thanks to this stupid mating bond, I can't even be mad at you!"

Kieran meets my eyes again, a faint smile ghosting across his mouth. "I'll sleep in the doghouse, if that's what you want. You can punish me however you like, as long as you like it. Just ... know that I'm sorry. And when you're ready, I'll tell you everything. No more secrets."

I stare at him, arms crossed.

Gods, I want to smack him and kiss him at the same time.

And now he's grinning, because he knows exactly what just crossed my mind.

Grinning because he's winning.

"The fitting punishment for you is no sex until further notice." I snort.

Kieran gasps, clutching his chest like I just staked him in the heart. "Come on, even you can't stand that."

"Maybe not." I smirk, lifting a brow. "And maybe I'll miss it too, especially with you in bed next to me every damn night." I lean in slightly, voice dropping. “And maybe—just *maybe*—in the middle of the night, I will slip my hand down there ... and you’ll watch me. Hear me moan your name. Feel every tug of the bond as I chase that climax ... and when I finally shatter, you’ll still be lying there. Hard. And helpless. Because you don’t get to touch me after the shit you pulled.”

Immediately, I feel it—the arousal flaring through the bond like wildfire, burning hot and fast as the image sears into his mind.

It’s all Kieran can do before he lets out a low, guttural growl—and drops to his knees.

“You know you’re my mate and I love you forever,” he rasps, head tilted back, hunger and desperation burning bright in those storm-lit eyes. “And that was ... incredibly hot—but also very not funny.”

“Good.” I snort, stepping closer to him, but not close enough for him to touch me. “You deserve to suffer for what you did. And now, I’m going to go home, and you’re going to watch me walk away. Because I’m still mad, and you still have to pay.”

Kieran exhales dramatically. “How are you going to get home?”

“Gideon will take me,” I say. “You’re going to sit there, think about you did, and what you want to do to me. Do not show your face for a few hours.” I lift my chin, trying hard not to smile, even though I can’t wait to drag him into bed with me. “Then you’ll come home. You’ll cook. You’ll run me a bath. And you’ll sleep in the guest bedroom.”

“Cassandra ...” He groans, his voice hoarse.

Watching Kieran begs is so ... fucking hot.

But if we’ve got forever together, he needs to learn.

“Understood?” I ask.

He sighs, long and frustrated, but his eyes soften as he says. “Yes, my queen.”

I grin and slowly making my way out of the room, knowing damn well those golden and deep-blue eyes are burning into my back.

Gideon blinks at me outside the door.

Needless to say, he’s heard everything.

He shakes his head, offering me a hand.

“And you say you’re no queen,” he mutters, amused. “Not even Aurora can serve him his ass on a plate like that.”

Then we vanish home to the mountains, a victory smile on my face.

Chapter 34

It's been a few days since Aurora officially made it to the top of my enemy list with a red line underneath her name.

Kieran demanded that she apologise to me.

Aurora, of course, claimed it was his own fault for not telling me in the first place—said that her, dropping the bomb was an act of kindness.

To be fair, she did have a point.

But let's not pretend she did it out of the kindness in her icy heart.

I continue to work with Laia regarding the changes in my wardrobe. Aurora hasn't shown her face since—which has been great.

Until today, when all of us are attending a Council meeting.

She sits on one end of the table, looking smug and unbothered. Kieran and I sit on the other.

And all I can think about is setting fire to the obnoxious fur wrapped around her throat.

"We have found a way to sever your channelling link." Daphne starts with the best news I've heard in two weeks. Kieran and I glance at each other.

"And?" my mate asks.

"Would you like the good news or bad news first?"

Kieran narrows his eyes at her.

She shifts in her seat, clearing her throat. "Good news is ... it's just a potion."

"And?" he repeats, quieter this time.

I'd be shitting myself if he weren't the love of my life and used that cold, quiet tone with me. The other members of the Council exchange tense glances in silence.

"It might ... affect your mating bond."

The entire room is still. Nobody dares to breathe.

Kieran doesn't even blink. "No."

"Oh, don't be so childish." Aurora scoffs, arms crossing as she leans back like she's lost interest and can't wait for this to end. "She said it *might*, and if it *does* affect the bond, it's not like you both can't be together—or are you scared that without the bond, the magic will wear off?"

"I don't remember asking your opinion." Kieran turns to her, his eyes like blades. "Your job is to find a solution, not comment on my relationship."

Aurora's face flushes a sharp shade of red, but she clamps her mouth shut.

I swear I see pain flicker in those green eyes, but it disappears quicker than a heartbeat.

"I think you should at least consider it," Atticus says, cautiously. "You don't have to take it right now, but ... at least it's something."

Of course, he's going to side with his sister.

It must be complicated, working for Kieran while watching your sister be humiliated in front of the entire council.

"The answer is no," Kieran says without an ounce of hesitation. "It's not an option."

"Shouldn't Cassandra get a vote in this?" Skylar proposes—or perhaps just woke up this morning craving death.

But Kieran doesn't reply, just turns to me and waits quietly.

Oh, Gods.

I'm not sure whether to be grateful that he respects me enough to speak for myself, or slide under the table to hide from the pressure of everyone's eyes on me.

But if I want a place in this Court ... if I want them to respect me as Kieran's partner, I need to learn to find my own voice.

"I don't want anything to affect our mating bond," I say, my voice firm, my head held high. "But ... I suppose we can keep that as the very last resort, in case of emergency." Like I get taken by the rebellion, or something.

I sure hope not, but if something happens to me, there's no reason the entire Court should burn with me.

A proud smile paints across Kieran's mouth as he cocks his head towards me. "What she said."

No one else objects.

I might need to ask Kieran not to be so quick to play the my-mate-is-always-right card. I mean, I'm still new here. The last thing I need is for the entire Council to turn on me because their King blindly agrees with everything I say.

I'm not Queen—yet.

But I very well might never be, if I don't play these political games right.

Do I care if I get a fancy title? No.

I only care about how my actions reflect Kieran.

"In that case, I would like to bring up the official marriage oath," Felix says, steering the conversation elsewhere. "Have you thought about having a ceremony?"

And now I have to shift in my seat, trying not to choke on the very air I'm breathing.

"Mother of the stars." Kieran runs a hand through his hair. "Would it kill you not to record every bloody thing the moment it happens?"

The Oath Recorder just shrugs. "I'm only doing my job."

"Well, thank you for proposing to my mate before I did," Kieran drawls, dragging his gaze to me. I can feel heat flush my face.

Oh, Gods.

It's getting too real.

I entered the trials to bring back a dead boyfriend, quietly hoping to die in the process—and now I am bound to a Fae King for life, and we're talking about our wedding.

"What's the rush?" I ask quietly. "The final trial hasn't even started yet."

"Precisely why we should have it soon," Felix mutters. "I figured you might want your friend Lucas to be there."

Implication hangs in the air—the possibility that my one and only friend in this Court might not make it.

A wedding with no family, no friends.

A wedding amongst strangers.

For a moment, I can't utter a word. I am still absolutely over the moon that this mating bond happened—me and Kieran, bound by something more than just fate. But the truth is ... I'm about to begin a whole new chapter of my life with nothing to hold on to but him.

I didn't choose this.

I only chose Kieran.

And I have accepted what choosing Kieran means, but with this channelling link, I can't go home.

If we have the ceremony now, I won't get to show my mum the wedding dress. My dad won't give me away. Noah won't get a chance to mock me for finally looking like a proper girl in a gown.

There will be no bridesmaids. No party.

Just ... a wedding, and a forever.

Suddenly, I realise how difficult this will be.

I forget we're still tethered by the bond until Kieran reaches for my hand, his finger lacing mine as every bit of my grief crashes into him, too.

"There won't be any ceremony for now," he says to Felix. "You already recorded the bond. That's enough."

I squeeze his hand back, a silent thank you.

I'm far from ready for this conversation. I need some sort of stability—and maybe a new role. Something else to anchor me. Something that gives me purpose beyond just being Kieran's wife.

The meeting ends not long after that. Daphne is tasked to find another way to fix the mess that is our channelling link. Aurora slips out without saying a word. The others linger, casually chatting as they walk out the room.

Kieran turns to me. "I want to show you something."

"What is it?" I ask.

He offers me a hand—same as the first day. Same as every day since.

I take it without hesitation.

And in the blink of an eye, we vanish back to the mountains—to the little village tucked at its base, lined with small shops and cafés—Asterhollow. My most favourite place to wander lately. Cold wind brushes my face as I take in the familiar cobbled street.

"Are we going shopping?"

"I promised you no more secrets," he says, nodding his head towards one of the shops ahead. "If you're ready, I'll tell you more about this place."

I tilt my head. "Why? Aren't they just shops and restaurants?"

"They are," he murmurs, drawing a sharp breath. "But the Fae who work here … they were once humans."

I freeze, the autumn breeze suddenly turning ice cold in my lungs.

"You know what the trials were built for," he says, his voice low. "At the end of each one, the winner is given a choice: a wish, or a life here as Fae." He pauses, and I feel blood drain from my face. "It's their last test. One designed to prove just how corruptible your kind can be." His eyes meet mine. "And almost every single one of them chose to become a Fae."

Holy shit.

It takes me a minute to process that, but Kieran waits patiently.

When I finally speak, my voice comes out like a whisper.

"Are you telling me … that Lucas, Jordan, or Oliver will also have to pick?"

"Yes." Kieran exhales. "I know how this must look to you … but if you give me a chance, I will show you everything."

I swallow.

We are so different, Kieran and I.

And hatred runs deep in the foundation of this Court that I might one day rule beside him.

We're going to fight.

There will be countless things we disagree on in the forever we now share.

It will break me to watch other humans participate in these twisted mind games the next time an eclipse paints the sky.

Yet, he loves me.

Me.

The very thing his entire Court despises.

The very reason he fell.

He gave those who turn Fae jobs, and possibly homes, when he could have just tossed them on the street and let them fend for themselves.

There is more to this, I realise. So much more.

This Fae King is so complex. So relentless. So much.

And somehow, all mine.

I am in.

I am all in.

With a steady voice, I say, "Show me."

Chapter 35

"This is James." Kieran introduces me to the owner of the lovely café we always seem to end up at, Cassiopeia. I have seen him many times, but never once did it cross my mind that this male was once a man. "He's been living here for over eighty years."

Eighty?

"Milady," James says, bowing his head with respect.

"Please," I quickly say. "I'm not a lady."

He furrows his brows. "But you are Lord Kieran's mate."

"I'm not a lord." Kieran exhales. "But yes, she's my mate."

Lord. Prince. King. It's fascinating how people keep calling him these titles, even when he insists on just being "Kieran."

"Forgive me. I thought—"

"It's fine, James," I cut in softly. There's no need for formality here. "You've been here for eighty years?"

"Yes." He nods politely. "In human years, it would be much less, but I don't think anyone in my past life remembers me now."

Aurora said a month here is only four or five days in the human world. That means ...

"It's been thirteen human years," Kieran says, probably sensing me struggling to do mad maths in my head.

Wow.

I could be pregnant, give birth, raise a whole baby—and barely a year would pass for my family.

Think of how awkward the conversation would go, if I visited my parents with a toddler.

I wonder if his family is still looking for him. Some parents never stop searching for a missing child, even decades later. Loved ones rarely let go ... especially when there's no closure.

"Why?" I clear my throat, keeping my tone neutral. I'm merely trying to understand, not to judge anyone. "Why did you stay?"

"Honestly? I was tired of how fragile I was as a human," he says, as if it wasn't even a big, life-changing decision. Or perhaps it's just been too long ago that he doesn't fully remember what the weight felt like. "As a Fae, wounds heal faster. I'm much stronger. Rarely ever get sick. I'm going to live forever—and I have magic."

And ... I can see why that would be tempting.

"Forgive me if this sounds like an interview. You don't have to answer if you don't feel comfortable," I say quietly. "But ... what about your family?"

Kieran glances at me, before leaning in to whisper, "I'll give you both a minute."

He steps outside without waiting for a response. And I know why he's doing it—James won't feel entirely at ease answering personal questions with the King of the Fallen hovering in the corner.

"I don't have anyone," James replies at last. He looks no older than forty, even though he's been here for eighty Fae years. I wonder if he stopped aging the moment he was turned. "All I had was debt. I gambled everything away. My wife left. My son wanted nothing to do with me. I came here to wish for a fortune to pay it all off—but I knew, deep down, I'd have gone back to gambling. I'd probably end up dead in a gutter, and no one would care."

Every soul selected for the trials is broken in one way or another.

James was exactly the kind of corrupted human the Court needed to parade before the stars.

"And you realise what this is all for, right?" I ask carefully.

"Yes." He nods. His expression doesn't change. "When you live here long enough, you start to understand Kieran's ambitions. The reasons behind the things he does." He pauses, glancing towards the glass window, where my mate waits outside. "He doesn't actually want to hurt humans, you know. If he can help it, he won't. His only goal is to prove that his kind—our kind—shouldn't be punished for the crimes their humans commit. That it's okay to be flawed. He doesn't even want to go back to the other Court. He just ... doesn't want any more of his people to fall."

For a beat, I don't know what to say.

On one hand, I don't agree with how things are done in this Court.

On the other hand, I understand why, and I'm struggling to wrap my head around how hard all of this is for Kieran.

His family is cruel—too cruel. They cursed him, trapped him here, all because he dared to build a home for the Fallen. So, Kieran retaliates the only way he knows how—by showing them their precious little humans can be just as monstrous.

And in a meantime, there are still Fae—twisted, bitter ones—who believe Kieran should kill every human to ever step foot inside this Court.

Now he's here, caught in the middle, trying to save them both.

"Are you ..." I hesitate, then finally say it. "Are you happy here?"

The question earns a gentle smile. "I have a home, own a business, and married the love of my life."

I can't help but smile with him.

"Kieran made his point, and then he gave us new lives," he murmurs. "Of course, it's unfortunate when there're deaths in the competitions. But I do believe that part was a compromise. Something the Council insisted on to keep the peace. To satisfy those who still demand blood. That's why they hold funerals. It's their way of honouring the price, while keeping the machine running."

It's a huge statement—those words from him.

I feel them like a slap on my face, the numbness expanding in lazy waves so slowly they seep through every part of me until I'm soaked with them.

I haven't heard everything.

But I have heard enough.

I thank James and wish him a good day before stepping outside. Kieran turns to meet my eyes—and it's all I can do before I throw my arms around him, holding him like I'm afraid he might disappear any second.

"Oh," he whispers. "Does this mean I can sleep in the bedroom again?"

"It means I love you," I breathe, murmuring against his chest. "And yes ... you can move back to the bedroom—if you promise to stop carrying everything on your own. I am your mate. From now on, we share the weight. Together."

Kieran exhales, stroking my hair gently, his touch so delicate—so out of this world. "It's not something you need to bear, Little Star."

"But I will." I pull away just enough to look into those eyes. "I'm your partner, Kieran. We're in this together. You wanted forever—this is how we do it."

The storm-lit eyes soften, like fire turning to embers—still fierce, but warm and steady. He lifts a hand to my face, fingers gently brushing my skin. A quiet sigh escapes him.

"I don't know where you came from, but I thank the stars for you every single night," he mutters, his voice hoarse. "You are ... incredible in every way. And it genuinely blows me away that you chose me."

"Says the one who built an entire Court to save thousands," I say softly. "It's your Court. And no, I don't agree with everything, but we'll work on it together, over time."

He smiles faintly, that familiar glint returning to his eyes. "So ... starting with James was the right call, huh?"

I roll my eyes. "Unless you bribed him to say nice things about you."

"Swear to the stars, I didn't. What'd he say, anyway?"

"He said"—I pause, a sweet smile tugging at my lips—"you gave him a new life."

Kieran arches a brow. "Well, guess we're his regulars now."

"I suppose so." I laugh.

"Come," he says, taking my hand in his. "Let's introduce you to the others."

And by others, Kieran means the rest of the humans who chose to stay—the ones who turned Fae. The whole village is full of them. They speak easily with me, sharing stories of their trials, the lives they left behind, and the magic they now hold. Most of their powers are simple—healing, warmth, speed.

One of them asks when I plan to turn Fae.

I have no answer for that.

They joke that I should do it before I turn thirty—to preserve the beauty, they say.

All I can do is laugh.

It's easy for them. Their human lives are long gone. But mine? I haven't fully come to terms with my new responsibilities as Kieran's mate yet. My life has flipped upside down, again.

For now, I want to take one thing at a time.

"Will I be able to pick what kind of magic I want, if I turn Fae?" I ask as we settle onto the balcony back home, tea in hand. Kieran uses his power to warm the seat again.

"That'd be nice, wouldn't it?" He laughs, lifting his own cup. "But no, it doesn't work like that. The stars choose for you."

"Interesting." I blink. "What about wings?"

"Those, too."

"Ugh. So if I don't like them, I'm stuck with weird wings for the rest of my life?"

"Some Fae don't even have wings," Kieran drawls, slowly sipping his tea. "And you can magic them away. You don't have to wear them all the time."

"But you have them out most of the time."

"Yes, because I'm sexy beyond resistible."

I narrow my eyes at him. Should have known he was going to say something like that.

Kieran grins. "Does that mean you want to turn Fae eventually?"

"Not any time soon," I murmur. Even the thought makes my stomach twist. "But I don't want to be a cranky old woman when you're still thirty, hot, and sexy."

He throws his head back to laugh this time, loud and unfiltered. "I'll still find you adorable, trust me. Though the hardest part would be watching you grow old and ..."

He can't even say it.

But I feel it, hot and heavy in my chest.

"Come on, Kieran," I say, smirking now, trying to lighten up the mood. "You won't be attracted to a fifty-year-old me the way you are now. And sex with an older lady could be ... challenging. Back pain and all that."

He looks at me like he's imagining growing old with me—an easy and comforting thought.

An impossible one for him.

"I'll turn Fae eventually," I whisper, leaning closer. "Can't leave you to mourn me for eternity now, can I?"

It's the best solution for us—the only right one.

But one I'm not ready for just yet.

Joy flickers in his eyes. Kieran reaches for my hand, then lifts it to his lips. "I'm not going to ask that of you. You can take all the time you want. I'll wait—even if you want to do it when you're forty."

"You heard what the others said. I have to do it when I'm still young enough." I laugh. "So I look pretty forever."

"You're already pretty forever."

Who would have thought the brooding King of the Fallen turns into a soft-hearted, I-love-you-and-I'll-give-you-the-moon kind of partner behind closed doors?

"You know, we never celebrated our mating bond," I say, tilting my head, the biggest smile on my face. If he were human, this would basically be like an engagement party. "Maybe we should go out. Have a nice meal tonight."

"If you promise I get to take off whatever fancy dress you slip into the moment we're home." His smirk deepens. "It's been too long."

"Gods, it's only been a few days."

"That's a few days too long."

I sigh, shaking my head, but can't stop my stupid smile.

We finish our teas, and I start trying on the hundred dresses and gowns Aurora approved and had Laia deliver—and according to the King of the Fallen, they all look shit on me. Kieran is making me change again and again just to catch a glimpse of me naked like he hasn't already seen every inch of me.

I finally have to kick him out of the room.

Peace, at last.

I slip into a black sequined gown with long sleeves. It matches my ring and hugs my curves like it was made to demand attention—sexy but still elegant. Just the right amount of both.

I look at my reflection in the mirror, my face flushed as I realise Kieran and I have only been to one date, when we grabbed lunch that time after ... well, making up from the five days he avoided me. But tonight will be something special, a celebration. Sure, we live together and are way past that, but something about going out with him, just the two of us, like a normal couple, makes my stomach twist with giddy nerves.

And now that all my things are here, I can finally dress properly.

I put on some jewellery, paint my lips, and finish with my favourite perfume.

I don't know what the Fae put in it, but I honestly can't get enough.

Neither can Kieran.

"You look ..." He pauses, already pulling me into his arms the second I step out of the room. "Gods, what did I do to deserve you?"

"You're too much." I laugh but kiss him anyway. It's always impossible not to with Kieran—my red lips be damned. I'm sure Kieran can sort out the smudge with a flick of his magic.

We haven't even left the house, but his hands are already wandering down my body—one sliding down my back, the other at the nape of my neck. Gods, I love how Kieran touches me, craving it like I need it just to stay sane.

It was hell sleeping alone in that massive bed. We've barely touched until now, and I'm realising just how much I've missed it. I'm starved for it.

"Do you think maybe we could"—he breathes, his lips grazing down my neck, biting it, voice rough with need—"leave a little bit later?"

"Hm," I purr. "Tempting."

But before he can persuade me any further—

Kieran jerks back. Stiffens. Horror spreads across his face.

Then, he starts coughing, choking. Violent and desperate.

I freeze.

A few seconds later—it hits me, too.

The burning sensation in my throat, the air leaving my lungs. All of a sudden, I'm struggling to breathe. Panic rips through me.

Within moments, we're both on the floor, gasping, choking, Kieran crawling towards me with wide, terrified eyes.

My head spins. My vision fractures.

I can't breathe.

We can't breathe.

What is happening?
What is happening to us?

Chapter 36

Cold.

It's so cold.

Sensations start to creep back to me, pricking every bit of my skin as the numbness leaves my body in slow, painful waves. My head feels heavy as stone. My vision is blurry.

I blink, again and again, until the darkness turns into light, burning low but disorientating.

The cold seeps in from the damp, hard floor beneath me. My breath comes shallow, my teeth clattering. Icy water drips from the ceiling above—no, not ceiling—stone.

Some sort of ... cave.

Where am I?

Is this a dream?

It takes me a long, aching moment to realise that what I'm seeing is real. Every fibre of my body protests as I push myself up, my heart pounding in fear and confusion. I look around ... and realise that I am in a holding cell built into the rock, thick, rusty bars sealing me in.

What—

How did I—

For a breath, I'm convinced the rebellion has me. That they've dragged me here. I try to piece my last memories together—I was in the village, talking to James and the others. Then Kieran and I went home. We got dressed. We were about to go out, and—

Mother of the stars.

Kieran.

Everything slams back into me in an instant. I remember now. The kiss. The heat of his hand. And then choking. Gasping. Crawling towards each other—

I stop breathing.

Oh, Gods—Kieran.

"Hello!" My hands slam against the bars, my voice raw and urgent as I scream at the top of my lungs, hoping to catch someone's attention—anyone who might be able to tell me what the hell happened to Kieran. To us. "Please, can anyone hear me?"

I don't know why I'm here. And I don't care.

The image of Kieran's face—straining for air, eyes wide with fear—burns into me, tearing every breath from my lungs.

He's not here.

He's hurt.

And I don't know where he is.

Gods... oh, gods.

Please.

Please.

I scream until my throat aches, but the cell stays silent. It's too damn dark. Too cold. My black sequined gown is now damp with dirt, clinging uncomfortably to my skin. Autumn feels like winter in this cell, ice clawing its way to my slow-beating heart.

Something happened.

We were hurt.

Wait—

But I'm not.

I'm not anymore.

That means Kieran is not hurt.

Relief crashes over me, but I don't stop shouting. I can't, not until I know what the fuck is going on. Not until I see for myself that Kieran is alive and well.

But nobody comes.

No one at all.

My knees buckle, my heart in shambles. My fear a monster clinging to my shadow.

No one comes.

I wait and I wait, alone in the dark with nothing but a flickering light and the cold to accompany me.

Like a reaper waiting patiently for my heart to slow until it stops.

And still, no one comes.

Warm.

It's too warm.

This is not just a holding cell, I realise.

It's a torture chamber.

Just when my heart is slow enough for sleep to take me, when my body begins to surrender to the cold, the air swells with heat—enough to drag me back. To keep me breathing.

And then, just when I start to feel almost comfortable ... it vanishes.

The chill seeps in again, slower this time.

No.

This can't be happening.

Kieran will feel all of this too.

I rest my aching body against the wall of the cave, trying to focus my mind somewhere else, but it's no use. Each shiver, each gasp will cut through the bond like a blade.

I'm hurting Kieran, and I can't stop it.

Please.

For what feels like forever, I just sit there, too cold to move, too broken to speak, enduring the hell this cave forces on me.

It breaks me, then pieces me back together.

Again.

And again.

A part of me begs for the final breath—to end this agony.

But I can't.

If I die, Kieran dies with me.

So I breathe, even though it hurts.

I don't know how long has passed, but then I finally hear it—

Footsteps.

It takes everything in my power to force my eyes open. The world swims at first, fractured and all blurred, until the shape resolves—tall, winged, framed by the bar.

Atticus.

"Oh gods ... Atticus," I rasp, my voice shredded raw. My throat feels like sandpaper, my lips cracked. I haven't had a single drop of water in forever. I try to push myself up, but I can't.

He can help.

He can get me out of here.

But—

Why hasn't he moved?

Where's the urgency?

Why—why is he looking at me like that?

"Atticus ... what's going on?" I murmur, panic rising. "Where is Kieran?"

"Where is Kieran?" he repeats, stepping closer, his face half shadowed in the dimmed lit light. "Are you kidding me right now?"

"What—"

"Why, Cassandra?" he snaps. "Are you trying to check if your plan worked? If he actually died?"

I freeze. It's like the air in the entire cell is sucked out.

My ... plan?

"Atticus, what are you—"

"Thanks to you, he's now lying in bed, barely alive." His mouth curls in a cruel scoff. "Got to hand it to you. Iron-laced perfume? Clever. I genuinely didn't see that coming. You wore your little mate act so well ... but they don't call it a rat if you see it coming, do they?"

Oh, Gods.

He thinks I did this.

Is that why I'm in this hell hole?

My perfume was laced with iron?

"I don't know what you're implying," I manage slowly, muscles screaming as I drag myself closer to the bars, "but I didn't do this. I don't know anything about the perfume ... and why would I poison him when I can feel his pain through the bond?" I choke. "Please ... take me to Kieran."

"No," he spits. Not even a second of hesitation. "The link is severed. We made sure of it."

"What?" The sound tears out of me. "No, no, Atticus, our mating bond—"

"You poisoned him. What the fuck do you care if it's still there?"

"But I didn't!" I shout, fear creeping in, taking over every bit of my body. My hand grips the bar so hard its bites into my skin. "I swear to the stars, I didn't do this! You've got the wrong person!"

But he just stands there, not even blinking.

The cell is icy, but it's nothing compared to the look in Atticus's eyes—sharp, glacial, utterly unforgiving. I have never seen him like this ... and I doubt those who have ever lived to tell the tale.

"I trusted you," he murmurs. "I asked you to keep an eye on Jordan and Florence ... and then you went and did this?"

"For fuck's sake, I didn't do it!" I yell. "You can't just keep me in here! You don't even have proof! What if someone is trying to frame me?"

He shakes his head like he's already made up his stupid mind and nothing is going to change it.

"Actually, you're wrong," he says, and for all the handsomeness he possesses, his smile has never been so ugly. "Because Kieran's out, I am—by law—acting High Lord of this Court." He steps closer, shadow falling across me. "So yes, Cassandra—I can keep you in here."

What is going on right now?

This has to a joke.

There has to be some sort of mistake.

Where is everyone else?

Gideon? Skylar? Virgil?

Even Lucas?

Did they all just swallow this lie without a second thought?

"I want to speak to Gideon," I demand. He's been glued to me for weeks. He knows there's no chance I could have done this.

"You're not in the position to request anything here."

"I am your King's mate," I grind out.

Atticus leans in, a wicked smile on his face. "There is no King in this Court. However, there is a High Lord—and right now, that's me."

I am lost for words.

I have never known Atticus to be so ruthless, so—irrational.

I don't understand.

What the fuck is wrong with him?

Then it clicks.

How he's acting High Lord, how no one has been in here, how I have had no chance to speak, to defend myself.

Oh Gods.

The ugly truth hits me like a heavy blow to the skull.

"It's you," I snarl, rage flooding my veins like wildfire. "You fucking did this." I spit the words like venom. "You are the rat!"

His eyes flicker. A flash of lightning in the dark.

And I know. I just know. It's him.

"That's a bold accusation," he says casually, arms crossing. "You should be careful, Miss Thorne. I could have your head, you know."

"Kieran would never let it happen!"

"Kieran isn't here, is he?" He arches a brow, his green eyes too delighted for someone whose King lies on death's doorstep. "Who knows if he'll ever regain consciousness?"

I grip the bars until I feel my skin split. Fear bleeds into fury.

"I'm going to kill you," I swear, then again, louder. "When I get out of here, I'm going to fucking kill you."

"*When* you get out of here?" Atticus scoffs. "That's rather ambitious."

"So is treason," I snap. "I don't know what your angle is, but this Court will never be yours."

"Oh, Cassandra ... you really are naïve, aren't you?"

I don't reply, just stare at that face, wishing I could smack the smugness right off it.

Kieran trusted him.

We all trusted him.

"The Court is already mine."

Chapter 37

I don't know what day it is.

In fact, I don't know if it's day or night.

All I've had to eat are slices of bread hard enough to knock someone in the head. A guard brought them to me, along with some water and a bucket for me to use—another cruel form of humiliation. The guard left without looking at me or saying a word, even though I was practically on my knees, begging.

I drift between nightmare and torture—the cold slows my heart enough for me to sleep, then the warmth wakes me up and sends me straight to hell.

I haven't gotten a clue how much time has passed when Virgil pays me a visit.

His face is tight, jaw clenched. I can see conflict in those eyes as he steps closer to the bars.

The man commands a non-Fae army.

I know why he's here.

"Atticus," I murmur, voice barely there, "sent you to torture me, didn't he?"

He lets out a quiet breath, his face grim, as he glances up like the sight of me physically pains him.

"I don't want to do this, Cassandra," he whispers.

"Then don't."

"He's the High Lord now."

"*Acting* High Lord," I correct. "But so what? Is this how it's going to be? Kieran is down, and you're helping him kill his mate? Where is your loyalty, Virgil? Kieran's going to wipe you off the earth when he recovers—you know that."

He doesn't reply, just looks at me. His eyes darken at the mention of Kieran's name, and my heart drops.

"He's still alive," I ask slowly. "isn't he?"

"Yes, he is," Virgil says, exhaling. "But I don't know, Cassandra. We're watching him closely, but he seems ... worse every day."

"Then something is wrong!" I snap. "Who's watching him? You can't trust Atticus, do you hear me? Get him away from Kieran!"

"I can't." He groans, low and frustrated. "You don't know what's going on out there. With Kieran down, the rebels took the opportunity to riot, spreading propaganda that you tried to kill your own mate, and Kieran was soft and stupid enough to let it happen. We had to move the rest of the contestants."

My blood roars in my ears.

This whole time I've been locked up in this frozen hell whilst my name's being dragged through the Court.

"Virgil, I know you're not stupid," I say, my voice shaking with rage. "I wasn't given any chance to explain myself. No question. No trial. I woke up in here, and Atticus had already decided I was guilty. I'm going to say this once—one last time." I lean in closer to the bars. "I. Didn't. Do. It."

His expression doesn't change. He only lets out another breath.

"I believe you," he mutters under his breath, glancing over his shoulder as if to check if we're still alone. "But Atticus found you and Kieran. He's got the story airtight. And I can't prove anything—yet."

"You believe me?" I blink. Are my ears playing tricks?

"Yes, but unfortunately, the only one who can prove your innocence refuses to see you."

"Who?"

Virgil folds his arms, gleaming black wings tucked in tight. "Aurora."

I snort. "You might as well kill me now, Virgil. No way in hell she's going to help me. If anything, she might even be working together with her brother. They've got me right where they want me—out of the picture. Atticus gets the Court. Aurora gets Kieran."

He narrows his eyes. "I know you and Aurora don't exactly see eye to eye, but she would never hurt Kieran."

"How do you know that?" I ask. "Kieran broke her heart, humiliated her, and was going to marry me."

"I know," he says, voice low, a warning. I can't believe she's got him wrapped around her finger, too. "Because she'd rather kill you than Kieran."

Huh.

Fair point.

"Isn't that great? The only person who can help me won't do it because she hates my guts." I lean in to the cold wall, my voice hoarse. "Do what you have to do, Virgil."

"Just tell me what happened. I don't want to hurt you, but I need to give Atticus something."

"I don't know what happened," I say quietly, exhausted from just breathing. "One minute we were making out, and the next we were crawling on the floor, unable to breathe."

Virgil drags a hand down his face, his jaw ticking. "And you don't know where the perfume came from?"

"I bought it a while ago …" I exhale, my teeth starting to clatter again as the cold seeps in deeper. "But it was left in my room at the Court for weeks before my things were moved into Kieran's place. Anyone could have gotten in."

"True. But it's not easy to buy iron dust here, Cassandra. I'm going to do some digging in to—" Virgil stops mid-sentence as loud noises cut through the cave.

Metal cranks. Kicking. Groaning.

"Oh, you've got to be shitting me," the Night Blade Commander mutters, staring at the newcomer.

I move my stiff neck slowly, barely seeing through the dark.

A figure emerges from the shadows, sword in one hand, dagger in another—panting, eyes wide, ready for war.

Lucas.

Oh, Gods.

"I told you to stay put," Virgil shouts, throwing his head back like he's so sick of all the shit that's been dumped on his lap lately. "Where the fuck are you planning on breaking her out to? There's nowhere in this Court we can't track you."

"I don't fucking care," he says, voice tight as he glances over at me. "Mother of the stars, what have you guys done to her?"

"The cell did that to her," Virgil replies, eyes fixed on Lucas, who's still pointing his weapons at him. "You know you're not going to get past me with those, right?"

"Yeah, well." He wipes the sweat on his forehead with the back of one hand. "Try me."

"I'm not going to fight you, idiot," Virgil says with a long, weary sigh. I can't see his face from here, but I'd bet a fortune that he hasn't even flinched. "But there's no way you can get her out of this cell."

"At least I'll try." Lucas scoffs. "What did do you guys even do, huh? Fuck all. All that talk about supporting Cassandra as Kieran's mate is bullshit. Something happened, and you've already decided she's guilty."

"Watch it. I'm not your enemy here."

"You're standing between me and my friend—I think you are."

His tone is low, dangerous. I have never seen Lucas fight, but from what I keep hearing, he's more than capable of taking down a few Fae in the sparring ring. Though, I'm not sure he can handle Virgil.

"Even if I step away, you still won't get her out." Virgil raps his knuckles against the metal bars, the noise echoing too loudly in my head. "Atticus used blood magic. Only he can open it."

Nothing really shocks me anymore, but I can see how hard those words slam into Lucas.

He curses, furious and defeated.

"Don't," I whisper, trying to reach for him, but lifting my arm feels impossible. "You'll get in trouble, too."

"No, no, Cass." He drops his weapons, crouching in front of me, the rusted bars between us. "This can't be it. I won't let you go down for this."

"I'm going to pretend I didn't see you here, Lucas." Virgil exhales, already turning away. "Now, I'm going to see what the hell you did outside, and you'd better be gone by the time I'm back."

Lucas doesn't answer. He doesn't even look at him. His hand reaches for mine as Virgil's footsteps fade. I try to smile, but it probably comes out all twisted and pathetic. My lips are cracked. Blood is all I taste.

"Gods, you're freezing," he mutters, shrugging off his coat and shoving it through the bars. "Wear this."

"Thanks ... but you just wait—ten minutes from now, it will be boiling in here."

Terror blooms across his face. His breath catches.

"I can't believe they're doing this to you. I'm going to fucking kill them all."

I shake my head, breathless. "It's Atticus ..."

"Atticus? What did he do?" he asks, his voice sharp as he helps the coat over my shoulders. "What the hell even happened? All I've heard is you poisoned Kieran, and the next thing I knew all hell had broken loose. No one would tell me anything. It took me days to find out that they were keeping you here."

"I probably don't need to tell you this, but"—I pause, coughing as my lungs are about to fail me—"I didn't poison him. Someone laced my perfume with iron dust."

The colour drains from his face. He turns awfully still for a whole minute.

"What is it?" I whisper.

"Did you ..." He shifts, swallowing hard, hand squeezing mine. "Did you just say your perfume?"

"Yeah ... that's what Atticus said."

"Oh, Gods." He blinks, then lurches to his feet, terror flicking in his terrified eyes. "What the fuck have I done?"

"What—"

Lucas starts pacing relentlessly, panic pouring off him in waves until it seeps into my own chest. The movement makes my stomach churn. I have barely eaten in days, but everything inside me is threatening to rise back up.

"Lucas," I say, keeping my voice steady, though my pulse is thundering. "What did you do?"

"I—" he starts, but stops again, clutching his temples with a ragged curse. "Fuck!"

"You're scaring me." I wince. "Please ... just tell me."

He glances back, and the look in his eyes slows my breathing quicker than the torture chamber—it's anxious, apologetic, and utterly broken. He steps closer, but instead of crouching, he's on his knees this time, begging.

"Remember the promise I made to Florence that day I paid for your daggers and Tessa's?"

I swallow hard.

Oh, Gods.

No.

He said—he said he would do her dirty work in exchange for those blades.

"A few weeks ago, she called in her favour and asked me to give Atticus a bottle of perfume," he admits, eyes dropping to the ground. "I didn't think anything of it. Thought it was an easy task—so I did."

"You ..." I choke, my mind refusing to wrap around it. "You gave it to Atticus."

He nods slowly, then runs a shaky hand across his face. "He must have switched it with yours. Cass, I—"

"No," I cut in, my body trembling with pain—only this time, it's nothing physical. "Lucas ... what have you done?"

“I didn’t know! I swear to Gods, I didn’t know!” he says quickly, trying to reach for me, but I drag myself back. “Cass, I’m sorry!”

“You almost killed me,” I sob, raw, blinding agony ripping through every inch of me. “You almost killed Kieran! I told you that promise was a bad idea!”

“I had no idea!” His voice cracks, desperate. “Fuck—Cass, I’m going to fix this, all right? I’m going to get you out of here!” Then he’s on his feet again. “Just ... please, let me fix this. I’ll be back as soon as I can.”

I don’t answer. I can’t say anything at all. The hard lump in my throat is making it hard to breathe, let alone speak. Lucas looks at me one last time—those sorry eyes cutting deeper than any blade—before disappearing into the dark

And I sit there, sobbing, screaming, the echoes my only company.

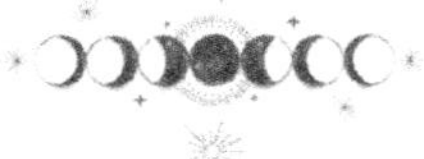

For so long, I just lie there, in the cold, the warmth, the wet floor.

I don’t speak. I don’t move when Virgil returns, until he eventually gives up and walks away.

I just lie there.

Part of me thinks this is it—this is my punishment from Declan. I am lying on the floor exactly like how those people left him to die.

This has all been my punishment.

This whole thing from the beginning.

And then, I hear them—footsteps. More than one set.

A pair of elegant shoes stops just beyond the bars.

"Oh, dear," the person murmurs, her voice thick with mockery—or maybe pity.

Aurora.

Lucas brought Aurora.

And now I wish I really was dead.

"Please ..." I rasp, my voice shredded, my throat raw. Pain is all I feel. "Please—Aurora ... just kill me."

I can't do this anymore.

It's too much.

I'm freezing.

Then I'm boiling.

My lungs drown in fluid that I choke back up. Fever claws at my skin. Cold gnaws at my bones.

It hurts.

Gods, it hurts too much.

"Stop that." Lucas's voice cuts through the clouds in my head, sharp with urgency and anger.

But I just whimper uncontrollably.

I don't know what he wants from me.

Kieran might not even live.

And I don't want to be here if he doesn't.

"Kill you?" Aurora snorts, smugness practically dripping off of her. "Killing you would be too easy for what you did to Kieran."

I don't even have the strength to defend myself anymore.

I don't move.

I don't blink.

"Aurora, we talked about this," Lucas snaps. "She didn't do it. Look at her!"

"I am, and I'm loving what I'm seeing so far."

"For fuck's sake, this is not why I brought you here!"

Aurora exhales, probably wearing that bored-out-of-her-mind expression, but then she crouches in front of me, the skirts of her gown brushing the filthy ground. "Tell me, Cassandra—did you try to poison your own mate?"

I open my mouth, but nothing comes out. I try again, and manage at last. "No."

Then, nothing.

I hear nothing but utter silence.

When I finally look up, her face is pale as paper.

"You're telling the truth," she breathes, her voice trembling, like one single word knocks the wind out of her lungs. "But ... but Atticus didn't lie when I asked—"

"He didn't have to lie to make up a story," Lucas cuts in. "Your power is seeing truths, not detecting lies."

What—

Is that why Virgil said she's the only one who could help me?

My mind swims.

She saw the kiss marks Kieran glamoured.

She went still when she realised I loved him.

Oh, Gods.

She's a walking truth-detector.

"I don't ..." Aurora falters, panic ripping through her green eyes. I've never seen her speechless before. "I don't understand ... why would Atticus—"

"Wake up, Aurora," Lucas mutters, his voice rough as he places a hand on her back. "You know why."

A part of me truly believed she was in on it.

But looking at her now—at the devastation in her face—I realise she's a victim, too.

We both love the same male—the one her own brother poisoned.

For a long while, no one speaks. Lucas doesn't even dare to breathe too loudly, and I just lie there, drifting in and out of consciousness.

Until Aurora's shock hardens into anger.

Until it bleeds into rage.

"Step back," she orders. There's no ask in that tone—only demand.

Lucas moves without hesitation.

I always knew there was something buried beneath her beauty and elegance—I just never knew how dangerous she could be until she curls her fingers into a fist and crushes the metal bars like they're nothing.

The cell swings open.

Of course.

Blood magic.

She has the same blood as Atticus.

Lucas's eyes widen, and a second later he's inside, scooping me into his arms and carrying me out of the cave so fast my mind can barely keep up with what's happening.

"Get her out of here," she says behind us, voice still shaking with fury.

"To where?" Lucas demands.

"Gideon." She exhales hard, as if trying to steady herself again. "Take her to Gideon. He'll know what to do."

"What about you?"

Her gaze cuts like shattered glass. "I have a bone to pick with my brother."

Chapter 38

It's so damn bright outside I can barely keep my eyes open.

I didn't know Lucas was this strong, but it feels like he's been carrying me forever. Fresh, cold air scrapes at my lungs, my breathing short and shallow. I hear noises—birds, footsteps, ragged panting.

Someone speaks. Someone else argues.

I must have drifted out of consciousness again, because the next thing I know I'm lying in a bed, the fire crackling beside me, and someone is touching my cheek.

"Try to drink this," a voice offers. I know that voice—it's Gideon. "It will make you feel better."

"Gideon?" I murmur, trying to open my eyes, but they are so damn heavy. Everything is a blur, but I make out the object he's lifting to my mouth—a small glass jar.

Oh, please, I need them to dose me up with all the Fae medicine they've got.

I take it without hesitation. The medicine tastes bitter on the tip of my tongue, but a hell of a lot sweeter than death, so I drink it all. Every last drop.

"Where's Kieran?" That's the first thing that comes out of my mouth. I blink. Once. Twice. Until my eyes adjust to the surroundings. Gideon sits beside my bed. Lucas slouches in an armchair near the door. The walls are dark wood. The only decoration in this place is a single painting hanging crooked above the mantelpiece.

This isn't anyone's home.

A cabin. A safe house, perhaps.

"He's at home, resting."

"I don't understand." I shove the blanket aside, trying to get up, and failing miserably. Gideon catches me just in time and helps me back into bed again. "Why is he not better? Your medicine healed me overnight when I was stabbed."

"Iron dust is different." Gideon sighs. "But first of all, you need to sit down and eat something."

"I don't want to eat. I want to see Kieran."

"Yes, because Lucas risked his life to save you just for you to be reckless and walk right into a trap."

That sentence lands like a punch to the ribs.

I sink into the headboard, staring past him. I can't imagine what it's been like for Kieran—days and days of not knowing what's going on. Does he even know about the riots? Does he know about me?

I can't imagine he does.

And I pray Atticus hasn't whispered in his ears, twisting the truth and painting me as a villain.

"What do we do, Gideon?" I ask, trying to gather every bit of myself together. If I'm going to fight, I have to be strong.

"You focus on not dying, for now," he says flatly. "We can't risk taking you to him, Cass, as much as we want to. If Atticus captures you again ..." He pauses, eyes hardening. "It won't be pretty. And if anything happens to you, Kieran will burn this Court to the fucking ground." He rises to his feet. "I made soup, and I'm going to heat it up. You need to eat and rest for now."

It's not fair.

Not at all.

I don't want to rest. I have barely moved in days—or however long it's been—and all I want is medicine in my veins and a blade in my hand.

I can fight.

I want to try.

But then reality sinks its teeth in.

I don't even know what kind of messed-up black magic Atticus has up his sleeves. If Kieran made him acting High Lord, he must be powerful.

"I should have turned Fae," I mutter to Lucas, my fingers curling into fists. "At least I could've fought."

"Or died with that same perfume."

"But I wouldn't have been so pathetic," I counter.

"You don't mean that," Lucas murmurs, stepping closer to take Gideon's seat beside me. "You didn't want to turn Fae, Cass. Not now."

No, but I do want to save Kieran.

I would do anything to save him—just like he'd take that throne to save me.

It's dangerous, what we have.

But nothing else matters if we're not together.

"How did it become like this, Lucas?" I ask, my voice starting to break again. "We didn't come here for this ..."

"Yeah, tell me about it." He scoffs, raking a hand through his dark hair. "I don't even know what's going to happen to us, but I guess this is our life now."

"I suppose you're right."

And if I'm going to be immortal, this won't be the last crisis we face. I imagine the Fae must take things for granted sometimes, thinking they have forever to chase what they want—until something like this creeps up on them, ripping them of all their hopes and dreams.

I don't want forever. I just want one more day with Kieran.

"We'll find a way," Lucas whispers, squeezing my hand, but I'm not sure he believes it.

I eat in silence, a simple soup tasting almost decadent after days of stale bread. Laia comes by later and helps me to the bath, where I wish I could stay until all the problems magically dissolve into the water.

I fall asleep again not long after. My mind screams "wake up," but my body knows better—it needs more rest. The Fae medicine drags me under, and the low murmur of Gideon and Lucas in the next room becomes a lullaby.

Chapter 39

The air is different.

The bed feels strange, yet weirdly familiar.

I open my eyes slowly. The senses hit me all at once—the soft hiss of the rain against the roof, the warm smell of cinnamon spiced coffee, the faces hovering over me—

Oh, Gods.

I jolt upright so fast my soul nearly rips free from my body.

I blink, again and again—and my *family* is still gathering around me.

Mum.

Dad.

Noah.

"Sweetheart," Mum says from the chair beside the bed, reaching for my hand, but I snatch it back.

Oh, Gods.

What—

What. The. Actual. Fuck.

For a heartbeat, I think I'm still in a coma. That I was in a major accident and dreamt it all up—the Court, the Fae ... Kieran.

Because this—this can't be real.

I'm home.

But my ring is still on my finger.

I didn't dream him up. I *was* at the Court.

"She looks like she's seen a ghost," Noah says. "That Fae—Gideon—he warned us you might react like this."

Gideon brought me here!?

"How long—" My voice cracks, panic spiking in my chest. "How long have I been back?"

A month in the Court is four to five days here.

Even a single day could be a week.

"Oh, Gods, I have to go back. I have to—"

"What are you talking about?" Dad rises to his feet, but I'm already halfway out of bed. "Cassandra, you've been gone for nearly two weeks! We had no idea if you were dead or alive. You can't just leave again. I won't let you!"

"I'm sorry, Dad," I say, panic rising. "I wish I could stay. I really do, but—it's been two months for me, and Kieran—Kieran needs me."

Gods, I hope he's still alive.

If anything happens to him, I—

"Gideon also said you'd say that," Noah cuts in, arms crossed. "I don't know who this Kieran is, but there's no way in hell we'd let you out of our sight again. He said he'd be back when he could, but I already told him to fuck off."

"Noah, you don't understand." I shove past him, rifling for a coat. "I promise I'll come back and explain everything, but right now I have to go."

"How, exactly?" Mum asks.

I stop breathing.

I ... don't know.

Fuck.

Realisation wakes me up harder than the cold in the cell. I run through every possibility in my head—and find no answer. The Court only reveals itself during a celestial event. The Fae can leave when they want, but they can't stay here, or they will fade into nothing.

And Kieran can never leave.

There's no one here to take me to him.

No one at all.

"No ..." The word breaks on a whimper as tears sting hot behind my eyes. "I can't stay here. I can't—"

It's been what—at least three days over there? And Gideon hasn't come back.

I have no idea what's happened. What if Atticus captured him and Lucas? What if he captured Aurora, too? What about Kieran—is he even alive?

"Oh, Cassie ..." Mum steps in, wrapping her arms around me. "I don't know what's going on, but please—don't do this to us again. At least talk to us. Make us understand."

I don't know how to.

How do I compress two months into words? Two months that weren't just a slice of my life—they were an entire life.

I choke, and my tears break free. Because all I can think of is Kieran—alone, injured, in bed. Not knowing where I am.

And I can't get back to him.

My finger grips the ring so hard it hurts.

My lifeline.

All I have left of Kieran.

It takes me forever, but I tell my family everything.

The trials. The rebellion. The mating bond. Kieran.

And I see every emotion crash into them like waves to the shore—their despair, their confusion, and their disappointment.

I wasn't coming home to stay.

I picked life at the Court over them.

I never thought I would come back so soon, but now that I'm here, I have a chance to say everything that I didn't. Everything I should have said.

"You're telling us"—Noah is the first to break the crushing silence. I brace myself for judgement—"that you have a whole other life at the Court. Fell in love with a Fae King, became his mate, and were going to live there with him forever until a civil war broke out?"

I flinch. "Yes."

"You're out of your damn mind."

Exactly the reaction I expected from him.

From all of them, really.

"You have just met this Fae—this Kieran," he presses. "I thought you did all this for Declan."

"I did." I narrow my eyes, my voice tightening. "And it's killing me that I can't anymore. I'll probably never stop blaming myself. But what did you want me to do—stay in the trials and condemn the rest of the Fae to die because somehow the stars decided to bind me and Kieran together?"

"They're Fae, for goodness' sake! Why do you even care about them?!"

"Because I love one of them, you fool!"

The words rip out of me, leaving the room in stunned silence. My parents flinch, like the sound itself wounds them.

"I'm sorry I left. I was in a very dark place, all right?" I force out. "I tried to break up with Declan the night that he died, and I haven't stopped blaming myself. But the Fae aren't all like what we've been told. And it's not like I planned on falling in love—not that I care what you think. But right now, I don't have time for this. I need to go back."

"So what? Are we supposed to just let you go?" Noah's voice cracks, sharp pain flashing in his eyes. "Do you have any idea what those two weeks did to us? Mum cried herself to sleep every night. Dad barely ate—while you were off living your best life with the Fae King."

I can barely breathe.

And maybe I deserve it.

"Noah, that's enough," Mum says at last, her hand tightening on his arm.

I look away, shame and guilt stuck in my throat.

"I'm glad you're okay," she whispers. "But ... in a way, I feel like we lost you along with Declan that night. Maybe it's our fault that we didn't try harder to pull you back. I should've asked you to move in. I should've never let you be alone."

It must run in the family, the art of blaming ourselves.

"Mum," I breathe. "It's not your fault. Nothing was going to stop me. I'm really sorry ... I wish it wasn't like this. There's just ... too much going on right now. And I promise, I will try to find a way to come back. We'll have a proper talk. I won't be gone forever." Maybe Gideon could bring me back, or take them to the Court for a visit one day. I don't know yet. But I will find a way. "But when Gideon comes back, I will leave with him."

"You're talking about marching into a war," Dad mutters. It's a struggle for him to get the next words out. "How will we even know you're still alive?"

Truth is, they won't.

And I might not survive it.

All I know is Atticus is probably keeping Kieran alive but weak enough that he can't act. He knows the Court won't survive without Kieran—and if Kieran is still breathing, there's a chance we can still turn this around.

If not, then that's it for me. For everyone.

But how do you tell your parents that?

"I have to do this, Dad," I admit, knowing how impossible I'm being—asking them to let me go. "Please ... try to understand. I'm not leaving because I want to. I wish I had more time with all of you, and one day we will ... but not right now."

Silence drapes over us, heavy as the storm outside. Rain is still pouring down like the sky was crying with us.

The truth is painful, but it's better this way.

At least now they have closure.

"If a day here is a week over there, Gideon could be back any minute," Mum says quietly before forcing a smile. "I'd say we should ... have a proper meal. Spend one last day together."

I bite down the tears threatening to spill and nod. "I'd really like that."

It's been so long since I've tasted Mum's cooking, and I savour every bite like it's my last.

No one cooks like her. Gods know she's tried to teach me, but I'll never be half as good. Having a feast at the Court every day is great, but I've missed the simplicity, the warmth, of Mum's home-cooked meals.

I hope she can cook for Kieran someday.

I picture him meeting my parents—how awkward it'd be when Dad puts on the what-do-you-want-with-my-daughter scowl, acting all tough and demanding respect, whilst Kieran stands there, calm, polite, older than both of them put together. As disturbing as that is.

We play board games after dinner—something we haven't done in a long time. It's strange, how you always think you have forever with your parents. Life sweeps you up in a confused, spiralling wave, and you put other things above your family because you think they'll always be there.

Until one day, they aren't.

These are such simple things—eating, talking, shuffling cards—but my aching heart is so full. Full but heavy with worry. I hold on to every laugh, every joke, but each minute that ticks by is absolute torture.

What is taking Gideon so long?

It's two in the morning, and my parents are clearly tired, but no one moves to go upstairs. I know exactly why.

"I won't leave without saying goodbye," I say eventually. "So you don't have to sit here all night."

My parents glance at each other.

"It's not just that," Dad mutters. "But I don't think I can sleep, knowing this could be my last night with you."

"Dad ..." I breathe. "You have to sleep at some point."

He huffs. "I used to say that to you when you were a kid."

"Well, you grow up and start telling your parents what to do." I cross my arms, but my smile never falters. It's just how life is, isn't it? We grow old and take care of our parents instead.

Except ...

Once I turn Fae, I'll have to watch my parents die, and live forever without them.

I know that it would happen eventually, even if I stay human, but the thought of watching everyone I love slip away—leaving me behind—is terrifying.

Mum's laugh still rings in the room. She shakes her head. "I can't believe you're going to be a queen."

I blink, blood rushing to my cheeks. "Well—who knows if Kieran will ever take the throne."

"Oh, I'd like to be a queen's mother."

... Did that really just come out of Mum's mouth?

I think we've had too much wine.

Dad snorts. "I haven't approved yet."

"Me neither," Noah adds.

I throw my head back, rolling my eyes. They both pulled the same stunt with Declan, grilling him like he'd committed a crime, when I first introduced him. Unbelievable.

"Please," Mum says, wine glass in hand. "He's a king. What more do you need?"

"I don't know ... a dowry?" Noah shrugs. "Surely a king can cough up a handsome sum."

I hiss. "Are you seriously putting a price tag on me?"

"If he's just going to snatch you away, we've got to make it worth something. Can't have you live a royal life all by yourself, sis."

And here we go, yapping at each other like we're teenagers again. Mum and Dad let out the same long-suffering sigh in unison.

"First, I've got to hope the Court is still there for me to rule." The sarcasm turns bitter at the end of the sentence. "I can't believe it's taking Gideon this long."

"That's because he isn't coming," a cool, almost-bored voice answers from the doorway.

Every drop of blood drains from my face.

Atticus.

I'm already on my feet, standing between him and my family.

"What have you done to him?"

"Nothing. I don't even know where he is." Atticus shrugs, his fingers tracing lazily along the cabinet by the door like he's admiring a piece of art. "You have a lovely home. Not sure why you'd trade it for ours."

"Who's this?" Noah steps beside me.

"Ah—where are my manners?" The prick smiles, stalking closer and extending my brother a hand like this is some kind of dinner party. "Name's Atticus."

"What—the rat of the Court?" Noah spits, not an ounce of fear in his eyes.

Atticus doesn't even bother to deny it anymore.

"I see my reputation precedes me." He lowers his hand, gaze dropping to me. "Seeing as you're dying to come back, I thought I'd save you the trouble and escort you myself."

"I'm not going anywhere with you," I say through clenched teeth. Mum is behind me now, Dad at my side.

"Did you think that was a question?" He tilts his head, smiling—then drags his eyes to my parents. "I wonder if your parents would like to see where you live."

"Like my daughter said—we're not going anywhere with you," Dad says flatly.

I love him for standing up for me, but he doesn't know what these Fae can do. I don't even know what Atticus can do.

And now he's threatening my parents.

What do I do?

I don't have my daggers, and I've got nothing to use against magic.

I've got no choice.

Atticus is going to hurt them—or hurt me and make them watch.

No one can help me here.

Gods, I've never felt so helpless like this past week. And now I really wish I was Fae. That the stars had given me something to fight this piece of shit. Anything.

"Where are you taking me?" I ask, and immediately feel Mum's hand tightening painfully around mine.

"You can't go with him, Cass," she whispers.

"Not back to the cell," Atticus says casually. "Somewhere far more ... exciting."

"I want to see Kieran."

"You'll see him," he drawls. "Eventually."

Something in his tone tells me he doesn't mean in this life.

I turn to my mum, taking both of her hands—and she already knows what I'm about to say.

"No ... love, no." Her voice cracks, head shaking in a desperate, silent plea.

"I have to."

"No, you don't," Noah snaps. "Cass, don't even think about this."

"I don't have a choice, Noah." My eyes flick to Atticus behind me. Wherever he's taking me, it won't be anywhere good. But if he wanted me dead, he could have killed me any time in that frozen hell.

He needs something.

Why go through all this trouble to drag me back?

He wants some leverage, or to make a statement.

Either way, it will get me closer to Kieran.

"I will send word as soon as I can," I promise them, even though it might not even be possible. "Don't worry, you'll hear before you even know it."

It's better this way, leaving on my own terms, so they don't have to see him hurt me—or get hurt themselves.

"No." Dad's voice is steel, his shoulders squaring as he steps forward. "I won't let you take her."

Atticus shows no emotion, as if my dad is nothing but air to him. His eyes remain fixed on me as he says, "You sure about that?"

"Don't do anything stupid," I say under my breath.

"I think you should say that to your father."

Gods. When did he become this unbearable?

"It's okay, Dad."

"No, sweet pea, it's not."

I nearly burst to tears at that nickname—the one he used to call me when I was a little girl. And now his little girl is about to walk straight into a trap.

I can't bear to look at their faces. I can't stand the desperation in their eyes. Part of me almost wishes Atticus would wipe their memories, because this moment will hurt them longer than forgetting ever could.

"I will be back before you know it," I say with a steady voice. "Time moves faster over there, remember?"

"That's not funny," Noah mutters.

No, it's not.

But I pull him into a hug anyway—tighter than any hug we've ever shared. Then Mum, whose sobs echo in my skull. Then Dad, who refuses to let me go.

"I love you," I whisper, trying not to cry for their sake, even though my throat burns and my eyes sting. "I love all of you."

I let go and leave quietly with Atticus at my back. The sobbing gets louder with every step, until it eventually fades into the night. I don't look back.

I can't.

At least this time, I got to say goodbye.

I should be thankful for that.

"Let's go," is all Atticus says once we're outside.

I take his hand, and the world rips apart.

A few seconds later, light slams into me. Night turns into day. The moon and stars vanish, replaced by a bright, blue sky and sunlight. Cold air burns my lungs as I steady myself, blinking at the endless sprawl of trees around us.

Where are we?

This looks like—

The forest.

It feels like the same one from the first trial. Only this time, the branches are bare, and the air carries the sharp bite of late autumn.

"Welcome to the third trial," Atticus says beside me.

My head snaps to him. "What?"

"The rules are a little different this time. Originally, we planned to dump all contestants in here and let you rip each other apart. Last man standing wins. But then ..." He pauses, a smile blooming across his face. "I figured it's more entertaining to let a few angry Fae hunt you all instead. You know—for fun."

"What the actual fuck—Atticus!"

"Ah, yes." He holds up one finger, and with a flick of his wrist, both of my daggers materialise into his hands. "Just to make it fair. The others came in with weapons."

I freeze, cold air trapped in my chest.

He tosses them on the ground, then bows with mock grace.

"Good luck, Your Majesty."

Chapter 40

I've got to find Lucas, or I'll die alone in here.

Hell, at this point, I'd even take Oliver or Jordan. We are all being hunted down like animals. This is no longer a trial. It's basically a sport for them. We're outnumbered, and the brutal truth is only a miracle can save us right now.

It's just the matter of how long we can manage to stay alive.

I intend to make that as long as humanly possible.

I pick up my daggers. The moonstone blade gleams faintly. Danger is nearby. Gods, at least Atticus could have given me a proper outfit. The dress I'm wearing is anything but practical.

I squint at the sky. The sun is disappearing beyond the tree line, the air warmer than a usual morning, so I'm going to assume it's almost late afternoon. I don't know which way is north, or even if I'll survive if I make it out of the woods. There's no telling that people at the Court won't try to kill me, too.

But the problem isn't just being hunted.

It's being hunted at night, once the sun sets.

Okay, Cassandra, be logical. You haven't slept all night. Soon you'll be hungry. You're going to need water. Maybe a fire?

But a fire at night might attract some unwanted attention.

No fire at all and I'll freeze to death by sunrise.

Either way, I need to find somewhere to hide.

I start moving quietly, fallen leaves making crunching noises under my feet—not ideal. But then again, an ideal situation would be me at home, in Kieran's arms, warm and safe—not stalking through a death trap.

Just hold on, Cassandra.

He's alive.

He has to be.

I hold on to that thread of hope with every breath that I take. After a while, I spot a tree tall enough to climb and get some visibility. The last thing I want is to wander deeper into the woods without knowing what's out there.

I strap both daggers to my boots and start climbing, praying that I don't step on my own dress and plummet to my death.

I try to go as slow and as steady as I can. Speed is not my concern here. Only staying alive.

Every branch scrapes my skin, and I lose count of how many blisters this tree so generously gifts me.

Then my foot slips, and my dress snags on a jagged edge, tearing with a loud rip. I nearly scream, but I stop myself just in time. My heart leaps up my throat, all twenty-three years of my existence flashing before eyes as I hold on for dear life.

For a second, I really think this is it, but my trembling hands are still holding on, and splinters have made a lovely home on them with my blood as their swimming pool.

I'm okay.

Still alive.

I try to slow my breathing, giving myself an imaginary trophy for still being brave enough not to cry out when I slipped.

Then, when the shaking finally stops, I keep going.

It feels like forever before I'm finally high enough to see the surrounding woods. The sun has already vanished beyond the horizon, leaving only steaks of orange and purple bleeding across the sky.

And all I see is trees.

Nothing but this endless, suffocating forest.

The sweat on my forehead turns to ice as my breath grows heavier. A cold breeze slams into me from every direction.

There is nowhere out.

For a brief moment, I let myself panic. I need to feel it, to let it tear through me, before I force it to pass so I can think straight again. I squeeze my eyes shut, listening to my own heart drumming, trying to control my breaths until they stop hitching.

Okay, Cass.

Time to find shelter.

Food and water.

Focus on the things you can control.

The descent is painfully slow. My limbs are tired and trembling, but I can't risk resting. Pretty soon the forest will be swallowed in pitch black, and I don't want to find out what lurks here in the dark.

My legs feel like jelly when I finally touch the ground again, shaky and weak. I have a feeling that if I sit, I might never get back up again.

So, I keep moving.

There has to be water somewhere.

It's getting darker and darker by minute, shadows stretching long, my moonstone blade now shimmering brighter in my hand.

Somewhere behind me, a howl cuts through the trees—somewhere far too close.

Please don't tell me there are wolves in this forest.

I quicken my pace, but the howling multiplies, overlapping with sharp barks. Not one wolf—several.

Oh, this is bad.

Really bad.

I run.

Branches whip at my face as I sprint, my lungs screaming, heart pounding in my chest. I don't look back, but the barking is closer now—shapes darting through the trees on either side of me, their eyes glow yellow in the darkening sky.

Then, my stupid dress betrays me again. I trip and hit the ground hard. For half a heartbeat, I can't see anything, until a thunderous growl tears through the dark, so close it rattles my bones.

I scramble to my feet just as the first wolf lunges at me—no, not wolves. They are larger, broader. Their jaws could snap a normal wolf in half.

Direwolves.

Holy fuck.

My daggers flash up on instinct. I swing, catching its shoulder, not deep enough to kill but enough to make it yelp and skid back, blood splattering across the twilight dagger.

And all of the sudden, raw, hungry energy slams into me. It tears through my veins like a blast of magic.

I freeze, staring at the blade. The blood seeps into the steel like it's feasting on it.

I might not die here after all.

The other two lunge at me at the same time. I duck—so fast it terrifies me. Then I slash the one to the left, and another surge of raw magic tears through me, hotter, wilder. I can feel it pumping through my veins, like a beast trapped in a cage, roaring to be unleashed.

I embrace it, letting it consume me with a smile and open arms.

I growl, but my voice isn't mine. Every move is on instinct and faster than I can think. Even the wolves seem hesitant at the shift. They step back, circling and assessing me.

And this time, I launch myself onto one of them, nails digging into its fur, riding it like I'm trying to tame a wild horse. The direwolf's head snaps to the side to bite, but I drive the twilight blade into its back, further than I probably could with my human strength. A whine tears from the wolf, loud and haunting.

I stab, and I stab.

The more I cut, the stronger I become—the weaker it is.

Another one catches me on the arm, desperately trying to save its mate. I cry out, bracing for flesh to tear, but it barely stings. Just a shallow scratch. No blood. No gaping wound. My arm is still intact.

Woah.

I've got wolf skin, too?

Let's fucking go.

A snarl rips out of me as I leap down and jump at the other one, like I'm on a mission to rid the forest of these creatures. My senses explode—every scent, every shift in the air, every heartbeat hits me at once. I crash down on them one by one, daggers slashing, ripping through fur and flesh.

Oh, how the tables have turned.

The prey takes a redwood throne and crowns herself the queen of the jungle. Direwolf heads adorn my house crest.

Blood sprays everywhere.

They yelp. I suck in more power.

Three direwolves turn to two. Two collapse to one. One falls into nothing.

I rip them apart. Every last one of them.

Thick, hot blood drips from my hair, splattered all over my clothes. I'm drenched, stinking of death and merciless victory.

I glance down at the carnage.

Wonder if direwolf meat tastes nice.

Well, meat is meat—if I throw it in a fire, it's dinner.

I crouch low and start hacking, crimson soaking into my hands. I carve enough for one meal, then flip one of the beasts over with the strength that shouldn't belong to me and begin skinning it.

It's cold, and I need something else to wear.

What's better than a direwolf pelt?

I grin through the gore, three direwolves' strength pumping in my veins.

I'd better get popular votes for this performance.

Chapter 41

The best part of having a wolf's ability? You can track anything.

I find water in less than half an hour.

It's freezing, but I dive in with no hesitation, scrubbing the dried blood off my skin and hair. If there's ever a time I can let down my guard in this forest, it's now.

And actually, it doesn't even feel that cold.

My night vision is clearer than day.

I hope this magic doesn't wear off for another week.

A part of me wants to rest, but I'm afraid this super strength will fade by the time I wake. I need to make the most out of it whilst I can, especially when I want to track down the others.

I scrub blood from my dress as best I can, wishing I could wear it beneath the wolf pelt, but it's still dripping wet. So I just wrap the skin tight around me, sling the dress over my arm, and drag along another carcass I haven't carved yet—who knows how long I'm going to be stuck here for. A girl's got to eat.

I follow the stream, senses sharpened, catching every trace of scent the forest offers.

Problem is, I don't know how to tell humans, Fae, and monsters apart.

I recognise one scent, though—blood.

So much of it. So close.

I follow the trail, the stench sharpening with every step until I find the source.

It's Oliver.

Bleeding into the cold dirt next to Leon—shapeshifter Leon—silver blood seeping from his corpse.

My guess is his nightmare came back to finish him. Maybe he managed to kill the shifter, but something else got to him instead.

I stand over the body, not a drop of pity left in me.

Good fucking riddance.

At least he's not entirely useless.

I need some layers.

I crouch beside his body, already tugging off his clothes. They're baggy on me, but anything will do at this point. *Let's see what else you had on you, Oliver.*

Hm.

A few snack bars. A knife. And a compass.

Great find.

I shove them all in my pocket—Oliver's pocket—and move on as quickly as I found him. Don't want whatever killed him to come back and get me too.

The moon is rising on the horizon, bright and yellow. Wind rattles the trees in the dark, its whispers haunting and echoing. I'd be scared shitless if it weren't for the power my twilight dagger stole. And as much as I want to keep hunting, I should probably find shelter while I'm still strong enough to drag this direwolf carcass around with me.

Sleeping on a tree sounds like the best move, but I can't risk leaving the carcass on the ground to attract other predators.

There has to be a cave or something.

I keep moving, eyes scanning every inch in front of me—until I finally spot a hole in the side of a hill, wide enough for a bear to crawl into. I drop everything and poke my head inside, using my wolf sense to sniff the air.

Empty.

An abandoned den.

My new idea of a haven.

I roll the carcass in first, then pile up enough dried leave to cover the entrance. The wolf pelt will keep me warm tonight, and the carcass is my brand-new mattress.

Home sweet home.

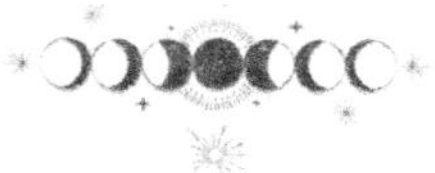

Something thick and slimy drips onto my arm. Then hot, rancid breath hits me like a gust. I snap my eyes open and come nose to nose with a giant serpent the size of horse, its eyes massive and hollow.

A scream tears out of me before I can stop it. I scramble for my daggers, hands slick with panic. The serpent jerks it head back, like even it wasn't expecting me to shriek in its face.

I no longer feel the wolf inside me, but I still slash it on instinct—with the wrong dagger.

Fuck!

The serpent rears back, its body thrashing against the den walls. A hit rattles the entire den, saliva dripping from sharp fang onto the dirt. The hollow eyes lock on me. I'm cornered—trapped at a dead end with nowhere to run.

I stumble, searching for the twilight dagger, but my hands are too shaky to grab anything.

The serpent launches itself, and for split second, my whole life flashes before my eyes, Kieran's voice ringing in my ears—

The world goes still.

I don't open my eyes until the ground shudders with a heavy thud.

The serpent lies sprawled, its skull split clean through by a spear that came out of nowhere.

Two Fae in black stand silhouetted at the den's mouth, wicked smiles curving their lips as they drag the serpent's carcass out. Their eyes gleam when they see me—their new prey.

"Well, well," one of them drawls, ducking his head inside. "If it isn't the King's little toy."

Without thinking, I throw the moonstone dagger at his face, but he snatches it out of the air like I've tossed him a ball.

"That's not very nice, my dear." He hums.

A second later, he's crawling inside. I clutch my twilight blade, but a single flick of his wrist and the dagger rips out of my hand and lands neatly in his grasp.

No!

I hurl everything I can find at him—rocks, twigs, snack bars. I kick and thrash, but he only laughs as his hand closes around my ankle. With one brutal yank, he drags me out into the daylight, my nails clawing at the dirt, leaving nothing but torn grooves in the earth.

The other one joins in, shoving me down hard, his weight pressing me into the ground. My skin crawls where he touches me.

"Where's your precious Kieran now, huh?" He sneers, laughter laced with cruelty. "Think he'll still want you after this?"

I spit in his face.

"You dirty little bitch!" The sentence comes with a slap so hard it makes my ears ring. "I'm going to ruin that body until you beg for it to end—then I'll wrap you nice and pretty and leave you at his deathbed."

The cold floods my chest as I realise exactly what they have planned for me. Panic claws up my throat. I thrash, kicking my feet as hard as I can and screaming at the top of my lungs, praying someone—anyone—will hear.

The prick who dragged me out of the den steps closer and starts unfastening his trousers, while the one on top of me slides his hand to my thigh—fingers digging in, bruising.

Disgust coils my stomach as he forces my legs apart with his knees, one hand pinning my wrists, the other tearing at my clothes—

And that's when the world erupts.

A blast of light and power shakes the ground beneath us.

"Hands. Off. My future wife." The voice is pure, lethal rage. "You fucking ghouls."

Kieran.

Oh, my Gods.

Every colour in existence leaves both Fae. They scramble to their feet, desperate to flee, but Kieran just curls his fingers into a fist, yanking them back through air with his magic without breaking a sweat.

He's here.

And he's well.

Mother of the stars.

"I should burn you both to dust right now, but that's far too quick for what you just tried to do," he says, voice low and shaking with fury. "This is your Queen. And you will remember to kneel before her."

He drags his fist downward. Both Fae collapse, their knees slamming into the dirt, faces twisted in agony as Kieran's power forces their spines to bow.

All while I'm still frozen in time at the sight of him.

Is he really here?

How?

And he recovered from the iron dust?

Oh, Gods.

The storm-lit eyes soften, his voice gentle as he asks, "You okay, Little Star?"

I blink.

I breathe.

And then I hurl myself into his arms, sobbing like a little kid.

Oh. My. Gods.

I thought I'd never see him again. I throw both of my arms around him, holding him so tight it hurts, feeling the warmth of him and realising he's real.

This is real.

My whole body shakes. My knees buckle. I cling to Kieran as my tears spill fast and uncontrollably. Everything that's happened in the past week crashes into me all at once—the frozen hell, the day with my family, the trial I was dumped into—but the entire world stills in these arms.

Calm. Safe.

Mine.

This is the only place I ever want to be.

"I thought you were almost dead," I choke out, cupping his beautiful face with dirty, trembling hands.

"Me?" Kieran smiles, head tilting. "Not before I marry you, love."

And now I cry again.

Gods, I can't believe him.

Last I heard he was on a brink of dying, and now he's making a joke about marrying me?

"What happened? How are you here?"

"Long story," he mutters, exhaling slowly. "First, what do you want to do with them?"

I turn to the two Fae still kneeling, drenched in sweat, their faces pale like their souls have already left their bodies. I wipe my tears with the back of my hand and pick up my daggers, flashes of their hands on me still in my head.

They didn't hesitate.

And if Kieran hadn't come—

I stalk closer. My twilight blade kisses the first one's cheek, dragging down painfully slowly.

"Please, milady. We didn't mean to—"

"Oh, now you didn't mean to?" I huff a cold laugh, pressing until the steel slices skin. Blood wells, and with it, a rush of stolen magic surges into my veins.

The Fae flinches.

"Maybe in the next life," I whisper, slicing deeper, dragging the blade lower, carving a thin red line all the way to his throat. He cries out in pain, but Kieran's power keeps him rooted. "You should think before you act."

Then I drive the dagger upward, just beneath his chin, burying it deep.

He gasps, choking on blood, his last breath stolen within seconds. More surges of magic slam into me.

The other one opens his mouth, terror spreading across his face, but no sound comes out.

"P—please, I'll do anything—"

"Aw, I'm touched." I offer him a smile, sweet and kind. Blood drips from my dagger in steady drops as Kieran releases the first body, letting it collapse in the dirt.

I step closer, tilting his chin up with the blade, forcing him to meet my eyes. "But you see ... I only need you to die, so—"

I breathe in deep, then drive the dagger slowly into his skull. The crack of bone splintering fills the silences, a grotesque lullaby. His eyes roll back, body convulsing once—then nothing. He drops to the cold dirt, dead before his body hits the ground.

Kieran blinks at me, arching a brow. "That was"—his breath hitches, storm-lit eyes burning—"so fucking hot. Some would say we're made for each other."

I run straight into his arms, and Kieran doesn't care how filthy or blood soaked I am.

Our lips find each other, and the world explodes back into colour.

"I missed you. Gods, I missed you so much," he murmurs into the kiss, hand slipping in my hair. "I'm sorry I was late."

"I don't care. You're here. You're here," I whimper, wrapping my legs around his waist, closing the gap between us as I kiss him harder, my heart racing frantically in my chest. "I'm sorry I poisoned you."

He laughs low in his throat. "A little dust can't kill me, but being away from you almost did."

Oh, Kieran.

Here I thought it was impossible to love him even more than I did.

Turns out I was wrong.

I refuse to let go, and Kieran kisses me like he might die if he stops—I purr into the kiss, seeing nothing but him in front of me.

Until a noise interrupts us from behind.

"Glad to see you're safe, Cassandra,"

I don't even think—I flick my wrist, and the stolen magic shoots out of me.

"Ow, that hurts."

I freeze, realising what I've just done—but Kieran only laughs and pulls me back into another devouring kiss. My head spins, bliss clouding everything ... until recognition hits.

Gideon.

Oh.

I just blasted *Gideon* for interrupting our kiss.

I pull away and find not only Gideon, but the entire Council, including Aurora, all in their fighting leathers and armour, flanked by a whole army of Fae and other creatures I don't even want to ask about.

I don't know whether to comment on the fact that they look like they have been to war—

Or mock Aurora for wearing trousers.

"Sorry, Gideon," I whisper, blinking at all of them. "What—" I swallow hard. "What's going on?"

"What's going on," Virgil says, smirking as he folds his arms, "is we just crushed the rebellion at the Court and came looking for you—because it'd be irresponsible for us to leave our King and you in this deadly forest alone. Though ... it looks like you both want to be."

My eyes go wide.

The rebellion is defeated?

And did he just say *King*?

I whip my head towards Kieran, and he's just grinning like he was just given a new toy.

"What do you say, love?" he drawls, amusement flashing in his storm-lit eyes. "Up for being a queen?"

Chapter 42
Kieran

Two nights ago

Fuck.

It's been too long since I last saw Cassandra, and I'm experiencing what is most likely the equivalent of drug withdrawal humans face. My chest is heavy, and I feel out of breath, even though I have barely moved much in almost two weeks.

I wish I could go to her, but I can't.

This fucking curse is killing me.

And I have something else I need to sort out first—something to end this chaos at the Court.

Cass is safe, and that's all that matters. I'd rather be tortured by this unyielding yearning than have her here when we're about to unleash hell on the rebels, though my heart breaks at the thought of her waking up in the human world against her will, not knowing what's happening to the rest of us.

She's going to kick my ass to the fucking moon when she's back, and there will be eternity for her to do that.

I have to make sure there'll be eternity for us.

Because nothing else matters if we can't be together.

Truth is, I've been fully recovered from the poison for a few days, but Atticus doesn't know that. He'd been putting iron dust in my medicine every bloody day to keep me weak and away from my mate—from everything he planned to take.

Or so he thought.

Whilst his rebellion group infiltrated the Court, my people had also been working in the shadows, tracking their every move, marking them in dark corners.

We made him think some of the Council members were loyal to him when they were all feeding intel back to me, Gideon, and Virgil—intel Atticus's big mouth stupidly bragged about because he thought he'd gotten his filthy claws on the throne.

My patience runs thin as a cobweb waiting in his grave.

Today, this ends.

"It's time," Virgil quietly says as I put on my coat. "Atticus is occupied with Florence. We've got to go now."

I nod, adjusting the collar of my coat. Apparently, I've made two bad judgements in the past decades. One being appointing Atticus as the Court's acting High Lord. The other is placing too much trust in Florence to supply us weapons—the very ones she's using to point at my throat.

She's always been a quiet one. She minded her own business, never complained, and did her job splendidly.

The only thing that's wrong with her is that she's fucking Atticus.

And he probably smooth talked, bedroom-eyed talked, hands-touching talked her into joining his sacred little crew.

Because what do you think "Atticus is occupied with Florence" means?

It's not the first time someone has lost a war because of a female.

And it won't be the last.

"You sure about this?" Gideon asks me for the tenth time, even though we've gone over the plans about five times already. I don't know whether to thank the stars that despite being my High Commander, his duty as my best friend comes first, or curse them because he's such a pain in the ass sometimes.

But mostly, I'm just thankful for Gideon.

"Why? Would you like to do it for me instead?"

Gideon scoffs, holding up both hands like he's saying, "Never in a million years."

Exactly.

Because who wants to carry the weight of the entire Court on their shoulders?

Certainly not me.

But I'll take that throne in a heartbeat if it means keeping Cass and the people I care about safe.

And maybe it has been a long time coming.

Maybe it's exactly what this Court needs.

A new day after centuries of chaos.

A king to put things into the right order.

"Let's go," I murmur as we step outside. A cold breeze blasts at me like a welcome-back kiss to remind me I'm not dead, and this next chapter is about to be a merciless one. It's been so long since I've stepped foot outside my own house. It's past midnight, and the cold chills my bones. Stars flicker overhead, some shooting across the midnight sky.

And I will admit, it's incredible to be blessed with magic—but I rarely ever use it to keep warm. Mainly because being cold reminds me I'm still alive and not entirely untouched. My arrogance needs to be squeezed back into a Fae-sized bottle, because I won't lie ... in the early decades of my life, there were times when my attitude and blazing hormones drove me to do things I could only bury my face in my hands in response to, if someone brought them up today.

Cass would never fall for that little shithead, let's put it that way.

My point is, no one is invincible.

I'm lucky to be standing here today, even after all this—the banishment from the stars, the riots, iron dust poison, to name a few—and I should never ever take this for granted.

It's time to right the wrongs.

We vanish to the River of Vows, where the rest of the Council members await with our High Priestess, Odenne. Felix is already seated, a scroll and a pen resting on his lap, waiting to record my next suffering like this is his idea of a Solstice morning.

Sometimes, I ask myself what I created his bloody position for. The male truly does his job like his life depends on it.

"You look nice," Aurora mutters as I stalk closer, her green eyes lowering to the ground. I have always thought she belongs amongst one of those shimmering stars in the night sky, but for the past week, that fierce light in her eyes has seemed to dull—for obvious reasons.

We both have our differences and could fight till we draw blood.

But I do care for her. I loved her for a decade, and although that love has turned into a bond between two friends, I still have that protective instinct in me. My chest floods with that familiar ache I can never deny when anything causes her pain. And that thing, unfortunately, includes me.

"Can't be crowned King without looking sharp now, can I?" I joke, hoping to lighten everyone's moods, but Aurora just exhales softly.

She finally meets my eyes again. There's something unreadable in her expression. Aurora has never been one to hesitate—she says exactly what's on her mind. But tonight, she opens her mouth and closes it again.

Then she finally manages, "You're doing all this for her—the things you never wanted to do for me."

I knew that was coming.

It's probably best we get that out of the way now.

I slide both hands in my pockets, my ring cold on my finger. For a moment, I look up at the night sky, exhaling slowly and letting memories of the life we shared together rise again.

It feels like a lifetime ago.

There were good times and equally bad times.

I can't deny we were happy once—but that's long gone now.

We just ... weren't right for each other, simple as that.

"Let's not go there, Aurora," I whisper, glancing at the others who have started to take their seats in this small chapel hidden just a few minutes' walk from the bridge Cass and I got fake married. "I'm sorry, all right?"

It's all I can say, really.

She simply exhales and walks to take a seat amongst the others quietly.

Odenne welcomes me to the dais with a bow that I return. I draw a deep breath before we begin. I have been dreading this moment for Gods know how long. But now that it's here ... it doesn't feel as horrible as I thought it would be.

There's only one thing in my head as she swears me in as the King of the Fallen—Cassandra.

I recite every single word of the vow, loud and clear, and drink every last drop of the Fae wine she offers as tradition demands.

There's no crown on my head—not yet.

But I can feel it in my bones—something this sacred ritual and the River of Stars bless my power with.

And then we wait.

We wait all night, taking our time as I claw back into bed, acting an ill male, so that Atticus leaves in the morning with another victorious smirk we're about to wipe off that face.

It's the day of the final trial. We know exactly how the rebels will let their guard down, thinking their friends will be hunting down the humans for fun—not realising they are about to be hunted, too.

We gather again in the Council Hall as soon as Atticus is gone. Aurora is playing her part, the hostess of the trials once again, whilst Daphne glamours a group of trusted Fae to take our place, showing our faces from afar—far enough for Atticus to notice, but not close enough for him to say hi and catch us.

"Any pep-talk before we go to war?" Skylar asks, arms crossed, and weapons drawn. "Your Majesty?"

"Mother of the stars." I wince. "Never call me that again will be pep-talk number one." *Unless your name is Cassandra Thorne and we are in bed.*

"Great pep-talk so far." Virgil hums low in his throat. "My shadowborn assassins marked some known rebellion members last night. They won't know it, but we'll see the marks."

Unlike Felix, I know I recruited Virgil for a reason ... but fuck me, the army he raises scares the shit out of me sometimes.

These shadowborn assassins are practically invisible, existing like silhouettes under moonlight. They can fight if commanded by the right person—and Virgil happens to be that person.

Thank fuck he wasn't the rat, because we would have all been in deep shit by now.

"My second pep-talk would be not to piss him off." I tilt my head to Virgil, who just grins. "And don't die."

"I'll try," Gideon drawls, hand resting on the hilt of his sword.

I let out a chuckle, low and anxious, taking in all the faces around me. The group of people who annoy the living hell out of me ninety percent of the time—but that's exactly how siblings and families treat each other.

We exchange one last glance. And one by one, we vanish to our agreed locations where the rest of our army waits in groups.

Only Gideon and I stick together. We walk right out the Council Hall doors, joining our group of soldiers and quietly taking down anyone passing by with an "X" marked on their chest, shouting the body counts between each other like it's a competition.

I cut, and slash, and kick, and punch.

I don't stop.

Every body I drop is another step closer to Cass.

But it doesn't take long for someone to alert the Fae gathered near the forest about us—and then all hell breaks loose.

Fire. Shattered Glass. Utter chaos from all directions.

I swap between helping Gideon and vanishing to see if I can locate Atticus anywhere, but he's nowhere to be found.

Then again, how do you find someone when you both can vanish into thin air?

So, I come back and do what I can for now.

I wipe the sweat off my forehead with the back of my hand, blood stained on my clothes—others', not mine—as a small army of Fae charges at us from the left, some marked by the shadowborn assassins. Gideon sees them too, and he's about to open his mouth—

But I curl my fist, reaching for that power resting in me, then unleash it.

I drag my fist down, and they all slip like the floor is made of oil. I clench the fist, crushing their bones into pieces without them so much as raising a finger our way.

"Oh, great!" Gideon shouts, throwing one hand in the air. "Take all the fun, why don't you?"

I shrug.

It's messy when we all fight with magic. Every one of us has unique abilities, and we would be here for weeks trying to play tricks on each other—not that we don't use our magic at all. But we do take pleasure in the art of stabbing and making our opponents bleed.

A low-life jerk cuts me in the shoulder when I'm not looking. I groan, but before I can return the favour with the tip of my blade, someone plunges a gleaming dagger into the back of his neck, cutting clean through the front before the dagger is drawn back, precise and beautiful.

The body drops, making a loud thud on the marble floor, revealing Aurora behind him.

Her face is grim, brows drawn tight.

I know that look.

"What is it?" I don't take my eyes off her, my voice tight.

"Atticus knows we're here."

"And?" I ask again, louder this time, hand blasting magic at anyone trying to get close, because something in her face tells me I should be listening to this very carefully.

"It's Cassandra." She swallows. "Atticus just dropped her into the trial."

One single name makes my heart leap out of my chest. Blood boils in my face, slowly spreading to every part of my body. The next stupid soul who tries to launch themselves at me disintegrates into dust before they can take their next step, scattering in the grey air with the rising smoke all around us.

"Go." Aurora says one word, already knowing my head is elsewhere. "We've got this."

And then I vanish, cursing Atticus's name and vowing to shred him into pieces when I see his fucking smug face.

He's dead.

He's fucking dead.

Chapter 43
Cassandra

It's been almost an hour since Kieran basically asked me to marry him without actually asking.

I would like to be excited about that part, but all of my thoughts disappear the minute we arrive back at the Court and witness the damage the riots and fighting have done to this beautiful place.

Gideon warned us that a fire had broken out, but I wasn't prepared for this.

The fire tore through the contestants' living quarters, leaving blackened walls and cracked glass in its wake. It's clear how much the rebels despised us from what they did to the whole block, doors ripped from hinges, windows shattered. The scent of smoke still clings to the air.

And the library—the library is gone.

They torched it all. Thousands of stories and centuries of carefully collected knowledge destroyed by hatred.

There are no bodies on the ground, but the blood splatters are still fresh in some parts.

Smoke burns in my lungs.

"We will rebuild it," Kieran whispers, throwing an arm over my shoulder, but my words are still stuck in the numbness. "It will be fine."

I nod—because that's all I can do.

"Where are the rebels now?" I ask. "And Atticus?"

"Some dead. The others fled. We put those who survived in prison," Octavia replies, glancing aimlessly at the ruins. "Atticus is still on the run, along with Florence."

Gods, this is such a mess.

"They won't get far. My creatures are after him," Virgil says.

I scratch my arms, not sure how to feel about any of this. As long as Atticus is out there, how can I feel safe? He could go after my family—threaten them.

"He won't get anywhere near you, or your family," Kieran whispers like he can read my mind through my expression. He lifts my chin up with his fingers, voice soft. "I'll send people to protect them."

The channelling link is no longer there, but he still sees me.

I'm so grateful for that.

"I'll go," Gideon offers. "I'll take some guards with me."

I look at him with gratitude. "Thank you, Gideon. Please let them know that I'm fine."

He nods, then he is already on his way.

Then I turn to Kieran, dread clawing its way up my throat, and I'm trying not to choke on fear as I ask the next question, "Please tell me Lucas is okay ..."

He glances at Virgil, who quickly nods.

"We pulled him and Jordan out of the trials. They're with the healers for now, but they're expected to fully recover."

Thank Gods.

I place a hand on my chest as a warm stream of relief spreads across it. Kieran softly rubs my back, as if to comfort me.

"We're going to debrief. Would you like to come with, or do you want me to drop you at home first and I can fill you in later?" he asks gently, one hand stroking my hair.

If this were any other day, I'd insist on going in with him. But after all this—the trial, the night, and the morning I had, and all this wreckage—I don't think I can.

"Please take me home?"

"Of course."

He takes my hand in his, and we both vanish to the house together. Nausea coils in my stomach as the world stop spinning, and I hold on to Kieran because I need something to anchor me after days of uncertainty.

"Do you want me to stay?" he whispers, picking me up in his arm in one single swoop. I gasp, but I'm too tired to resist—and it does feel lovely being carried inside like this. I shake my head in his arms. "Are you sure?"

"Your people need you." I can't help but mock, "Your Majesty."

"Yeah, about that." Kieran chuckles. "I'll explain when I'm back. You try to get some rest. Daphne already warded the house again so that Atticus can't get in. You don't need to worry about anything."

"You know that's easier said than done." I pull him closer for a kiss. "And I won't stop worrying until you're home."

"Keep doing that and I won't leave at all."

And there he goes—making me laugh again. After everything we've both been through, a few words from him and my world is bright again. "You have eternity with me. Go be a king."

"Fine," he mutters, pressing another hard kiss on my lips anyway before letting me down on the sofa. "You know, I'm going to need something to destress after all the headaches I'm about to go through."

I grin. "Then you'd better leave soon, so you can get the hell back to me." I brush my lips on his neck. "I'll have a bath. And maybe I just won't put anything on and wait for you in bed."

"Yeah, okay, going now," Kieran growls, but lingers for another kiss. "Gods, I fucking love you."

I burst out laughing.

Yeah.

Everything will be just fine.

We'll all get through this together. All of us.

Kieran came back after a few hours and filled me in on what happened in the past week whilst I was gone.

Turns out the army has been working quietly in the shadows—literally in the shadows, with Virgil's shadowborn assassins—to weed out the members of the rebellion from the inside. Every thread Atticus thought he had pulled just ... snapped.

With Aurora holding the scissors.

She's been acting as a spy this whole time.

She confronted Atticus after rescuing me from the cell. He tried to brainwash her into believing getting rid of me would get her Kieran, and she played along with it—then fed all the plans Atticus told her back to Gideon.

Aurora might be a sociopath, but she'd do anything for this Court. Even sacrificing her own brother.

It's so difficult to hate the bitch, honestly.

"So, let me get this straight," I say, trying to digest the information. "You suspected all along that it was Atticus?"

"Yep," Kieran replies, turning onto his side, his perfect hair flopping just too nicely on his forehead—and I have to blink, because it's been so long since we shared a bed and I still can't believe I am sharing one with this Fae.

"I mean, the perfume was an unexpected move, but I've suspected for a while. Every time I asked him to look into the rebellion, he always came up with vague information, then some people we captured got away too easily," he explains, running a hand through his hair. "Which was weird for someone so highly capable. So, I had a spy keeping an eye on him."

"Who?" I roll onto my stomach.

"You're going to love this bit." He grins. "Jordan."

My jaw drops. No noise comes out of me.

"Jordan?" The name tears out of me like a scream. "We're talking about the same Jordan whose eye you took because he groped Laia? The sex addict Jordan who's a pain in the ass to everyone? The one Atticus told me and Lucas to spy on because he could be working with Florence?"

"The very same." His grin deepens. "Don't you think that makes the perfect cover?"

I blink, speechless.

"I promised him a wish and his eye back," Kieran adds. "Did I trust him? Not entirely. But he ended up surprising me again and again. He gave me more valuable information than

Atticus ever did. And here's the twist—Atticus was convinced the bastard hated me and was actually working with the rebellion. When I was recovering, Atticus slipped more iron dust into my medicine every day, just enough to keep me weak. Then one day, he let Jordan handle the poisoning ... not knowing Jordan was my spy."

"Are you telling me I've got to thank fucking Jordan for the fact that you're alive?" I clutch my head like it might explode. "Why didn't you tell me he was working for you?"

"We needed your interactions with him to be authentic." Kieran laughs like he didn't just drop the most shocking plan of the century. "Jordan cut off the poison and kept feeding intel to Aurora and Gideon. I'd been fine for days, just playing weak. I was waiting for the perfect moment to catch Atticus off guard, and I knew you were safe at home." His eyes darken. "Until he found out and dumped you in that trial ..."

I stop breathing, reaching for his hand. I know from his eyes that the image of those Fae on me is still burning in his mind.

"We had to move quickly. The others were handling the rebellion, and I was looking for you." He breathes, squeezing my hand. "It took me hours. That fucking forest was brutal even for me. I keep thinking what would happen if—"

"Hey," I cut in softly, moving closer to him until our foreheads touch. "Nothing happened."

Kieran exhales, long and hard, then presses a kiss on my forehead. "I can't believe you killed three direwolves on your own."

"Oh, you should have seen me." I laugh. "I was a total badass."

"No, my love," he whispers, gently brushing his finger on my neck. "You're a queen."

And now I'm blushing like an idiot.

"So—when did you become a king?"

"Barely a day before I found out you were in the trial," he says, his voice sharp. "I decided I was done with it all. I needed to take the throne to end this rebellion once and for all. You wouldn't believe what kind of authority a single, stupid word holds. I was sworn in by the High Priestess, and of course, Felix had to record every miserable second of it. Wouldn't surprise me if the news has reached the stars we fell from."

An inappropriate chuckle bursts out of me. Gods, I wish I was there for it—Kieran being bored out of his mind, sulking his way through vows whilst Felix scribbled down notes to every word spoken.

"Just so we're clear, I don't really care about being a queen," I murmur, leaning in for a kiss. "I only care about you. And if being with you means playing queen and sitting through boring meetings or doing charity work, then that's what I'll do."

"I'd never expect anything from you," Kieran whispers, hand sliding to the back of my neck. "All right? Never. I only took the throne to keep you safe. You're in no way expected to live this miserable life of constant headaches."

And I'm grateful Kieran says that, I really am.

But ...

"No, Kieran, we already talked about this." I brush my thumb across his cheek. "We do this together. The good. The bad. The ugly. All of it. You don't get to decide which burdens you carry alone."

Kieran doesn't say a word, but his eyes say everything. No one has ever looked at me like this before—like I'm the most precious thing he's ever held. Love burns in them, fierce and unyielding. So does joy, and dread, all tangled together. And I know exactly why. Because once you have this—the thing that we have—you're terrified there's never going to be enough time in the world.

Even immortality wouldn't be enough.

His lips brush mine, breath unsteady, his voice breaking on a whisper. "Marry me." Then another kiss, a desperate plea. "Please?"

We are mates, and I know now what that entails.

I shouldn't be surprised.

But that really caught me off guard.

I blink, sucking in a breath, heart thundering like crazy. "First, you took the throne for me. And now this." I shake my head. "Can't believe this is coming from the same male who broke up with his girlfriend of ten years because he didn't want to be King."

Kieran furrows his eyebrows. "What is it going to take for you not to bring up Aurora when we're in bed, naked?"

I burst out laughing. "Sorry, it's just ..." I bite my lip, still grinning. "I can't believe you're doing all this."

He sighs. "It's not about what I'm willing to do. It's about who I'm willing to do it for."

And that's probably the truest thing I've ever heard. We always hear stories—people who have been together for years and never marry, then break up ... and the next person they meet, they marry instantly.

"I love you, Kieran," I whisper, pressing my lips on his for another hungry kiss. "And yes, I will marry you. On one condition—my family gets to attend."

The corner of his mouth curves into a smile, storm-lit eyes softening. "My dear, you're the Queen. You can do anything."

And now I have to climb on top of him to reward him for saying such lovely things. His hand immediately slips down my body, another in my hair, every touch scorching, aching.

But before I give in to the breathless need clawing at me, I pull away just enough to whisper, "So... what's going to happen to Lucas and Jordan once they've recovered?"

"Tomorrow, we hold a coronation. I'll make a statement, and both of them will be granted a wish."

My eyes widen. "Both of them?"

Gods, I can dance with joy right about now. That means Lucas can bring Declan back!

"Yes. They have both served this Court well." Kieran presses a kiss on my neck, one hand squeezing my ass like a warning that talking time's nearly over. "Jordan saved me. Lucas saved you."

And who's going to save me from being devoured by him in this bed again and again?

I lick my lips as I feel him harden against me.

Eternity sounds terrifying, but there's no one I'd rather spend forever with but him.

Chapter 44

It's the brightest morning we've had in weeks. Sunlight pours in through the thin layer of curtains, lighting up the whole mountains in shafts of gold and orange. Even the air feels different—fresher, cleaner, the start of something new.

One thing is for sure: even though our channelling link is no longer there, the mating bond is still intact, which Kieran and I are happy about.

And right now, we have so much more to look forward to.

Aurora arrives with Laia first thing, before I even have a chance to put a drop of coffee in my veins—of course, she has to make sure we're in our best dresses for the coronation.

"You look like shit," she says by way of greeting. "That hair needs divine intervention."

"Gee, thanks."

"Did you even sleep? Your face is puffy."

I narrow my eyes at her. "No, we wanted to fuck."

Her eyes narrow back. "You are both disgusting."

"You asked." I shrug, crossing my arms as she rifles through the rack of gowns she brought. As much as I hate her, I think I should make one thing very clear. "Hey, Aurora."

"Yes?"

"I—I really appreciate what you did," I start, dropping my gaze to my hands, fidgeting awkwardly. Laia slips to the corner of the room, clearly trying to give us some space. "You know, for me, for Kieran, and for this Court." My voice drops softer. "Thank you."

"Yeah," she says quietly, eyes still fixed on the rack.

"I mean it," I add. "I owe you one. And I'm ... really sorry—about your brother."

"Don't be," she whispers, finally turning to me. And for the first time—she doesn't bother hiding the pain in her eyes. "He used me, too. That night you got stabbed. I'm pretty sure it was him who put that dress in Laia's pile."

I clamp my lips together, not sure what to say to that.

Aurora smooths down her dress, a faint smile ghosting on her lips. "Let's make sure you look splendid today, shall we?"

This is weird ... in a good way.

She's extended an olive branch, and I'd be an idiot not to take it.

"I'd really like that."

Kieran walks in to see me smile at Aurora—and he immediately frowns at the sight.

"One of you is a shifter, isn't it?" he asks.

"Oh, shut up," we say in unison ... then our heads snap to each other in disgust.

Ew, I'm in sync with Aurora.

"Yeah, okay, that's really creepy," my mate decides, pointing to the door. "I'm out of here."

Aurora sighs. I roll my eyes. Laia chuckles, then immediately slaps a hand over her mouth when Aurora's glare shoots towards her.

But before we can get any further into this delightful morning circus, the door opens again.

"Sorry," Gideon says, raising one hand. "Didn't mean to interrupt your morning, but this idiot insisted on seeing you before the coronation."

"Lucas!" I drop everything and throw myself at him. Gods, he looks well. Only a few scratches on his face. "I'm so happy to see you!"

"Me too. I heard Atticus dropped you in the trial. I tried to find you, but—"

"It's all good, Lucas," I cut in gently. There are so many things to look forward to today. I don't want to drag my nightmare back into the room. But then I remember one thing. "I can't believe you two dumped me back at home against my will!"

"Oh, well—here I was hoping I'd redeemed myself by offering to take care of your family. They're fine, by the way. Virgil's best solders are taking over today." Gideon coughs, whilst Lucas just scratches the back of his head. "Sorry—we just thought that was the best thing to do while we dealt with the rebellion. Couldn't risk Atticus getting his hands on you again. Well ... until he found out and went to retrieve you."

"Don't ever do that again," I hiss, then turn back to Lucas. My irritation dissolves into excitement when I remember what today actually means. "And you are getting a wish."

"Yeah." His voice dips, eyes darting to Aurora—only for a second—before settling on mine again. "But you know what that means, right? I'll have to go home soon."

I force a smile, nodding.

I know.

I haven't stopped thinking about it since we survived the second trial.

But at least he's still alive.

And for that, I'm grateful, even if it means I'll be living here on my own.

I'll manage.

"Come on, you can stay a little while," Gideon says, nudging him with an elbow. "There'll be a huge celebration. You basically saved the Court. Chicks dig that."

"There are always celebrations." Lucas shakes his head. "You lot are insane."

"It'd be insane if there were no celebrations." Gideon winks.

Yes, don't we know it.

"Are you boys done yet?" Aurora chimes in. "We've got a lot to do over there."

"It's barely been five minutes," Gideon drawls, deliberately slowly, before glancing at Laia in the corner. "I haven't even said hello to Laia."

Of course—how can I forget?

Laia's cheeks flare pink, her lashes batting frantically. "Hello, Gideon."

"Oh please," Aurora mutters, sweeping towards the balcony like she can't stand to breathe the same air as anyone in love.

And Lucas—of all people—immediately follows.

Huh.

Am I missing something here?

I tilt my head, watching them disappear. Since when did Lucas have anything to do with Aurora? What could he possibly need to say to her? He was the one who convinced her to come see me in the cell that day...

Oh, dear Gods.

He convinced her. The Fae who looks like she hates everyone but herself. And he *convinced* her.

Is there something between the two of them?

Did he actually come to see her, not me?

Lucas? And Aurora?

Lucas and Aurora?

Oh, fuck.

I stare at Aurora the whole time she helps me get dressed. Hundreds of questions run through my head, but I manage to keep my mouth shut—mainly because I'm scared of what I'll uncover if I ask.

Are they involved?

Or are they just friendly?

Did they fuck?

How many times did they fuck?

Was she the mystery Fae he hooked up with and refused to name?

I am going insane.

Gods, Cassandra, keep it together. The whole Court is watching you and Kieran—literally.

I have never seen these many Fae in the Court before. Everyone has gathered to celebrate the coronation and the end of the trial. A new black throne gleams beside a golden one—the Court's signature colours.

The same colours Kieran and I wear today.

Aurora already prepped us on the schedule this morning, but my mind is a blank page as I walk hand in hand down the hall with Kieran. Heads bow in respect.

Oh, Gods.

Don't trip.

Don't fucking trip.

Kieran moves with maddening grace and his head held high—the same way he's always been since I've known him. Meanwhile, I'd have faceplanted by now if he wasn't holding me upright.

"Am I supposed to sit on the throne?" I whisper as we near the dais.

Kieran grins. "Or you can sit on my lap."

I hiss at him. "People are watching."

"And you don't need to change a thing, no matter how much they stare," he whispers, lifting my hand to his lips. "You look perfect today. And yes, you will sit beside me on the throne—exactly where you belong."

"Oh please." I chuckle under my breath. "I already said I'd marry you. You can stop hyping me up now."

But Kieran leans in to brush a kiss on my cheek like we're not in front of hundreds of Fae. "Never."

I sigh, but I'm unable to stop my smile.

We both settle on the thrones, now facing the public. I never knew you could see every single face from up here.

Aurora glides forward, her gown brushing the marble floor.

"Welcome," she declares with a dazzling smile. "Today, we celebrate not one, but three joyous occasions. The end of the trials. Peace in our Court. And of course—the new King and our future Queen."

Oh, brilliant. Aurora's just called me *future Queen.*

I think I'm going to faint.

Please don't throw eggs at me.

Or if they must, please let it be cooked eggs—at least it will be less messy.

I brace myself for the inevitable boo, but nothing comes.

Oh.

"Let us begin with the coronation," she announces, her voice carrying across the hall. She turns to Felix, who ascends to the dais beside the High Priestess I've met once at the River of Vows. In her arms rests a golden crown, shimmering like moonlight.

Aurora explained this morning that even though Kieran had already been sworn in privately, tradition demands it be repeated before the Court to make it official. Kieran rises to his feet, every inch the untouchable King. I stand beside him, my heart pounding.

I don't think I understand most of the vow they are repeating. I'm too busy trying to stand upright and not fall on my face.

Mother of the stars, is this what I'll have to do once we get married?

Yeah, I definitely need some training from Aurora.

I clasp my own hands to stop them from shaking, every hair in my body rising as Kieran kneels before the Priestess. She lowers the crown onto his head with reverence.

The moment he rises, the hall explodes into cheers and chanting, a sound so loud it feels like the ground is trembling under our feet.

I always knew the kind of respect Kieran commanded.

I just never realised, until now, how absolute it truly is.

"Thank you," Kieran announces, his voice echoing in the hall. "I know most of you probably thought this day would never come. Truth is—I didn't either." He pauses, glancing over his shoulder at me. "I've never been one for speeches, but let me make one thing clear: this Court is my home. You all know why it exists and why we do what we do. My goal has never been to rid the world of humans. It's to prove to the stars that we're all flawed. That nobody should be punished for it. Not us, and certainly not the humans, who never asked to be bound to us at birth."

I draw a deep breath. Once. Twice.

"Now, I can't promise that things are going to stay the same. As you can see, the stars decided to send me a human as my mate." He smirks. "But that's a conversation for the future. For now, I'll say this: we've been through hell these past few weeks. And not all of us survived it." His voice dips, weight pressing into each word. "The rebels will answer for their crimes. Rest assured that the families of those who lost their lives saving us will be well cared for. And today, we begin a new chapter."

The crowd nods in agreement.

"First, let's reward those who deserve to be rewarded," Kieran tilts his head to his Council. Beside them stands Lucas and Jordan. "Gideon—I appoint you as our new acting High Lord."

Gideon blinks, like he's been struck by lightning. "Me?"

"Yes, you," Kieran says, exhaling, the faintest smile tugging his mouth. "I was wrong to pick Atticus over you. And right now, there's no one else I trust with it."

A king who admits fault in front of his entire Court.

My Gods.

Gideon doesn't say anything for a beat, like he's still trying to process it. Then his lips twitch into a smirk. "Does that come with a pay rise?"

Laughter ripples through the crowd.

Oh, Gideon.

"What?" He laughs. "It's a fair question."

Kieran's face is bored, but his smile deepens. "Yes, you idiot, it comes with a pay rise."

"Fine, I'll do it." Gideon grins. "For the record, I was going to say yes anyway."

"Next," Kieran breathes, shaking his head at his best friend. "Aurora—it's safe to say we might all be dead if it weren't for you. For your devotion to the Court, I appoint you third in command."

Aurora's green eyes fly wide, shock breaking through her pretty face.

"Thank you for everything you did for us," he adds. "And yes, it also comes with a pay rise, and as many glamorous dresses as you like."

She flutters her eyelashes at him, her perfect lips curving into a smile. "Oh, I'm probably going to need a new house just to fit all those dresses, too."

"Mother of the stars, you lot are ..." Another sigh tears out of Kieran. He drags a hand down his face. "Fine, you can have a mansion."

"Thank you, my King." She dips low in a perfect curtsy.

Even I let out a laugh.

Such a beautiful day.

Everything feels like it's heading into the right direction.

Kieran announces more rewards to his people and doesn't forget to thank them for their loyalty.

Then he turns to Lucas and Jordan.

"Last but not least—our final trial was different from the usual ones we've had, but I can say that considering the circumstances, we'd all agree that both Lucas and Jordan have served us well. And for that—I would like to offer you each two options: a wish—or become Fae and live amongst us."

I swallow hard. I knew this was coming, but being Kieran's mate means I had to keep this a secret.

I can see the shock on Lucas's face.

"And my eye?" Jordan reminds Kieran.

"Of course, since you saved my life," Kieran says, lifting his hand—then with a flick of his fingers, Jordan's eye patch disappears, leaving only his new eye beneath it. He blinks fast, joy blooming across his face, and he smiles—a big, bright smile with gratitude that I have never seen from him before. "And you get a wish—just as long as you don't do anything stupid again."

Jordan lets out a sigh. "Here I thought I'd gained enough of your trust by now." He clicks his tongue. "I don't care about the wish. Can I please become Fae and work at the Court?"

And it goes exactly how Kieran said it would—almost everyone picks becoming Fae.

"You'll be provided with a house, and you can work here." Kieran nods. "We'll do the ceremony on the full moon, but I do have to warn you—it won't be pleasant."

"It's just a night, and I get eternity." He shrugs.

Kieran turns to Lucas. "And you?"

My heat is pounding in my chest. Images of everything we have been through over the past months slam into me all at once. Becoming friends with him. Losing Tessa. The fights we had. The laughter. The drinks we shared.

Going through the mirrored maze with him.

I have cried. Laughed. And cried. And laughed again.

He's the only person who ever really understood me.

And now—at last—we're getting Declan back.

I had a talk with Kieran this morning, assuring him he needn't worry about Declan. Once Lucas wishes for him back, Kieran will erase Declan's memories of me, and he will live as if I never existed in his life. We figured it's kinder than bringing him back just to tell him I entered a competition to save him, but I'm about to marry a Fae King.

Lucas looks at me with the usual warmth in his eyes—but today, there's sadness in them, too. My heart aches at the thought of him leaving.

He shakes his head slowly, his voice cracking as he says, "I'm sorry, Cass. I know what we came here for. But ... I can't go back to my old life. I don't even know what it was anymore."

The world stops. My breath catches.

No.

What is he—

"Lucas," I breathe, my hands trembling. "What are you saying?"

He doesn't look at me. He turns to Kieran. "I would like to become Fae."

Epilogue
Kieran

Time is peculiar here. I can't really explain myself how it works.

Winter creeps in, slow and merciless. Snow lies inches deep on the ground that only weeks ago was carpeted in brittle autumn leaves. The maroon and orange Cassandra so adores bleeds into blinding white across the whole Court.

Even so, streets stay busy. Shops celebrate the new season with decorations and warm spiced wine. The little things we've learned to appreciate since being banished from the stars.

It hasn't been all bad, the three centuries I've been here.

Sure, it was hell when it was just me and a few cranky bastards who wouldn't shut up about how miserable every bloody thing was. No restaurants. No markets. No taverns. Just endless fighting.

But over time, as more fallen Fae arrived, we adapted. We argued, we fought, we broke things and rebuilt them again—until slowly, we carved out a city. Our borders stretched. We even came up with our own festivals and traditions.

It became our home.

And no matter what anyone says, I couldn't have built this alone. The people made it what it is today, and I wouldn't trade anything for it.

Except Cassandra.

I would tear it all down, even turn human—if it ever came to that.

The truth is, no matter how much sweat and blood you put into something, you can never please everyone. There will always be those who undermine me, who rebel when they don't get what they want.

If I can resolve it, then fine, we'll sort it out.

But if they ever so much as lay a hand on my mate, then they fucking burn.

Precisely what's waiting for Atticus, when we finally catch him.

It's been weeks since the coronation, and the prick is still in the wind.

Gone. Just like that.

I don't know what unsettles Cass more: that, or the fact that Lucas is now Fae.

She has barely spoken a word to him since, and it pains me to see her like that, especially when I can't do a damn thing about it.

Though, I'll admit, part of me was relieved that I didn't have to bring Declan back. Believe it or not, I'm not a fan of welcoming my mate's ex-boyfriend into the picture. The stars are cruel bastards. Even if she asked me to wipe his memories of her, if fate dragged him to her once, it's bound to happen again.

But that's no longer my concern.

The fact that we have scoured every inch of this Court, using all the resources and magic at our fingertips and haven't found Atticus tells me one thing: he isn't here.

And I know he can't be in the human world. Not this long, anyway.

Which confirms the suspicion that's been gnawing at me, so I sent Gideon and Virgil out to patrol—outside the Court.

After four days, they return this afternoon, their brows drawn tight.

I thank the stars Cass is out in Asterhollow with the human-turned-Fae. It's one of the things she does every week now, and I think it's great she's found something of her own beyond politics.

"What is it?" I ask as they approach.

"You're never going to believe where we've been," Gideon mutters.

"Try me."

"We finally found them," Virgil says, his tone sharp as blade. "One of the other fallen courts."

I lean back on my chair, a grin tugging at my mouth.

"They call themselves the Court of Shadows, and we only stumbled them thanks to our shadowborn assassins." Gideon's gaze flicks to Virgil, whose chin lifts with the quiet pride of a general whose army just proved itself indispensable.

"Well, I assume by the fact that you two are standing here in one piece that they're not entirely hostile?"

"Not just that. They already know about us. About you." Virgil pauses, then produces an envelope and places it on the desk before me. "Word of you taking the throne has reached them, and they are requesting an audience—here, of course, since you can't leave."

I pick up the envelope. Inside, neat strokes of elegant handwriting in black ink scribble across the paper, sealed with an unfamiliar crest. A formal visitation request.

The date they propose is three weeks from now.

But it's the final line that makes my blood roar.

I believe our interests align, and it's time we talk about your brother.

Yours truly,
King Silas of the Court of Shadows.

The envelope turns into smoke a few seconds after I finish reading.

Neat trick.

"Oh yeah," Gideon flinches. "They love practical jokes over there. Even more so than us."

I laugh, the sound echoing off my office walls. "Let them come. I'll draft a response later."

"You don't think it's a trap?" Virgil presses.

I drum my fingers on the armrest of my chair, considering it for a minute. We have been here for over three centuries, and in that time I've heard whispers of other Fallen Courts. If they truly have known about us all this time and haven't attacked or reached out until now, then I doubt they are our enemy.

"We won't know for sure until they're here." I decide at last, voice hardening. "And if they're harbouring fugitives—" My smirk returns. "—then I need to know."

Atticus wasn't working alone. He couldn't have done.

The question is who was pulling his strings?

And then there's the mention of my brother. Very intriguing.

After all, I believe we all fell from the same Court. My family reputation precedes them. I wonder why King Silas waited until now to reach out.

I lean back, my grin deepening.

This is going to be fun.

TO BE CONTINUED

Acknowledgement

Writing this book was like riding a storm of passion and ideas that wouldn't stop shut up till everything was written down on the very last page. I didn't do anything else. I didn't want to eat. I didn't go out, or if I did, I was constantly thinking of Starfallen. It was mostly written on sleepless nights after my usual 9-5 and I'd sleep about four to six hours a night for two months straight... yes, even on weekends.

I could not not write. It was all I wanted to do. I fell asleep thinking about Starfallen, waking up with it being the first thing on my mind. And I'd dream of it in my sleep.

I have always been like this. Starfallen is the second English book I've ever written (my first one hasn't come out yet.), but since I was a teenager, I would stay up writing until birds started chirping outside. And I have done this with about forty other books I wrote in my native language, Thai. Once, I finished writing a whole 200-A4 page book in ten days. Yes, ten days.

I am insane. I know.

So, Antony, I apologise I barely saw you even though we lived in the same house, ha! And no words would be enough to thank you for your understanding and the support you have given me. All the checking ins, refilling my water, taking my plates aways, bringing me snacks, etc. I love you, and I am beyond thankful for you.

My dear besties, Melissa and Lena, you have both been there since the beginning. We have gone through so much in such short time. I am so proud of how we stepped out of our comfort zones and into this bookish world together. I'm forever grateful for the love and support you both have given me.

My original ten alpha readers, without you guys I'd have never thought of bringing Starfallen out to the world so early after just finishing it a few months ago. I was so sure I'd have to go back and work on the book big time after getting your feedback. How did you ALL gave the draft five stars, I'll never know. But it's your feedback that is part of the reasons this book is now out in the first place.

My Street Team, I have said it before, but I'll say it again: if this book does go places, I will have you all to thank for. I cannot believe I put together a group of 37 crazy ladies from different continents, and we all match each other's freak... The fact that when we kicked off the street team, most of you had only read three chapters of Starfallen and became so devoted to the point where you'd sell your souls for the book is still baffling and mind-blowing to me!

Our group chat is always chaotic in the best possible way. The way you guys support each other and keep sending each other gifts and books is honestly so heart-warming. You have made a terrifying place aka the internet a very positive place for everyone in the group. No bad vibes. Never any judgement. Always cheerful and hilarious. I know I have made friends for life since the first week. I fucking love you all, even if you give me headaches. And I shall continue collecting souls and breaking you guys like a dementor. Long live the worms. (Sorry, inside joke only.)

And to all of you who's holding this book in your hand... wow, it's still crazy to me that there are strangers out there who are reading my book! I thank you from the bottom of my heart. It's not easy being an indie author. Most of us never make it, but I always think that even if Starfallen became just one person's favourite book, that's enough. I hope you like this book if you have read this far. But it's okay, too, if you don't.

Do tag me on socials and come say hi. I promise I read every review and love hearing your thoughts about absolutely everything Starfallen related!

Thank you. Thank you. Thank you.

It's probably not common, but I do absolutely want to thank myself. For sticking with it all. It was beyond difficult when I started writing my first English book, Thalassian, and I couldn't have written Starfallen without it. I've learned and grown so much in the past six months, and I keep hearing people around me say "You should be very proud of yourself.", and I am incredibly proud of myself. It feels like an imposter syndrome sometimes. I genuinely do not know how to accept compliments most of the time. And every word everyone has said to me about Starfallen truly means the world.

I only started this indie journey not long ago and feel like we've come a long way. I am excited to see where this journey will continue.

Lastly, can someone kindly give Jordan (the chaotic one) a tissue? She's about to cry again.

Love,

Fern x

Printed in Dunstable, United Kingdom